WILD PRAIRIE ROSES

LENA NELSON DOOLEY
LAURIE ALICE EAKES
LISA HARRIS

BARBOUR
PUBLISHING

A DAUGHTER'S QUEST

Dedication

To our wonderful God and to Gateway Church in Southlake, Texas, where He has planted James and me for this season in our life. Lord, You are doing an awesome thing, and Your vision is so far beyond our reach. Thank You for letting us be a part of the miracle You are performing in this place.

Every book I write is also dedicated to my precious husband, James Allen Dooley. You are always there for me. You love me, cherish me, protect me, and make me laugh. These past forty-four years have been an amazing ride. I never want to get off.

Prologue

April 1867

Dawn sent fingers of sunlight between the Ozark Mountain peaks, bathing Constance Miller in warmth she needed on this early spring morning. She stood near a window, gazing out at the pastel colors spread across the sky by the rising sun, and thanked God for the beauty around her.

Raspy breaths across the room behind her broke the stillness and drowned out the first twitters of birds awakening to the new morning. How she hated the sound that meant her father's death could be imminent.

When the doctor had left yesterday, he had held out no hope for recovery. Without her father's strong presence in her life, Constance's future looked bleak. She couldn't farm this land by herself, and there wasn't a man on the mountain, or even in the valley below, who she would consider marrying. Where did that leave her?

Other young women had ventured far from their Arkansas mountain homes, but she felt no yearning to move away from here. Her gaze was drawn to the golden tint now rimming the tall budding trees, some with tender green leaves, that surrounded their home place. Spring was her favorite time of the year. It usually made her think of a new beginning. But the wheezing gasps coming from the man in the bed on the other side of the room signaled an ending instead. She clasped her arms tight across her chest and shivered in her flannel nightdress.

"Connie." Her father's rasping voice was hardly distinguishable. "Come here, gurl." The last word faded into nothingness.

She whirled and rushed to kneel at the side of the wooden platform covered with a ticking filled with dry corn husks. "I'm here." She removed the rag, which now felt hot, and dipped it into the cold water in a basin on the floor before replacing it on her father's brow.

His bony arm snaked out from under the covers, and his hand gripped her forearm with amazing strength. "You hafta promise me somethin'." His gaze bored into hers, and a fire of determination burned in his eyes.

"Anything, Pa." She wanted to keep him calm. Too much excitement could leach his waning strength too quickly.

"I ain't got much time." He stopped to take another noisy gulp of air. "You gotta listen real good."

Constance nodded and leaned closer to him so he wouldn't have to try to talk so loud.

"I done something real bad when I was gone."

She knew that war was ugly with men killing each other and all, but she didn't think he was talking about that aspect of the war. Surely her pa hadn't done much else. When she started to tell him that, he interrupted her.

"I come up with a plan to steal some gold from those Yankees. It was only Jim Mitchell and me who talked about it, but the next day, I knew God didn't want me to do it." His hold on her arm slackened. "The war made me lose my way for a bit." His hand dropped to lie motionless on the tattered quilt that covered his emaciated body.

She grasped her father's hand. "I knew you couldn't have done anything too bad, Pa."

His eyes fluttered open. "But someone did steal the gold, and they did it jist the way I planned. It had to be Jim." Once again his speech faltered, and his eyelids closed.

Constance moved her head closer to him once more and was thankful that the morning sun began to take the chill from the room as its rays crept across the rough wooden floorboards. "If you didn't do it, then you're not guilty of anything."

Her father opened his eyes again. They held a sadness that went straight to her heart.

"I'm guilty of two things. I hadn't oughta come up with the plan, and I never took the time to tell Jim about God." Once again he relaxed with his eyes closed.

"We all make mistakes, Pa."

"Not like these." He kept his eyes closed as he continued. "I cain't go to my rest unless you make me a promise."

Constance didn't know what she could do about any of this, but she didn't want her father fretting. "I'll promise you anything you want."

His watery eyes opened, and he stared at her face as if memorizing every inch of it. "Connie, gurl, you gotta go to Iowy and find Jim Mitchell. You gotta tell him about Jesus, then convince him to give back the gold."

She couldn't keep from showing her surprise. "I can't do that. The only time I've ever left this mountain was when I went to school, and that was only in the next valley. I don't even know where Iowa is."

"You gotta find out. Get that schoolmarm to help you. . .or the new preacher, but you gotta go. I won't rest easy unless you promise."

Constance stood and walked over to the table where the wash basin sat beside a bucket of water. She picked up the tin dipper and took a drink, noticing that the container was almost empty. That would mean a trip to the clear stream that ran down the mountain a few yards from the house. She dreaded leaving her father for even the few minutes that would take.

How could she make her father a promise like that? Uncertainty and fear crowded her thoughts.

His breathing became more labored and echoed in the stillness. He wasn't long for this world. *Oh God, what am I supposed to do?*

A loud snort was followed by her father calling her name again. She rushed over and fell to her knees on the floor, not even being careful about splinters this time.

"I'm here."

A faint smile lit his face for a fleeting moment. "You look jist like your ma." Then his eyes slid closed again, but he continued to speak softly. "If you stand at the window on the west wall of the cabin and count to the seventh board on the floor, you'll find my stash of money."

Constance's gaze went to the wall, and she counted over to where he was talking about. It looked like the rest of the unpainted floor.

"Where the boards come together, the one to the south ain't nailed down. Pick it up, and you'll find the money I've been saving. I meant to go find Jim m'self, but the good Lord had other plans. Jim wrote down the name of the town where his family lives on a piece of paper, and I kept it all this time. It's with the money."

All his energy must have been spent, because he went so slack that Constance thought he might have died right then. She laid her hand on his chest and felt the faint beating of his heart. Tears slipped down her cheeks, and she swiped at them with the backs of her hands. More took their place. She watched him sleep for a few moments before she went over to the board. Constance lifted it and saw a large rusty tin can with a rag tied on the top. She picked it up and took it to the table. After untying the dirty string and lifting the scrap of cloth, Constance's eyes widened at the large roll of paper money stuffed in the can.

She and her father had always had enough to eat and clothes to wear, but that amount of money would have made a difference in their life. Her father wouldn't have had to work so hard, and they could have had a few more nice things. Why had he let his guilty feelings rob them of a better life?

Chapter 1

Hans looked at the words he had painted on a new board: VAN DE KIEFT SMITHY. Today, he would hang it right after the stagecoach delivered his new anvil. Finally, he was a business owner. He'd worked hard as an apprentice for Homer and then continued working for him several more years before the blacksmith decided to retire on the farm he had bought about five miles from town. Of course, Homer planned to do all his own smithy work, so he wanted to keep his anvil.

The afternoon stage wouldn't arrive for a while. Hans might as well go ahead and hang the sign while he waited. He picked up several nails and stuck them in his shirt pocket. He shoved the head of the hammer into one of his hip pockets before picking up the sign. After standing in the street in front of the blacksmith shop for a few minutes, looking at the building, he decided to nail it up over the top of the large doorway. He set the sign against the side of the building and went inside looking for his ladder.

Hans wasn't excited about climbing on the thing. He never had liked heights. When the boys played in the hayloft while he was growing up, he tried to stay on the ground as much as possible. He closed the doors and latched them together before he leaned the ladder against them. After testing to see if the ladder was stable, Hans took a tentative step up. Another followed. How many rungs would he need to climb before he could reach far enough to attach the sign?

Good thing he was over six feet tall, so he could reach pretty high. He stepped down and decided to climb back up only four rungs. After hefting the sign over his shoulder, he took a firm grip with his other hand on the ladder. This time, his steps were slower. Finally, he felt secure, but he decided not to look down.

About the time Hans had the sign placed exactly where he wanted it, the ladder swayed. Cold sweat broke out on his forehead, and a voice came from behind and below.

"I'll hold the ladder for you, Hans, while you pound in those nails."

"Thanks, Sheriff." Hans didn't dare look at his friend but was glad he had come by. "I appreciate it."

He quickly pounded nails into the four corners of the sign and stepped back down the ladder. When he was standing safely on solid ground, he thrust out his hand toward the sheriff.

Andrew Morton shook it, then turned to look up at the sign. "It looks nice. You did a good job on the lettering."

"Mother made all of us learn good penmanship, even the boys. I'm glad now." Hans stood in the middle of the street with his hands on his hips to get the full effect. "Everyone should be able to see the sign most anywhere on the street."

He rubbed his hands down the legs of his denim trousers. "I'm going to leave the door closed. Isn't it about time for the stagecoach to arrive? My anvil should be on it today."

Hans started toward the station, and Andrew walked beside him. "I think I'll mosey that direction, too."

Constance glanced around the crowded stagecoach, trying not to show her distaste. The trip had been way too long and much too hard. Some of the people who shared the space with her didn't understand the importance of cleanliness. She could hardly wait to arrive at Browning City, Iowa. When she stepped out of this conveyance, she planned to breathe in a lot of clean, fresh air.

She pressed her hand down the length of dark green gabardine that covered her lap. When Constance had donned the traveling suit in Fort Smith, it had been the most beautiful outfit she had ever owned. She felt sure she didn't need to be ashamed of the way she looked.

Layers of dust almost obliterated the color of the fabric. Several times she had been given the choice of whether to spend the night at way stations and catch the next coach or continue on this one when the fresh horses were harnessed to it. Because of her eagerness to take care of her final promise to her father, she always chose to go on. Now she regretted it. The driver had told them that the next stop was Browning City, and she would arrive dirty with her traveling clothes completely wilted. Why was she always so impetuous? Mother had often warned her to take longer to make decisions. Why hadn't Constance listened?

The grizzled man who sat in the opposite corner of the coach leaned his head out the window and looked in the direction they were going before pulling back into the cabin. "I can see the edge of town up ahead. How many of us are stopping here?"

When Constance was the only one who lifted her hand, he smiled at her.

"I've got a brother who lives a few miles west of Browning City. I'll be getting off, too."

Constance glanced out the window in time to see several boys running alongside the vehicle as it began to slow down. A puppy romped around their legs. The houses on her side of the street looked inviting, each wearing a coat of whitewash or paint. None of those unpainted gray cabins such as hers back home in the Ozarks. Some houses had picket fences, while iron railings corralled other yards. This looked like a nice town. Too bad she was only here for one reason.

When the driver stopped the coach in front of the station, Constance noticed two men standing on the boardwalk, eyeing the people in the windows of the coach.

A tall, broad-shouldered man with blond hair long enough to touch his collar turned to his companion. "My anvil is probably in the boot. I'm sure no one wanted to lift it onto the luggage rack on the top." He stepped off into the street.

The driver opened the door. "This is your stop, miss. I'll get your carpetbag down for you." He stepped up on the front wheel of the coach to reach it.

Constance gathered her reticule and stood up as well as she could in the confines of the coach. She had been sitting so long her legs felt stiff. She planned on taking a long walk after she checked into a hotel or boardinghouse. Exercise would work the soreness out.

When she reached her foot down for the step, somehow she missed it. She realized that she would land on her face in the dirt. Just what she needed for her entrance into a new town. Constance grabbed onto the handle of the door, but it swung wider, taking her with it. After shutting her eyes, she took a deep breath, preparing for her inglorious landing in the street.

Instead, strong arms lifted her up and away from the coach. Her eyes flew open, and she peered into a handsome face with eyes the color of the sky above.

⊗⊷

Without thinking, Hans reached for the woman to stop her from hurting herself. When he lifted her, she felt like a feather in spite of all the layers of skirts that swirled around them. The green hat that matched her clothes was knocked askew and fell over one side of her forehead, almost covering one eye. Her arms clutched him around his neck as she opened her eyes and stared at him.

Everything around them disappeared. When Hans stared into her eyes, they flashed green and brown all at the same time. Golden flecks glistened in the bright sunlight. Fear, surprise, and a questioning look followed each other across her face, leaving her with a vulnerable expression.

Heat suffused his arms and every part of his body that touched her. His stomach began a strange dance that it had never done before, and then it turned over and knotted up. Hans had experienced reactions to young women before, but he had always been able to control them. This felt different—more personal and. . .somehow strange.

Some of the young woman's abundant brown hair fell out of the bun she wore low on her neck. Her cheeks turned red, and her rosy lips parted slightly. His mouth went dry, and Hans tried to swallow, never taking his gaze from her face. The most beautiful face he had ever seen.

As Andrew walked past Hans, he leaned close and whispered for his ears alone, "You can put her down now."

How long had Hans been holding her? He didn't want to look around because he was afraid of what other people might see on his face. Never had he experienced anything quite this intense. Uncomfortable, yet special somehow. Nothing in his life had prepared him for this moment.

Hans whirled and carefully made his way to the boardwalk. He gently set the woman on her feet and turned back toward the coach. He needed to get his anvil and hurry to his place of business.

"Thank you." Her soft words followed him, but he didn't turn around.

He only hoped she was not staying in town long. He wasn't ready to confront these strange feelings, and he surely didn't want to make a fool of himself.

Chapter 2

From the warmth she felt in her cheeks, Constance knew they must contain a blush that hadn't gone away. With her carpetbag sitting at her feet on the boardwalk, she glanced up and down the dusty street. Thankfully, a hotel was on the opposite side, down a ways. After the stage pulled off, she picked up her baggage and started toward the building. She kept her head down and only peeked around, hoping no one noticed what had happened.

As she took her first steps, some of the people standing around followed her with their stares. Even when she was in school, Constance hadn't liked being the center of attention. Her feelings of discomfort welled up and almost overwhelmed her. She wished she had never come so far from home and familiar things. If only her father hadn't asked her to make that promise. She couldn't break a deathbed promise, could she?

When she once again glanced around, the other people on the street were going about their own business as if they had forgotten her. Maybe her inglorious descent from the stage wouldn't haunt her for long.

The tall, handsome blond man who had rescued her strode down the street carrying a heavy anvil as if it didn't weigh much. When he had caught her as she exited the stagecoach, she felt the strength of those bulging muscles. The blacksmith in the mountain community near her home was an old man. Even though he was strong, he never could have had a physique like this smithy.

Constance started down into the street, almost missing the wooden step. . .again. She had to forget that man and pay attention to what she was doing. With as much aplomb as she could manage, she swept toward the hotel. She didn't want anyone to know how out of her element she felt.

Thankfully, the clerk at the hotel didn't seem to know what had happened. Her embarrassment had been on the other side of the coach from this building. He probably hadn't seen her descent and the aftermath, and apparently word of the event hadn't reached him.

"Are you alone, or is someone traveling with you?" The man peered up over his glasses as he handed her a pen and inkwell.

Constance dipped the nib into the black liquid, then proceeded to write her name on the register. "I'm alone." She opened her reticule and glanced up. "How much is the room?"

After he told her, she pulled out enough money to pay for a week, careful not to let anyone see how much she had left. Traveling alone was frightening enough without giving someone a reason to rob her.

Her room was on the second floor of the hotel, facing the street. She unpacked her carpetbag and placed the items in the chest of drawers beside the door. The pitcher on the washstand contained fresh water, so she was able to take care of her toilette.

Even though it was not quite evening, the strain of the journey pulled Constance toward the inviting bed. She laid down and closed her eyes, expecting to fall asleep immediately. However, her thoughts returned to the incident in the street. When she had missed the step, fear shot through her like an arrow, lancing the carefully constructed wall around her heart.

As the memory assailed her, Constance once again felt that strong arms were lifting her. She had never been so close to any man except her father. . .and he hadn't carried her in his arms since she was a small child. She didn't understand the flurry of emotions that scattered through her. Nothing settled them until her gaze connected with the man's beautiful blue eyes.

Could she call a man's eyes beautiful? Well, no matter. His were. And his expression held a special kindness that Constance wasn't ready to analyze. She hoped she would never see him again. At the same time, she hoped she would. Confusion ruled her thoughts, and she fell asleep dreaming about a tall blond man.

⚭

Morning sunlight pulled Constance from a deep sleep. For a moment, she didn't know where she was. Not in the mountain cabin on a mattress tick filled with corn shucks. When she turned over, nothing rustled, and the softness of the featherbed caressed her body in comfort. After she opened her eyes and looked around the room, which seemed luxurious to her, a loud rumble from her stomach reminded her how long it had been since her last meager meal. While she hurried to dress, the fragrance of bacon and biscuits from somewhere below teased her senses.

When Constance reached the dining room on the first floor of the hotel, the room was almost empty. She wasn't used to sleeping this late. While she stood poised in the wide doorway between the hotel lobby and the restaurant, a grandmotherly woman swathed in a large apron came through the door from what had to be the kitchen.

"Well, come on in if you're hungry." The woman's smile lit her eyes with laughter. "You've come to the right place." She ushered Constance to an empty table by one of the front windows. "Would you like bacon, eggs, and biscuits or flapjacks?"

"What are flapjacks?" Constance couldn't help looking puzzled.

"Some people call them pancakes or griddle cakes. I like to make them with buckwheat, and we have real maple syrup, not just cane syrup."

"That sounds good." Once again, Constance's stomach made a loud protest.

"I'll be right back." The woman bustled through the door and returned immediately with a mug and a pot of coffee. "Would you like a cup?"

While she sipped the hot beverage, Constance studied the street outside the window. Browning City was larger and busier than the small town near the home place. People on horseback, in wagons and buggies, and walking on the board-walks all seemed to have a purpose. Constance had a hard time imagining all she had seen in her journey. Even though she had read about these things in the books that filled the school library, to see them for herself made her feel almost giddy. To think, she probably never would have ventured as far as Fort Smith if her father hadn't extracted the promise from her. How was she ever going to find Jim Mitchell?

Constance didn't look forward to trying to get information about the man. People might get the wrong idea if she were too obvious with her questions. While she ate the wonderful flapjacks and bacon the waitress brought her, she devised a plan. She would make her way unobtrusively through the town, listening to conversations, trying to hear something about Jim Mitchell or his family. She didn't want anyone else to know about the gold before Mr. Mitchell had a chance to give it back on his own. That way, he might not get into trouble with the law.

❧

Hans was striding toward the mercantile when he noticed the woman from the stage crossing the street. Morning sunlight gleamed on the shiny curls that peeked out from under the brim of her bonnet. He'd heard his mother call that style coal shuttle. The way it tipped up in the back made the young woman look almost saucy.

He quickly glanced toward the front windows of the store so she wouldn't see him staring at her. *Wonder what she's doing in Browning City? Would she stay long?*

The bell over the door announced his entrance into the store where a customer could find almost anything. Hans moved toward the area where the proprietor kept nails. He had bent several this morning. For some reason, his aim must be off. Of course, he hadn't gotten as much rest last night as usual. The remembered feeling of that woman's soft body in his arms burned in his mind, chasing away sleep. Her lovely face with the large, multicolored eyes had beguiled him. He tossed and turned for hours before finally drifting into an uneasy slumber filled with dreams about an elusive woman who beckoned to him, then flitted away.

Hans shook his head and read the sizes written in pencil on the sides of the tins holding nails. Maybe he should get several different kinds. The bell above the door rang again, pulling his attention from the small metal spikes.

She had come into the mercantile, too.

Even though he turned back toward the hardware, the fragrance of flowers that accompanied her wafted toward him, reminding him of his torment during the night. Hans tried to keep his attention on what he was doing, but he was aware of her every move even though he didn't turn to follow her with his gaze. She glided around the store, stopping to finger different merchandise.

Several other customers clustered around the space, carrying on conversations. The woman moved near a group and looked at things on shelves nearby. When Hans glanced at her, she seemed to be paying more attention to the people than the merchandise. She looked up and noticed him studying her, so she moved on. She stopped near another group of people, fingering fabric as she covertly watched them.

Something didn't feel right to Hans. Was the woman trying to steal something? Surely she couldn't be a thief. He wanted to make sure, so he angled his body to where he could observe her without her knowing it. Of course, that put him near things he wouldn't be interested in, not in a million years. He just didn't want the proprietor to be taken advantage of by this woman. . .and he didn't want to believe that she could be dishonest—a pretty woman like her with a delicate air about her and the hint of some hurt lurking behind her eyes.

When she moved on, nothing was missing from the shelf, and her handbag was so tiny, it wouldn't hold much if she did try to stuff anything in it. But something about her didn't seem quite right. Her movements looked furtive, as if she had something to hide.

❧

Finding Mr. Mitchell might be more difficult than Constance had thought. Although she spent almost an hour in the general store, listening to see if anyone would mention the Mitchell family, not one person did. Perhaps she should go elsewhere.

Out on the sidewalk, Constance decided to explore the town a little more. She walked the other way down the street, stopping to peer into windows when it was possible to do so without drawing attention to herself.

Soon she had passed several businesses and found her way into an area where houses lined the streets. One of them had a sign out front that proclaimed BARKER'S BOARDINGHOUSE. If Constance didn't find the Mitchells fairly soon, she might move there instead of staying at the hotel. Although her father had quite a bit of money saved, the cash wouldn't last forever.

She returned to the business section of town, hoping to eavesdrop on other conversations. A number of people milled around. She meandered about, trying to listen to conversations, but nothing helped her in her quest.

On one street, Constance noticed a school set a couple of blocks from a church. Back home in Arkansas when the circuit-riding preacher came through, they held services in the schoolhouse. She had never been in a building that was just a church. Maybe she would visit on Sunday, which was five days away.

Constance spent the next four days casually exploring the town, listening in on conversations but keeping her distance from people. One day, she went down a street that led to the livery stable. Just past that, a blacksmith shop stood with its wide doors flung open to the spring breezes. She stopped and quietly observed the man who had caught her when she fell. He pounded on red hot metal, forming what looked like a horseshoe. No wonder he had no trouble helping her. The strength she had felt in his arms made his work look easy, even though she knew it probably wasn't. Why was she spending so much time thinking about and observing him? No other man had ever spent so much time in her thoughts.

⌘

When Hans glanced up and saw the woman standing under the spreading branches of a tree down the street, he stopped hammering against the anvil. If he didn't, he would probably miss and smash his hand. It had taken all his willpower this week to keep his thoughts from dwelling on the way he had felt when he carried her the short distance from the stage to the boardwalk. While he stood staring, she turned and started back toward the center of town.

Hans plunged the horseshoe in cold water. Steam hissed up around him, bringing sweat to his brow. After placing the finished item on his worktable, he wiped his forearms and face with a towel and rolled down his sleeves. He pulled the doors closed and hurried up the street to follow the woman. Today, he intended to talk to her. Enough of this cat-and-mouse game they had been playing.

He almost caught up with her when she stopped to look at something in a store window. She turned and started back toward him, so Hans leaned against the front of the café in the next block. He heard a commotion in the alley that separated the two buildings and stuck his head around the corner of the building just as two boys started running toward the street. They weren't looking where they were going, and they should reach the end of the boardwalk about the time the woman would step down from it. If they collided with her, they would knock her into the dirt.

"Now where do you scallywags think you're going?" He grabbed each boy by the collar.

They turned angry eyes toward him.

"What are you doing, mister?" The tallest boy sounded belligerent.

Hans looked up in time to see the woman smile at the three of them. "I'm just trying to keep you from running into this lady."

The boys stopped resisting and glanced up at her. "I'm sorry," they said in unison.

She turned her smile on them. "It's all right. You didn't see me coming, did you?"

They shook their heads and thanked her before moving more sedately down the street, at least for a little ways.

"Thank you for saving me again." Her rich melodious words stretched between them, making an indefinable connection.

Hans felt tongue-tied, something he had never before experienced. He nodded.

She held out her hand. "My name is Constance Miller."

He looked at it a moment before engulfing it in his. "And I'm Hans Van de Kieft. I'm. . ."

"The blacksmith." She finished his sentence when he faltered. "I saw you working in your shop earlier." She looked down at their still-joined hands and gently extracted hers. "I'm glad to finally know your name."

While Hans watched Constance walk away, his heart thundered in his chest, and his stomach tied in knots again. He needed to talk to someone, so he started toward the parsonage. Hopefully, Jackson was home and had time to visit.

The pastor opened the door after the first knock. "Hans, come in. Mary has gone to the store or I would offer you something to eat."

Hans shook his head. "I'm not hungry." He was afraid that if he tried to eat, he wouldn't be able to swallow a bite. Of course, the sensation in his midsection wasn't exactly unpleasant.

"Well, that's a first, isn't it?" His best friend led the way into the parlor. "Is this just a social call in the middle of a workday, or did you come for a specific reason?"

Hans dropped into his favorite chair and leaned his forearms against his thighs, letting his hands dangle between his knees. "I kind of wanted to talk to you."

Jackson sat down and leaned back in his chair, resting one ankle on the other knee. "As a pastor or as a friend?"

"Both, I think."

"This sounds intriguing." Jackson's eyebrows rose in question. "How can I help you?"

It took a moment for Hans to verbalize his feelings. "Did you hear about me keeping that lady from falling from the stagecoach?" After his friend nodded, he continued, "Odd things have been happening to me since then. I'm not sleeping well, and when I do, I have strange dreams." He wasn't sure he had expressed himself in a way that could be understood.

Jackson didn't comment, just waited for him to continue.

"Actually, I just met her again, and when she shook hands with me, I had the same reactions I had when I caught her." He looked up hopefully, then back down at the floor.

"What kind of reactions?"

"I don't know. She's on my mind a lot, and I feel unsettled."

Jackson gave a soft snort, so Hans looked at him again. Jackson was trying not to laugh.

"Are you crazy or something?" Hans surged to his feet and moved around the room. "It's not funny. You're my pastor as well as my friend. I need to know what to do about these. . .feelings. I've always been able to control my emotions. Actually, no other woman has caused so much havoc in them. I know what lust is, and I don't believe that's what I feel, but I wonder if it's more than I should be feeling. I really want to get to know her, but I'm not sure she's honest."

A sober expression replaced the smile on Jackson's face. "I didn't mean to make light of what's happening to you. It's not a sin to want to get to know a woman. She may be passing through town, or she may be looking for a home here." He stopped for a moment as if mulling over something. "Just what about her makes you think she's not honest?"

Hans rubbed a hand across the back of his neck. "Nothing specific. I've seen her at the store a couple of times, and she didn't buy anything. She seemed to be listening in on conversations."

"Are you sure?"

Hans pictured the times, running through every move she made. "No, I'm not. But is it wrong to feel drawn to her since I don't know anything about her?"

Chapter 3

Bright spring sunshine gave Sunday a heavenly glow, increasing the intensity of the color of new leaves on the trees and of multicolored buds peeking between greenery on the ground. Constance felt confident that she would look as good as anyone else at the church service because she was wearing another of the dresses she had purchased before she left Fort Smith. Her straw bonnet was decorated with silk flowers that complemented the light green ribbon matching her gown. She had never worn a pair of white cotton gloves before, but the woman at the store assured her that most women wore them to church. Of course, Constance wondered how they kept them clean. Maybe she would remove them and put them in her reticule when she was in the building.

She loved all the beauty of the day, but something about this prairie land made her feel unsettled. The mountains back home seemed to hold the sky high above her. Here there was so much blue spread from horizon to horizon that it almost pressed down against her. She wished for a few peaks to lift it up.

As she approached the building with its steeple topped by a small cross that stretched toward the heavens, she was glad to see so many other people streaming toward it. Many walked in family groups, but others rode horses or wagons. A few had fancy buggies such as she had never seen before.

Although Constance wouldn't be in Iowa long, she might like to meet a few other Christians. Back home, the circuit-riding preacher didn't get to their settlement more than once a month. On the other Sundays, her family and their neighbors had an all-day singing and dinner on the grounds. It was the highlight of the week, a time when everyone rested from the hard labor of their days and enjoyed Christian fellowship. Constance missed a lot of those gatherings while her father was sick, and she left home soon after he was buried. She shed her tears of grief during the long hours of the night, because her days were busy.

She had traveled first to Fort Smith, where she had spent a couple of weeks obtaining her wardrobe and learning about travel by stagecoach and about the state of Iowa. After that, she had headed to Browning City. During that time, Constance had felt very alone, afraid of the people around her. Not one of them had reached out to her. Hopefully, today would be different. She knew she could trust people who loved God.

When she entered the building, light from outside came through the frosted

19

windowpanes that lined the sides of the room. A single, stained-glass window above the hand-carved pulpit drew her attention. The Good Shepherd held a tiny sheep in His arms against His snowy robe. As a child, she had heard the story behind the picture. Constance walked down the center aisle and chose a seat about halfway toward the front of the sanctuary. She slipped off her cape, folded it, and placed it on the bench beside her. Then she removed her gloves and put them in her reticule on top of the cape.

Constance continued to study the picture, finally noticing other tiny sheep dotting the hillside in the background behind Jesus. Flowers scattered around His feet. She had never seen anything as beautiful as the window, and she basked in the warmth it brought to her heart. A faint hope rose that God would take care of her and help her keep the promise to her father.

Soon after she sat down, the service began. When the pastor finished the opening prayer, a woman went to the pump organ, and a profusion of musical notes filled the room. The hymns they sang were familiar to Constance, so she joined in with all her heart.

When she put her wrap on the seat beside her, it made an effective barrier between her and those who shared the same pew. Not having someone sitting with her didn't detract from her enjoyment of the service. By the time the pastor started his message, she was glad she had come, even though she didn't know anyone.

" 'The secret things belong unto the Lord our God. . . .' " The pastor read a verse from Deuteronomy that Constance had never noticed before. " 'But those things which are revealed belong unto us and to our children forever, that we may do all the words of this law.' "

Of course, Constance loved the New Testament, and she read it much more often than she did the Old Testament. But these words spoke straight to her heart. Too bad Mother's Bible had fallen apart more than a year before. If she still had it, she would look up the words and read them for herself. While the preacher continued his message, Constance started to pray silently that God would help her find Mr. Mitchell. She could conclude her business with him and return to her beloved mountains before very long.

❦

Since Hans had started having a hard time going to sleep, sometimes he overslept. Because of this, he slipped into the church after the singing started and took a seat on the back pew. He didn't usually sit that far back. It made him feel as if he were a spectator instead of a participant in the service. He liked to be close to the front so nothing would distract him from worship. Jackson was a biblical scholar, and his messages always gave Hans a lot to think about. Often, he would return home and reread the passage of scripture and mull over Jackson's words for days, noting how they applied to his own life.

When he was settled in his seat, Hans glanced toward the front. His attention snagged on a woman sitting about halfway down on the opposite side of the aisle. The tilt of her head and set of her shoulders caused his heartbeat to accelerate. He glanced down and took a deep breath before raising his head again. There were other single women in the congregation, but none made him feel this way.

Besides, maybe Constance Miller wasn't single. Just because no one came with her didn't mean that she didn't have a husband back home. At that thought, something unsettling dropped into his chest.

She probably was a believer. She sang every word of the hymns without looking at a hymnbook. The church only had a few scattered around the pews anyway.

Hans noticed that no one sat beside her. For just an instant, the idea of taking that empty space entered his mind, but he dismissed it, turning his attention to the words of the song. How could he be so interested in a woman he might not be able to trust? Besides, it would start gossip about both of them.

∝≈∾

After the final prayer, Constance picked up her cape and fastened it around her shoulders before gathering her handbag and gloves.

"Hello." The cheery feminine voice came from behind her.

Constance turned to see a woman not much older than herself. A smile wreathed the petite woman's face.

"I'm Mary Reeves." She held out her hand. "I don't believe I've met you."

While she took the proffered hand, Constance replied, "I just came to town last Monday. My name is Constance Miller."

The other woman gestured toward the back door where the pastor was shaking hands with people as they left the building. "That's my husband, Jackson. We'd like to have you join us for lunch. I have a roast in the oven, and we usually invite anyone who is new to share a meal with us."

Constance liked the woman's sincere smile. Maybe having dinner with them would be a good thing. She might find out something about the Mitchell family that way.

"Thank you."

As they made their way toward the door, Mrs. Reeves introduced Constance to several other women. They each welcomed her to both the church and the town. Maybe Constance would be able to make a few friends while she continued her quest.

∝≈∾

It wasn't unusual for Jackson and Mary to invite Hans to eat with them, so he gladly accepted Jackson's invitation. As a single man, he always welcomed a home-cooked meal.

"I'll be there in a few minutes." Hans squinted against the bright sunlight. "I finished fixing that kettle for Mary. I'll go fetch it. I know how much she uses it."

While he strode toward his shop, his thoughts returned to the Miller woman. There was some mystery about her, some secret she kept hidden. Why did she invade his thoughts so much? He didn't need to get involved with anyone who wasn't completely honest, did he?

He stepped up on the porch to the parsonage, and Jackson opened the door before he could put the kettle down and knock. "I watched for you. I know that thing is pretty heavy."

When Hans walked through the doorway, he almost dropped what he was carrying. The woman who had filled his thoughts and dreams so much this week sat in a kitchen chair talking with Mary.

"Come on in, Hans," Mary called from the kitchen. "I've invited Miss Miller to share our meal."

Miss? Mary called her *Miss.* Hans could only hope she was right. That is, if he really were interested in the woman.

⟡

When Mary started to introduce Constance to the blacksmith, Constance stopped her. "We've met. Mr. Van de Kieft has protected me from harm more than once."

She should have known that the other woman wouldn't let the subject drop. After they were seated, Mary wanted to know all about it. While they enjoyed the wonderful food, Constance and Hans had to recount both instances. It was interesting to hear the experiences from his perspective. By the time they were through with the stories, all four of them were laughing, and the atmosphere felt much more relaxed.

Constance offered to help Mary wash the dishes, but the other woman insisted that they leave them soaking in the dishpan. "I can wash dishes anytime. I want the chance for us to sit down and really get to know one another."

Mary brought cups of strong coffee into the parlor on a tray that also contained ginger cookies.

"Thanks, Mary." Hans took a couple of the large sweets in one hand. "These are my favorite."

"That's why I made them yesterday."

Constance wondered why the large man had such a strange expression on his face, as if he was surprised by what the pastor's wife said.

"But Jackson just invited me after the service." Hans sank his teeth into the cookie and sighed around it.

"Oh, I know, but we talked about it yesterday." Mary smiled at her husband, and Constance felt a sudden longing for someone to love like that. "But we didn't know that Miss Miller would be attending church this morning. Wasn't that a pleasant surprise?"

For some reason, Constance got the feeling that they weren't surprised at all. Now why did she feel that way?

Mary sat demurely on the sofa beside her husband. "So where exactly did you come from?"

Constance was just taking a sip of the hot beverage, and the abruptness of the question almost made her choke. Mary certainly got right to the point. "I've lived in the Ozark Mountains of northern Arkansas all my life."

Hans set his cup down on the coffee table and leaned back in his chair. "So what made you leave Arkansas?" His eyes narrowed, and she got the feeling that her answer was very important to him.

She glanced around the room, then out the front window. "This is a pretty area."

Constance turned back and took a nibble of her cookie. Looking at him out of the corner of her eye, she could tell that her answer didn't satisfy him. Constance was beginning to like this man, but she wasn't sure she wanted him asking too many personal questions.

Mary reached over and patted Constance's hand. "Wasn't it rather dangerous to travel alone? Didn't you have anyone to come with you?"

Tears sprang into Constance's eyes, and she tried to blink them back. "My mother has been gone for several years, and I. . .lost my father recently."

"Oh, I'm sorry." Mary's expression contained distress. "I didn't mean to bring up sad memories."

Constance swallowed a couple of times, trying to dislodge the lump in her throat. "It's part of life that you have to get used to."

Finally, Jackson joined the conversation. "That doesn't make it any less sad for the person who experiences the loss. Can I pray for you?"

When Constance nodded, they all bowed their heads. Jackson's prayer contained words of comfort that helped her move beyond the pain of the moment. When he finished, they sat for a few silent minutes. She had about decided that it was time for her to leave, but Hans cleared his throat.

"So why did you come to Browning City?"

What could she say without giving too much information? Constance groped in her mind for some way to answer truthfully. She stood and walked over to peer out between the curtains. Trying to find out something about the Mitchells by listening unobtrusively hadn't worked. Maybe she could trust her secret to these people. . .or at least part of it.

"Hans." Mary's voice sounded gentle. "Maybe Constance doesn't want to tell us. We shouldn't put her on the spot like that."

Constance turned toward the group. "That's okay. My father asked me to come find his friend from the war." She clasped her hands tightly in front of her waist. "Do any of you know Jim Mitchell?"

Jackson looked from his wife to Hans then back. "I believe a family by that name owned some land near the Mississippi River, but I don't think anyone has lived on the farm for more than a year."

Constance returned to her chair and perched on the front of it, clasping her hands in her lap. "Is it very far from here?"

"We're several miles from the Mississippi, and if I remember right, the farm is northeast from here." Jackson shuffled his feet against the rug. "I'm sorry we couldn't be any more help than that."

She stood and looked toward the hall tree where her cape hung. "You've helped me a lot. I needed friends, and you welcomed me into your home and fed me a delicious meal. But it's time I got back to the hotel."

Mary followed her into the foyer. "I hope we can become good friends."

"Thank you. I would like that."

Constance donned her cape and gloves and slipped out the door. She knew she was running away, but she had always been totally honest. Trying to keep a secret was becoming a burden to her heart.

Hans didn't stay long after Miss Miller left. He couldn't even remember what Jackson, Mary, and he had discussed in those last moments. His mind was on the story that Constance had told them and on the part of the story she left out. *Why is she so intent on finding this man? Is she interested in him in a romantic way?*

That thought felt like a spike sinking through his chest. He didn't care what she did. But she should be too young for her father's friend, shouldn't she?

Chapter 4

After leaving the parsonage, all Constance could think about was the fact that a Mitchell family owned a farm close to the Mississippi River, not too far from Browning City. That was probably Jim Mitchell's family. How could she find out? The question was her first thought on awakening Monday morning.

She paced from one side of her hotel room to the other trying to think what her father would do if he wanted to find them. Surely, he would go out there to the farm to see if anyone had returned. He might even try to get into the house and see if they left any indication where they might be. Constance could do that, couldn't she? Or maybe talk to a neighbor who might know where they went and when they would come back.

How would she find the farm? She didn't know anything about Iowa, except the portion she had seen from the windows of the stagecoach. If she had it figured out right, the Mississippi was east of Browning City. Did one of the roads lead east out of town? She could just follow that. Maybe it would be a good idea to talk to the sheriff and see if he knew where the farm was. She didn't want to ask Pastor Jackson and Mary about it again. It wouldn't do to arouse too much attention from anyone. They might ask more questions than she wanted to answer.

Constance went to the open window and leaned out to check the temperature. The spring breeze didn't feel cold, so she didn't put on her cape, just her bonnet, before picking up her reticule and going downstairs.

Thankfully, the hotel wasn't on a street where she could see the smithy. While she made her plans, the blacksmith's face often intruded on her thoughts. He didn't really know much about her. Although he had been kind to her, she knew he couldn't possibly be interested in her except as a casual friend. It wouldn't do any good to pay much attention to him. After she found Jim Mitchell, she would be on her way back to her beloved Ozarks.

The walk to the sheriff's office didn't help clear her jumbled thoughts. The door to the office stood open, so she stepped inside. The sheriff had his back to the door, tacking up a wanted poster. Constance had never been in such an office before. The room had a utilitarian feel to it, bare of decorations, unless you wanted to count the posters. They made her shiver in disgust. She didn't want to see outlaws, even if they were mostly drawings. She cleared her throat.

The sheriff whirled around. "Well, what can I do for you, little lady?"

Constance didn't like being called *little lady*. "My name is Constance Miller, and I've come for some information."

The sheriff held out his hand. "I'm Andrew Morton, and I'll help you if I can."

She barely touched his hand with her fingers when they shook hands. "I'm trying to find someone."

The sheriff took off his hat and laid it on his desk. "Have a seat." He gestured toward the chair in front of the desk while he leaned against the front corner of the large, plain wooden piece of furniture. "Who are you looking for?"

Constance cleared her throat again, this time because it felt so dry. "One of my father's army buddies. Jim Mitchell."

He scratched his stubbled cheek and stared into space for a moment. "I think he's the son of a family that owns a farm near the Mississippi."

"That's what I heard."

"I haven't seen hide nor hair of any of the Mitchells for almost a year." He moved behind the desk and dropped into his squeaky chair. "Why do you want to find Jim?" He leaned his arms on the desk and stared intently at her.

Constance squirmed, trying to find a more comfortable position on the hard wooden seat that was so tall her toes barely touched the floor. "My father wanted me to find him. Before he died, he made me promise to do that."

"I'm real sorry to hear about your father. When did you lose him?"

Tears sprang to Constance's eyes, and she removed a hanky from her reticule and blotted them away. "Several weeks ago."

The expression on the sheriff's face turned sympathetic. That brought more tears to Constance. She was sure that by now her nose and eyes must be red-rimmed. She blotted them again with the now soggy bit of cloth.

"Would you like me to go look for him?" He began tapping a pencil on the wooden desk in a brisk cadence. "I probably could go next week."

Constance stood. "No, thank you. If you could just tell me how to get to the farm, I'll go myself."

He rolled up out of his chair and towered over her. "I can give you directions, but I'm not sure it's a good idea for you to go out there alone. I know you came on the coach by yourself—"

"How do you know that?" She knew it wasn't polite to interrupt, but she wanted to know where she stood with this lawman.

He chuckled. "I was standing with Hans when the coach drove up."

"I suppose you saw me fall." Constance knew how to make her tone icy. Hopefully, the man would take the hint.

His grin widened. "Actually, you didn't exactly fall. After you stumbled, Hans—"

As if their words called him, the blacksmith stepped through the doorway. "Andrew, I finished shoeing your horse, so I decided to bring him—" He stopped short and glanced from the sheriff to Constance.

The room felt extremely warm. She wished she had brought her fan. Hopefully, she didn't look too flushed. She even thought about grabbing one of those wanted posters and fanning herself with it.

"Hans." The sheriff skillfully took control of the conversation. "Miss Miller came to ask directions to the Mitchell farm. She wants to go there by herself. I was just starting to tell her it really isn't safe for a single young woman to travel out in the country alone."

Hans nodded. "I agree. Outlaws occasionally roam the back roads. She would be easy prey for them."

Constance stood as tall as she could, stiffening her back. "Thank you for your concern, but I don't want to wait until next week when the sheriff could check it out for me. I want to finish my business with Mr. Mitchell and return home as soon as possible." She turned toward the lawman. "If you'll be so kind as to give me the directions. . .maybe you could write them down, so I won't get lost."

The sheriff sat back down and pulled a tablet and pencil from the top drawer of his desk. "I can't stop you from going, so I'll write the directions so you won't get lost, but I still don't think it's a good idea."

❧

"I'll go with her."

Hans stuck his hands in the back pockets of his trousers. So much for forgetting about Constance Miller. Not only would she be in his thoughts, he was going to spend at least a day with her.

"Oh, but I couldn't take you away from your work." She started to reach for his arm, but then let her hand drop. He followed her actions with his gaze.

He turned to look in her beautiful face, a face that held a very becoming blush. "Work's a mite slow right now." He watched her indecision dissolve into acceptance. "It might take most of the day, so I'll pick you up at the hotel at nine o'clock in the morning, if that's all right with you."

Her nod was almost imperceptible.

"Here are the directions." Andrew handed the piece of paper to him. "I think you know where this is."

Hans studied the notes and crude drawing. "*Ja*, I know the place. We won't have any trouble finding it." He stuck the paper in his shirt pocket and turned to go.

"Thank you, Mr. Van de Kieft." Her soft words followed him into the street, the melody of them once again playing on his heart.

As expected, Hans didn't get much sleep that night, either. At one point, he stood by his bedroom window and stared at the stars. "*Vader* God, why is this happening to me?"

When he spoke out loud to the Lord, he wished for an audible answer in return, but it didn't come. However, peace stole over his heart. Maybe God had everything under control. Maybe it was His will for Hans to spend time with this woman.

Since she had expressed her desire to return to Arkansas, he needed to guard his heart. If he got too close to her, he would be hurt when she left. When he finally fell asleep, he slept longer than he planned and had to hurry to get everything ready to pick her up.

Nine o'clock had passed when he pulled the wagon up in front of the hotel. While he tied the reins to the hitching post, Constance came out on the boardwalk.

"Will I need a parasol to protect me from the sun?"

Because the walkway was a couple of feet from the level of the street, Hans had to look up at her. "Yes, bring one. The road we'll follow has shade in some places, but not in others."

He stood with his hands fisted on his hips and watched her go back into the building. Her clothes were more sensible for a ride than anything he'd seen on her so far. The brown skirt and matching top wouldn't show the dust too much, and the fullness of the skirt would make it easier for her to get up into the wagon. Of course, he would be glad to help her. As tiny as she was, he could just swing her up. That thought reminded him of the other times he had touched her. The familiar knot tied itself in his midsection.

As soon as they passed the edge of town, trees lined the roadway. Even though the leaves on many were just coming out, they provided respite from the sun. Constance folded her sunshade and laid it behind her in the conveyance. "What's this stuff in the back of the wagon?"

She eyed the folded quilt as if it were a coiled serpent. After she returned to the hotel yesterday, all kinds of doubts tormented her. Could she really trust this man? He had protected her from harm twice before, but were his intentions honorable today? Maybe possible outlaws weren't the only danger on the trip.

"It will take us more than an hour to reach the farm." The man didn't take his eyes off the road when he talked to her. "The basket contains food for our lunch, and I brought the quilt in case we have to eat on the ground."

"Thank you." She was always thanking the man. Why hadn't she realized that they would need to eat while they were gone? She could have asked the hotel kitchen to prepare them something. If she were back home, she would have known what to do. Here she felt almost like a fish out of water. Everything was topsy-turvy, and she didn't always think straight.

They rode along for more than an hour without saying anything. Constance watched the countryside change from fairly flat land with lots of trees to small rolling hills with tall grasses blowing in the wind. Soon after they left the shelter of sparse shade, she once again unfurled her parasol. Holding it kept her hands busy.

Mr. Van de Kieft wasn't talkative. At first, she was glad. What did they have to talk about anyway? Then she decided that he was either just being stubborn or he was ignoring her. She didn't like to feel ignored.

"Have you always lived in Browning City?" Her question must have startled him, because he gave a slight jump.

He turned toward her and studied her expression for a moment. "Not always."

Was that all he was going to say? "So where did you live before?"

He kept his eyes on the road ahead. "My family came here from the Netherlands when I was only ten years old. We had a farm north of Browning City."

Once again, silence stretched between them. When it became uncomfortable to Constance, she asked another question. "You said 'had.' Are they not there now?"

When he shook his head, the shiny blond hairs that barely touched his collar stirred in the soft breeze. "No. My father's only brother and his family came to America after we did. He settled in Pennsylvania. My parents decided to move close to them."

Constance stared at him. "And you didn't go with them?"

He guided the horses around a bend in the road before he answered. "I was serving as an apprentice to the blacksmith and didn't want to go." He glanced at her as if looking for her reaction.

"Do you hear from them?"

"Ja, we write letters all the time."

When they finally turned down the lane that led to the farm, Constance was glad Hans had thought to bring food. Her stomach gave a very unladylike rumble.

"Are you hungry?" His words surprised her, because he hadn't said anything for quite a while.

"I believe I am." *How embarrassing!* Because they were once again riding in speckled shade, she folded her parasol and put it behind her.

"We should be at the house pretty soon. Let's check to see if anyone is living there first."

They soon rounded a bend in the lane that revealed a meadow reaching all the way to the edge of a bluff. Although she could hear the river flowing below, they seemed to be high above it. On the other side of the meadow, a house nestled between trees at the edge of a forest. What a beautiful setting for a home.

"The house looks deserted." Hans pulled on the reins, and the team came to a full stop. "If you want to, we could eat closer to the edge of the bluff, and you can take in the view."

She turned toward him. "That's thoughtful. I would enjoy it very much."

"The horses have plenty of grass to eat here. After we've finished our meal, I'll try to find some place to water them."

Hans set the brake and stepped over the side of the wagon. When he was on the ground, he turned and placed his hands on her waist. Before she realized what was happening, she stood on the ground beside him. It took a moment for her to catch her breath. The man really was strong to lift her so effortlessly over the side of the vehicle. The warm imprint of his hands on her waist lingered, making her uncomfortable.

He headed toward the back of the wagon, and she followed. "I can carry the quilt." She tried not to sound breathless but didn't quite make it.

"Mary was kind enough to fix the food for us." Hans smiled at Constance. "She said to tell you to enjoy it."

"I'll be sure to thank her the next time I see her."

Soon the quilt was spread under the shade of a tree far enough away from the edge of the bluff to be comfortably safe. Constance enjoyed the view while Hans unpacked the picnic basket. The tantalizing fragrance of fried chicken called to her stomach, and it rumbled a response.

"I can't exactly remember my geography. Is that area across the river still Iowa?"

Hans looked up from his task. "No. That's Illinois. The river is the eastern boundary of Iowa." He pulled a large jug of fresh water and two tin cups from the basket. "Our food is ready."

❦

Constance sat on the other side of the quilt. Hans was glad he could face her and study her while they ate. After she finished arranging her skirt around her, he handed her a blue granite plate, a silver fork, and a red-checked napkin.

The food tasted wonderful out in the spring air. Besides the chicken, Mary had included biscuits, cheese, and pound cake. As they ate, their conversation took many turns, but they learned a lot about each other. For the first time, Hans felt really comfortable around Constance. Comfortable enough to ask the question that burned a hole in his heart and mind.

"Why did your father insist on you finding this Mr. Mitchell?"

Constance paused with her tin cup halfway to her mouth. Her gaze bore into his before she turned her eyes away from him. For a moment, he didn't think she was going to answer.

"He wanted me to give him a message."

"It must be a very important message." He waited for her response that never came.

The way she stayed turned away and wouldn't look at him confirmed the suspicions Hans harbored. There was much more to the story than she was willing to reveal. What was she hiding? If it wasn't something bad, why was she so secretive?

Chapter 5

Constance walked toward the house. Hans met her going the opposite direction, leading the horses to the spring-fed pool they found quite a ways into the woods. While he watered them, she gazed all around the meadow. The house looked pretty large. Maybe the Mitchell family needed a lot of space. She wondered how many people lived here.

Each side of the building contained at least two windows. She had never seen this many on a house in the country before. Hoping to get a look inside, she pushed aside the bushes that grew in every direction from their position beside the house. Unfortunately, curtains obstructed her view of the room. After trying two more windows and receiving several scratches on her hands, she gave up. She walked the perimeter of the house at a distance far enough away to avoid touching the prickly plants.

The walls looked sound. Constance stepped up on the front porch and turned around. Since the meadow gradually rose from the edge of the bluff to the level of the house, she could see far into the distance. Even though she missed the mountains, she would enjoy seeing a view like this every morning. Facing east, the morning sunlight would warm the house, but when the heat of the afternoon sun beat down, the trees surrounding three sides of the house would keep it cool.

Constance moved over by one of the narrow, square columns supporting the roof of the porch. If she owned a house like this, she would put a couple of rocking chairs out here. It would be a good place to sit in the evening, watching twilight creep across the landscape.

After enjoying this scenario, she turned to check the front door. If it wasn't locked, maybe she could slip into the house. She had never gone into anyone's house without them inviting her in, but the place was deserted. It wouldn't hurt to look around.

Just as the latch clicked open, Hans came around the side of the house. "It's time we started back."

Disappointed, she pulled the door closed again. She wanted to be alone when she checked out the house. At least now that she knew the way to the farm, she could come by herself.

After they were seated in the wagon, Hans clicked his tongue to the two horses. "There's another farmhouse not too far from here. Maybe we could stop and see if the neighbors know anything about this family."

Constance turned to look at him. "That would be helpful. Tha—" She gulped on that word.

"Constance, you don't have to thank me for every little thing I do." He sounded amused.

She gripped her hands in her lap. "My mother taught me to be polite." She peeked up at him.

He nodded, but she noticed he kept his thoughts to himself.

She did, too. Constance had a lot to think about. Why would a family just leave such a nice place sitting empty? Where did they go? When did they plan to come back? Would they ever come back?

Hans turned the team onto a lane that led back through a copse of trees. He knew there was a farm on the other side. Soon the wagon emerged into an open field with a house on the east side.

"Hallo." His shout must have startled Constance, because she jerked and grabbed onto the seat. "Anybody home?"

A man carrying a pitchfork came out of the barn and started toward them with the tool across one shoulder. They met halfway to the house.

"What kin I do for you?"

Good, he was friendly. Hans knew that not all farmers liked people coming onto their land. Since this house was hidden from the road, he had been afraid the owner wouldn't welcome them.

Hans hopped out of the wagon and shook the man's hand. "We're trying to find out something about the Mitchell family who live between here and the river."

"You and your missus want to come up to the house for a cold drink of water?"

Hans knew that if the man knew they were unmarried and traveling alone, he would get the wrong idea about Constance, so he didn't correct the man. He wasn't sure Constance noticed. If she had any questions, he would answer them after they were on the road again.

"We had some just a bit ago. Thank you, anyway. What can you tell me about the Mitchells?"

"You're not the law, are you? No one's in trouble?"

Hans shook his head. "Constance's father wanted her to look up his army buddy, Jim."

The farmer stuck the pitchfork into the dirt and leaned one arm on the top. "Jim and his brother came back after the war." He pulled a bandanna out of the back pocket of his overalls and wiped the sweat from his forehead. "They was 'round here for a couple of years." He stuffed the handkerchief back into the pocket but left most of it hanging out, probably to dry.

"About a year ago, both the old man and his wife took real sick. The brothers tried to nurse them back to health, but it didn't work. After their parents died, those boys hightailed it out of here, and we ain't heard from them since." He put his other arm across the one on the handle of the tool. "Can I help you with anything else?"

Hans scuffed his toe through the dirt on the lane. "Has anyone else been interested in the farm?"

"Not so's I know. Jim and his brother asked us to look after the place for them. We keep an eye on it, but I haven't seen anyone nosing around."

Hans studied the man's expression. He felt sure the farmer was telling the truth, but since this farm was cut off from the road by all the trees, the man might not know if anyone went up there.

"Thank you for the information." Hans stuck out his hand, and the farmer shook it before hefting the pitchfork back across his shoulder.

The man pointed to a grassy area on the other side of the lane. "You can turn your wagon around over there. There ain't no soft spots where you kin get stuck."

Back out on the road, Constance finally spoke. "You didn't tell him we weren't married."

Hans nodded. "I know."

"Why not?"

He glanced at her to see if she looked angry. Thankfully, she didn't. "I thought it would be better for your reputation if he didn't think you were single."

"But isn't that lying?"

"I didn't tell a lie. I just let him think what he wanted to."

This conversation was taking them nowhere. Hans wished he could get her to open up to him and tell him the real reason she was so intent on finding Jim Mitchell. There could be all kinds of reasons. Maybe her father promised her to Mr. Mitchell, and he wanted her to fulfill the promise. But she didn't look as if she were trying to find her intended.

Could there be some other, less legal reason she wanted to find the man? That thought kept nibbling at him, making him feel unsettled.

❦

They arrived back in Browning City mid-afternoon. Constance felt tired. She didn't think she would have been so exhausted if she'd been able to get the man to carry on a conversation on the long trek. As it was, she felt that Hans didn't quite trust her. Maybe he guessed that there was more to her promise than she had told him. There was, but it wasn't really any of his business. Talking about unimportant things would have made the time go faster.

She tried to get him to notice the country they drove through. His monosyllabic answers effectively cut any conversation short. Constance would have just as well traveled alone for all the company he was.

Hans stopped the wagon in front of the hotel and hopped out. By the time Constance stood up, he was on her side of the wagon, ready to help her down. This time, he took her hand and held her steady as she stepped over the side onto a spoke of the front wheel.

When she stood on the ground, she looked up into his face. "I appreciate the way you helped me today."

"Constance. . .Hans." Mary came out the front door of the hotel. "I've been looking for you. I guess I didn't realize it would take this long to go to the farm." She stood on the boardwalk and smiled at them.

Hans offered Constance his arm and escorted her to the steps where the boardwalk broke for the alley. By the time they were at the top of the steps, Mary stood beside them.

Constance let go of his elbow and turned to the pastor's wife. "Why were you looking for us?"

"Actually, I was looking for you." Mary took Constance's arm and pulled her toward the hotel lobby. "Let's sit in here so I can tell you what I found out."

After the two women waved at Hans as he departed, they sat on a sofa beside one wall. A tall bushy plant made the spot feel secluded.

Mary looked as if she were about to explode with excitement. "Mrs. Barker owns the boardinghouse."

"I've noticed it on the other side of town."

"Well, she's a really good cook, but she doesn't like to bake. She had a woman who did all her baking, but the woman fell and broke her leg. Mrs. Barker needs another cook. I thought you might like to do it, if you know how to bake, that is. You would get a free room at the boardinghouse, and she'd pay you some, too." Mary talked so fast, Constance couldn't get a word in edgewise. "I know you won't be here long, but maybe you could stay until the other cook is on her feet and able to work again." When she stopped talking, she turned an expectant expression toward Constance.

Baking was one of Constance's favorite things to do, and she was good at it. She wanted to stay in town until she could locate Jim Mitchell, anyway. Maybe she should do something to bring in money instead of spending so much of her savings.

"That sounds like a good idea." Constance smiled at Mary, joining in her excitement. "I know how to bake lots of things."

Mary stood. "Do you want to go meet her right now?"

When they arrived at the boardinghouse, Mrs. Barker stood on the porch talking to a couple who rented a room from her. Mary and Constance waited on the front walkway until the trio finished their conversation.

"Mary Reeves," Mrs. Barker called from the porch. "What are you doing standing out there in the sun? Bring your friend up here for a cool drink of water."

Constance followed Mary up the steps, and the two women sat in inviting cushioned rocking chairs. These were just the kind Constance imagined should be on the front porch of the Mitchell's farmhouse.

"So what brings you here?" The proprietor of the boardinghouse dropped into the third rocker.

Mary leaned forward. "I want you to meet Constance Miller. She's new to town, and she knows how to bake."

At that last statement, Mrs. Barker's face beamed. "Does she now?" She peered at Constance over the top of her glasses. "Are you looking for a job?"

Constance wasn't sure why she felt so nervous. Maybe because she had never had a job in her life. "I understand you need someone for a while. I won't be here too long, but I could stay until your other cook comes back to work."

The older woman tented her fingers under her chin and stared out at the treetops across the street. After a moment, she turned back toward Constance. "So what exactly do you know how to bake?"

Constance had expected to be asked such a question, so she had a ready answer. "It's been said that my biscuits are the lightest ones in the holler back home. I always make berry pies in the summer. We dried peaches and apples so we had those kinds of pies all year round. No one has ever complained that my crusts were tough."

Mrs. Barker rocked her chair back and forth. "This is sounding better all the time. Is that all?"

"Well, my pa was partial to yeast rolls, but sometimes I made potato rolls or sourdough rolls when we couldn't get the yeast."

"My mouth is watering just from the telling." Mrs. Barker smacked her lips. "What about cakes?"

Constance didn't want to brag too much. She'd done enough of that in the last few minutes to last all year. But she needed to give Mrs. Barker enough information so she could make her decision.

"My pound cake always gets eaten first on Sundays when we have dinner-on-the-grounds. I can make other kinds, too. Apple spice, pumpkin, several others."

Mary rocked contentedly and gave Constance an encouraging smile.

"Would you be willing to show me what you can do?" Mrs. Barker sounded eager.

"Do you want me to make biscuits for dinner tonight? There's time." Constance felt a spark of excitement inside.

Mrs. Barker stood up. "Come right on in. Mary, are you going to stay and visit while we do this?"

The beef stew simmering in a large kettle on the back of the stove filled the kitchen with an enticing aroma. Constance realized with a start that she was hungry again. She would enjoy eating here.

"Since you're having stew"—Constance hooked one of Mrs. Barker's aprons over her head and tied it behind her back—"why don't I make a pan of corn-bread, too?"

"Sounds good to me." Mrs. Barker started putting containers out on the table. Then she turned toward Mary. "You and Pastor Jackson would be welcome to stop by for supper."

After Mary agreed, she left, presumably to tell her husband about the invitation.

Mrs. Barker sat beside the table, greasing baking tins, while Constance got started mixing the dough. They chatted while they worked, and soon Constance knew she would like to live here and work for this woman.

When the first pan of lightly browned biscuits came out of the oven, Mrs. Barker exclaimed, "Constance, you have a job if you want one."

Constance dusted the last of the flour from her hands and smiled at the other woman. "I want one."

"Then you can move your things from the hotel after supper. Come upstairs, and I'll show you your room."

⊗

After dinner, Pastor Jackson and Mary walked back to the hotel with Constance. He waited in the lobby while the two women went upstairs. Constance pulled her carpetbag out from under the bed and carefully packed her belongings in it.

"I'm glad you could help Mrs. Barker this way." Mary stood by the window, gazing out into the twilit evening.

Constance stopped folding her unmentionables. "It'll help me, too. I won't have to be quite so careful with the rest of Pa's money." She went over to the other woman and gave her a quick hug. "Thank you."

Mary turned back toward her. "I can see God's hand in all of this, can't you?"

Constance nodded. Of course. How could she ever have gotten this far without God's help? But why couldn't she find Jim Mitchell, and why did God want her here in Browning City, Iowa, if she couldn't?

Chapter 6

Constance stood looking out the window of her upstairs room in the boardinghouse. A nearly full moon shone through the cold night air, lighting an inky sky that contained pin dots of stars. A soft breeze ruffled the leaves recently emerged from their buds on the trees. She felt so far from her mountain home.

Time and distance hadn't really dulled the pain of being alone. Even though she tried to keep all her grieving to the nighttime hours, some days it was extremely hard to keep up the strong front she maintained before others.

The little girl inside her wanted her mother back. Had it really been three years since Ma died? That event so soon after Pa returned from the fighting seemed to change him more than the war had. Maybe that was the reason he wasn't able to fight off his final illness.

Tears streamed down her cheeks, and she didn't bother to rub them away. Not only did she long for a comforting hug from her mother, she wished she was still a little girl who could climb up in her daddy's lap and lay her head on his shoulder. How safe she had felt there.

She turned back toward the pleasant room. Mrs. Barker made the rooms homey. Constance had never had things this nice when she grew up. Mother did make quilts out of the good parts of their worn-out clothes, and she used every scrap left over from making new things, but her quilts were more utilitarian than beautiful. Constance crossed the room and ran her fingers along the honeycomb pattern so different from Ma's nine-patch quilts.

If Pa had used more of the money he saved, they could have had nicer things. It wouldn't have been soon enough to save Ma, but. . .her mind couldn't even imagine what it would have meant.

The tears came faster, flowing down and spotting the multi-colored cover. Constance pulled it back and slid between sheets smoother than she had ever slept on before. Even the ones in the hotel weren't this nice. She turned her face into the pillow to muffle her sobs and cried for her losses and for what might have been. But there was something more inside her that she couldn't explain. Some deep longing she had never felt before.

Because she slept fitfully, Constance was up before the chickens, as her mother would often say. She bathed her face in the cold water left in her pitcher, hoping it would erase the ravages of a night spent in grief. She peered into the looking glass above the washstand. Her skin only had a few red blotches on it. By the time she was dressed, more natural color filled her face.

Constance pasted on a smile, took a deep breath, and opened the door. When she reached the kitchen, it stood empty, silent, and lonely. She went to the black cast-iron stove and stirred the embers, adding more wood from the pile on the back porch. While the fire built up, she put ground coffee and water in the blue graniteware pot and set it on the back of the stove.

By the time Mrs. Barker came into the kitchen, the room had warmed, and the smell of fresh-brewed coffee filled the air. Constance stood beside the table, cutting biscuits from the dough she had patted out on its floured surface.

"Why, Constance." Mrs. Barker went over to pour herself a cup of coffee. "You don't have to get up so early. I usually stoke the fire and start the coffee." She turned and leaned against the cabinet that held the empty dishpan and a bucket of water.

Constance continued cutting the dough and putting the biscuits in a greased pan. "I woke early, so it didn't make any sense to lie abed." Although she didn't glance up, she could feel Mrs. Barker looking at her.

"I have a rolling pin."

Constance turned to look at her employer before concentrating on her task. "I don't really like to roll the biscuits. I know I did last night, but I was just getting used to this kitchen. They will be lighter if I don't work the dough too much. I just pat it to the thickness I want."

Mrs. Barker came over and glanced at those in the pan. "I never thought of doing something like that."

Once again, Constance felt the woman looking at her. She raised her head and smiled at her employer.

After setting her cup on the edge of the table away from where Constance worked, Mrs. Barker studied Constance's face as if she were reading a book. "I see a hint of sadness in your eyes that I didn't notice yesterday. Are you homesick for your family?"

Constance swallowed around the lump in her throat, a lump that was probably made up of more tears waiting to be released. "I don't have any family left." She sobbed on the last word.

"Oh, you poor dear."

The sympathy in Mrs. Barker's voice released some of that reservoir of tears. Constance reached up and swiped them away.

"I think you need a mother's hug."

Comforting arms engulfed Constance and didn't let go. She enjoyed them for a moment before she stepped back. "Thank you." Here she was thanking someone again. She stiffened her spine and went back to her task.

"I'm here for you anytime you need me." Mrs. Barker bustled over and placed a skillet on the stove. Then she started stirring eggs together to scramble.

At breakfast, Constance paid closer attention to catch the names of the people at the table. Two men named Theodore and Thomas sat beside each other. She could tell by all their similarities that they must be brothers. Short in stature, their balding heads had tufts of hair around the sides and back that stood straight up, and their eyes twinkled when they laughed. Not only did they look almost identical, their voices sounded similar, and their gestures followed the same patterns. They kept talking about working at the mercantile. From what they said, they must be employees, not the owners of the place.

Martha Sutter was the schoolteacher, and Sylvia Marshall talked about the clothing she designed for a customer, so she had to be a seamstress. Constance wondered where she did her work. The new couple who rented a room yesterday afternoon was quieter, listening to the others. However, when Martha asked their names, they told her they were Ed and Francis Owens. They didn't say much else except that they were looking for a farm to buy, so they might not live in the boardinghouse very long.

"Mrs. Barker, how is Selena?" Constance wondered who Sylvia was inquiring about.

"She's still in a lot of pain." The proprietress shook her head as if dismayed. "Her sister came in from their farm and took her home with her. She wanted to be sure she was well cared for. The doctor is concerned because the break wasn't a clean one. He's afraid it might take awhile to heal."

The other cook. Constance said a silent prayer for the woman.

Constance baked all morning. Mrs. Barker wanted bread so they could have sandwiches for supper. She gave Constance canned peaches to make pies for lunch, and Constance made a pound cake to have at suppertime. All the work felt good. It had been too long since she felt such a sense of accomplishment.

When everyone came in for supper, Hans arrived. He told Mrs. Barker that he wanted to eat at the boardinghouse that night. He was tired of his own cooking. Somehow, Constance had a hard time picturing the gentle giant toiling over a hot stove. She wondered what he cooked.

"You're welcome to eat here anytime." Mrs. Barker smiled encouragement at him. "I can always use the extra money."

Constance ate quietly, listening to all the conversations around the table. She hoped they would mention something that would help her finish her quest.

"Mrs. Barker, this pound cake is the best one I've ever eaten." Hans stuffed a forkful into his mouth, and a smile lit his face.

"Thank Constance." The woman gestured toward her. "She's my new baker." Hans stared at Constance. "I didn't know you were looking for a job."

She dropped her hands into her lap. "I wasn't. Remember Mary was waiting to talk to me when we returned to town?" He nodded, and she continued. "That's what she wanted to tell me. That Mrs. Barker needed someone to bake while her cook recovered. It sounded good to me. I have a better place to stay than the hotel, and I can save my money."

"If you're going to bake every day, I just might have to eat here every night." Hans laughed.

Some of the others joined in. Their compliments about her baking abilities encouraged Constance. Maybe she was supposed to be here right now. If only someone would mention something about the Mitchell boys, especially Jim.

The thought of Hans eating here every night caused an unsettled feeling in her. Why did the prospect of seeing him every day make her happy?

Hans had been surprised to learn that Constance had a job at the boardinghouse. Pleasantly surprised, since the things she baked were so delicious. When he told Mrs. Barker he might eat there every night, he meant it as a joke. After she agreed, he knew it was just what he wanted to do. Maybe by being there with everyone sharing their days, he would be able to find out what Constance was hiding. And the food was far better than anything he put together.

For the next few nights, he showed up right when the meal was being served. Every night, Constance made a different kind of dessert. If Hans didn't work so hard, he might get fat eating all those rich sweets.

Since his family had moved away, he lived alone. He hadn't felt lonely until he spent so much time with other people around the table in the evening. Maybe he wasn't created to be solitary. He had friends, but when he went home after work, the evenings seemed to stretch on forever.

Today was Saturday, and several people from outlying farms who came to town to pick up supplies also brought items that he needed to repair for them. A couple even had him shoe more than one horse, which they would take home when they left town later. His day was long, almost past the supper hour at the boardinghouse.

When he arrived, everyone was finishing their meal and ready for dessert. He had just walked in as Mrs. Barker had told him to do, but when he saw all the empty dishes on the table, he turned to leave.

"Hans." Mrs. Barker hurried around the table to greet him. "I thought you would be coming. I told Constance to put a plate in the warming oven for you." She turned to look at the young woman. "Why don't you get it for Hans while I pour his drink?"

Constance carried the covered plate with two thick, quilted potholders. When she set it in front of him and lifted the cover, the smell of fried chicken, mashed potatoes, and gravy caused his stomach to rumble. He hoped no one noticed, but just before Constance turned away, he noticed a twinkle in her eye. It looked good there. Too often, her face held a sad expression.

Mrs. Barker patted Constance on the shoulder. "You sit down and finish your food. I'll get the apple pie for everyone."

Constance slipped into the empty chair beside him. He felt her presence so strongly that, even if his eyes had been closed, he would have known she was there.

Mrs. Barker returned carrying two plates of pie, which she set in front of the two single women who roomed with her. "What kept you so long, Hans?"

Everyone turned to look at him expectantly. He didn't like the feeling of being the center of attention. "I had lots of customers today. Then I went home to clean up. I didn't want to show up at your table in dirty clothes or with dirty hands."

A chorus of chuckles went round the table, and conversation resumed. Hans enjoyed the excellent food while everyone else except Constance ate dessert. One by one, they excused themselves and left the room. Then Mrs. Barker took her empty plates into the kitchen.

"I've been wanting to ask you something, Constance." When he said her name, she looked at him instead of the food on her plate. "I have a buggy, and I would like to pick you up and take you to church in the morning." Her expression told him that she might want to decline his invitation. "I know you walked last week, but the boardinghouse is farther away, and the weather is getting warmer. We could even ask Mrs. Barker if she wants a ride, too. Would that be all right with you?"

Constance stopped eating and put her fork down. After a long moment, she turned to smile at him. "That would be nice, Hans."

Mrs. Barker agreed to go to church with them, but she planned to go out to see Selena after the services. The people who lived on the neighboring farm to Selena's sister had offered to give her a ride out there and even bring her back to town.

⋘⋙

On Sunday, the sanctuary of the church welcomed Constance like an old friend. How could she have gotten to feel so at home in such a short time? Hans stayed outside talking to one of the farmers, and that suited her fine. She sat in the same pew where she had sat the week before and looked up at the Good Shepherd. Mary turned around in the front row and smiled at Constance. Several times this week, the two women had spent time together.

Just before Pa came home from the war, Patience—Constance's best friend all through her growing-up years—had gotten married and moved to Little Rock. At first, they wrote letters to each other. Then when Patience and her husband had a baby, the letters became few and far between. It had been months since she had received one. Already, Mary had become a good friend to Constance, filling the hole left by losing Patience.

Before Jackson stood up for the opening prayer, Hans came down the aisle and asked her if he could sit beside her. She slid over and let him be by the aisle. Constance hoped no one got the wrong idea. Mary glanced back again, and her smile widened.

After the final prayer, Mary made a beeline up the aisle, stopping beside Hans. "Jackson and I would like to invite the two of you over for lunch. Today, I left a meatloaf in the warming oven."

A big smile spread across the man's face. "I really like your meatloaf."

Constance wondered if there was any food he didn't like. She'd seen him eat a lot of every supper at the boardinghouse. She wondered if Mrs. Barker was charging him enough for his meals.

"So how about it, Constance?" Mary's eyes pleaded with her. "We really enjoyed last week."

Constance glanced around the room that was rapidly becoming empty. "Won't other people want to spend time with you, too? They might not like you spending so much time with someone new."

Mary's face held an incredulous expression. "No one will care. Most of these people hurry back to their farms to take care of livestock. Besides, we've had supper with three different families this week. So please say you'll come. I know Mrs. Barker doesn't serve meals to the boarders on Sunday."

How could she say no? Jackson had helped her start finding the Mitchell property, and Mary had found her a job. Besides, she really enjoyed this couple. She glanced up at the tall man standing in the aisle beside her. If she were truthful with herself, she had to admit that spending time with Hans could be interesting, too. It couldn't hurt to do it one more time, could it?

Chapter 7

That man really does like your meatloaf." Constance laughed at the memory of Hans's appreciation.

At least today Mary let Constance help her with the dishes. While Mary washed, Constance dried and stacked them on the table. Later, she would help Mary put them up. Then next time she came, she would know where they went in the cupboard behind the curtains that hung above the dishpan.

Mary's eyes twinkled in amusement. "That's why I made such a large one. He did eat quite a bit, didn't he?" After plunging a plate in the rinse water, she shook off the excess and handed it to Constance. "He's been here before, but you have to agree that it takes a lot of food to fuel a man that large."

Constance felt the warmth of a blush make its way up her neck and into her cheeks. She had been thinking the same thing. Not only was Hans handsome, but he was also strong and well-built. Of course, a lady shouldn't have noticed a man's build, but how could she miss it? She placed the dry plate on top of the stack on the table and turned back around. His muscles rippled when he ate, as well as when he worked.

Mary had a speculative gleam in her lively eyes. She put her hands on her hips and laughed. "You already noticed that, didn't you?"

Constance tried to think of something to change the subject, but just then the topic of conversation came through the back door, accompanied by Jackson. "Here come the men." She ducked her head and polished an already shining piece of silverware.

Mary turned toward her husband. "So what did Hans think?"

Constance wondered what Mary meant. The men had stepped outside while the women cleaned up the table, but Constance hadn't known that there was an ulterior motive.

Jackson put his arm around his wife and pulled her close to his side. "He agrees with me. We can do it, and he will help."

"Help with what?" Constance laid the damp towel on top of the cabinet beside the wash basin and folded her arms. "I'm missing something here."

Hans smiled at her, and for a moment, her breath caught in her throat. Then he turned toward Jackson. "Our pastor decided we should use the extra land behind the parsonage to start a large garden. Several members of the

44

congregation don't have access to an area where they can grow vegetables. We could either let them help with the garden, or we could give some of the excess produce to those who need it most."

Jackson pulled at the button at his collar. "All the details haven't been worked out, but Hans has agreed to help with the project."

"I'd like to help, too." For several years, Constance had been in charge of growing the produce for her family. "I have a lot of experience."

"This is sounding better all the time." Mary smiled up at her husband.

When Constance saw the look of love Jackson gave his wife, she wondered if a man would ever look at her like that. She longed for it.

"One of the reasons I wanted to see if Hans would help is that I don't want Mary to do too much."

"It won't hurt me." She tapped his shoulder with a playful nudge. "We'd like the two of you to be the first to know. Sometime in late autumn, there is going to be an addition to the Reeves family."

Constance clapped her hands. "Oh, Mary, that's wonderful. Jackson is right. You shouldn't do too much. Let the three of us do most of the work."

"Along with other parishioners who want to help," Jackson added.

"Friday is usually a slow day at the smithy." Hans gazed out the back door at the property. "I'll come over and start plowing."

Jackson left his wife's side and leaned one hand against the doorpost. "I'll be free to help you. We should be able to put in at least a couple of acres or more. That will grow quite a few vegetables."

Constance turned to Mary. "Do you have a root cellar?"

"Of course."

"Then maybe you should plan on at least an acre of potatoes. They last a long time in a root cellar and can be used in so many ways."

Before Constance and Hans left that afternoon, the four of them had planned how to lay out most of the rows. Jackson and Hans decided to call their undertaking the Community Garden.

❦

When Hans arrived at the boardinghouse for supper the next day, his mind was full of all the plans they had made. Without hesitating, he told the others around the table about what was going on. Thomas and Theodore asked a number of intelligent questions about the undertaking.

"I, for one," Theodore said, "would like to help with this garden. We always had a large one when we were growing up, didn't we, brother?"

When Thomas nodded, his fringe of hair bobbed. "That's one of the things I miss by living in the boardinghouse in town. I really like to work in merchandising, and someday, I hope to own my own store, but I do miss the feeling of fresh-turned earth between my fingers." He got a faraway look in his eyes.

Hans would have never guessed. These brothers dressed like businessmen and talked a lot about their work. "We can use all the help we can get. The plot contains several acres."

Theodore turned toward Mrs. Barker. "How would you like to have fresh produce all summer?"

A big smile spread across her face. "If we have too much to use, I could always can some for the winter. Then our meals would be more than meat and potatoes in the coldest months."

Soon conversation buzzed around the table. Hans leaned back in his chair, enjoying all the fuss. This idea fueled so much interest, the group took on the feel of a real family.

"Mr. Van de Kieft." Martha Sutter leaned around Constance. "Do you think I could let my older students help with the project? Some of them live on farms, but many live in town. It would be good experience for them."

Hans turned his attention toward Constance. "What do you think?"

She cupped her chin with one hand. "What a wonderful idea! With so many people helping, maybe Mary won't feel that she has to do too much."

Hans nodded, wishing he could touch her chin the same way. "I'm going to start plowing next Friday."

"I'm usually off on Fridays." Thomas looked at his brother. "I'll help with the plowing. Maybe my brother can help us with the seeds."

"Consider it done." A pleased expression stole over Theodore's usually solemn face.

Sylvia wasn't very talkative, but she chimed in, "I can help when you start planting. Just let me know."

Mrs. Barker got up to start serving the angel food cake Hans had been eyeing ever since he sat down. "It looks as if you have almost a full crew just waiting to help you, Hans."

"I'm sure Jackson will be glad for so many willing hands." The piece of cake she set in front of him had to be six inches high. The man who married Constance would be blessed indeed. For some reason, that thought didn't set too well with all the food he had eaten.

Work on the garden progressed at a fast pace. Constance helped all she could, but Pastor Jackson had asked her to try to keep Mary occupied in pursuits that weren't too strenuous. That wasn't an easy task. Mary often insisted that the work helped her gain strength she'd need to deliver the baby.

Constance was so caught up in the baking at the boardinghouse and working with Mary that she didn't think very often about her promise to her father.

About a month after she came to Browning City, she and Mary were in the parlor of the parsonage, working on tiny clothing for the baby. Constance had hemmed a flannel blanket, and now she was crocheting an edging around it. A knock sounded at the door.

"You stay there," she said to Mary. "I'll see who it is."

Hans stood in the late afternoon sunlight that slanted onto the porch. Golden rays highlighted his hair and deepened the intensity of his blue eyes. He held his hat in his hands.

"Come in, Hans." She stepped back, and he entered.

"Don't get up, Mary. I came to see Constance."

Constance noticed that Mary had a satisfied look on her face just before she bent to make more tiny stitches in the gown she worked on.

"So what can I do for you, Hans?"

He put his hat under one arm and reached toward his shirt pocket with the other. "When I went to the post office to check for my mail, the postmaster asked me if I would give you this." He pulled out a slightly wrinkled, smudged letter.

"I wonder who that's from." The only person who had ever written to Constance had been Patience, but she couldn't know that Constance was in Iowa.

Hans grinned. "Open it and see." He didn't seem to be in any hurry to leave.

Constance dropped onto the sofa and studied the missive, turning it over and over. The words written on the outside were her name and General Delivery, Browning City, Iowa. The only people she had told where she was going were their closest neighbors. Bertram and Molly Smith had helped her get through the death of her mother and then the death of her father. She had thanked God for their presence in her life.

Hans still stood in the doorway to the entry hall. "Are you going to open it or not?" He sounded like a child who couldn't wait to open Christmas or birthday presents.

She turned it over, released the sealing wax, and spread the page flat. She knew the Smiths didn't have a lot of schooling, just the elementary grades available in their holler. There weren't many from that area who went as far in school as she had.

The writing looked spidery, but she was able to make out the words:

Constance,
We don't know if'n yore coming back to yore home place or not. If yore not, would ya consider sellin it to me.

Constance glanced down to the bottom of the page to be sure it was written by Bertram. It was.

I been savin' money hopin' to get more land. If'n yore willin, I could pay ya a fair price.

When she saw the figure he had written as a fair price, she could hardly believe it. The amount was more money than she had ever dreamed of owning at one time. With that much, she could live comfortably for quite a while.

"Is it bad news, Constance?"

She glanced up at Hans. While she had been reading the letter, he had taken the chair across from her. She could feel his intense stare as if it were a physical touch.

"No." She let the hand holding the letter fall into her lap. "I wouldn't call it bad news. I just don't know what to think about it."

"Is it something you want to share with us?" Mary didn't take her eyes off of her sewing. "You don't have to if you don't want to."

Constance glanced from one to the other. "You two and Jackson are my best friends here, so I don't mind telling you. Maybe you can pray for me to know what to do." After picking the letter back up, she read it to them.

When she mentioned the money, Hans widened his eyes at the amount, so she asked, "Do you think that's fair?"

He stood and paced across the room, turning his hat in his hands. "I don't know anything about your property. That would buy a pretty good farm around here. . .but do you really want to sell?"

"I don't know what I want to do." She folded the paper in half several times, then thrust it into the pocket of her skirt. "Bertram and Molly are looking out for things while I'm gone. I know that when—if I go back, I'll have to hire someone to help me. I can't do everything by myself. I'm not sure I can afford to do that. There's a lot to think about."

Hans stopped his pacing and stared out between the front curtains at the waning light. "Have you ever thought about staying here in Iowa?"

He turned back and their gazes connected and held for a long moment. How could Constance answer his question? Just thinking about being here with her new friends, including the man who stood across the room from her, brought happiness to her heart. Maybe mostly because of him. She couldn't tell him that.

"I like it here, and I feel an accepted part of the community, but I also have to fulfill my father's dying wish."

Constance noticed that even though Mary continued sewing, her gaze occasionally darted from one of them to the other. "So, Mary, what do you think?"

Mary put her work in her lap. "I think you were right when you said that you needed prayer. When Jackson comes home, and it should be anytime now, we should seek the Lord about this."

Hans stood clutching his hat in one hand, staring at Constance. She felt his gaze again.

"That would be nice. However, I need to go to the boardinghouse and help Mrs. Barker with supper." Constance stood.

"Why don't you come back after supper? You come, too, Hans." Mary laid her sewing in the basket at her feet.

"Ja, I agree." Hans came back to stand beside Constance. "May I walk over there with you?"

&

After Constance and Mrs. Barker finished doing the dishes, Hans escorted Constance back to the parsonage. "So have you been thinking a lot about that offer in the letter?"

She nodded. "Have you?"

"Ja." He had thought of nothing else.

What would it mean if Constance sold her farm? Would she stay here in Iowa? Did he want her to? Of course he did, but was it God's will for her to stay? Hans wanted God's best for her, but he hoped that didn't include taking her away from Browning City. The thought of Constance getting back on the stage and riding it out of town caused a pain deep in his heart.

There were other things to consider. Even though Constance said he was one of her best friends, she was still keeping some secret from him. In her busyness, she had stopped talking about the promise and finding Jim Mitchell, but today the letter had brought the issue to the forefront again. His heart told him he could trust her, but his mind couldn't get past the fact that she might be hiding something bad from him. Because of the way she had thrown herself into the life of the town, he couldn't imagine her wanting to find Jim Mitchell to marry him. There had to be something else. But what could it be? Maybe she would tell them tonight.

&

After the four of them had prayed for a while, Constance remembered the scripture from the first message she had heard Jackson preach. Something about the secret things belonging to the Lord. That night when she was alone in her room, she walked to the window and looked out at the spring night. All kinds of plants and trees wore the splendor of their spring renewal. That splendor had been hidden through the winter, kept by God, awaiting the time to reemerge. Maybe the things in her life were like that, too. Was God keeping some things secret, waiting until the right time to reveal them to her?

Dear God, is there a reason You have not helped me find Jim Mitchell? Is the time not right? I wish You still talked to people today. Is my new home supposed to be in Browning City away from the place where I experienced so much grief?

She pulled from her pocket the letter Bertram and Molly sent. After going over to the bureau, she spread the paper in the light from the candle. She traced each word with her finger. When she came to the amount of money, her finger tingled almost as if the numbers were alive. *Am I supposed to accept this offer?*

In the early morning light, she took out the unused paper, quill, and ink she had bought when she moved into the boardinghouse. Carefully, she dipped the nib into the black liquid and spread her answer across the parchment. Then she dripped blood-red sealing wax to seal the message. After breakfast, she would post it.

Chapter 8

Constance threw herself into working in the Community Garden. Doing the things she grew up with made her feel like a productive part of the town. After baking in the morning, then having a noon meal at the boardinghouse, she spent most of each afternoon either in the garden or with Mary.

Spring in Iowa was different from spring in the Ozarks but just as beautiful. Sunshine coaxed flowers to peek through partially opened buds. Robins hopped along the ground searching for worms. They and other birds were particularly fond of the soil Hans had turned over for the garden plot. As leaves began to fill the branches of nearby trees, the twittering of birds building nests lent a special musical background to the work. Constance hummed along with them while she pulled the weeds trying to grow between the rows.

Some days, several other people joined her in her toil. When Hans was one of them, she liked to watch him out of the corners of her eyes. His well-developed muscles rippled as he worked with a hoe or planted another row. She wondered how his shirt kept from ripping, he filled it out so well.

That thought brought a blush. She felt the warmth creep up her neck and onto her cheeks. Hopefully, if anyone noticed, they would just think it was the sunshine giving her the rosy cheeks. She quickly averted her gaze and kept her head down.

One day, she decided it surely had been enough time to receive an answer from the letter she had sent the Smiths back in Arkansas. When she arrived at the post office, several other people stood in line to pick up mail. She had to wait her turn to talk to the postmaster.

She took her place behind a man she had never seen before. When he reached the front of the line, he and the postmaster started a long conversation. Since she was the last person in line, she wandered around the room, looking at various notices tacked up on the walls. Anything to make the wait more bearable.

The man talked really loudly, and one word stuck out to Constance. He said the name Mitchell. She started back across the room to ask him if he was kin to them, but he continued talking, and she could hear every word.

"It's too bad about those boys. I think they just lost their way after their parents died."

The postmaster nodded his agreement.

Constance couldn't hold in her curiosity any longer. "Excuse me, sir. Were you talking about Jim Mitchell by any chance?"

The man turned toward her and nodded, his scraggly beard bobbing up and down in rhythm with his head. "Yep. Him and his brother."

"I've been trying to find Jim Mitchell. He and my father were in the war together." She tried not to sound too eager.

"Well, I was just telling Hiram here"—he gestured toward the man behind the desk—"that both those boys got in a gunfight in a saloon north of here, and it didn't end good for them. They both died from their wounds."

Shock robbed Constance of speech for a moment. Jim Mitchell was dead. If that was true, she would be released from her promise, wouldn't she? But what about the gold?

"Where did you say this happened?" She stared up into the man's face, trying not to show him how interested she was in his answer.

He scratched his cheek through the beard. "Let me see. I think it was at Camden Junction. It's about a five-hour ride north of Browning City. I heard tell they are both buried there. Seems like they were the end of the line for the Mitchell family in these parts. It's just too bad. I always did like their parents."

Camden Junction. Constance would have to find out where that town was located. Maybe she could go there and be sure this man knew what he was talking about.

After finding out that she didn't have any mail, Constance walked slowly back to the boardinghouse. What did all this information mean to her? How she wished that God would talk to people today. She wanted to ask Him what she should do about all that was happening in her life.

That gold had to be somewhere. Maybe it was on the farm. Tomorrow after she finished baking, she would go out there and see for herself. She knew Martha planned to take her students to work in the garden, so no one would miss her.

All the time she worked in the garden that afternoon, she wanted to tell Mary what was going on, but she didn't want to worry her. Maybe if Constance found the gold and gave it back to the government, then she would feel released from her promise to her pa. No one needed to know what Jim Mitchell did. She didn't want to give his family a bad name now that he was gone. . .if he really was.

The next day, she started baking earlier than usual. By the time Mrs. Barker got to the kitchen, Constance had a couple of pans of biscuits all ready for breakfast. She had started making double the amount of bread every other day, so she wouldn't need to bake bread today. There was enough left from yesterday's baking. By the time Mrs. Barker had breakfast ready, Constance had enough pies made to last through supper.

"You really are in a hurry." At least Mrs. Barker didn't sound upset. "Do you have special plans for today?"

"I just thought I would spend some time looking around the countryside today. Maybe I have spring fever." Constance kept her eyes on her work.

"You know, Constance, if you want to take a day off from the baking, it would be okay. You do more than your share of the work around here as it is." Mrs. Barker came over and gave Constance a quick hug.

Tears sprang to Constance's eyes. Mrs. Barker made her feel more like a family member than an employee and boarder.

When she finished helping clean up the kitchen, she went by to see Mary. After they visited a few minutes, Constance told her that she wanted to explore the area for a while. Mary didn't seem concerned, so Constance soon left. She walked to the livery stable, being careful not to go by the smithy on the way. When she stepped into the large shadowed barn, an older man came out of one of the stalls.

"Can I help you, miss?" The man leaned his pitchfork against the wooden rails.

"I'd like to rent a horse." Constance tried not to look nervous, even though the anticipation of maybe finding something today made her almost quiver.

The man looked her up and down, but not in a bad way. "Have you ever ridden before?" He must have been sizing up her abilities. He probably didn't want an inexperienced rider to hurt one of his animals.

"Yes, we had a horse when I was growing up. I used to ride it across the mountain to school."

He stood with his hands on his hips. "So it's been awhile?"

"At least two or three years." Constance didn't like being put on the spot like that. Why couldn't the man just rent her a horse and quit asking questions?

He went into the open tack room and took a bridle off a hook on the far wall. He turned and strode down to a stall at the other end of the structure. After opening the gate, he went in and put the harness on the animal, then led the horse toward her.

"This here horse is gentle but has enough spirit to make your ride a good one."

"Thank you, Mr. . . ?"

"Jones. Charlie Jones."

She took his proffered hand and shook it. "I'm Constance Miller. I'd like to rent the horse for most of the day. Should I pay you now?" She had some money tucked inside the waistband of her riding shirt. She'd find a way to remove it privately when she needed to.

"Naw. We can settle up when you get back." Charlie rubbed the horse's neck and gave it an affectionate pat.

He went through the open tack room doorway and brought out a side saddle. Constance hadn't ever seen one. She had just read about them. They sure looked different.

"I don't know how to use one of those." Constance pulled on the sides of her split skirt. "I've always ridden straddling the horse."

She watched Mr. Jones go back and exchange the saddle. He hefted it up on the back of the animal that stood patiently waiting.

"What's the horse's name?"

"Blaze, but it's talking about this"—he pointed to the white slash down the horse's face—"not about how fast he runs." He chuckled at his own joke.

Even though Constance didn't think his words were that funny, she laughed. She didn't want to insult the livery manager. After using the mounting block to get up on the horse's back, she turned him toward the street and started riding east. It didn't take her long to get a feel for the animal, and soon she was moving along at a good pace.

⌘

Hans headed toward the livery stable with some harness he had mended for Charlie. In his pocket, he carried a shriveled apple from his root cellar. He liked to give Blaze a special treat when he went by his stall. Maybe he'd take the horse out for a ride, since he didn't have much work right now.

"Charlie, I've got your harness." When Hans went from the bright sunlight into the shadows of the stable, for a moment he couldn't see anything. "Where are you?"

"Over here mucking out Blaze's stall."

Hans hung the harness on its usual hook before meandering down the length of the building. He leaned his forearms on the top rail of the enclosure and put one booted foot on the bottom rail. "So where is Blaze? I brought him a treat."

"I reckon you'll have to wait a bit before you give it to him." Charlie didn't let up working while he talked. "He probably won't be back for quite a while yet."

Hans dropped his foot back to the dirt floor. "Someone rent him for the day?"

Charlie stopped and peered intently at him. "Yup." He looked back down at the pile of soiled straw he'd pulled into the middle of the stall. "Some woman. Kind of pretty, but I don't think I've seen her before."

Hans straightened and shoved his hands into the back pockets of his trousers. "What did she look like?"

"I tole you she was pretty. A little bit of a thing, but she knew how to ride a horse." Charlie started forking the straw into his barrow.

"Did she have brown curly hair?"

"Don't know how curly it is, but her hair was brown. She had it pulled back into her sun bonnet." He hefted another forkful into the conveyance.

"Did she tell you her name?" Hans hoped the thought that came into his mind was wrong.

"Yup. I don't let anyone take out a horse without leaving me their name. Constance Miller." Charlie leaned the pitchfork against the back wall of the stall and picked up the handles of the wooden wheelbarrow. "Anything else you need? I gotta go dump this mess."

"How long ago did she leave?"

Charlie stopped short and set the barrow down on its legs. "You sure do have a lot of questions this morning. Why do you want to know?"

"Miss Miller is a new friend of mine." Hans knew in his gut where Constance was going. Why didn't she ask him to go with her? Guess she hadn't believed him when he'd warned her about possible dangers out there. "I thought I might try to catch up with her. I'm not sure she understands all the dangers that could lurk outside town."

"Why didn't you say that right off?" Charlie started down the row of stalls, then stopped. "Blackie here is the fastest horse in this stable." He opened the gate, went in, and closed it behind himself. "He's a little skittish, but you can handle him okay."

Hans started for the tack room to pick up the saddle he used when he rode. "You didn't tell me how long she's been gone."

"About half an hour, I reckon." Charlie led the horse toward Hans.

Hans made quick work of saddling Blackie. Then he leapt into the saddle and hightailed it down the road heading east out of town. He didn't want to ride the horse too hard, but anything could be going on out there. It wasn't often that renegade former soldiers or other highwaymen roamed this road, but it could happen at any time. . .even today.

❧

When Constance left the edge of town, she urged the horse into a gallop but soon slowed down. The countryside spread around her with an abundance of grass, trees, and wildflowers in a rainbow of colors. She wanted to enjoy all the glory of spring that surrounded her. Unlike her first time outside town when she felt as though the sky pressed down on her, she realized how comfortably the gentle rolling hillocks undulated across the landscape. The beauty of the land bubbled with life, and birds soared above the trees she passed occasionally. Small fluffy clouds rested against the robin's-egg-blue sky but didn't block out any of the sunlight.

Since the horse could move faster than a wagon, it shouldn't take as long to arrive at the farm, so she wasn't really in a big hurry. It felt good to be on the back of a horse, and it was easier to ride the road cut across this wide-open prairie instead of up and down mountainsides, where the animal had to pick its way between rocks and brush. She didn't have to watch where her horse stepped as closely here as she did back home.

Even though Constance saw farmhouses, they all sat far from the country road she traveled. A feeling of isolation and loneliness crept upon her. Then she remembered the warning Hans had given about the possibility of meeting outlaws out here. Why hadn't she thought of that before she left town? Maybe she should have asked him to come with her, but surely he was too busy.

Constance watched the shadows among the groves of trees she passed. Could someone be hiding there waiting for an unsuspecting traveler to come along? If so, the outlaw wouldn't get anything from her. She hadn't brought a handbag, and most of her money was hidden under the mattress in her room at the boardinghouse. She knew she should think about putting it in the bank, but she hadn't expected to stay in Browning City so long.

Blaze must have sensed her apprehension, because he became skittish, sidestepping a little. Constance had to concentrate on controlling the beast. Then she heard it. The sound of approaching hoofbeats. Her heart beat a loud thunder, and fear tasted metallic on her tongue. They were still a long way off. She glanced over her shoulder and saw a lone rider gaining on her. Should she turn off the roadway and hide? It was probably too late for that.

They had been riding so long that she didn't want to push Blaze any harder. What should she do? She hadn't seen a farmhouse for quite a while. If she came upon a lane leading to one, maybe she should take her chances there.

She ventured one last glance over her shoulder, trying to gauge how long it would be before the man overtook her.

The closer Hans got to the rider up ahead, the more certain he was that it was Constance. It hadn't taken as long to catch up to her as he had feared it would. Hopefully, she wouldn't resent him for coming after her. For some reason, he felt as though he had to protect her—from harm and from herself.

Remembering those moments in Jackson and Mary's house when their gazes had connected and everything around them had dropped away, his heartbeat sped up to match the fast clip of the hoofbeats. Constance was wearing a dark brown riding skirt that flapped behind her in the wind. A green blouse and sunbonnet completed her outfit. Hans was sure the green flecks in her brown eyes would be prominent today. He imagined her smiling up into his eyes and almost lost his tight hold on the reins. He couldn't do that while they were traveling so fast.

Constance glanced back and seemed to speed up a little. Didn't she know who he was? Maybe not. She could be scared, thinking he was an outlaw. It served her right for not being more careful. If he thought she could hear him, he'd call out to her, but he was still too far away to make his words heard over the sound of two sets of pounding hoofbeats. He leaned over Blackie's neck.

When his attention returned to the rider up ahead, Hans felt his heart leap into his throat. Blaze had stepped into a rut or hole, and his right front leg gave way under him. He went down. With horror, he watched Constance roll with the animal before she let go of the reins and flew away from him. At least Blaze didn't land on top of her. If he had, he would have crushed her.

Knowing that it wasn't good for Blackie, Hans urged the horse to go even faster. What if Constance was hurt? His heart stopped beating for a second before rapidly returning to its fast cadence.

When they approached the spot where Constance lay, Hans pulled back too hard on the reins. He would have to apologize to Blackie later, but he had to make sure Constance was all right. He leapt from the horse's back and dropped the reins, knowing that Blackie wouldn't wander far from where he left him.

Constance was too still, and her face looked as white as the snow that had covered the countryside not too long before she arrived in Browning City. Her long eyelashes fanned across her cheeks in a dark brown smudge. Even her lips, which usually were a healthy pink, looked a strange bluish tint. *Oh God, please don't let her be dead.*

Hans dropped to his knees on the grassy verge beside her. A faint pulse beat at her throat, and her chest rose and fell in shallow breaths. What should he do now?

Chapter 9

Constance floated in blackness, trying to find a tiny speck of light. No other sensation registered in her muddled brain. The sound of hoofbeats rapidly approaching caused her heartbeat to accelerate right along with them. She felt the pounding of each hoof beneath her. Would the horse run over her? And why would a horse be coming toward her when she was asleep?

She realized she wasn't in her bed. Instead she was lying on something hard. Constance rubbed the fingers of one hand against the surface, only moving a couple of inches. Grass. . .the ground beneath. . .a pebble or two. Where was she, and why couldn't she open her eyes? She tried to take a deep breath but could only grasp a shallow one.

The horse stopped short, and a man's voice whispered, "I'm sorry, Blackie."

She heard the animal's huffing breath and the warm earthy smell of lathery sweat. The man's voice sounded familiar. She couldn't quite remember why. Maybe if she lay really still and thought about it, the answer would come to her.

"Oh, Constance, what am I going to do now?"

Hans. At the whispered question, an image of his face swam into her mind. The fragrance of heat and masculinity that she associated with the blacksmith invaded her senses. She forced her eyes open a bit. He leaned over her, only a breath away. For a moment, the look of concern—and something else—in his eyes called to something deep inside her. Sensations she had never experienced surged through her, warring with unrest and unnamed pain.

When Constance's eyes fluttered open, Hans leaned back away from her, hunkering with his feet under him. Healthy color finally suffused her face, and her breathing sounded more normal.

"Are you injured?"

She stared up at him without saying a thing, so he sat down on the soft, green grass near her head and lifted it into his lap. The fall had knocked her bonnet off her head, but its ties held it against her back. All of the pins that usually held Constance's hair had scattered, so her curls spilled around her, setting off her lovely face.

His desire to run his fingers though the glistening softness made his hand tingle. Hans looked up at the sky and took a deep breath. He needed to concentrate on making sure Constance was all right. He would have to deal with his runaway emotions later.

"I don't think so." The whisper was almost softer than the breeze that cooled them.

Hans stared into her eyes, which had darkened to almost chocolate brown. He loved the myriad of colors that they exhibited. *Hazel.* He'd heard someone call that color of eyes hazel. Whatever shade they were, he could almost drown in them.

"I'm going to lay you back down. I want to check on your horse. Then we'll go back to town."

Constance felt bereft when he left her. Carefully, she eased into a sitting position. Her hair tumbled down to her waist, and finally, she could breathe easier. While being totally aware of Hans's every move, she glanced around, trying to find some of her hairpins. Mother had always told her that a lady wore her hair up instead of letting her curls riot down her back. She picked up all she could reach without moving too much. While she gathered her hair into some semblance of a bun, Constance watched Hans.

He approached Blaze, talking in a soothing tone. The horse shuffled over, favoring one front leg. Probably that was the reason they went down. She hoped he wasn't hurt too bad.

She glanced back and noticed a particularly deep rut cut crossways in the road. She should have watched where they were going instead of urging the horse to go faster. They could have avoided the hole. Why hadn't she paid more attention to what she was doing?

Hans had gotten his hand on the bridle. He reached into one pocket, pulled out something, and held it under the horse's mouth. Blaze nipped the item and chewed contentedly, allowing Hans to check out his front leg.

"Is he going to be all right?" Constance pulled her bonnet back onto her head, hoping it would hold the hair in place long enough to get back home.

Home. The boardinghouse. . .and Browning City, was beginning to feel like home to her. She was glad she had written to Bertram and Molly, telling them she would sell them the farm and having them send her all the personal items still left in the cabin. She didn't know if she would stay in Iowa, but she wanted the comfort of having a place where she felt safe and accepted, maybe even loved, by wonderful people.

Hans led Blaze over to the large black stallion he had been riding. He attached the reins to the back of his saddle and gave both horses a few loving pats before he turned back toward her. Anticipation poured through her as his long stride brought him closer.

Hans strode over to where Constance sat on the ground. She hadn't stood up, but she had tamed her hair. Too bad. He liked to see it tumble over her shoulders. The Bible was right when it called a woman's hair her glory, and Constance's had looked glorious spread across his lap awhile ago. He took his thoughts captive by the time he reached her.

"Let me help you up."

When he reached down, he placed his hands on either side of her waist and lifted her into a standing position. She trembled, and he pulled her into his arms. . .just to support her while she got her bearings, right?

"Do you hurt anywhere?"

"All over, I think." Her words spoken against his shirt brought warmth to his chest, inside and out.

He swept her up into his arms and walked toward Blackie, thankful that the horse was so powerful. Carrying two people shouldn't tax him too much.

"We'll have to ride together. I don't want to injure Blaze's leg any more than it already is."

Constance clung to his neck with both arms. "Will he be all right?"

"Yes." He stared straight ahead, not wanting to look down into her eyes, which were too close for comfort. "He just doesn't need to carry any extra weight back to town."

Hans swung Constance up onto Blackie's back, then mounted behind her. The ride to town would be exquisite torture, but he didn't mind. They would have to go slow because of Blaze's injury. Hans wanted to savor the feel of Constance in his arms for as long as it lasted. It might be the last time they would be that close.

Finding it hard to control his emotions, Hans studied the landscape around them. He should have gone riding sooner. Spring was his favorite time of year. Everything looked bright and fresh. It reminded him of the hope of renewal that the Lord gave every day. A profusion of colors spread around them, but he couldn't concentrate on any of them.

When he was near Constance, the fragrance of some flower floated around her. This close, it filled his senses. He had to get his mind onto something else.

"What in the world were you thinking, coming out here alone?" He knew he sounded harsh, but she needed to understand the risk she took.

She stiffened in his arms.

Why did men always think they were right? Constance gritted her teeth before she lashed out at him. After all, he had rescued her. . .again.

"I didn't think about it being dangerous."

"I'm sure you didn't." The steel in his tone cut like a knife. "Were you headed toward the Mitchell place?"

How did he know that? Could he read her mind? "Yes. I wanted to see if anyone had come home."

They rode in silence for a few minutes before he said anything else. She could feel the tension coiled like a tightly wound clock in the man behind her.

When he finally spoke, his tone wasn't as strident. "I would have come with you to keep you safe."

Of course, he would have. If he had come, she would have had to tell him more of her reasons for searching the house, and she didn't want to do that. At least not yet.

More of the muscles in her body began to announce their presence, aching and sore. Maybe she was hurt more than she thought. Riding on a horse for a long time didn't help.

"What is so important that you felt you had to go out there alone?"

The question hung unanswered between them. She wasn't going to tell him another thing.

As they continued to amble along, the rhythm of the ride lulled her, and soon she slumped against him. Even though his muscles were taut, they gave a welcome warmth and cushioned her exhaustion.

⨯⨯⨯

Hans knew the moment Constance fell asleep. He hoped she hadn't hit her head too hard. He knew that it wasn't good for a person to go to sleep so soon after a head injury. Hopefully, she was just tired.

He held the reins with one hand and pulled her closer with the other arm. Holding her cradled in his embrace felt somehow right. When he got home, he was going to have a long talk with the Lord about what to do about this woman.

When Hans stopped the horses outside the doctor's office, Constance stirred in his arms. He took one last moment to enjoy her essence before she was fully awake.

She stretched as she sat up away from him. "Where are we?"

"Dr. Harding's house." Hans slipped off the horse, then reached back for her.

"I don't need a doctor."

Hans helped her down, and when her feet reached the ground, her knees buckled. He held her up, then pulled her against him. "We've been on the horse a long time."

He was glad the doctor lived on the edge of town, and there weren't any people in sight. They might misconstrue why he was riding and holding her in his arms. He didn't want anything to sully her reputation.

Constance pulled back. "I can stand up."

"Are you sure? Let me help you inside."

This time, she didn't argue. They walked slowly, and she limped a little.

When Hans knocked on the door, the doctor answered. The older man took one look at Constance and stepped back, giving them plenty of room to enter. "So what happened?"

"She was thrown from a horse." Hans looked down at her and read the pain in her eyes. "I don't think she's hurt too bad, but we had a long ride back to town."

"Bring her into my exam room." Doc Harding led the way. "Did it knock her unconscious, young man?"

"Yes. She was just coming to when I reached her." Hans picked her up, and this time she didn't object.

While he was laying her on the bed in the examining room, Mrs. Harding bustled through the door.

"I'll take over now, young man, and my wife will assist me." The doctor was all business. "You can come back and check on her later."

Hans glanced at Constance, and she nodded. "I need to get the horses to the livery stable anyway. I will be back, though."

❧

When Hans walked out of the room, Constance relaxed. Having him near kept her in a constant state of unrest. She didn't want to think about why.

"Let's have a look at you." The doctor, an older man with a shock of white hair and unruly brows over kind eyes, reminded her of one of her neighbors back home. "Where do you hurt?"

"All over, I think." She tried to laugh, but even that caused pain.

The doctor's wife took Constance's hand. "I'm Wilma Harding, and this old sawbones is my husband. He just wants to help you, but he'll have to examine you. Would it be all right if I help you out of these clothes and into a gown?"

Constance cut her eyes toward the tall man.

"I'll be waiting right outside until you ladies are finished."

When the door closed behind him, Constance let go of the breath she had been holding. Wilma Harding got a voluminous white gown from a chest beside the door. She helped Constance slip it over her head before she started removing her clothing under the covering. Constance was glad that she didn't have to undress completely in front of the woman.

Soon the doctor returned and started prodding various places on her body. "You already have some bruising. Did you land on your back?"

She nodded.

"Then you need to turn over."

After Constance settled on her stomach, Mrs. Harding put a soft pillow under her head. Then she took Constance's hand once again.

"I'm trying not to hurt you," the doctor explained, "but there must have been some rocks under you. A few of these bruises look like they go pretty deep. You're going to be sore for a while."

He straightened up, and Mrs. Harding helped Constance rearrange the gown.

"I don't think you have any broken bones." Dr. Harding stroked the white goatee on his chin. "Since you were unconscious for a bit, I want to keep you under observation for a while."

Constance tried to sit up. "But I have a job." Mrs. Harding gently pushed her back down on the bed. "I bake for Mrs. Barker."

The doctor stared at her for a minute. "Someone will let her know where you are."

~~~~~

While he rode Blackie to the livery stable on the other side of town, Hans prayed for the doctor to know how to help Constance.

Charlie stood in the open doorway of the stable with his thumbs tucked under his suspenders and watched Hans ride toward him. "What happened to Blaze, and where is Miss Miller?"

By the time Hans had dismounted, Charlie was examining the horse's front leg.

"Blaze stepped into a rut while going pretty fast. When he went down, Constance was thrown to the ground. I wasn't too far back down the road, so I helped them. I left her at Doc's."

Charlie nodded. "Good. . .good. I've got some liniment that should help this soreness. It shouldn't take too long for Blaze to be completely restored."

"If it's all right with you, I'll keep Blackie a while longer."

"Yup. Go right ahead." Charlie led Blaze into the stable.

With determination, Hans turned the horse around and rode away.

Chapter 10

When the doctor finished with Constance, he asked his wife to stay with her. He didn't want Constance to go to sleep for a while since she hit her head when she fell.

Mrs. Harding sat beside the bed. A knitting basket rested on the floor beside her chair, and a mountain of something filled her lap. Her clicking needles punctuated the conversation.

Constance liked the woman. Her tender, helpful heart shone through everything she did.

"How long have you been in Browning City, Constance?" Mrs. Harding switched directions on the blanket or whatever it was going to be.

"More than a month." Constance wished she wasn't lying so flat. She would rather face the doctor's wife more comfortably. "Several weeks. I would have to count up to be sure." She looked all around the room, trying to see if there were any more pillows anywhere.

The knitting landed on the basket and spilled onto the floor. "Do you need something, dear?" Mrs. Harding leaned forward, and her kind eyes studied Constance's face.

"I just thought if I had more pillows, I would be more comfortable."

The other woman bustled back to the chest beside the door and pulled three puffy pillows from its depths. After placing them behind Constance's back, she sat down and picked up her work.

"Now, where were we?" The rhythm of stitches continued as if there hadn't been an interruption. "Where did you live before you came here?"

Constance knew the woman was trying to keep her occupied, but she wasn't sure she wanted to tell her every detail of her life. "I've always lived in the Ozark Mountains of Arkansas."

Before another question was forthcoming, thankfully, a knock sounded on the front door of the house.

"I'll be right back. Just don't go to sleep while I'm gone."

In her mind, Constance followed Mrs. Harding's footsteps up the hallway. She heard the front door unlatch and muffled voices carry on a conversation. The other woman's voice sounded vaguely familiar, but because the two women spoke so softly, she wasn't sure who exactly. Soon, two sets of footsteps came back down the hallway.

"Constance, look who came to check on you." Mrs. Harding preceded the visitor through the doorway.

"Mary." Constance was glad to see her friend. "How did you know I was here?"

The pastor's wife smiled at her. "Hans came to tell me. We agreed that you shouldn't go back to your room at the boardinghouse. I'm going to take you to the parsonage to recover. He should be here soon with a buggy." She turned toward the doctor's wife. "That is, if it's all right with you."

"I've enjoyed having her, but I do believe it would be better if she were with good friends." She picked up her knitting and moved it away from the chair. "Why don't you sit down and visit with Constance? I'll go get you some coffee."

Mary sank into the chair but put a restraining hand on Mrs. Harding's arm. "I don't need any coffee. Hans should be here soon."

Almost before Constance realized what was happening, she rested once again in the strong arms of the man who rescued her. Hans carried her out to the waiting carriage and placed her in the cushioned rear seat. Then he lifted Mary up to sit beside her.

He drove slowly toward the parsonage, probably to keep from jarring Constance too much. The man's thoughtfulness touched a place in her heart. No one had ever taken such good care of her. She was usually the one seeing to other people's needs.

Mary kept up a running commentary all during the ride. At the house, Hans lifted Mary down, and she proceeded up the walk to open the door.

When he lifted Constance from the vehicle, she started to tell him that she could walk. He didn't give her a chance, because he swept up the walk and into the house very quickly. Instead of taking her into a bedroom, he set her down in an overstuffed chair in the parlor.

"Thank you, Hans." Mary hovered near. "Why don't you come back and share supper with us? I'm sure Jackson will want to hear all about your exciting day."

Hans tipped his cap. "I'd be obliged." He turned to Constance. "I'll go tell Mrs. Barker what happened so she won't expect you back for a few days."

After he left, Constance exclaimed, "A few days? I should be okay by tomorrow."

Mary sat on the end of the sofa nearest her. "We don't want to rush it. It will be my pleasure to have you here."

"But you're going to have a baby. You shouldn't have to take care of me."

Mary laughed. "Oh, Constance, not you, too. Jackson acts as if I'm made of blown glass. I'm perfectly healthy, and I will love having you here with me for a few days."

When Hans returned for supper that evening, Constance still sat in the comfortable chair. He was glad to see that healthy color had returned to her face.

"Mary won't let me lift a finger. I could get spoiled if this continues." The twinkle in Constance's eyes went straight to his heart.

"I don't think you have to worry about that." He pulled a straight chair near hers. "I hope I didn't scare you when I rode toward you. Was that why you rode faster?"

Constance's gaze dropped to her hands, which she twisted in her lap. "I probably owe you an apology. I should have listened to you about the dangers of riding alone. When I heard you coming, I was afraid you were a highwayman."

She turned her eyes toward him, and her expression held true remorse. "We both made a mistake. Let's just forgive each other."

"Ja, forgiveness is a good thing."

Supper with his three best friends loomed as a blessed promise. *Best friend? Is that all Constance is?* But she couldn't be anything else until she opened up to him completely. He had prayed about her often, and he felt that God wanted them to be together, at least for now. Even though they had spent a lot of time together, she still held something back.

He wasn't getting any younger, and he had asked God often enough to bring someone into his life for a lasting relationship, but there was no one else who interested him—not before Constance came to town, and especially not now.

After watching the happiness marriage brought to both Jackson and Mary, Hans wanted the same thing for himself: A woman who would be the helpmeet scripture speaks about. A woman to share the same dreams and goals. A woman to be the mother of his children and who really wanted those children. He didn't even know if Constance liked being around young ones.

He turned his attention to the woman in question. "Do you have any brothers or sisters back home?"

Sadness fell like a veil over her face. "No. I'm an only child. If there had been anyone else, maybe Pa wouldn't have sent me on this quest."

Perhaps he had misjudged exactly why she was looking for Jim Mitchell. If she were going to marry the man, she wouldn't have said that, would she?

"When you marry, are you looking forward to having children, Constance?"

She narrowed her eyes in a thoughtful faraway look before answering. "I hope God gives me lots of children. I didn't like being an only child." She turned a dazzling smile toward him. "Hans, why all the interest in my future?"

Since he couldn't think of how to answer that, he was glad that Mary called them to supper.

⚭

Finally Constance was back at the boardinghouse. When she made her way to the kitchen that morning, Mrs. Barker expressed gratitude for having her back. While Constance worked, her thoughts returned to the last few days. She hadn't planned on staying at the parsonage for more than a week, but until yesterday, each time she expressed a desire to go home, Mary had discouraged her.

Hans had spent a lot of time with her. She liked him, but when he was in the room with her, something inside her felt agitated. . .or more alive. She wasn't sure which. She wondered if he didn't have much work at the smithy. He was always underfoot. Probably since she had resumed her job, he would only come by at suppertime.

Constance felt as if she were in some kind of suspension, not able to make plans until she could fulfill her promise to her father. She even tried to talk to God about it, but He seemed so far away. Her questions about why He had taken her ma and pa hit the ceiling and bounced back. She had even asked Him to help her find Jim Mitchell, but that prayer also didn't seem to reach heaven.

Maybe she should just continue with the search herself. The sooner, the better.

A few days later, after she had made an extra supply of baked goods, she told Mrs. Barker that she wanted to take the next day off.

Early in the morning, she ate her breakfast, wrapped leftover biscuits and bacon in a rag, and set out for the livery stable. She knew Hans wouldn't like her going off by herself, but she had to finish this before she could move on with her life. After all, the man wasn't her keeper.

⚭

Hans enjoyed the freedom of being able to see Constance so often when she was at the parsonage. After she went back to work at the boardinghouse, he had to catch up with his work, but each evening at supper, he worked the conversation with Constance around to what she was going to do the next day. If she said she was going anywhere, he kept an eye out for her, trying not to let her know that he was watching her. Somehow, he knew she wouldn't appreciate it. That woman needed a keeper. . .or protector, and he was just the man to do it, whether she agreed or not.

Last night, Constance had seemed evasive when they were talking. Something was up, and he figured it had to do with going back out to the Mitchell farm. He went to the livery early and rented Blackie for the day. By the time she came, rented Blaze, and started on the road toward the farm, he was already on the way. But he went across country, from one copse of trees to the next, never getting very far from the road.

Sure enough, Constance galloped down the road not long after he left town. He kept far enough away so she didn't see him, but he was careful not to let her completely out of his sight. Soon she slowed to a comfortable pace. As he watched her, she seemed to be taking the time to enjoy the countryside, but she headed straight down the road toward the farm.

Hans would like to enjoy the surroundings, but he didn't want to take the chance that she was really going somewhere else. He kept his attention on her.

Constance rode directly up to the house. She dismounted beside the front porch and tied Blaze's reins to one of the supporting columns.

Hans dismounted far enough away so Constance couldn't hear him approach. While he led Blackie, Hans watched her knock on the door. After a short time, she tried the door, opened it, and walked in. He picked up his pace, hoping she wouldn't hear him.

A loud shriek accompanied a crashing sound that came from inside the house. Hans jumped on Blackie's back and urged him into a run. When he was almost at the house, he jumped out of the saddle and hit the ground running. His footsteps pounded up the steps and across the porch.

When Hans burst through the door, Constance could hardly believe her eyes. What was he doing here? And why did he have to come at just that moment? She must look awful.

She had been walking across the room when the floorboards gave way with a crash. They were rotten and couldn't hold her weight. She had feared she was going to fall a long way. Instead, the root cellar was shallow, so when she fell, her head remained above the floor. She didn't even want to look at Hans, knowing that she was surrounded by a cloud of dust and splintered wood. She was afraid to move too much, because some of the sharp boards could pierce her body.

"Constance, what have you done?" His shout made her angry.

"What have I done? What are you doing here?" She tried to put her hands on her hips, but shards of wood scraped her wrists. She burst into tears.

Shock and confusion covered his face. "I'm going to help you, Constance. Don't move until I get there."

With both arms out as if to break a fall if it came, Hans walked toward her, testing the floor boards as he came.

The sight that had greeted Hans when he burst through the door brought the upheaval of an earthquake to his emotions. Constance had been covered with dust. Only the whites of her eyes stood out from the dirty color that cloaked her from the top of her head all the way down as far as he could see of her in between broken boards. The jagged wood that reached toward her looked like menacing arms of death. He whispered a quick prayer for her safety and his own wisdom.

He shouldn't have yelled at her. It was a reaction he hadn't been able to tame. Now he must help her, and to make matters worse, she had started sobbing.

"Please don't cry." He tried to sound soothing. "I'm going to get you out of there."

Most of the boards that made up the floor of the room were all right. Just the few down the center had been weak.

"Look at me, Constance." His stare willed her to turn her gaze toward him.

When she finally did, the despair he saw almost brought him to his knees.

"You need to trust me completely. Don't move until I tell you to, and only move in the direction I say. Okay?"

She finally gave a slight nod, fear from her gaze spearing through him.

"I'm going to pull this board up." He indicated which one. "Please don't move toward it in any way."

"Okay." Her whisper resounded through the silent room.

He gingerly worked with the board, pulling it away from her body, then ripped it out and threw it to one side of the room. It landed with a *thunk* and a cloud of dust against the wall. One board on each side of it needed to come out before he could rescue her. Taking great care, he pulled each one out. Moving carefully, he scooted near the edge and reached for her.

Hans grasped her wrist. "It would help if you held on to my wrist, too."

Constance turned her arms until she could latch onto his. They tightened their interlocked grips, and he pulled her up. When she stood on both her feet, she pulled from his hold and started trying to brush her clothes with her hands.

He grabbed her arms to stop her. "Constance, it won't do any good. Look how much debris is clinging to your skirt."

"Eew." She made a face. "I don't like bugs on me."

In among the dust that layered her clothing, he saw cobwebs and insects clinging in clumps. "Let's get you outside and see what we can accomplish together."

Docilely, she followed him. Hans was glad she hadn't argued. Maybe this wasn't as bad as it seemed.

"If I break a branch off of a bush, we can use it to brush you off." He jumped off the porch and headed toward the nearest thicket.

When he returned, she stood in the grass not far from the porch. He started brushing her below the waist in the back. She turned slowly allowing him access to her whole skirt. Meanwhile, she used her hands on the front of her bodice. He could brush off her back.

After they finished, he noticed the tracks of tears on her dirty cheeks. He pulled a bandanna from his back pocket. "You might want to use this to wipe your face."

She swiped it up one side and down the other, smearing more than removing the dirt. He didn't want to point it out to her, because she didn't seem to be in a very good mood. Who could blame her? But it was her own fault.

"Constance, what were you thinking?" His harshness should show her just how foolish her actions had been.

Instead, all his words did was inflame her anger. "What were you doing following me?" Her hands fisted on her hips, and she glared from behind the dirt masking her face.

"Didn't you learn your lesson the last time you rode out alone?" He knew his tone was even louder, but the woman wasn't listening to his good advice.

"I am an adult. I don't need a keeper." Her volume grew to match his.

Two could play the same game. He placed his fists on his own hips. "Yes, you do. What would you have done if I hadn't followed you? You couldn't have gotten out of there without hurting yourself more." What he wanted to do was shake some sense into her.

He reached for her arms, and she burst into great heaving sobs. Hans pulled her toward him and cradled her against his chest. *Lord, what am I going to do with Constance?*

Chapter 11

The bell over the door of the mercantile jingled, alerting Constance that someone else had entered the store. She glanced toward the front and sighed. Hans stood so tall and broad-shouldered that he blocked out most of the light from the glass in the door. She fought against her own heart. Just the sight of the man caused it to flutter in her chest of its own accord. She took a breath, trying to calm down. Yes, he was handsome. Yes, she enjoyed spending time in his company. But the man had become her shadow. Wherever she went, he went.

She moved down the aisle and stopped to finger a roll of lace. The intricate creamy pattern would look good decorating the collar of the brown dress she had on today. The frippery didn't hold her attention long. From across the room, she felt every move the man made. Probably she shouldn't touch any more fabric because her palms were beginning to sweat. What was wrong with her?

Granted, Hans had rescued her a few times, and she was thankful for that. More than thankful, really. What would she have done if he hadn't come along? She shuddered to think about it. Somehow he had decided that she needed a keeper, and he was the man for the job.

Constance turned to walk between other counters containing a myriad of products. Up ahead, she spied shiny new shovels leaning against the back wall, and an idea took root in her mind. The gold had to be somewhere. Perhaps Jim Mitchell had buried it on the farm. She could use a spade like that to try to dig up the treasure.

She didn't want to alert Hans to what she was thinking, so she turned to look at the candy sticks. Constance was partial to peppermint. She also liked horehound. Her mother had used them to help when Constance had a cough, but she never felt as if they were medicine. She could almost taste them now, and a craving took up residence in her mouth.

After choosing two of each of the sugary confections, she pulled her coin purse from her reticule. While she finished paying the clerk, Hans stopped beside her. She could feel his heat, even though he was at least a foot away from her.

When the other man went to help another customer, Hans leaned one hand on the counter. "Good to see you, Constance. So you have a sweet tooth."

She held one of the sticks toward him. "Would you like one?"

He smiled, never taking his eyes from her face, as his hand closed around her fingers. "You don't have to buy me one."

"I know I don't." She tried to turn on all her charm. "I just wanted to be nice."

"Thank you." He still held her fingertips along with the candy. He pulled it to his lips and bit a chunk off the end. The *crunch* sounded almost as loud as her thudding heartbeat.

The gesture seemed much too intimate for a public store. Constance hoped no one watched them. Heat stole its way into her cheeks.

Hans took the candy from her with his other hand, not letting go of her fingertips. For a moment, the world around them melted into nothingness. Constance was held captive in his warm gaze, and the room seemed to empty of air. She gulped a shallow breath, and he slowly released his hold on her.

"See you at supper tonight." He turned and sauntered away as if nothing had happened.

How could he? Everything in her world had shifted, and he apparently didn't feel a thing. She watched him walk out the door.

She turned and stalked to the shovels. The sooner she fulfilled her promise, the better. Her life had just become much too complicated. Maybe she should leave this place as soon as possible.

⌘

What was I thinking? Hans berated himself as he hurried toward the smithy. The exchange with Constance had quickly escalated into something where he was no longer in control.

Lord, what am I going to do? The woman. . .Constance does things to me that I don't understand. Should I keep my distance until she is honest with me? But, Lord, she needs a protector. No telling what she would do without someone to rescue her. Why do I feel so drawn to her?

At least the store was a very public place. The desire to pull her into his arms and kiss her had almost overwhelmed him. That's why he had turned and run. Why had he gone to the store? Right. He needed to pick up some things Evan Cooper, the owner, needed repaired. Now he would have to make another trip, but not while Constance was still in there. How much control could one man have?

He knew she needed protecting, but he would have to keep more distance between them. She hadn't been out of town for a couple of weeks, and nothing had happened to her. Maybe he could relax a little, let her get on with her life. She hadn't done anything to make him think she would try striking out alone again. When he saw her at supper each night, her happiness and contentment radiated through the room.

He figured that she had almost forgotten about the reason she came to Iowa, and he felt sure her letter had told those neighbors back home that she would be making her home in Browning City for now. Whistling as he walked, he returned to the smithy in time for the livery owner to bring in three horses for shoeing.

⚬⚬

Constance glanced down the street toward the smithy. Hans was out front shoeing a horse. Since he hadn't been back long, he should be occupied for a while. She needed to test out her theory that the gold was buried on the farm.

She hurried to the boardinghouse and put on her riding clothes. After stopping in the kitchen to tell Mrs. Barker that she would be gone most of the day, she headed to the livery. Soon she rode Blaze back to the boardinghouse to get a large tow sack that contained the shovel and a rope. She hadn't wanted to take them to the livery with her because Charlie might notice and ask questions.

Feeling at one with the horse, she spent the ride to the farm in a pleasant lope. After she arrived, she led him to the spring quite a ways into the woods behind the house. Constance tied the rope to a small tree, giving the horse plenty of room to graze and reach the water when he was thirsty. Taking the shovel and sack, she went back to the front porch, where she sat down on the edge and glanced around.

If I were a man, where would I hide the gold? There were plenty of places. Would Jim Mitchell have wanted to keep it hidden from his parents and even his brother? Maybe he would bury it in the edge of the woods behind the house. She left the sack on the porch and walked around the building, carrying the shovel.

It had rained often this spring, bringing forth a multitude of plants and flowers. That also helped keep the ground from being so hard. The loamy soil under the trees turned easily. She dug at the base of one tree then another. When she didn't hit a strongbox very soon, she moved on to other trees.

Dirt streaked her hands and arms, and the work caused sweat to pop out on her brow. She swiped it away with her forearm, then noticed the muddy smear on her arm where she had pushed up the sleeve when she first felt the heat. Probably there was one on her face, too. At least no one would see her like this. She went back to the spring and knelt on a rock ledge beside the pool. She reached into the cold water and rinsed her hands and arms before splashing some on her face.

Why didn't she wait until she had a drink before she did that? Now the water in front of her was dirty. Constance moved along the side until she came to a spot where the water was clear and clean before she cupped her hands to bring the soothing liquid to her mouth. Most of it drained between her fingers.

She stooped farther down, with her face almost at the surface of the pool and tried again, hoping she wouldn't lose her balance and fall in. As wetness trickled down her throat, the cool liquid soothed her thirst.

"So, Blaze, are you enjoying your rest?" Constance walked over to the horse and patted his neck.

The shadows thrown by the trees around her gave her a lonely feeling. If only she could find the gold soon and be on her way.

She returned to the clearing that contained the house. Maybe he hid it in the root cellar. After the fiasco of the last time she had entered the house, she didn't look forward to going in there again. But she had watched the way Hans carefully tried out each board before he put his full weight on it. She could do that.

After taking a deep, fortifying breath, Constance walked into the dim interior. She tested every board that was left in the floor of the main room. None of them gave way. The trapdoor to the cellar was in one corner of the room, near a window. She pulled back the curtains, and sunlight streamed through the space, highlighting the hole in the floor. She lifted the trapdoor and placed a tentative foot on the steps cut into the rock supporting the house.

Constance tiptoed down and bent her head so she could move around. She felt like an old woman the way she had to walk. She plunged the long shovel straight down into the dirt over and over, trying to find the treasure. The only hard thing she hit was the rock foundation.

When her back ached so much that she couldn't stand it another minute, she went back to the opening and climbed out. After letting the trapdoor down over the hole, she turned around in the sunlight. *What a mess!* Dirt covered every inch that she could see of herself. She felt sure there were no clean spots on the part she couldn't see either.

Now what should she do? Maybe Jim Mitchell hid it in front of the house. After hiking the shovel onto her shoulder, she went back outside and started to work. She turned over some dirt, pushed the shovel deeper into the soil several times, then moved on to another place. Methodically, she made her way back and forth across the meadow.

When Constance finished, she hadn't found anything but rocks, roots, worms, and bugs. What a waste of time. If she had been back home with her father still alive, he would have made use of the worms and bugs to go fishing.

She went back to the porch and dropped to sit on the front edge. Where had Jim Mitchell hidden the gold?

She tried to figure out reasonable things that could have happened. Perhaps he had other men help him, and one of them hid the gold. Maybe they all wasted their ill-gotten gain in riotous living. She had heard that ungodly men often did that. Since she had done everything she could to try to fulfill her promise to her father, maybe it was time to give up and get on with her life.

Constance smiled at the last thought. What would getting on with her life entail? The question brought a familiar face into her mind. Sparkling blue eyes that had darkened almost to navy when they were last in the mercantile. The only blond hair that she had ever wanted to run her fingers through. That man was too disturbing for her peace of mind.

When he lifted her hand and took a bite of the stick of peppermint she held, for a moment she had thought he was going to kiss her fingertips. Just as quickly, she wanted him to, even though there may have been other people near them. She didn't know if there were because all of her attention concentrated on the tall, brawny man whose eyes haunted her dreams, whether she was sleeping or awake.

She relived his full lips closing around the candy, and Constance wondered what it would feel like to have them touching hers. When that thought entered her mind, she touched her fingers to her mouth, and a sigh escaped from her soul. These thoughts were too disturbing, so she jumped up and started toward the spring. She might as well clean up and prepare to ride Blaze back to town. After glancing around the clearing, she knew that she couldn't leave without filling in all those holes, but first she needed a cool drink of water.

❧

What was I thinking? How often had Hans asked himself that question since Constance fell out of the stagecoach into his waiting arms? More times than he wanted to count. She was constantly in his thoughts, making a home for herself that he didn't want to disturb.

When Charlie came back to pick up his horses, he mentioned that Constance had rented Blaze for a ride. Now Hans raced down the road toward the Mitchell farm. He had become complacent, and Constance had just been biding her time. What was so important that she had to keep going out there and endangering her life? Was she looking for something? If so, what could it be?

Maybe her father had given Jim Mitchell something that he wanted Constance to retrieve. It made sense. Even though sometimes Hans had thought something wrong was going on, the explanation could be as simple as that. Why hadn't he trusted Constance? Given her a chance to tell him in her own time?

Hopefully, his haste wouldn't be needed, because she wasn't in any danger, but something pushed him on. For some reason, he felt that Constance needed him today. Surely it wasn't because she was in peril again.

When he approached the farmhouse, he slowed Blackie to a walk. Fresh tracks led toward the house, but when they turned off the dirt road, they were swallowed up in the thick grass. He looked up from the tracks and couldn't believe his eyes.

The meadow in front of the farmhouse was pockmarked by many places where someone had been digging. He walked Blackie between them, being careful to keep the horse from stepping in one of the holes. Even by the porch was evidence of more digging. At the bases of the trees on the edge of the woods that surrounded the meadow on three sides, holes looked like some kind of open wounds in the earth.

Hans dismounted and stepped up on the porch. The recesses of the house weren't as dark as they had been the last time he was there. He glanced around inside and noticed that some of the curtains had been pushed back so that sunlight poured into the room.

"Constance, are you here?" His words echoed in the empty space.

Through the hole in the floor, he noticed that someone had been digging in the cellar, too. After carefully making his way around the opening, he opened the two doors that led off the main room. Both of the other rooms looked undisturbed. All the furniture, as well as the floor, wore a heavy coat of dust.

Where can she be?

Outside once again, Hans took a deep breath and walked toward the edge of the cliff.

Chapter 12

Before Constance tried to get all the dirt off her hands and face, she made an attempt to remove the soil from her clothing the way Hans had before. A branch from a nearby bush worked fine on the front and sides, but she couldn't reach the middle of her back. She must look a sight with most of her clothing freshened and a streak running down one side. She'd make a pretty good skunk, wouldn't she?

That thought introduced the idea that these woods could contain one of those notoriously malodorous creatures. Hadn't she heard somewhere that they were nocturnal animals? Hopefully, any that lived near here were. Being on the receiving end of a spray from one of the black-and-white-striped animals would completely ruin the day.

What about her problem with her clothing? Constance walked over to a sturdy tree and rubbed against it with her back. Maybe that would help some.

Since she had done everything she could to clean off her dress, she knelt beside the clear pool. She had been so preoccupied when she was here earlier that she hadn't noticed the abundance of smooth pebbles that lined the bottom. Varying shades of browns, black, and white—some with shiny specks—formed a beautiful mosaic created by nature. Constance dipped one fingertip into the water, and ripples spread in ever-widening circles.

Her life was like that. She had spent so many years settled into her home in the Ozarks, but now her life spread across two state lines. Who knew where it might lead? She hoped that she presented to the world as pleasing a picture as the rocks in the bottom of this spring.

Another picture whisked into her mind, blurring out the pool and bringing a catch to her breath. Scenes played one after the other. Hans catching her in his strong arms with a startled expression in his blue eyes. Hans working in the Community Garden, taut muscles rippling with the rhythm of his work. His white teeth sinking into the peppermint stick with his lips wrapping around it, barely missing her fingertips. These thoughts did nothing to cool off Constance from her previous labors. If only she had her folding fan that rested in the top drawer of the chest in her room at the boardinghouse. She would put it to good use.

Constance shook the thoughts from her mind and concentrated on washing her hands, arms, and face. Then she pulled her sleeves back down and buttoned her cuffs.

She walked over to the grazing horse. "Blaze, it won't be long until we start back to Browning City."

As Constance approached the edge of the woods, she thought she heard a male voice. Were there other men? She only heard one. Who could that be? Did she need to hide from the man?

She carefully worked her way between the bushes and trees without making a sound. When she peered around the trunk of one of the last large trees between her and the meadow, she saw a man standing near the edge of the bluff. Immediately, she recognized his clothing and the way he stood proudly with his head flung back. The sunlight glinting on his hair gave his locks a golden glow. What was Hans doing here?

He hadn't noticed her, and he continued to talk with a loud voice. She wondered if he was calling to someone across the Mississippi. Surely the river was too wide for him to be heard, even though he was shouting. Then she heard him say, "Lord." She stealthily moved closer to the house until she could understand every word.

❦

"Lord, what am I going to do about Constance? You know how I feel about her, but is it Your will for me to spend so much time with her? How can I keep her safe if she won't tell me the truth? What is she looking for, and why won't she let me help her? Lord, I need some answers from You, and I need them as soon as possible."

Hans stared at the patchwork of cultivated ground across the river. Some farmer over there had started his spring planting. Too bad no one was working this farm. This year's planting season would soon be over. He thrust his hands into the back pockets of his trousers. Trying to take his mind off Constance only worked for a few seconds.

"Help me here, Lord. I really need You."

The snapping of a twig cut into the silence at the end of his sentence. He whirled and stared straight into the face of the woman who caused him so much unrest.

For a moment, her eyes widened. "Hans," she called to him. "What are you doing here?"

He loped across the meadow, being careful not to step into any of the holes. "I could ask you the same question." He gestured toward one of the pockmarks. "Why have you been digging here?"

Constance heaved a deep sigh, seeming to consider how to answer. During the lull, he reached her side. He had to grip his hands into fists to keep from reaching out to her; then he thrust his fingers into his back pockets.

She stared at him a long moment before answering. "Come sit down on the porch with me. I'll feel more comfortable talking to you there." She turned and led the way.

After she sat, he dropped down onto the wooden porch but not too close to her. He wanted to keep his wits about himself, and being too near Constance would muddle his thoughts. "What are you going to talk about?"

She turned her head and stared off into the distance. "I know you've been really helpful to me. . . ."

After her words faded off, he waited. Surely she had more to say.

"I guess you want to know the real reason I'm looking for Jim Mitchell."

He nodded, then realized she couldn't see his movement from there. "Ja."

⤜⤛

How could Constance tell her story without Hans getting the wrong impression of her father? She was tired of hiding things from Hans. Maybe the absolute truth would be best in this circumstance. She turned to look at him, and his intense scrutiny almost crumbled her defenses.

"I told you that my father made me promise to find Jim Mitchell."

"Ja." He nodded again. "I remember."

The way he said it, she felt that his memories contained more than her comment about the promise. What if he was also remembering the moment in the mercantile? Heat crept into her cheeks, so she turned back to study a flock of birds heading north in the intense blue sky.

"It's kind of a long story."

"I have plenty of time." His tone held finality.

Constance knew she would have to tell him everything, even if it meant that Hans wouldn't trust her. . .or like her. . . anymore. "My father was a good man. He came back from the war changed. I don't think he ever got over it before he died." She glanced back at Hans. He didn't look disgusted yet.

"Ja. I've seen other men who were affected by the fighting." Hans lifted a foot onto the edge of the porch and leaned an arm on his upraised knee.

"I didn't know about any of this until he was dying. That's when he extracted the promise from me."

Constance didn't know why it was so hard to talk about what happened. She should just blurt it out. She had spent enough time with Hans to know that he was an honorable man. He would understand. She studied his hand that hung in the air. Maybe not looking at his face would make it easier.

"While they were together in the fighting, my father worked out a plan to steal a gold shipment from the Union soldiers." After that sentence, she ventured a glance at his face.

Hans shifted until he could lean back against the post holding up the roof of the porch. "I heard about that shipment being stolen. Is that what you're looking for?"

Disappointment wrinkled his brow, and she winced.

"Yes, but not for the reason you're probably thinking. You see, my father didn't take part in the robbery. He was a Christian. He said the war made him forget for a while, but he couldn't go through with the plan, and he thought he had convinced Jim Mitchell not to do it, either."

A look of relief softened Hans's expression. "Then who stole the gold?"

Constance took a deep breath before she continued. "The only person with him when he planned the job was Jim Mitchell, and the robber or robbers carried it out just the way Pa planned it. He was sure Mr. Mitchell did it."

"And he wanted you to come get his share." Now disgust colored his tone.

"No!" She was sure he would never believe her, but she might just as well finish the story. "Pa wanted me to tell Mr. Mitchell to give back the gold. Pa had been saving money so he would have enough to travel here and talk to him, but then Pa got sick. Just before he died, he told me where his savings were hidden and made me promise to convince his old friend to do the right thing. I never knew it would be so hard to fulfill that promise."

After she finished, she sat with her hands clasped in her lap, waiting for his comment, certain this admission would drive Hans away. Why would he want to protect her now? He evidently thought she was part of the whole bad mess.

"So all these holes were looking for the gold." His statement of the fact sounded almost like a question.

Constance nodded, not even turning her head. "I thought if I could find it and give it back to the government, I would have fulfilled the promise to my father."

Hans stood and moved in front of her. "Look at me, Constance."

She complied. With the bright sunlight behind him, she couldn't read his expression.

"None of this is your fault. You shouldn't have had to shoulder the burden alone." He reached out and took her hand in his. "I wish you had told me before. I could have helped you decide what to do."

With a tug of his hand, he pulled her to stand in front of him. Too close in front of him for her comfort.

"So what do I do now?"

⊱⊰

Her question shook him. So did her inquiring gaze. As a man, he wanted to be able to fix everything for her, but how could he take care of all this? Where should he start?

"First let's get these holes filled. I'll help you." He glanced around the clearing, feeling more in control since there was something tangible to accomplish. "Where is the shovel you used?"

"Down by the spring." For the first time in weeks, her heart felt lighter. "That's where I have Blaze grazing near the pool."

Hans went to Blackie and picked up his reins. "Let's take Blackie, so he can get a drink."

While they walked, silence stretched between them like a living thing, but he had to come up with a viable solution. If he tried to talk, it would muddle his thoughts. Maybe they should go see the sheriff. Andrew would know the best way for them to handle it. Hopefully, Constance would agree.

The glen in the middle of the woods looked idyllic, like some place from one of the fairy tales his mother read to him and his brothers and sisters when he was a young boy. Sunlight broke through the branches that arched over the spring-fed pool, making the surface sparkle and glisten. This would be a special place to own, yet the farm stood desolate. What a waste. Hans wondered what would happen to the property if the brothers never returned.

Constance went over to Blaze and talked softly to him while Hans watered Blackie.

"I'll leave Blackie grazing here with Blaze." He led the stallion to a spot in the tall grasses not far from the other horse; then he picked up the shovel that leaned against a boulder beside the pool, hefted it to his shoulder, and started toward the meadow.

"I wish I had another shovel." Constance skipped every few steps to keep up with his long stride.

Hans silently berated himself for not noticing sooner. When he shortened his steps, they walked together. He didn't talk, because he was mulling over all she had told him today.

As they reached the edge of the woods, he stopped and pulled the spade down. "You use this, and I'll use my hands."

She turned her eyes toward his face, and they darkened to a deep brown. "I don't want to make you do that. It's my fault the holes are there in the first place. I can use my hands."

He picked up one of hers and laid it on his palm. Such a tiny, dainty thing. Her fingers barely reached the base of his. "It would take you a long time to fill in even one of the places. I can do it easier."

Hans knew that he should let go of her hand, but it rested against his callused palm, soft and creamy, even after all the work she'd done today. "You take the shovel, Constance."

When he reluctantly dropped her hand, her expression changed to one of disappointment. It mirrored what he felt. "You start here in the shade. I'll go out there in the sun. I'm used to it."

As Hans knelt beside a hole, he glanced back at her. She stood watching him for a moment, then turned to the holes at the bases of the trees. While she scraped the dirt back where it came from, he did the same. He filled a hole, then patted it down, leaving only a little mound that would settle with the next rain.

They worked for a while with just the breeze and forest sounds breaking the silence. Hans felt peaceful accomplishing something for Constance. This was the way a husband and wife would work together. That was what he really wanted, a wife to work alongside him and share everything with. *Lord, You're going to have to help me with this. Did You bring Constance to Browning City because she is the wife I have prayed for?* That new thought made his heart feel lighter.

"Constance." His voice sliced through the meadow like an intruder. "We should go talk to the sheriff when we get back to town."

He glanced at her. She had stopped working and stared at him. "I'm not sure that would be a good thing."

Hans stood up and brushed his hands on his trousers. "It's the only thing to do. Andrew Morton is a friend of mine. He'll give us good advice about all of this."

She stood the shovel up and clasped both her hands around the handle, staring out across the river. "Since I don't have any other ideas, I guess you're right."

Hans could tell that she wasn't completely convinced, but it was a start. *Right, Lord?*

Chapter 13

Constance hadn't realized just how heavy the burden of the promise had been until she no longer carried it alone. Telling Hans was the smartest thing she had done in a long time. He was an honorable man, wise enough to handle her promise with discretion. Except for the first few minutes when he thought she was telling him that she had come here for the gold, he had been nothing but supportive. And he gave no indication that he thought any less of her father for coming up with the plan to steal the gold. He understood how a man's outlook could be skewed by the circumstances of a war.

She had become used to having Hans around all the time, and now Constance knew that she really didn't want that to change, no matter what she felt before. Now that she understood his concern for her, she welcomed it. No one had ever paid that much attention to her needs, not even her parents.

If things were different, maybe there could be a future for the two of them. . .together. Of course, he didn't think of her that way, but she could imagine them sharing their lives. Hans was the kind of man Constance wanted to marry. A man who knew how to protect a woman. A man who took charge of things with wisdom. A man with blue eyes that could melt the coldness from any heart, especially hers.

While they finished filling in the holes, all she could do was think about the man who worked in the too-warm spring sunlight, cleaning up her mess. Even in that task, he sheltered her by having her do the easier holes in the shade.

"Constance, are you about finished?" Hans stood over her.

How could such a large man move so silently? She hadn't known he was near until he spoke her name. Then the sound of his voice wiped everything out of her mind except the fact that he was so close. Heat made its way up her cheeks. She couldn't remember ever blushing as much as she had since she met this marvelous man.

After giving a final pat with the shovel to the mound of dirt she had scraped together, she stepped back. "That's the last one."

Constance ventured a glance at his face, and his smile almost took her breath away. She turned and started through the woods toward the spring.

He moved beside her, matching his steps to hers. "It'll feel good to get all this dirt off us, won't it?"

She nodded, hoping he was looking at her. She was afraid that if she spoke again, her voice would tremble, and that would never do. The poor man didn't need to be burdened with the fact that she felt more for him than a friend should. Probably, that fact would embarrass him and ruin their wonderful friendship.

They got a drink, washed up, and led the horses over to the water for one last time. Hans thought about the last few minutes. He wasn't sure exactly what had changed between him and Constance, but something had.

He helped her up into Blaze's saddle before he mounted Blackie. "We've agreed to go straight to the sheriff's office. Ja?"

Constance nodded before she looked at him. In the shaded glen, her eyes looked a smoky brown. The green flecks were hardly discernable. For the first time, he really noticed how long her brown lashes were. He wasn't sure he had ever seen any woman with such lashes. Of course, he didn't pay that close of attention to other women's individual features. He cleared his throat and clicked his tongue to start the horse.

Because they rode the horses at a fast clip, they didn't talk on the ride back to town. When they could see Browning City up ahead, Hans eased back on the reins. Constance followed his lead, and they rode into town at an easy walk. Hans hoped Andrew would be in his office and not out somewhere taking care of trouble. He wanted to get this talk over with before Constance changed her mind.

They had almost reached the building that housed the sheriff's office when Andrew came out, placing his hat on his head as he closed the door behind him.

"Wait up, Andrew."

The man peered at them and quirked an eyebrow as they stopped their horses and Hans dismounted. Before he could get Blackie tied to the hitching post, Constance slid to the ground, too.

"What can I do for you?" Andrew stood with his arms crossed, but his star was still visible on his chest.

Hans held Constance's arm as they went up the steps to the boardwalk. "Do you have time for us to talk?"

The sheriff looked from one to the other, then opened the door and held it for them to enter in front of him. "Miss Miller, please have a seat. I'll see if I can rustle up another chair for you, Hans."

"That's all right. I can stand." He moved over and leaned against the wall, crossing his arms.

Andrew took off his hat, placed it on a hook on the wall, then dropped into the chair behind his desk. "What's this all about?"

Constance glanced back at Hans.

"She has a story to tell you. Then we want your opinion."

Constance turned around and clutched her hands in her lap. She told the story in a fast monotone. Hans knew it was hard for her because she didn't know Andrew very well. He wanted to make it easier on her but understood after what she had told him that she needed to do it herself.

While Constance told the story, she kept her gaze trained on the boards at her feet. She didn't think she could continue if she tried to look at the sheriff. When she finished, she raised her head and ventured a glance. The man just looked thoughtful, not censuring.

After a moment, he stared her straight in the eyes. "That's an interesting story. I've heard rumors about a gold shipment being stolen, but I never heard from anyone who knew for sure that it really happened. A lot of rumors fly around every time someone new comes to town with a tale. I do think that if it happened, the government would have moved earth and heaven to find the gold. Maybe it was stolen, and they did find it. No one knows for sure. If a gold shipment was stolen, and if it never was found, I don't think Jim Mitchell had anything to do with it."

He leaned back in his chair and engulfed his chin with one hand. Constance could hear Hans shuffling behind her. What should they do now?

The sheriff cleared his throat. "The Mitchell family was real close. Those boys loved their parents. If Jim had any gold, I think he would have used some of the money to pay the back taxes on his folks' farm. Mr. Mitchell had been feeling poorly for a few years, and he wasn't able to work his crops enough to keep up. Jim wouldn't have let his father go through all the worry if he'd had a way to prevent it."

Constance gave him a tentative smile. "Thank you for your time."

Andrew stood up and leaned on the desk. "You know, those boys lit out of here right after their parents were buried. I haven't heard from them for quite a while."

She arose from her chair. "A man at the post office told me he heard that both the brothers were killed in a gunfight at Camden Junction. I'd really like to go there and check out their graves before I give up. I did make my father a promise."

"Now, young lady, I understand, but it wouldn't be a very good idea for you to go there alone, and I won't have time to take you for another week, probably." He took his hat back down off the hook. "I'm on my way out to a farm where there's been some trouble. I have to make sure everything's all right, and I don't know how long it'll take."

Hans stepped forward. "If Miss Miller wants to go before you can take her, I'll accompany her."

When they left the sheriff's office, Hans escorted Constance back to the livery, where they left the horses.

"I need to go to the mercantile." Constance turned to leave the stable.

"I'll walk along with you."

Constance would be glad to have him with her, but she didn't want to take him from something else he needed to do. Hadn't she bothered him enough already? "Don't you need to get back to work?"

"There's nothing that can't wait."

Just as they stepped up on the boardwalk in front of the store, Mary Reeves exited the establishment. "Hans, Constance, how good to see you. I wanted to ask you to come over for dinner if you can."

Hans rented a buggy and went to pick up Constance to take her to the parsonage. Mrs. Barker welcomed him into the parlor of the boardinghouse, then went to tell Constance that he had arrived. He hadn't spent much time in the room, so he ambled around, looking at all the things scattered over various pieces of furniture. His quarters behind the smithy were adequate, but all these doodads did make this room more homey. Maybe he needed a woman's touch. He didn't know any man who would think to put those frilly things on the tables or buy tiny statues to place on top.

He wondered what kind of things Constance would add to a room to make it her own. Would she sew filmy curtains like the ones that framed the front windows? He had cut the backs out of a couple of old shirts with torn sleeves and tacked them over the windows so no one could see in at night.

Footsteps approaching the doorway drew him from his thoughts. He turned to see Constance waiting for him. A smile lit her face, bringing a grin to his. She looked a lot different than she had earlier in the day when her clothes were covered with dust and her hands were grimy. A vision of feminine grace and. . . loveliness in a fluffy dress the color of spring grass. It brought out those green highlights in her eyes. He walked toward her, wanting to take her in his arms and hold her near his heart.

Hans wondered what she would do if he did. Probably scare her spitless. She had let him help her when she needed it, but he was sure that the thought of being more than friends had never entered her mind.

"I brought a buggy so we won't have to walk." He wished he could think of something more intelligent to say to her.

"Thank you, Hans." The musical lilt of her voice caused a flutter deep inside him.

He held out his arm, and she slipped her hand in the crook. When she did, he caught a whiff of the fragrance of spring flowers that wafted from her. This could be a rather long evening while he tried to rein in his emotions.

Constance stopped to gather her skirts in her hands so she could step up into the buggy, but Hans caught her from behind with his strong hands on her waist and lifted her as if she were light as a feather. She knew that wasn't true, but the man did make her feel tiny.

While he went around in front of the horses, she arranged her skirts so every edge was inside the buggy. It wouldn't do to have a stray breeze lift them and reveal her ankles or something even higher on her limbs.

The other side of the buggy shifted when he applied his weight. She liked the way the vehicle rocked in rhythm. She could get used to having that in her life.

"It's a lovely evening for a drive, Hans." She kept her gaze trained on the passing scenery.

"Yes, it is." He spoke softly, but it sounded very close.

Constance turned to find his eyes on her instead of the road. She reached into her reticule and pulled out her ivory fan. After unfurling it, she tried to cool her face, which she felt sure was flushed.

Thankfully, the parsonage wasn't far, because that last interplay made her feel tongue-tied. He must have experienced the same malady, because there was no more conversation.

She thought about climbing down from the buggy while Hans tied the horses to the hitching post. The memory of his hands on her waist stopped her. Constance wanted to feel it at least one more time. She furled her fan and placed it back in her handbag.

When Hans stood by her side of the buggy and looked up into her eyes, the twilight darkened the blue in his to almost black. Or was there another reason his gaze seemed so intense? Once again, he easily lifted her to the ground. For just a moment, she wanted to lean toward him, hoping he would engulf her in his strong arms. She whirled around and started up the walkway toward the porch. He quickly moved in step beside her.

"I'm sure we aren't late." Laughter laced his tone.

"I'm glad you're here."

Constance hadn't noticed Jackson on the porch until he spoke. She smiled at him.

"Now we can eat." He rubbed his stomach. "Delicious smells have been coming from the kitchen for some time."

Mary stepped through the door. "I thought I heard voices out here. Come on in. Dinner's ready."

As usual, conversation flowed freely throughout the meal, but Constance had a hard time keeping up with it. Her attention wandered often to the man who sat across the table from her.

～❧～

Hans had a hard time keeping up with the conversation. When he ate at the boardinghouse, Constance sat beside him. And the last time they ate a meal with the Reeves, he hadn't admitted to himself just how strong his feelings for her really were. Every time she spoke, he took the opportunity to study her. Since her times out at the Mitchell farm, her creamy skin had taken on a golden hue, and her cheeks were a more healthy pink. She looked vital and alive. Now that she had been totally honest with him, everything about her called to his heart.

At the end of the meal, he couldn't remember a single bite he'd taken. Only the evidence of food having been on his plate assured him that he had eaten.

"Actually, I need to tell the two of you something." Constance gestured toward Jackson and Mary as she spoke.

Jackson leaned back in his chair and gave her his full attention. "As a pastor or as a friend?"

"Both, I think." Constance stood and started gathering her silverware onto her plate. "I'll help Mary with the dishes; then we can talk."

Mary touched her arm. "No, you won't. The dishes can wait." She stood. "Let's go into the parlor. It will be more comfortable in there."

Even though Constance tried to change Mary's mind, it didn't work.

Once in the other room, Constance sat in a straight-backed chair. Mary and Jackson took places on the sofa, and he placed his arm around his wife. Hans took the chair that matched the one where Constance sat. He wished he were closer to her, so he could give her moral support, but maybe this way was better.

For a few minutes, Constance told them all she had said to him and the sheriff. Jackson and Mary looked intrigued.

"That's some story," Jackson said as soon as she finished. "Do you really think there is gold out there at the farm?"

Constance took a deep breath. "I'm not so sure after what Sheriff Morton said. I think I've done all I can about the gold."

Relief shot through Hans. He had hoped she wouldn't let the search consume too much of her life. He agreed with Andrew. If the gold really was stolen, he didn't think it was anywhere near Browning City or the Mitchell farm.

Jackson continued to study Constance. "But you're not satisfied with your quest, are you?"

"No." She rubbed her palms together. "I want to be sure that Jim Mitchell is really dead. If he isn't, I need to continue to search for him."

"Didn't you say Andrew would take you sometime next week?" Compassion filled Mary's face and her tone.

"Yes." Constance sounded hesitant. "But I really wanted to go before then."

She gazed at Hans, and he felt her expression travel straight to his heart. He wanted to ease her burden in any way he could.

"I told her I could escort her to Camden Junction, but we have one problem."

"What problem?" Constance sounded surprised.

"Well, it's at least a five-hour journey on horseback. A buggy would take even longer. We couldn't make it there and back in one day."

Constance looked puzzled. Her expression changed the moment she realized what he was getting at. "Oh, even if we had separate rooms at the hotel, it might not look right." Her voice had a catch in it, and she looked discouraged.

Mary gave a soft clap. "I have a wonderful idea. My parents live in Camden Junction. Father is the doctor, and they have a large house. I'm sure they would be glad for Constance to stay with them. I want to send Mother some vegetables from the Community Garden. This would be a good opportunity. I could write Mother a note for you to take with you."

Hans watched Constance's expression while her friend talked. By the time Mary finished, hope had replaced the look of discouragement.

"I think that is a good idea, Constance." When he spoke, she turned a grateful expression toward him. "When would you like to go?"

"I can't go tomorrow because I was gone from the boardinghouse kitchen today." Constance looked thoughtful for a moment. "I could bake double everything tomorrow, and we could go the next day." She smiled at him. "If you aren't too busy, Hans."

He would never get tired of hearing her speak his name. This time it came out softly with great emotion, rendering him speechless.

Just as Mary had said, her parents welcomed Constance into their home with open arms. She would have known Mrs. Carter was Mary's mother without having been told. They looked just alike and more like sisters than mother and daughter.

Even though they arrived mid-afternoon and the Carters weren't expecting them, Mary's mother insisted on feeding them right away. While Hans took care of the horses in the barn behind the house and Constance freshened up in a bedroom on the second story, Mrs. Carter must have been busy. When Constance came down the stairs, a cold feast spread out across the table in the dining room.

A knock sounded on the back door.

"Oh dear, I hope it's not someone coming to take Doc away from us right when we want to get acquainted with Jackson's and Mary's friends." Mrs. Carter wiped her hands on a tea towel and stuck the end of it in her apron pocket before opening the door. "Come on in, Mr. Van de Kieft. You didn't have to knock."

"Hans." He still held his hat in his hand. "Please, call me Hans."

Constance watched him from the doorway. She could tell that his smile captivated Mrs. Carter almost as much as it did her.

"Of course, Hans. I hope you're hungry." Mary's mother bustled over to the cabinet and picked up a tray that contained thick slices of ham and cheese.

The table already held a platter of some kind of bread. It was darker than any Constance had ever made. Maybe Mrs. Carter would give her the recipe before they went back home.

A crock of homemade pickles added a piquant air to the room. A hint of spices, vinegar, and even sweetness. Sliced tomatoes and onions covered another plate. Constance hadn't realized how hungry she was until she looked at all the food.

The doctor returned from his office in the front of the large first floor, and they all sat down to eat. After he blessed their food, Mrs. Carter passed each plate to Constance first, then to Hans. He must have been hungrier than she was, because soon his plate was piled high.

Conversation flowed freely here, just as it did at Jackson's and Mary's house. After the Carters asked several questions about their daughter and her husband, they moved on to getting to know Hans and Constance.

When Mrs. Carter found out that all of Constance's family was gone, she patted Constance's hand. "We'll just have to make you a part of our family."

Constance almost felt like another daughter, filling a void she hadn't known existed in her heart.

At the end of the meal, Hans pushed back his chair. "I think I'll go and see about a room at the hotel."

"A fine meal, my dear." Dr. Carter patted his stomach before turning toward Hans. "You don't have to do that. We have plenty of bedrooms."

Red suffused Hans's cheeks, and he cleared his throat. "Thank you for your kindness, but it would be better for Constance's reputation if I went to the hotel."

Constance widened her eyes. She hadn't thought about where Hans would sleep. The man was amazing—always thinking about her. Her heart fluttered at the thought. If only she was more than a friend to him.

"After you return, Hans"—Constance looked down at her hands—"do you think we could go to the cemetery? I'd like to get that taken care of today."

He nodded and turned to go. "I'll be back soon." He spoke over his shoulder.

Hans hurried in the direction the doctor had told him. Constance had reacted to his comment about her reputation, but he didn't know why. Would he ever understand women, especially Constance?

After obtaining a room for the night, he went to the sheriff's office. That would be a good place to find out about what had happened.

It wasn't a pretty story. The Mitchell brothers did indeed start sowing wild oats after their parents died. He wondered if that loss was the root cause of their wild living or if the war had affected Jim too much. Whichever it was, both brothers had been buried at the back of the cemetery away from the churchyard. Plain wooden crosses marked the place, and their names had been painted on the crossbars with black paint. Already the letters looked weathered. Sometime soon, they would be completely obliterated. What a waste of two lives.

Hans really didn't want to bring Constance here, but he knew she wouldn't rest easy until she saw the graves for herself. He hoped it would end her need to follow her quest.

He went back to the Carters' house to get Constance. When they returned to the cemetery, she stood for a long time just staring at the plain crosses. Then, to his surprise, she dropped to her knees in the grass beside Jim Mitchell's grave.

She clasped her hands in front of her. "Mr. Mitchell, I'm so sorry my father didn't come to see you sooner. I wish he had. Maybe your life wouldn't have ended like this. He wanted to tell you about your need for God. When he couldn't come because he was too sick, he asked me to tell you. But we both failed. I hope someone else told you about God before you died."

The last few words were so faint that Hans could hardly make them out. Constance stayed in that position for a few moments; then she started to cry. At first, tears made their quiet way down her cheeks, but soon she sniffled and then sobbed. Hans felt as if his heart were breaking. He couldn't leave her there, so he pulled her up and into his arms, cradling her against his chest.

She continued to cry for a long time. All the while, Hans held her tight with one arm and gave her comforting strokes on her back with the other hand. He occasionally murmured what he hoped were comforting words. The rest of the time, he prayed silently for her sorrow and pain to be eased. How he wished he had the right to do more.

Chapter 14

The next day when Constance and Hans arrived back in Browning City, they went straight to the parsonage. Hans helped her down from the wagon seat and handed her several packages wrapped in brown paper and tied with twine. She started up the walkway, and he picked up the last four bundles left in the back of the wagon.

He caught up with her halfway to the house. "I'll take your carpetbag by the boardinghouse before I return the wagon to the livery."

She smiled up at him. "Thanks. I want to spend awhile with Mary if she's not busy."

He nodded. "She'll want you to be there when she opens all these parcels from her mother."

"Yes, she probably will." Constance stepped up on the porch. "I've missed being with Mary. It's been more than four days since we spent any time alone. We have a lot to talk about."

"I'm sure you do." The twinkle in his eyes carried over to the tone of his voice.

Maybe it was time for her to talk to Mary about her feelings for Hans. . .or maybe not. She'd see how the afternoon progressed.

Mary opened the door after Hans knocked. Her eyes widened when she saw all the packages in their arms. "Come in." She stepped back and pulled the door farther open.

"Where do you want us to put these?" Constance smiled at Mary's look of bewilderment.

"What are they?"

"We're not sure. Your mother gave them to us just before we left this morning. . .along with a basket of food for us to eat on the way home. It was enough to feed an army." Constance glanced toward the parlor. "Do you want these in there or on the table in the kitchen?"

Hans stood quietly and listened to the exchange. Constance welcomed his presence but knew she would wait until he was gone before she asked Mary all the questions that were whirling in her brain.

Mary turned back toward the kitchen. "Let's put them on the table. Then we can spread out all the items and see what they are."

Hans dropped the ones he carried beside hers on the shiny wooden surface. "I need to get to the smithy and see if I've missed anyone. If I'm not there, they just tack a note up on the door." He turned toward Constance. "Would you like me to come back and pick you up to go to the boardinghouse?"

She smiled at him. "Thank you, Hans, but no. I've ridden more miles than I want to remember in the last few days. The walk will do me good."

Mary went to the door with him, but soon returned. "Let's see what Mother sent. I can hardly wait. Why don't you open some of them while I open the others?"

She sounded like a child at Christmas. Of course, no one Constance knew ever had this many presents at that holiday.

Constance started trying to untie the knot on the bundle closest to her. The knot resisted, and she became frustrated with her efforts.

"Do it like this." Mary pulled the twine around one corner, then off the package.

As the paper from each bundle unfolded, the two women ooed and aahed. Baby gowns, blankets, knitted hats, sweaters, booties, safety pins that people had started using on diapers, and hemmed flannel diapers spread across the table. The last parcel contained a soft cotton nightgown and robe for Mary. Pink embroidered roses clung to vines that climbed all the way up the front of both garments.

Tears sprang to Mary's eyes. "Mother must have started working on these as soon as we let them know that we were going to have a baby."

"They're wonderful." Constance knew that the tiny stitches had taken a lot of work. "Your mother really loves you, and she already loves her grandchild."

After Constance helped Mary take the items up to the bedroom that was being turned into a nursery, the women returned to the kitchen for a cup of tea. Mary asked all about the trip, and Constance gladly told her the many details. They each drank two more cups of tea before they were through discussing the subject.

"You have something else on your mind, don't you?" Mary's perceptive question caught Constance off guard.

"Yes. I want to ask you about a thing that happened the day I went out to the farm, when Hans came and helped me fill in the holes."

Mary set her cup down and gave Constance her full attention. "I can see it's important to you. What happened?"

Constance studied the design worked into the tablecloth before answering, but her thoughts weren't on the pattern. She was trying to formulate the words into a sensible explanation. "Hans didn't find me immediately. He saw the holes and piles of dirt beside them. When I came back from the spring, he stood near the edge of the bluff talking to God."

"That sounds like Hans." Mary nodded. "He likes to seek the Lord about anything that bothers him. So what did he say?"

Constance clasped her hands together on the tabletop. "It's not so much what he said exactly. It's more the way he said things. . . . I know this doesn't make any sense, but I've never heard anyone talk to God that way. His head wasn't bowed, and he sounded just the same as he would talking to Jackson or us."

"That's because he was talking to his best friend. . .Jesus." Mary turned concerned eyes toward her. "Constance, what do you believe about God?"

What a surprising question. No one had ever asked her anything like that. What did she believe about God?

She stared out the window and watched two birds circling around while building a nest in the branches of the tree. One would go down and retrieve some grass; the other went for tiny twigs; then they both returned to the bower. She needed something specific, like the purpose the birds had to provide shelter for their eggs. Instead, her thoughts flew around without landing.

Mary waited patiently, allowing her to gather her scattered thoughts.

"I know that God created the world and all that's in it."

"That's a start." Mary smiled at her. "What else?"

Finally, things started to settle into a pattern. "He loves us, and He sent Jesus to die for our sins. Now they're both in heaven, and when we die, we'll go to be with God. Right?"

Mary picked up her spoon and stirred her cooling tea. "That's right as far as it goes. Have you ever asked Jesus to save you from your sins?"

Constance nodded. "When I was nine years old." She remembered the brush arbor meeting years before. What the evangelist said finally made sense to her. She had asked her mother to walk to the front with her, and everyone had come after the service to welcome her into the family of God.

"Have you studied the scriptures and grown in your faith since that time?"

Mary's question made her squirm in the chair. "We went to church when we could get there, but the circuit-riding preacher only came maybe once a month. The other Sundays, we had all-day singings with dinner on the grounds. I really like the singings and the fellowship of sharing the meal with neighbors."

Two grooves formed between Mary's brows. "Do you read your Bible and commune with Jesus?"

"I read Mother's Bible until it fell apart." Constance traced the pattern in the tablecloth with her finger to keep from seeing the pity she imagined in Mary's eyes.

"We can take care of that. I'll give you an extra one we have. I think I know what your problem is." Mary sounded decisive.

Constance looked up. "What is my problem?"

"No one has ever told you that you can have a close relationship with Jesus right now, have they?" Her eyes probed deep inside Constance, exposing her heart.

"I'm not sure what that means."

Mary took a moment as if gathering her thoughts, too. "When Jesus went back to heaven, He left his Holy Ghost with us. And He wants to be a part of our everyday lives. He wants to be the Lord of our lives and help us with everything we face. Does that make any sense to you?"

Constance got up and walked over to the window. The bright sunlight and beauty all around reminded her that God loved her through His creation. Could He really want to take part in everything in her life? Didn't He have enough to take care of? How would it change what happened to her?

She turned back to look at Mary. "I think I understand what you're telling me, but how does that work?"

"What happens when you pray now?" Mary's question didn't answer hers.

"Well, I ask God for strength and help, then hope everything will be okay. Many times it isn't."

Mary came to stand beside her. "You talk to Him way up in heaven, you mean?"

Constance nodded. "How do you pray?"

Mary's smile lit the room. "I imagine I pray much like Hans did. Jesus is my friend. He listens to me, and I listen to Him. He really cares about my life."

One thing Mary said caught Constance's attention. "What do you mean, you listen to Him?"

A faraway look came over Mary's face. "Sometimes, He talks to me through scripture. Other times, He drops thoughts and assurances into my heart. He even speaks to me through Jackson, both as my husband and as my pastor. I have a personal relationship with Him. When you ask Him to direct your life, He will give you peace in your heart. The Bible talks about a peace that passeth understanding. If I'm not certain about whether He wants me to do something, I see if I have a peace about it."

Constance sat back down and took a sip of her stone-cold tea. At least it wet her throat, which was dry from all the talking.

"So how do I do that?"

Mary studied her intently for a moment. "You just pray and ask Him to show you what He wants you to do in every situation and relationship you face. He's a gentleman. He won't force you to involve Him in your daily life and do what He wants."

A gentleman. Maybe that's why Hans was such a gentleman. He tried to treat others as Jesus did. "I'd like that, but I'm not sure exactly what to say or how to say it."

Mary sat down across the table from her and reached to take her hands. "You just talk to Him as you would talk to me. Tell Him what's in your heart. If you want me to, I can say a phrase, and if you agree, you can repeat it."

Finally, Constance didn't feel as if she were wandering through a strange forest without a map or compass. "I'd like that. Should I bow my head?"

"If you want to, but your head doesn't have to be bowed to talk to Him."

Constance decided she wanted to, because she was sure this would be a sacred time. A time she would want to remember forever.

"Jesus, I ask You to lead me through my life."

Constance thought about this sentence, then repeated it.

"I want You to take part in everything I do and show me how You want me to live."

This time Constance repeated the words immediately.

"Thank You for loving me and wanting to have a deeper relationship with me."

These words tumbled from Constance's heart as well as her mouth, and something happened. She could feel the presence of Jesus so strongly that it invaded every part of her. Tears became a waterfall down her cheeks. Love filled every part of her heart. More love than she had ever known existed. She bowed silently before the overwhelming presence, basking in Him. All her life, she had wanted this, but she hadn't known exactly what it was that she was looking for.

She wondered why no one had ever told her about it. Maybe someone had, and she hadn't understood what they were talking about.

Constance wanted to share it with everyone in the world, but for right now, she would just spend time with Him, letting Him establish His peace and love in her heart.

⟨≈⟩

When Hans went to the boardinghouse for supper, he could hardly wait to see Constance. Spending most of three days this week with her made him miss her when they were apart. *Lord, what's going on here?*

Mrs. Barker welcomed him to the table, but he didn't see Constance. He glanced toward the doorway to the kitchen as she came through, carrying a large platter of fried chicken. One of his favorites. His stomach gave a loud growl in response to the fragrance that filled the room.

Mrs. Barker cut her eyes toward him and grinned. "So, Hans, did you miss my cooking while you were away?"

"Ja."

He turned his smile toward Constance as she took the seat beside him. Too bad she wasn't across from him as she had been in Camden Junction. Something looked different about her. He couldn't decide what. As usual, wisps of hair that weren't confined into the bun at the base of her neck framed her face. Her eyes were a different thing altogether. They sparkled with an inner light that intensified the golden flecks. Why had he never noticed this before?

Hans had spent a lot of time studying Constance as she sat across from him at the Carters' house. He shouldn't have missed anything this startling.

"So, Constance." He had to clear his throat to dislodge a lump. "Now that you've found out everything you needed to find, will you go home to Arkansas, or will you stay in Iowa?"

She looked up from putting food on her plate and paused with the spoon in her hand. She took a moment to answer. "I really like Browning City."

Good. That's what he wanted to hear.

"Even though I miss the mountains, the view from the bluff over the Mississippi River is almost as good." She put the spoon back in the bowl and passed it to him.

He heaped mashed potatoes on his plate, ready to add the delicious cream gravy that was one of Mrs. Barker's specialties.

"I've made a lot of friends here." Constance glanced around the table at each one there. "More than I had back home."

Hans passed the gravy boat to Thomas and nearly dropped it. Hans wiped his sweaty palms along his pant legs. Paper crinkled in his pocket.

"I forgot." He reached into his front pocket and extracted an envelope. "When I was at the post office, Hiram asked if I would be seeing you this evening. Wanted me to give this to you." He handed the letter to Constance. "Looks like it came from Arkansas."

Constance nodded and stuck the letter in the pocket of her apron.

After supper, he asked if she wanted to go for a walk before it got too dark. She glanced toward her employer and started to shake her head.

"You go ahead, Constance." Mrs. Barker made a shooing motion with both hands. "You did most of supper for me, so I'll do the dishes."

They stepped out into the mellow twilight. A gentle breeze stirred the leaves on the trees, and the chirping of birds settling down on their nests accompanied the symphony of crickets and frogs. Hans always liked this time of evening, and today he would enjoy it even more because he was spending it with Constance.

When they walked down the street in the quiet neighborhood, their shoulders almost touched. He felt her presence beside him as a tangible connection.

"Didn't you want to see what the letter said?" He smiled down at her, thinking that if he had his arm around her, she would fit just right against his side.

"I took a peek when I removed my apron. The Smiths are buying my farm.

They'll send all my personal possessions in a crate and the money in a strongbox on the stage."

He walked silently for a few steps, then stopped beneath the branches of a cottonwood tree, facing Constance. "Does that mean that you don't have any ties back there now?"

When she turned her gaze up to connect with his, the new sparkle shone, even in the shadows. "Yes, it does. I'm now a permanent part of Browning City society." She smiled, lighting the whole area around them with the force of it.

That smile warmed Hans all the way through. He could get used to experiencing that feeling. He wondered what she would do if he smoothed his fingers across her cheek. His hand ached to do that very thing.

After he left Constance at the boardinghouse, Hans started toward his lonely quarters behind the smithy. It had never seemed that way before Constance came to town. He stopped and stared up at the twinkling lights in the sky. The full moon bathed everything in a glistening glow.

"Lord, something's different about Constance. Does it have anything to do with You?" He waited and listened for the still small voice that whispered a quiet "Yes" into his heart. "Is she the woman You created for me? Am I supposed to court her?"

Peace descended deeper inside him, and he felt as though he was on the road that God had laid out for him since the beginning of time. He would court her, but first he had to do one thing.

The next morning after he fixed a quiet breakfast for himself, Hans headed straight to the office of the county tax collector. The man had an office in Browning City.

"What can I do for you, Hans?" William Lawrence stood up from the chair behind a large desk and held out his hand. "All your taxes have been paid."

Hans shook hands and nodded. "Ja, I know. I wanted to check on the Mitchell farm. Andrew said the parents were really behind on their taxes."

Mr. Lawrence clucked his tongue. "It's a sad situation. I had hoped that when the boys returned, they would be able to help their parents. But it didn't happen."

"Are there any other heirs?" Hans hoped not.

"None that we've been able to find." The man sat back down and took a ledger from one of the drawers in his desk. He opened it and ran his finger down the page. "It's scheduled to be in the auction next month, sold for back taxes."

Hans tried not to smile at someone else's difficulty. "Would it be possible for me to pay all the back taxes and redeem the property before the auction?"

Mr. Lawrence rocked in his chair for a moment. "Well, we've never come up against that question before. I don't see why not. All the county wants is the back taxes. Are you sure you want to do that? It's quite a large sum."

"Ja." Hans stuck his hands in the front pockets of his trousers. "I have quite a bit of money saved. I knew I would want to have a house eventually."

The tax collector picked up a pen and wrote on a piece of paper. "If you bring me this amount, I'll make sure the property is deeded to you."

Hans studied the number for a moment. He could handle it. "Okay, you'll have it in the next few days." He folded the paper and put it in his shirt pocket before holding out his hand. "Nice doing business with you."

All the way back to the smithy, Hans whistled and started making plans.

Chapter 15

Several people came to the smithy on Saturday with work for Hans. He was glad for the business, but some of them needed their things right away, so he had to put his plans on hold. Hans needed a large fire in the forge, which made the June day extremely hot. He wished he could remove his shirt and work without it, but there were too many people in town today. He didn't want to offend any ladies who might come with their husbands to the nearby livery or to the smithy.

Hans laid his tools on the long table beside one wall of the cavernous room, then reached for the bandanna in his back pocket. After wiping the sweat from his brow, he hung the wet cloth across a bar by the door. Good thing he brought extra handkerchiefs today.

He wished he had time to talk to Jackson. His friend could help him decide the best way to approach the next few days. After spending several hours talking to the Lord last night, Hans was convinced that God brought Constance to Browning City for several reasons. The main one was to meet him.

His parents had taught their sons the proper way to court a woman. A man should approach the man who was the protector of the woman and ask his permission first. Constance didn't have a father, brother, or uncle for him to talk to.

When Hans went over in his mind all the times he and Constance had been together, he realized that there was a possibility she already felt something more than friendship for him, but he wasn't sure. How could he bring up the subject to explore their feelings? His ran deep, but he couldn't always put them into words. Maybe Jackson could tell him what to do. Any suggestions would be helpful.

As he returned to shaping a horseshoe against his anvil, every pound of the hammer contained some of his frustration. Rhythmical beats of iron against iron rang through the building and echoed into the street.

"Are you trying to beat that thing to death?" Jackson's laugh followed his question as he came in out of the sun. "It sure is hot in here." He took off his hat and fanned his face and neck.

Hans plunged the finished shoe into the bucket of cool water, and steam hissed in a cloud, adding to the oppressive heat. After a moment, he jerked the piece of shaped metal back out of its bath, shook the water off, and put it in the bucket that held several more. He laid his hammer on the table, then pulled off his apron and placed it beside the tool. After grabbing another bandanna, he headed toward the doorway.

"Let's get out in the breeze for a while. I'm ready for a break." Hans finished wiping his face, hands, and forearms, then hung the cloth beside the first one. "So what brings you by the smithy? Do you need something repaired?"

Jackson shook his head. "No. I just felt that I should come by and see you."

Hans laughed. "You must have been listening to the Lord. I've been bending His ear enough this morning, wishing I could talk to you."

Jackson waved toward a bench that sat in the shade of a giant oak tree across the road. "Do you have time to sit a minute?"

Hans led the way and dropped onto the wooden seat worn smooth from years of use by weary travelers. "I can take a little while."

After sitting beside him and propping one foot on the other leg, Jackson asked, "So why were you telling the Lord that you wanted to talk to me?"

Hans rubbed the toe of his boot in the thick layer of dust in front of them, making lazy circles. "I need some advice."

Jackson waited a moment, probably expecting Hans to continue, but he didn't. "About what?"

"I've developed strong feelings for Constance."

The last thing Hans expected was the laugh that exploded from his friend. It drowned out the rustle of leaves in the branches above, and the birds stopped chirping.

" 'Strong feelings,' huh? Just how strong are these feelings?"

"I'm not going to tell you if you're going to laugh at me." Hans tried to sound offended, but he knew he didn't succeed. "I'm trying to be serious here."

Jackson sobered and draped his arm across his upraised knee. "I'm sorry. I shouldn't have laughed. It just took you long enough to recognize what you're feeling. You do love her, don't you?"

How did Jackson know? Hans had just realized it the other day. "Well. . .ja."

"So what are you going to do about it?" Jackson cut right to the crux of the matter.

What could he do? "I'd really like to court her, see if she cares for me, too."

"I don't think you have to worry about that." Was Jackson a mind reader? A pastor wasn't supposed to take part in that kind of hocus-pocus, was he?

Hans ran a hand around the back of his neck. "I wish she had a father for me to ask. That's what my parents taught me to do. I'm trying to decide how to go about it."

Jackson stared up the street toward the center of town. "Why don't I ask her to move into the parsonage with Mary and me? My wife's getting tired much quicker these days. Constance could help a bit around the house, and she would be under my protection. You could take your time courting her and convincing her that you love her."

Hans wiped his sweaty palms down the legs of his denim trousers. "All right. That sounds like a good idea to me. I've noticed a difference in her attitude toward me lately. She might care something for me already."

Jackson laughed again, then held up his hand. "I'm sorry. It's just funny to me. Mary and I have both known for a long time that you love each other. We were just waiting for you to realize it, too."

"Does everyone in town know?" Hans couldn't have kept the exasperation out of his tone if he had wanted to.

"I doubt it." Jackson set his foot down in the dirt beside his other one. He leaned his forearms on his thighs and clasped his hands. "We just know you better than anyone else does."

❧

Constance had always loved going to church. Probably because of the music and spending time with friends. Today was different. When she walked into the wooden structure with sunlight shining through amber-tinted windows that lit up the whole space, she felt as if she were really going into the Lord's house. God no longer seemed way off up in heaven. Her heart was so full of His love that she didn't think she could contain it.

She slipped into a pew halfway down the center aisle, on the left. After taking her place, she bowed her head and shut her eyes, basking in His presence. Her life had made a drastic turn. Had it only been two days ago? Such a short span in the twenty years of her life. Finally, her heart was full of a deeper love than she had ever imagined. She wanted to pour it out on everyone she met. To tell them what they were missing by not having a deeper relationship with the Lord.

Constance opened her eyes and glanced around. Mary came through the side door that led back toward Jackson's tiny office. Usually she sat on the front pew, but today, she came back and joined Constance.

"So how are you feeling?" The kind expression in Mary's eyes probed deep into Constance's heart.

"I've never felt so good. . .about everything. I don't think life could be any better."

Mary patted her hand. "Have you heard anything from Selena lately? How is she doing?"

"I'm not sure." Constance did feel some hesitation at the mention of the woman's name. "Mrs. Barker is going out to check on her this afternoon. It's been long enough that she could have healed. Then I would be out of a job."

"That's wonderful." Mary's exuberance surprised Constance. "Jackson and

I wanted to ask you something, anyway. Are you coming over to the house for lunch today?"

Constance glanced down at her friend's expanding figure. "I really don't want to make extra work for you."

"You always help when you're there. I like having you around." Mary's last words were almost drowned out by the introduction to a hymn being played enthusiastically on the pump organ.

Constance nodded before she turned toward the front. Just as the song leader told everyone to stand, Hans appeared in the aisle beside her and asked if he could sit with the two women. Constance gladly slid closer to Mary. The only thing that could make her life even better would be if the Lord caused Hans to fall in love with her as she had fallen in love with him. With a secret smile, she joined her alto voice in harmony with his mellow baritone as they sang about God's amazing grace. Today, she understood in a new way what the words to that favorite hymn meant.

After the service, Hans took Constance and Mary to the parsonage in a buggy while Jackson stayed to talk to those who wanted to shake hands with him. By the time he arrived at home, the table was set and most of the food rested in pretty bowls scattered around the large oval.

Hans pulled out a chair for Constance, then took the one on the other side of the table. Once again, he made her feel cared for. If only that care could turn to something deeper. She unfolded her napkin and placed it in her lap while glancing up at the man. He was so handsome and strong, but his greatest strengths were his moral character and love for the Lord. Almost as if he could feel her gaze, he turned his eyes toward her. The warmth of his gaze made her wish a breeze would blow through the open windows to cool her cheeks.

"Let's thank the Lord for our blessings." Jackson extended a hand toward both Hans and Constance while they took hold of Mary's hands, and everyone bowed their heads.

Jackson prayed wonderful prayers, but Constance had a hard time keeping her mind on the words today. If only she had been able to sit in the place across from Jackson, then Hans would be holding her hand. She had felt the strength of those hands when he placed them around her waist to hoist her onto a horse or up into a buggy or wagon. She'd seen the calluses on his palms. Would they feel rough clasped against hers, or would they cause a delicious sensation in her stomach the way his hands on her waist did?

Constance didn't realize that Jackson had finished blessing the food until he and Mary released her hands. She should be ashamed for letting her thoughts wander the way they did during the prayer, but she wasn't. Today, everything was too wonderful for that.

Jackson placed several pieces of roast beef on his plate and passed the platter to Constance. She took some and gave the rest to Mary. It smelled so good, but when her gaze collided with Hans's, her stomach turned over, and she didn't know if she would be able to eat a thing. His eyes compelled hers to continue the connection, and she gladly complied. Jackson had to clear his throat before she noticed he held a bowl of steaming mashed potatoes toward her.

Somehow, Constance got through the meal without spilling anything. She had to keep her peeks at Hans to a minimum to accomplish that.

When Mary finished her last bite, she placed her fork on her plate. "Constance, Jackson and I would like you to move into the parsonage with us."

Constance turned her full attention to her friend. "I might not have a job for long, but I could still live at the boardinghouse. With the amount of money I received for the farm, I can afford it. I could start looking for a house to buy."

For some reason, that statement brought a frown to Hans's face. Why would he care if she bought a house?

"There's more to our idea." Jackson smiled toward his wife. "Mary is getting tired more quickly. I would appreciate it if you could help her. I know you do when you're here, but if you lived here, things would be easier for her."

Constance thought about the idea for a moment. "I really would like being here all the time, and if I helped Mary, it would be almost as though I was paying rent."

"Ja." Hans's enthusiastic agreement surprised Constance. "That would be a good thing."

Mary stood and started gathering dishes to take to the kitchen. "Then it's agreed. Jackson and Hans can help you move your things as soon as Mrs. Barker says Selena is coming back."

❧

Things couldn't have worked any better for Hans. Mrs. Barker had returned with the news that Selena was hoping to return to work right away, so he and Jackson moved Constance to the parsonage on Monday. He had been spending every evening over there for two weeks.

Constance cooked wonderful meals, and he ate with them. He hoped Mrs. Barker wasn't disappointed to lose one of her regulars for supper. Tonight Constance promised fried chicken. His mouth watered just thinking about the crunchy goodness. Her mashed potatoes and cream gravy were the best he had ever tasted.

Tonight would be special. Just that morning, Hans had heard from the tax collector that everything was in order. He now owned a farm that ran along the bluff above the Mississippi River. Of course, the house needed quite a bit of repairing, but he could go out there on days when he didn't have too much work, and soon it would be restored. He could hardly wait to surprise the woman he loved.

When the meal was over, Constance got up and started toward the kitchen with a load of dishes. As usual, Mary insisted that since Constance did so much during the day, she and Jackson would take care of the washing up. His friends had given him every opportunity to be with Constance. They were almost as excited about his courtship as he was, but he hadn't shared his secret with them.

When Constance accompanied him on this walk through the late June twilight, she seemed a little agitated. He took her hand, hoping she wouldn't pull away. Maybe the connection would calm her.

"Is something the matter, Constance?" Hans stopped beside a field that bloomed with a profusion of multicolored wild flowers on the outskirts of town.

She turned toward him, not letting go of his hand. "I don't feel that I'm being fair to Mary and Jackson. I moved into their home to help her, but every evening she insists that she and Jackson will do the dishes." Her upturned eyes clouded over with concern.

He laughed and took her other hand. "I have a confession to make, Constance. I wanted to court you the way my parents taught me I should, but you weren't living under the protection of your father or another male relative. I talked to Jackson about it, and he suggested that you move in with them."

While he talked, Constance's eyes grew larger. "Court?"

He pulled her closer to him and lowered his face almost to touch hers. "Yes, court. As in, I'm in love with you, and I want to marry you."

"Marry me?" Her voice took on a dreamy quality.

"I'll even kneel before you and propose to you if you want me to."

She pulled her hands from his and framed his cheeks with them. "Oh, Hans, I have been praying that God would allow you to fall in love with me."

Her face was so close that he couldn't resist. He dropped a feathery kiss on her lips. "So will you marry me, Constance?" Even he could hear the husky quality of the question.

Hans slipped his arms around her and pulled her closer. They fit together like a hand in a glove. After waiting for her faint "Yes," he once again touched her lips with his, this time settling his more firmly on hers. Her shy first response set his body to smoldering. Then she matched the fervor of his caress and a bonfire burst forth inside him. All he could think about was the fact that the woman he loved returned his love. They would spend their lives exploring the depth and breadth of what that meant. His caresses lingered as long as he could allow without losing control.

When he pulled back from the embrace, he was glad that they were in a deserted area. However, he knew that if he didn't want to defile her purity before the wedding, they would need to spend most of their time in the company of others.

⚮

When Hans pulled back from the embrace, Constance felt cool air take his place. She had never imagined the depth of love two people could share. What started as a simple kiss had turned to something much more. Something that could consume her. Being married to this marvelous man promised things she had never imagined. She came to Browning City on a quest for her father, but perhaps the real quest had been from God—to find the man He had created for her.

Epilogue

Hans thought he wanted to get married right away, but Mary and Constance changed his mind when they said it would take them at least a month to plan the wedding. Since Constance didn't have any family left, he thought they would just stand up before Jackson and let him perform a quiet ceremony and not bother with guests.

However, Constance had lived in Browning City long enough to make friends, and the women at the church liked having a reason to celebrate. Every evening when he went to the parsonage for supper, the list of people who were helping the two women had grown.

Maybe their way was best. It would give him time to make the house livable. The first few days, he went out to the farm alone, but soon he let Jackson in on the surprise. To keep the women from knowing what was going on, Jackson came to the smithy each day without telling them where he was going. When Hans finished fixing the things at the smithy that people needed right away, the two men went out to the house. While they worked together, they did a lot of talking about life and marriage. Hans felt he would be a better husband because of his friend's thought-provoking advice.

⬤⬤⬤

Mary and Constance went to the mercantile to buy the fabric for her wedding dress. Since Hans complimented her most when she wore green, they chose a watered silk the color of grass in summer.

Constance had always liked the assortment of pretty lace the store carried. They chose a spool in a creamy hue to trim her frock. After they completed the purchases, Mrs. Barker came over to help them sew.

"I miss having you at the boardinghouse." The older woman began to stitch the many panels of the skirt together. "But I'm so happy you and Hans are getting married. I've always thought highly of him. If I had been younger, I might have pursued him myself."

When Constance exclaimed, "I didn't pursue him," the other two women laughed. Then she realized her former employer was teasing her.

"I'm going to have Selena make you a wedding cake." A warm smile spread across Mrs. Barker's face. "They have several kinds of dried fruit at the mercantile. She can make a rich spice cake filled with fruit and nuts."

While they worked, Constance couldn't help wondering about Hans. Before he had asked her to marry him, he sometimes came by the house to see her during the day, but he hadn't since.

"I've noticed that Hans goes out of town almost every day. I've seen him, and sometimes Pastor Jackson, riding in a wagon away from town." Mrs. Barker tied off the end of her thread, then cut it close to the seam, being careful not to snip the delicate fabric.

"Maybe they're helping one of the farmers." Mary got up from her chair and stretched her back. "I can't sit in one position too long. How about if I get us something cool to drink?"

While Mary was in the kitchen, Constance turned toward Mrs. Barker. "Do you know about any houses to rent?"

"I haven't heard of any." The other woman pulled a length of thread from a wooden spool. "Of course you and Hans could live at the boardinghouse if you need to. I'm sure his quarters behind the smithy wouldn't be adequate."

Constance had mentioned to Hans that she wondered where they were going to live, but somehow the subject was changed before he answered. If it was up to her, she really didn't want to start their married life at the hotel or the boardinghouse. She had hoped for a little more privacy. She didn't want to hurt Mrs. Barker's feelings by expressing this desire.

The day before the wedding, two wooden boxes arrived on the stagecoach for Constance. Jackson had been in town when they arrived and brought them home to her. Constance remembered seeing one of the boxes shoved under the bed, but she hadn't thought about it in a long time. Jackson pried the lids off both of them for her, and she and Mary went through the contents. The little cabin in the mountains held meager possessions, and the best of the linens and dishes were in the first crate. The one from under the bed contained a china teapot with hand-painted flowers and matching cups nestled between crushed pieces of old newspapers, along with fancy doilies in a deep ivory shade. The edge of an envelope was visible on one side.

Constance pulled it out and saw her name in her mother's handwriting. She carefully opened the message and tears filled her eyes as she read.

Dear Daughter,

I met your father back in Virginia and married him even though my parents wanted me to wed a neighbor. When we came to the Ozarks, I brought these things. I want you to have them as a reminder of the life I lived before I fell in love with him. My grandmother brought the tea set from England when she came to marry my grandfather, and she crocheted the doilies while I was growing up. I want you to have something that belonged to my family.

Wherever she and Hans lived, she would place these things in a place of honor. One day, perhaps she could pass them on to their daughter.

⊗

The wedding day arrived bright and sunny. Hans had told Mary what he and Jackson had been doing. He asked her to make sure all Constance's belongings were packed. Hans had bought a special trunk for her to use.

The ceremony took place in the church, and the sanctuary was full. More people attended than he had expected, but he was glad for Constance. Since she didn't have a family, she should be surrounded by a host of friends. After the service, they all went to the schoolhouse that was empty for the summer. The women had spread a feast, and a pile of presents filled one table. After they ate the delicious meal, he and Constance took quite awhile opening everything and thanking everyone. It looked to Hans as though they received everything they could possibly need for their new home.

Finally, everything was loaded into the wagon, which also contained the trunk Mary had packed and enough food to feed them for several days. Everyone crowded around, giving them last-minute good wishes. Constance looked so happy it dazzled him. Hans felt almost as if his heart was too full of the love he felt for this beautiful woman, his wife.

He lifted her up onto the bench seat, wishing he could have taken her home in the new buggy he had purchased, but they needed the wagon to transport both her things and the wedding gifts. As they drove away, people continued calling out blessings on their marriage.

When they were out of sight, Hans put his arm around his bride and pulled her close to his side. He glanced down into her lovely face. "I love you, Constance Van de Kieft."

She leaned closer into his embrace. "And I love you, too, Hans."

He pulled on the reins, and the well-trained team slowed to a stop. The kiss at the end of the ceremony had been chaste. Now as his lips met hers, he poured all his suppressed emotions into the depth of the kiss.

When they separated a long time later, he had a hard time catching his breath, and her eyes shimmered with tears. "What's wrong?" He cupped her cheeks with his hands.

She smiled into his eyes. "Nothing's wrong. I'm happier than I have ever been."

With his thumbs, he gently brushed away the moisture from her cheeks. "Then why the tears?"

"They're tears of joy." At her words, he knew he still had a lot to learn about her.

Hans picked up the reins and started the horses. They couldn't get to the house soon enough for him. With one arm, he pulled her back to his side.

"Where are we going, husband?"

Husband. He liked the sound of that word. "We're going home."

"What do you mean?" Constance snuggled even closer.

"I have a surprise for you."

She pulled away a little and looked up into his face. "We're headed in the same direction as the Mitchell farm."

"None of the family is left, so I bought it for us. You liked the view from the bluff."

Constance sat up straight and stared at him. "But the house is such a mess."

"It's all right. We can fix it however you want." Hans had to struggle to hide the smile that wanted to burst forth. He could hardly wait to see her reaction to what he and Jackson had accomplished.

When they were close enough to barely see the house, Constance's gaze searched for it. "You cleaned up around the house, and there are two rocking chairs on the porch." Her last word was almost a squeal.

Her hand on his arm tightened. *Wait until you see inside.* He stopped the horses and helped her down from the wagon. They hurried up onto the porch. He opened the door and swept her into his arms to carry her across the threshold.

After Hans set her on her feet, Constance turned in a complete circle. He enjoyed watching the play of emotions across her face as she saw the new floor with a braided rug Mary had given them and all the furniture that filled the room.

She turned toward him. "Oh, Hans, everything is beautiful. I can't believe you did all of this and kept it as a surprise for me. I've never had a home this wonderful."

She stood on tiptoes and pulled his face down toward hers. When their lips met, her kiss swept him away on a rising tide of love.

How thankful he was that Constance had come on her quest. It not only had led her to Iowa, but it had also settled her into his heart and now into the home where they would build a family surrounded by love.

Lena Nelson Dooley

Lena is an author, editor, and speaker. *Wild Prairie Roses* is her twenty-third book release. A full-time writer, she is the president of DFW Ready Writers, the local Dallas-Fort Worth chapter of American Christian Fiction Writers. She has also hosted a critique group in her home for over twenty years. Several of the writers she's mentored have become published authors, too.

Lena lives with the love of her life in North Texas. They enjoy traveling and spending time with family and friends. They're active members of their church, where Lena serves in the bookstore, on the Altar Ministry team, and as a volunteer for the Care Ministry and Global Ministries.

The Dooley family includes two daughters, their spouses, two granddaughters, two grandsons, and a great-grandson.

You can find Lena at several places on the Internet: www.lenanelsondooley.com, lenanelsondooley.blogspot.com, and her monthly newsletter is at lenanelsondooleynewsletter.blogspot.com. You can also visit her on Shoutlife, Facebook, and Twitter.

TARA'S GOLD

Dedication

To my aunt Janelle, who's always been an example to me on how to serve God with one's whole heart.

Chapter 1

July 1870

*T*ara Young stuck her hand into the satin lining of her fringed jacket. The thin paper crinkled between her fingers, assuring her of its presence. All she had to do was carry the message into the mercantile and pass it to the young clerk who worked there. A simple task considering her last assignment. Stopping in front of the sheriff's office, Tara measured the distance between herself and the front door of the store. Ten steps, maybe eleven. A quick look down the boardwalk, which ran parallel to the town's whitewashed storefronts, confirmed her assessment that no one was paying attention to her.

And why should they? There was no reason for anyone to sense anything out of the ordinary with her presence in the busy passageway. She looked like any other fashionable young woman out for a day of shopping for ribbons or perhaps a peek at the latest dress fabric that had just arrived from the East. There was no cause to suspect her of carrying confidential information on the war. No grounds for anyone to guess she was a spy for her country.

A man stepped in front of her, his boots clanking on the wooden flooring. The afternoon sun caught the shiny ivory handle of a gun beneath his black overcoat. Tara swallowed hard. The moment of truth had arrived. And this time, she was ready.

Tara's head smacked against the back wall of the stagecoach, jarring her from her slumber. She sucked in a deep breath of air and held herself upright, hoping the other five occupants of the horse-drawn vehicle hadn't caught her snoring. Two trains, and now a stagecoach that had seen better days, had been enough to prove to her the inconveniences of traveling. How was a lady supposed to endure mile after mile of wheels jarring at every rut and fellow passengers snoring like an off-key church choir?

Sighing, she glanced down at the fawn-colored material of her traveling suit and winced at the condition of the garment. When she'd purchased it two weeks ago, it had been one of the most stunning ensembles in the store, guaranteed by the saleswoman to travel with ease. Now the folds of fabric were wrinkled, covered with a layer of dust, and stained with coffee. Any positive first impressions she'd hoped to leave with her new employers were bound to be sadly lacking.

The man beside her, who oddly enough resembled the ruffian in her dream, shifted his weight, causing his elbow to gouge into her side. By the end of her journey to Browning City, she'd be bruised from head to toe, if not from the two men between whom she sat sandwiched, then from the rickety springs and constant bouncing of the stagecoach.

He nodded his apologies, then turned toward the small window overlooking endless miles of rolling hills and farmland. As the hours continued to pass, there had been little change in the scenery. Cornfields seemed to have swallowed up every inch of the fertile soil, interspersed by only an occasional farmhouse or apple orchard.

Iowa.

She knew little about the state except for stories from her aunt Rachel, and more recently, memories from the pages of her aunt's journal. A sudden bout with cholera may have taken her beloved aunt away from this world, but in her short lifetime, Rachel Young had traveled from San Francisco to London and had seen more of this world than Tara might see if she lived to be a hundred.

A second glance at her attire brought a frown to her lips. Her aunt would have arrived at her destination in the height of fashion with barely a crease to show for her venture. Tara, on the other hand, seemed to have more in common with an Iowa farmer's wife than with a cultured lady. It was the latter role that had allowed her aunt to work above suspicion as she carried messages across enemy lines as a spy during the recent War Between the States. No one had anticipated Rachel Young to be anything other than a charming and beautiful socialite.

But expectations often ran sour. Tara stared at the heart-shaped stain on her skirt. Hadn't she always wanted to be like the other women in her family? Courageous and spirited. Even her parents, despite her mother's somewhat eccentric behavior, had worked for the Underground Railroad, helping dozens of slaves find freedom in the North, something President Ulysses S. Grant himself had attested to with a letter of recognition.

But most of the time she wasn't convinced it was even possible for a young woman of nineteen, as herself, to live up to the high standards that had been placed upon her.

"Miss Young?"

Mrs. Meddler's raspy voice brought Tara out of her reverie. A bright smile erupted across the face of the older woman who sat across from her. While Agnes Meddler's thin nose was too long and her brown gingham dress most unfashionable, at least she had been a pleasant source of conversation. The four men sharing the cramped quarters with them, on the other hand, had spent their time either sleeping or passing the bottle, much to Tara's disgust.

"Look outside." Mrs. Meddler jutted out her pointed chin. "We're almost there."

Tara strained her neck to look out the window. The dozing man beside her, his greased hair now plastered with dust, blocked most of the view, but if she stretched high enough she could catch a framed snippet of the terrain. The tops of the cornfields waved in the warm summer wind like a friendly greeting, but she could see no signs of houses or people or even Browning City.

Tara lowered her brow. "Are you sure we're almost there?"

"We're not more than a quarter of an hour away, I believe." The woman leaned forward in her seat and caught Tara's gaze. "No matter what anyone tells you, there's no better state than Iowa. Fruit trees, walnut trees, corn as far as the eye can see, and did you notice the lavender wildflowers? We call them wild bergamot, and they are but a sample of summer's colorful offering. . ."

Tara barely listened as the woman chattered on regarding the vast resources Iowa possessed and its good citizens. She hoped Browning City would boast something other than wildflowers, cornfields, and pleasant companions. While it might not offer all the cultural opportunities or the latest collections of fashionable clothing from Europe, she hoped it would at least offer a shaded city park or perhaps an ice cream parlor to provide a refreshing relief from the heat.

Of course, choosing to leave the comforts of the city had been her decision. Three weeks ago, she accepted the job as a companion for two of her distant elderly relatives, Thaddeus and Ginny Carpenter, in Browning City. But she hadn't taken the job for the income. Her aunt Rachel's journal mentioned a cache of gold lost by the Union army just waiting to be recovered—by her. She knew the Bible well enough to know that it was a sin to store up treasure here on earth, but this was different. This was her one chance to prove she could live up to her family's reputation and bear the Young name proudly.

When Mrs. Meddler hadn't been gossiping about how the sheriff had finally hired a deputy, or that the Dutch blacksmith and his wife recently had been surprised with twins, Tara had spent her time formulating her ideas to find the gold. And she was ready to put her plan into action.

Tara pressed her hand against her coiffed hair, wishing she had a chance to freshen up before alighting from the stage. A quick check with her fingers confirmed her suspicion that the combs had slipped beneath her velvet bonnet the saleslady had described as a regal shade of plum. And her skewed bonnet was no different from her misaligned life. Besides having the striking auburn color that ran in the Young family, she was the misfit who had never done anything that could even be considered courageous. Leaving the city to come to Iowa had been the first step to correct that image.

Fifteen minutes later, the stage came to a stop. Tara grasped the handle of her small beaded carpetbag, forcing herself to relax the tight muscles in her shoulders and still the flutter of butterflies in her stomach. She exchanged pleasantries with her short-term companions and disembarked with Mrs. Meddler while the driver unloaded their trunks.

From the edge of the station platform, she scanned the western horizon where the sun was already making its descent toward the rolling terrain. Mrs. Meddler had informed her that to the north lay the main street of town. Two dozen businesses, at the most, lined the wooden boardwalk, advertising their trades on hanging signs or hand painted on windowpanes. It was a far cry from Boston.

She tried to ignore her disappointment. "So this is Browning City?"

Mrs. Meddler laughed. "What did you expect? Chicago?"

Tara cleared her throat, wondering how the woman had managed to read her thoughts. "Of course not, but I. . . Really, it is beautiful with the sunlight shimmering through the clouds like a painted mural." She turned to her new friend. "And if the citizens are even half as nice as you say they are, then how could I not be happy here?"

Despite her sudden trepidation over the situation, Tara tried to sound convincing. The sky was beautiful, and she was glad to have a friend. Those two things, at least, were true.

"Will you be all right if I leave you now?" Worry shone through Mrs. Meddler's smile. "I do hate leaving you here all alone when you don't know a single soul in town besides me."

Tara gripped the handle of her bag. "Really, Mrs. Meddler. I'll be fine. Mr. Carpenter assured me that he would meet me here at the station, and I'm sure he will be along any minute."

At least, she hoped she was right. Surely her employer would be prompt when it came to time. After days of traveling, she wanted nothing more than a hot bath and a soft mattress on which to sleep. She'd then feel fresh enough tomorrow to put her plan into action.

Mrs. Meddler paused at the edge of the platform. "If by chance you do need to find me, just go into town and stop by the hotel and ask for me by name. It would be a pleasure to extend our visit over a cup of tea. Which, by the way, you must do once you are settled into your new position."

Tara smiled as the woman embraced her. "Thank you for your kindness, Mrs. Meddler. I'll take you up on the offer for tea one day soon."

Forty-five minutes later, Tara checked the time on the gold locket she wore around her neck. Clearly she'd been wrong about two things. Not only was Browning City far from the bustling town she'd hoped for, Mr. Carpenter obviously had no sense of time. Both revelations made her uncomfortable. Except for the stationmaster, who'd disappeared around the back corner of the building a few minutes ago, the place was deserted.

After pulling a lace handkerchief from her bag, she wiped the moisture from her forehead. She hadn't counted on the weather being so humid. From the edge of the platform she looked down Main Street. Painted houses with picket fences skirted the edge of the town. She wondered what it would be like to live in such a quiet place. The Carpenters lived outside of town on a farm, meaning she'd be even more secluded. The very idea of being so isolated made her stomach clench.

"Excuse me, ma'am."

Tara spun around at the sound of a man's slurred voice.

"These here your trunks?"

"Yes, they are." When the driver had unloaded them from the stage and set them down, she'd seen no problem with where they'd been placed. She certainly wasn't in anyone's way. "Why do you ask?"

"No reason, except. . .you're a fine-looking woman." He took a step toward her.

Tara froze. Although he dressed as a cowboy, with denim jeans, chaps, and a bowler hat, there was no doubt in her mind that he was out to round up something other than cattle tonight. Sunlight caught the butt of a gun partially hidden inside his shirt.

Tara looked around, but the stationmaster was nowhere in sight. The knot in her stomach tightened. She measured the steps between them as he came closer. Five steps, maybe six? Why was it that in her dreams she was courageous and ready to face any challenge, but in real life all her instincts demanded she run the other direction?

She had to ponder the question only a fraction of a second. Deciding her trunks weren't worth her life, she bolted across the platform toward the dusty street, running until she felt the ironclad grip of the man's fingers encircle her arm.

⁓

Aaron Jefferson dismounted his horse, trying to brush away the past five hours of dust with a few measured sweeps of his hand. Nothing but a hot bath was going to get rid of all the grime he'd gathered from the long trek across the state.

Scanning the horizon, he worked to stretch out his legs and sore back muscles. Before him lay the same rolling hills he'd seen for the past three hundred miles. Or so it seemed. At least he'd made it to his destination. The sun would be setting in less than an hour, and all he wanted was a hearty meal and a good night's sleep before another full day's work tomorrow. A lame mount hadn't been on his schedule.

Aaron checked the front hoof of the mare and frowned as she flared her nostrils at him. The rambling station on the edge of Browning City was in view.

Surely there'd be someone who could help him find a farrier to care for his horse, even at this hour.

This latest setback, though, seemed to be a simple quandary compared to the mounting pressure of his current government assignment. Patting his front pocket, he felt the folded letter of introduction and wondered if this town, like countless others before it, would prove to be nothing more than another wild goose chase. So far, none of his leads on the missing pile of Union army gold had gotten him any closer to the truth than when he first started. And Browning City was his last stop.

A scream rippled through the early evening air. Tugging on the rim of his Stetson to block the piercing rays of sunlight that hovered on the edge of the horizon, he caught the silhouette of two people struggling on the station's platform. Instinct kicked in, and he ran toward the commotion. Ten yards closer made clear that there was a woman in trouble.

By the time he reached the bottom of the stairs, she'd managed to hit the man over the head with her handbag and break away from his grip. She glanced behind her before running straight toward Aaron. In the next instant, he caught a glimpse of skirts and petticoats flying at him as she stumbled down the platform stairs and into his arms.

He braced himself at the impact and struggled to keep his balance. "Are you all right, ma'am?"

"I think so." She hiccoughed and stared up at him with tear-rimmed eyes. "He grabbed me, and. . ."

The trickle turned into a flow of tears. He kept his arms around her waist to steady her, then glanced up at the man who'd assaulted her, not sure who he should deal with first. Outlaws he could handle. He'd dealt with ruffians, bank robbers, and even managed to hold his own in a gunfight or two. A panic-stricken woman was another bag of beans entirely.

He nodded toward the man who was still reeling from being clobbered in the head. "Do you know this scoundrel?"

Her face paled. "I've never seen him before in my life. I was waiting for someone when he came at me."

The man stumbled toward the top of the stairs, looking disoriented. Aaron took the steps two at a time until he came face-to-face with the woman's attacker. The smell of liquor permeated the man's breath. There was nothing Aaron hated more than a man showing disrespect to a woman, and he wasn't about to let this troublemaker get away with it.

The man tried to shove him away. "This ain't none of your business, mister. And besides, I was just trying to have some fun."

The muscles in Aaron's jaw tensed. "I don't know where you're from, but where I'm from, we don't treat our womenfolk this way."

The man tried to swing a punch at Aaron, but missed. Aaron placed one solid punch on the cowboy's jaw and laid him out flat on the wooden platform.

Aaron shook his hand and tried to ignore the sting across the back of his knuckles as he hurried back down the stairs. "You won't have to worry about him for a while."

She covered her lips with her gloved hands. "You punched him."

"I'm sorry, ma'am, but his intentions were quite obvious."

"Of course, it's just that. . ." She cleared her throat. "Thank you."

Aaron noticed the strands of auburn hair that peeked out of the woman's bonnet as she looked up at him. "Really, it was nothing. Nothing any other respectable man wouldn't do in the same circumstances. . ."

He let his jumbled words trail off, and for a moment, he saw nothing besides the clear depths of her gaze. Blue eyes peered out from behind long lashes, and he found himself staring into two of the most striking blue eyes he'd ever seen. She was pretty when she smiled. Beautiful, in fact. Aaron blinked and shook his head. Just because her skin was as smooth as porcelain and her lips full, and her figure. . . He turned away from her, putting a stop to the ridiculous thoughts. Since when did he fluster over a woman just because she happened to fall for him? Literally.

Aaron tugged on the brim of his Stetson. Something told him that he'd just stumbled on something far more dangerous than a stolen cache of gold.

Chapter 2

Tara began to gather up the contents of her beaded bag, which had spilt across the ground when she'd whacked her assailant in the head. She wasn't sure what had just transpired between her and the handsome stranger standing beside her, but it was all she could do to keep her hands from trembling.

"What are we going to do with him?" She nodded at her attacker, who was slowly coming to.

"I'll handcuff him and take him to the sheriff." He dug into the pouch attached to his saddle and pulled out a pair of metal handcuffs.

Her eyes widened. "You're a lawman?"

"Something like that."

She wasn't surprised. He'd taken control of the situation as though it were an afternoon stroll in the park, while she, on the other hand, had managed to lose all sense of propriety and had panicked. As always. She shivered as she watched him take the stairs up to the station platform. Of course, her shaken nerves had nothing to do with the fact that she'd just gazed into the eyes of one of the most handsome men she'd ever seen. His eyes were brown, but not just any shade of brown. They were a rich toffee color with flecks of gold around the rims.

She shot another glance at him as he secured the prisoner's hands behind him. She barely saw the drunken cowboy. Instead, she noticed the lawman's coal black hair curled slightly around the nape of his neck. Stubble on his face gave him a rugged look, but the gentleness she'd seen in his eyes caused her pulse to quicken. She picked up her handkerchief, now covered with dust, crammed it into her bag, and bit her lip. Her rescuer's solid stature and strong jawline certainly weren't the reasons her heart was pounding. No, it had to be from the drunken man who'd left bruises on her forearms.

"I shouldn't have panicked." She grabbed the last item and shoved it into the bag, speaking her thoughts aloud. "I should have held my head up and demanded he leave me alone."

"Pretty hard to do with a man who's not only twice your size but also drunk. You had every right to be afraid." He dragged his prisoner to his feet. "And hitting him over the head with your bag took a bit of courage if you ask me."

Tara frowned. There was a big difference between courage and reacting out of sheer terror. Clutching her bag with one hand, she tried to straighten her bonnet, which was now completely askew. "I thought I left behind the high crime of the city, but I must have been mistaken."

He led the man down the stairs. "Where are you from? Des Moines?"

"No. Boston, actually."

"Unfortunately there's a bad egg in every lot whether you're in Boston, Philadelphia. . .or Browning City, Iowa." His grin left a dimple on his right cheek. "Let me be the first to properly welcome you, as most Iowans would, and assure you that not all of us are like this ruffian. Some of us are actually quite. . . well. . .quite nice."

"I'm sure you must be right." A shadow crossed the man's face, erasing his pleasant smile, and she wondered if she'd said something to offend him. "So you live here?"

"Originally, though I haven't lived here for a number of years."

"Then I'd say we've both had quite an interesting welcome to Browning City."

He raised his Stetson and scratched his head. "Can I take you somewhere? I don't think it's safe for you to be here alone."

"That has become perfectly clear. But I. . ." Tara paused. Where should she go? She could take up Mrs. Meddler's hospitable offer and stay the night at the hotel. But what would Mr. Carpenter think when he eventually showed up, and she wasn't at the station? If he showed up at all.

She turned at the sound of a squeaky wagon coming toward the station. "Perhaps that's Mr. Carpenter now."

"For your sake, I certainly hope so."

A moment later, the wagon pulled up beside her, and a man who looked to be as old as Moses stepped on the brake. "Miss Young?"

"Yes. Mr. Carpenter?"

"Welcome to Browning City, young lady. It's mighty good to see you." His wrinkled face was swallowed up by a toothless grin as he slapped his hands against his thighs. "And right on time, I might add."

"Right on time?" Tara's eyes widened in surprise.

"As always." Mr. Carpenter pulled a gold watch out of his pocket and flipped it open. "Five o'clock on the dot. Last stage pulls through here at this time three days a week."

"But Mr. Carpenter, it's well past five—"

"A fine piece of work, isn't it?" He stared at the engraved picture on the outside of the watch. "My father bought this beauty in London before immigrating to America in 1793. Gave it to me on my sixteenth birthday, only two weeks before he was killed by a bull in our back pasture."

"Oh my. I. . .I'm sorry." Tara glanced at her toffee-eyed hero, who looked to be as taken aback as she was by the eccentric man in denim overalls and a starched shirt.

"Not to worry," Mr. Carpenter said. "That was over five decades ago, I'd say, and a body has to eventually go on with his life."

"I suppose you're right." Tara quickly calculated the man's age. She knew her grandmother's second cousin had been older, but this man had to be close to seventy. "In any case, it is good to finally meet you."

"Hop into the wagon then. My Ginny has chicken-fried steak and mashed potatoes on the stove and hates it when I'm late for supper."

Tara's mouth watered. Hopefully Mrs. Carpenter's cooking was better than her husband's sense of time. She paused, glancing at the platform. "I do have two trunks."

"I've got 'em."

Mr. Carpenter nodded his thanks to the lawman, who picked up the first one and set it in the wagon bed. "Sampson will take care of them once we get to the farm."

Tara fiddled with one of the beads on her bag, wondering if she dared ask the obvious question. "Who's Sampson?"

"A fine man, he is. Lost his hearing in one ear when a cannon exploded beside him during the war, but other than that, the man's in perfect health. A good thing now that my Ginny and I are getting a bit up in years." He pulled out a handkerchief from his pocket and blew his nose. "Canning pickles tomorrow."

"Sampson is?" Tara shook her head, trying to follow the conversation while her trunks were being loaded.

"Of course not. The missus. She thought you might enjoy such a task. Nothing like a crisp, firm pickle."

Pickles? Tara scrunched up her nose. Did she dare tell her new employer that the only pickled fare she'd ever tasted had come straight from her grocer's shelves? She'd understood her job description to be more refined, like answering correspondence, reading pages from Charlotte Brontë or Henry David Thoreau, and perhaps a bit of simple cooking. Pickles weren't included in her definition of a cultured supper or dinner.

Tara climbed up into the wagon, wondering if she'd been a bit hasty coming to Iowa. Certainly finding the stash of gold would be worth any inconvenience, but beside the fact that Thaddeus Carpenter happened to be her grandmother's cousin, it occurred to her how little she knew about the man and his wife.

"Been some trouble?" Mr. Carpenter pointed a bony finger at the prisoner who lay hunched over on the stairs. "You must be the new deputy."

"He's not the new deputy." She sat down on the hard seat. "But that man tried to attack me, and this other gentleman came to my rescue. He's a lawman."

"Then I appreciate your kindness, sir." Mr. Carpenter handed Tara the reins and slowly started to climb out of the wagon. "I'd like to get down and shake your hand for taking care of this young woman."

Something cracked in the old man's joints. Tara winced as she watched him ease his way toward the side of the wagon.

"Mr. Carpenter. . ." Her voice trailed off as he slowly lifted one leg to the edge of the wagon.

"Sorry, but I'm not near as spry as I was a few years ago. Takes me a bit of time."

"Please, don't worry about getting down." With his Stetson between his hands, the stranger hurried over to the wagon to shake Mr. Carpenter's hand. "The trunks are in the back of the wagon, and I'm headed for the sheriff's office. No doubt this young woman is ready to get home."

"Once again, then, we're in your debt." Mr. Carpenter took the reins once more and winked at Tara. "I'd say it's time to get home, missy."

Hanging on to the edge of the seat with her fingertips for balance, Tara braced herself as the horses started down the dirt road at a steady trot. She turned back to take one last look at the lawman who'd rescued her as they made their way out of town and realized she'd forgotten to ask him his name.

❧

Aaron escorted his prisoner through the doorway of the sheriff's office, thankful the woman's attacker was too drunk to have put up a real fight. He knew he was far too tired to deal with the scoundrel.

"What have we got here?"

At the sheriff's question, Aaron shoved the prisoner into a wooden chair and stepped up to the sheriff's desk. The uniformed lawman sat with an apple in one hand and a newspaper in the other, apparently feeling as if there was little need for him to be patrolling the streets of this cozy community.

"My name's Aaron Jefferson. I've got a letter of introduction."

He handed the bearded man the letter. The sheriff lowered his glasses to the tip of his nose and peered over the top of the octagonal lenses. "Says here you're working for the United States government."

"Yes, sir." Aaron rotated the brim of his Stetson in his hands. "Hadn't meant to meet you under these circumstances, but not only is this man drunker than a passed-out coon, he attacked a woman tonight at the station."

The sheriff gave a cursory glance at the accused before setting down the letter. "Bud Pickett's about as harmless as they come. All talk and no action."

Aaron shook his head. "Not this time. He's drunk, and I'm certain he left marks on the woman's arms."

"Bud, what have you gone and done?"

Bud banged his head against the brick wall behind him. "I ain't done nothing but try and talk to a woman. Nothing against the law about that, is there, Sheriff Morton?"

"It is when you grab her and scare the living daylights out of her," Aaron countered.

"I said, I's just trying to talk to her, but then he comes and handcuffs me like I'm some criminal."

Aaron rocked back on his heels. "There happens to be a big difference between talking and attacking—"

"All right, enough, you two." The sheriff held up his hand. "Normally I wouldn't take kindly to someone cuffing up one of my citizens and dragging him in here, but if you're telling the truth, Mr. Jefferson, I suppose you didn't have a choice. Now, what was the woman's name?"

Aaron stared at the wanted poster hanging behind the sheriff's desk and drew a blank. Had he even asked her? Surely he'd remember something as simple as whether or not he'd asked for her name. He lived his life paying attention to detail and drawing information from people without them knowing what he was doing. He stroked his chin and felt its rough stubble. Obviously, blue eyes and long, dark lashes had not only left him tongue-tied, they had rendered him temporarily senseless as well.

He rested his hands against the desk and leaned forward. "I. . .I don't know what her name was."

"You don't know her name?" The sheriff balanced his chair on its back legs and eyed him warily. "And how do you propose I follow up on this incident when you don't even know the name of the woman involved? Seems like for a lawman you're a bit lacking in your investigative skills."

Aaron's fists tightened at the comment. "She's staying with the Carpenters on a farm outside of town."

The sheriff nodded and set his glasses down on the desk before rubbing his eyes. "Ol' Thaddeus Carpenter and his wife Ginny. Heard they had some relative coming from the big city. Hope she knows something about farmwork and making pickles."

"Pickles?" Aaron leaned forward. "Why's that?"

"Don't get me wrong, we all love the couple, but Thaddeus can be quite a character. I hope she knows what she's getting into."

One didn't have to be a genius to pick up on the fact that Mr. Carpenter might have been a bit senile, but he also couldn't quite picture the man's newly hired help canning pickles and assisting with the farm chores. While her dress might have been a bit weathered from the trip, she certainly hadn't bought it at a small town mercantile. She'd been poised and educated, and he was quite certain that the woman had been raised as anything but an Iowa farm girl.

Aaron cleared his throat. "You're kidding me, right?"

"And why would I do that?"

"I don't know, I just. . ." He shook his head. It wasn't his place to worry about someone he hadn't even properly met. "Never mind. Listen, I've been on the trail all day and need a bite to eat and a good night's sleep. If you don't mind taking care of Mr. Pickett—"

"Not at all. I'll keep him here overnight so he can sleep it off."

Aaron put his hat back on and turned to leave. "Good night, then."

Shoving his hands into his pockets, he left the sheriff's office, disturbed over his own behavior. For a man intent on leaving a professional impression, he'd certainly messed up this time.

No matter what his usual resolve, his brief encounter with the young woman had left him daydreaming of auburn hair and striking blue eyes. In the past, he'd never had trouble ignoring most women, spending his time, instead, putting everything he had into his assignments. And certainly no woman had ever gotten in the way of his career. He had no time for love and courtship. Maybe one day, when he'd finally proved he was just as competent as his father and his father's father, he'd settle down and start a family. Until then, he'd stick to chasing down leads for the United States government. Besides, most of the pretty girls he managed to meet weren't exactly the kind he imagined himself marrying.

Until tonight.

Aaron kicked at a loose rock on the boardwalk, even more determined to put the fair lady out of his mind. He hurried down the street toward the hotel. Ten thousand dollars in gold lay somewhere between here and the Mississippi River, and all a woman would do would be to get him into trouble. No, Mr. Carpenter's newly hired help could stick to making pickles and slopping the hogs for all he cared. He had to get back to work.

Chapter 3

Tara groaned at the insistent knocking on her bedroom door. She rolled to her side, drawing the covers over her head. Light had barely begun to filter through the window, and she had no plans of rising before the sun did. She rolled onto her back and frowned. Something was wrong. The bed was lumpy, the sheets were scratchy. . .

The past few days came rushing to her like a whirlwind. Her long trip to Iowa, Mr. and Mrs. Carpenter, and the cramped room on the second floor that would be hers as long as she stayed with them. She yawned, willing whoever was at her door to go away. She'd spent half the night tossing and turning on the uncomfortable mattress, and the other half dreaming about the handsome lawman rescuing her from the hands of a ruthless villain.

Someone knocked again.

"Miss Young?" Mrs. Carpenter called to her.

Tara sat up, trying to determine if she'd heard an edge of panic in the older woman's voice. What if one of them was sick? Nursing had not been one of the requirements for the job she'd taken.

She pulled the covers up under her chin. "Is something wrong?"

Mrs. Carpenter seemed to take her question as an invitation, because she crept into the room, moving directly to tug back the patterned curtains hanging along a small window. "I do hope you got a good night's sleep, Miss Young, because it's going to be a beautiful day."

Tara frowned and glanced out the window tinged with the faint light of dawn. Besides its pale yellow glow, the only other light came from the candle stub the woman held. Certainly these farm people didn't actually rise before dawn.

Tara worked to stretch a kink in her neck. "What time is it?"

"Five thirty." Light from the candle flickered across the older woman's face, catching her widening smile. A rooster cried out in the distance, but other than that, the morning lay shrouded in a canopy of stillness. "Thaddeus and I always rise by five, but I let you sleep in a bit today, as I know you must be tired from your long journey."

Tired from her long journey? As if that were even in question. Tara had just spent the past four days battling overloaded trains and coaches, sick passengers, and bad food, and now Mrs. Carpenter wanted her to jump out of bed and face the world before she'd had sufficient time to catch her breath.

"I am a bit tired." Pulling the edge of the thin quilt around her, she worked to keep the frustration out of her voice.

In all good conscience, it wasn't Mrs. Carpenter's fault that Tara's expectations of living on a farm had been too optimistic. Such a place could never compare to the modern conveniences of her home in Boston, where they had amenities like piped-in water and an indoor necessary. Perhaps she'd simply always taken for granted her own amply stuffed feather bed and linen sheets along with the many other things farm life obviously lacked.

Tara stifled another yawn. "I'm just not used to waking quite so early."

"Don't you worry about a thing, dear." Mrs. Carpenter tugged on the top of her mobcap, with its puffed crown and ribbon trim—a fashion that should have been disregarded decades ago, in Tara's opinion. "You'll get used to it. Early rising is good for a body. You'll sleep better at night, as well."

Tara bit her tongue at the string of complaints that threatened to erupt, trying instead to focus her mind on what her aunt Rachel had taught her from the Bible. *He that is slow to anger is better than the mighty; and he that ruleth his spirit than he that taketh a city.* Or in her case, better a woman who doesn't complain about a little hard work and lack of sleep than one who loses all sense of propriety while attempting to uncover a lost fortune of gold for the United States government. Pulling her robe around her shoulders, she sent up a short prayer that God would find it within Himself to grant her both an extra measure of patience *and* the cache of gold.

Mrs. Carpenter set the candle on a dresser covered with framed daguerreotypes, bric-a-brac, and a thick layer of dust. "I've got breakfast on the stove. Didn't want you to have to worry about that on your first morning here. Then we've got a busy day ahead of us. We're in the middle of pickling, you know."

Pickles? Mr. Carpenter had been serious?

Five hours, six hundred pickles, and countless pots of boiling water later, Mrs. Carpenter suggested they stop for a meal of ham, beans, biscuits, and a sampling of a previous batch of their homemade pickles. Tara tried to hide her aversion to the cured cucumber, quite certain she had no desire to look at another pickle let alone eat another one as long as she lived.

Mr. Carpenter's wooden chair squeaked beneath him as he sat down at the dinner table, causing Tara to wonder if it would hold up under the man's slight weight. Like the Carpenters, everything in the whitewashed farmhouse was old-fashioned, shabby, and worn. The walls were covered with faded paint; the mahogany furniture, with its carved feathers and eagle medallion ornamentation, most certainly came from another century. Even the cookstove was an outmoded cast-iron beast that was slower than yesterday's stagecoach.

Mr. Carpenter stabbed a piece of ham with his fork. "I was wondering if you could do me a favor this afternoon, Miss Young."

Tara fidgeted in her seat across from him. She had hoped that her duties would be minimal, giving her time to follow up the clues in her aunt's diary, but she was beginning to fear that wasn't going to be the case.

She forced a smile. "Of course. I'd be happy to do anything you need me to."

He helped himself to a second serving of beans while his wife fluttered in and out of the kitchen making sure they had everything they needed. "The post office was closed by the time I went to fetch you last night, and I have a letter that needs to be mailed."

Tara wiped the corners of her mouth with a cloth napkin, wondering if she'd just received the answer to her prayer. "And you'd like me to take it into town?"

Mrs. Carpenter sat down at the table, a second jar of opened pickles in her hand. "It's an easy drive into town, but the wagon is hard on poor Thaddeus's joints."

For the first time all morning, Tara's smile was genuine. "I'd be delighted to help. I'll have to change my clothes and freshen up a bit first—"

"Of course, my dear." She exchanged glances with her husband. "There are a few eligible bachelors in town, and I remember how important it was to make a good impression as a young woman who had yet to step into the joys of matrimony."

Tara scooted her chair back and shook her head. "Oh, but I didn't come here to find a man to court me. I came here to. . ." She stopped herself before the word *gold* slipped off her tongue. "To work for you, of course."

Mrs. Carpenter reached out and patted her hand. "Just don't be thinking that we won't give you any time off. We know how important it is for young people to enjoy themselves."

Mr. Carpenter nudged his wife with his bony elbow. "If I'm not mistaken, our Miss Young has already found herself a possible suitor. Remember I told you last night that a stranger saved her from a drunken scoundrel at the station?"

Tara gasped. "Why, I don't even know who that man was—"

"You did mention to me that he was handsome, Thaddeus." Mrs. Carpenter cocked her head and smiled. "Ahh, new love. There's nothing sweeter."

Tara shook her head. "I really don't think—"

"Don't mind my dear wife, Miss Young. She's a bit of a romantic, I must say, and she always manages to find a way to play matchmaker, don't you, dear? After fifty years of marriage, I suppose she simply wishes the same happiness we've found on others."

Tara closed her mouth. The last thing she wanted in her life right now was her own private matchmaker, but it was obvious she wasn't going to get a word in edgewise. She watched as Mrs. Carpenter leaned toward her husband and whispered something in his ear. He caught her hand and laughed.

"My wife just reminded me of our own courting days." Mr. Carpenter's gaze never left his wife's face. "Ah, the good Lord was gracious to bring us together. He may not have ever blessed us with children, but He's allowed us to live out our days on this earth together."

Tara crushed the napkin between her fingers, as something stirred within her. The love between the Carpenters was obvious, and she couldn't help but find herself growing attached to this odd yet endearing couple. Her own parents loved her, but they spent most of their time running the family business and staying involved in various patriotic activities.

With the last bite of her meal gone, Tara washed the dishes and changed her clothes before heading toward the barn. Making her way gingerly across the hay-strewn shelter, she once again questioned her sanity for coming to Iowa. At home, she would have stepped out the front door of her house and straight into an awaiting carriage. But Browning City was a far cry from Boston.

At least she'd been taught how to drive a wagon back in Boston and wasn't completely helpless. Even riding had been done with little effort, though, as the stable boys would get the horses ready for her. Holding her gloved fingers against her nose, she followed the cheerful whistles of Sampson, who was cleaning out one of the stalls with a wide smile on his ebony face.

"Mr. Sampson?"

The man continued his tune, seemingly oblivious to the fact that she was calling him. She'd almost forgotten. The farmhand was partially deaf. She regarded the dusty floor and raised the hem of her skirt an extra inch for good measure before taking another step closer.

Tara eyed the pale mare in front of her and raised her voice. "Mr. Sampson?"

The horse's head jerked toward her and its ears laid flat. Tara stumbled backward and slammed into a wooden post.

"Miss Young. . ." Sampson held up his hand to stop her before approaching the animal with quiet, soothing words.

He stroked the horse's shoulder and turned to Tara. "Horses scare easy, miss. Never come near 'em from behind. You're liable to startle them."

Tara stared down at her handbag. "I'm sorry. I—"

"And always make sure the horse sees ya before comin' near. They ain't aggressive, but they does frighten easy." He looked at her and smiled. "Don't worry, miss. After a few weeks of livin' here, it'll be easy for ya."

Tara grasped the edge of the post behind her, feeling foolish. There was no hiding the fact that she was a city girl. Even from an uneducated farmhand.

She cleared her throat and raised her chin. "Mr. Carpenter wanted me to go into town for him. I have driven a wagon before."

Sampson's broad smile showed off his white teeth. "Give me five minutes, miss."

"Thank you, Sampson."

The broad-shouldered man set down his shovel and went back to whistling his tune. Strange how a man could appear so happy when his job was nothing more than mucking stalls and working in the field.

True to his word, Sampson had the wagon hitched and ready in a few short minutes. Perched on the narrow bench, Tara was overcome with a feeling of freedom for the first time since leaving Boston. The pungent smell of vinegar that had permeated the Carpenters' kitchen as they poured the boiling brine over the dozens of green cucumbers was now replaced with the faint scent of wildflowers that dotted the landscape as she headed toward town.

Tara smiled. Her aunt's journal was tucked safely in her bag, and she was finally ready to put the first part of her plan into action. Armed with the name of one of her aunt's informants, she was determined to track down the whereabouts of the missing gold.

She reached up to ensure that her summer garden hat, with its spray of flowers, was perched securely atop her head. Feeling the need for an extra measure of confidence, she'd chosen to wear one of her favorite dresses, a gray poplin walking dress trimmed with two flounces and paired with a matching short jacket edged with lilac trim. Making a good impression on the sheriff was the first step in her plan to extract the necessary information from the lawman. Honesty, beauty, and a bit of womanly charm had always proven to be a highly persuasive combination.

Twenty minutes later, she stood in front of the sheriff's office. Taking a deep breath, she stepped inside. The sheriff sat at his desk, engrossed in a stack of papers.

Tara cleared her throat and stepped up to the small room that wasn't even half the size of her sitting area back home. "I'm sorry to disturb you, Sheriff."

The middle-aged man looked up, rubbing his graying beard with his fingertips. "Sheriff Morton. Good afternoon."

The lawman stood, knocking over his chair in the process. He stumbled to pick it up, then scattered the pile of papers with his elbow. "Excuse me, please, I. . .I'm not usually quite this clumsy." A dark tint of red covered the man's cheeks as he hurried to pick the papers up.

Once he had collected the items and placed them back on his desk, she reached out and shook his hand. "My name is Tara Young, and I can't begin to say how pleased I am to meet you, Sheriff Morton."

"Really?" Fiddling with his pencil, the man sat back down and peered at her over the top of his octagonal lenses. "Please have a seat. The pleasure is definitely all mine."

She sent him her most flattering smile. "Thank you."

"You're from out of town?"

"I'm from back east, actually, Boston. I just arrived in town last night."

"Then you must be the Carpenters' relative who's come to help them out."

Tara's brows rose. "I see that word spreads quickly in a small town like Browning City."

"That is one of the potential drawbacks of living in such a quiet community, but to most of us, the advantages far outweigh the disadvantages." The sheriff laughed. "What can I do for you?"

Tara clutched her bag against her chest. "I know you must be terribly busy with your work protecting the good citizens of this town—"

"Please." He held up a hand of protest. "Don't worry. There's always time to assist a beautiful young woman such as yourself."

"You're too kind." Tara leaned forward and lowered her voice. "Since you are a man of the law, I hope I can be assured of your complete confidentiality in what I'm going to ask you."

The sheriff removed his glasses and raised his thick brows. "But of course. I wouldn't be able to uphold the law if I was a man who couldn't keep confidences, now would I?"

Tara nodded. "I'm happy to hear you say that, because what I need to discuss with you is rather. . .delicate to say the least."

He set his pencil down. "I'm listening."

Confident she now had the man's full attention, Tara continued. "My aunt, who sadly passed away suddenly last year, worked as a spy for the North during the recent War Between the States, and in reading through her journal, I came across some entries that, well, I simply couldn't ignore."

"Entries about what?"

"A cache of gold stolen from the Union army that is rumored to be buried somewhere in the area."

Sheriff Morton leaned back in his chair and let out a deep belly laugh. "I hate to disappoint you, Miss Young, but I've heard more rumors about that missing gold than there are jackrabbits in our cornfields. Not too many years back a woman arrived in town who believed her father had a role in the heist, but no pot of gold ever turned up. Even the government claims that it exists, but I've been sheriff here for nearly thirty years, and I can promise you that if you go after that gold around here, you're only going to be chasing ghosts. There's no gold. Least not in my territory."

Tara ignored the sting of disappointment, but she wasn't finished yet. "I've got a name."

The sheriff cocked his head and eyed her warily. "A name? What do you mean?"

"My aunt mentions a man named Schlosser in connection to the gold."

"Schlosser. Richart Schlosser." He rubbed his beard. "If I remember correctly, Mr. Schlosser moved away three or four years ago. Lived on a farm a few miles out of town. All I can suggest to you is that you talk to the land agent and see if he has an exact record of when the family lived here. But if you ask me, you're better off spending your time caring for the Carpenters rather than chasing some alleged pot of gold."

Tara frowned at the man's last comment. Beauty and charm might give her an advantage at times, but it seemed they did little to ensure one was taken seriously. She stood and stepped behind the chair. It was time to end their conversation.

"I do appreciate greatly your taking the time to talk with me about this, Sheriff."

"I'm at your service any time, Miss Young." He stood and moved to the edge of his desk where he tapped his fingers against the hardwood. "There is one other thing, I almost forgot. I have the man who attacked you last night locked up in the jail. He's slept off his stupor, and I've given him a thorough lecture. Unless you feel compelled to press charges. . ."

"No, please." The last thing she wanted to do was make an incident out of the situation. "I think I'd rather put the entire episode behind me."

Tara nodded her thanks, then stepped out onto the boardwalk. While she was embarrassed over her reaction toward the drunken man and would rather forget the discomfiting moment—except perhaps the encounter with the handsome stranger—she was even more disappointed about the sheriff's reaction to the gold. Of course, she wasn't certain what she had been expecting. At least the visit wasn't completely in vain. She'd seen the land agent's office on the outskirts of town, and would take the time to inquire after the whereabouts of Mr. Schlosser once she delivered Mr. Carpenter's letter.

Tara crossed the street toward the post office, careful to avoid the patches of black mud that filled the street. She secured her hat with one hand as a gust of wind tried to blow it off her head. The last thing she needed was her summer hat to end up with a thick coating of Iowa mud.

At the edge of the boardwalk, an envelope fluttered to the ground in front of her. She caught it, then searched to find its owner. Her heart thumped as she looked up into the toffee-brown eyes of the handsome stranger who had rescued her the night before.

Aaron gazed into the familiar face of the woman who'd filled his dreams the night before, and he somehow managed to stammer an awkward, "good morning."

Her bubbly laugh sounded as light as the tinkling of a bell. "It's already afternoon."

"Of course." Aaron frowned, feeling suddenly foolish over his obvious display of nerves.

She held up one of his letters that had blown out of his hands. "Is this yours?"

He took the envelope, allowing the tips of their fingers to touch in the exchange. "Thank you. I was on my way to post the letters and there was a gust of wind. . ."

For a moment, an awkward pause hovered between them. Of course, she knew that. Aaron swallowed hard, wishing he didn't feel quite so happy to see her. With his information coming straight from Washington, his arrival in Browning City had been planned out in detail. He was to arrive, spend the morning mapping out the town and its occupants, visit with the sheriff, then interview those he felt might have information regarding the events that led up to the disappearance of the gold five years ago. His itinerary didn't include falling for the first beautiful woman he encountered. Not that he'd actually fallen for her. But it was true that he hadn't stopped thinking about her.

He tapped the envelopes against the palm of his hand. "I hadn't expected to see you again."

She lifted the edge of her skirt and stepped onto the boardwalk. "Actually, since Browning City is no metropolitan center, I would think that the odds of us running into each other were actually quite high."

"True." He took off his Stetson and followed her toward the post office. "I wanted to apologize for not introducing myself properly last night. With all the commotion, it seems as if I completely forgot my manners."

She stopped, turning to face him as a slight blush crept up her cheeks. "It's only natural that the formalities would get pressed aside in such a situation."

The explosion of a gunshot ripped through the afternoon air as a bullet ricocheted off the painted sign above their heads. Aaron grabbed her arm and shoved her through the doorway of the post office out of the line of fire.

Chapter 4

"Are you all right?"

Tara nodded as she stared into the face of the man who had managed to prevent her from harm for a second time in twenty-four hours. She crouched inside, beneath the window of the post office, willing the shots to subside. Someone screamed. The window shattered above them, sending thick shards of glass across the wooden floor.

" 'Fear thou not; for I am with thee. Fear thou not; for I am with thee. . .' " She repeated the scripture over and over, mumbling the words aloud.

Aaron crouched next to her, leaning on his palms. "Isaiah chapter forty-one?"

She nodded at his question, surprised he knew the verse. "So you believe in God?"

"Especially at moments like this." He pulled his gun out of his holster and checked the barrel. "I've faced death a time or two in my life and know that I don't want to leave this world without the hope of spending eternity with Him."

A gun fired again, exploding through the afternoon air like a blast of dynamite. Tara struggled to breathe. While she, too, believed as a Christian that the good Lord would one day take her home to live with Him forever, she hadn't expected that moment to be now. There were still a few things she wanted to take care of on this side of eternity first.

She lowered her head and tried to take a handful of slow, deep breaths. Aunt Rachel would have strutted out the front door of the post office and given the gunman a severe tongue-lashing for his disrupting the afternoon of the good citizens of this town. Her father would have found a way to disarm the man before marching him to the sheriff's office. She, on the other hand, was ready to hang up her fiddle and run. If the odds weren't so overwhelmingly high that she would get shot in the process, she had half a mind to do just that.

The lawman beside her lifted her chin with his thumb and caught her anxious gaze. "It's going to be all right, you know."

His calm voice washed over her like a soothing balm. She stared into his toffee eyes and wished she could transport this moment to another place in time. He gazed back at her, and she wanted to believe that what he said was true. His lips curled into a smile, and her stomach flipped. She turned away, fiddling with one of the beads on her bag. How could she entertain thoughts of romance when any minute a bullet could ricochet off the brick wall, signaling the end to one or both of their lives?

Still crouched, she wrapped her arms around herself and rocked back on the heels of her lace-up boots. "How do you know everything's going to be all right?"

"Trust me."

The silence that followed was as loud as the screams and gunfire that had permeated the afternoon seconds before. Tara held her breath. No one moved. It was as if time hovered between them, not wanting to go forward and uncover the final dreadful moment of the standoff.

The lawman signaled her with his hand. "Come with me."

He hurried her behind the counter of the post office, where three other women and two men sat huddled against the wall. One of the women cried silently, while another one simply stared straight ahead, her face void of expression.

He reached out and grasped Tara's hand. "You'll be all right here. I've got to stop him."

"No!" Tara's eyes widened. She tugged at his sleeve as he moved to leave. "He'll kill you."

"I'll be fine. I'm a lawman, remember?" He squeezed her hand. "And besides, I'm hanging on to those words from Isaiah."

Tara clenched her jaw together as he crept around the counter. God might be with them, but that certainly didn't always stop bad things from happening. And if he got shot. . .

She tried to steady her rapid breathing, but instead her pulse raced even quicker. The whole situation was ridiculous. Here she was caught in the cross fire of some madman, terrified something was going to happen to a complete stranger. She didn't even know his name. Pressing her back against the wall, she squeezed her eyes closed and tried to ignore the whispers of the others huddling beside her. How could it be that instead of a quiet town among the rolling hills, fruit trees, and cornfields of Iowa, she seemed to have landed in America's treacherous frontier?

She chewed on the edge of her lip. The whole reason she'd left her parents' home and moved here was to prove to herself that she could handle a challenge. . .that she wasn't the spoiled rich girl some of her acquaintances had accused her of being. . .that she wasn't the terrified individual who was right now sitting in a volatile situation about to faint from fear.

Someone shouted.

Her fingernails bit into her palms as she squeezed her hands shut. She had to know what was happening. He had saved her life. She wouldn't let him die in some futile attempt to hold on to his honor.

Keeping her head below the top of the wooden counter, she gathered up the thick folds of her dress material in one hand and scooted across the floor. One of the older women reached out and tugged on the waist of her skirt.

"What in the world do you think you are doing, miss?"

Tara glanced back at the woman. "I've got to know what's happening. He's—"

"This is not a time for curiosity." A scowl crossed the older woman's face. "All you can do right now is pray that man of yours doesn't do something foolish and get himself killed."

Her man? Tara frowned. That certainly was far from the truth, but it didn't matter at the moment. She knew exactly how high his chances were for getting killed, and she didn't need to be reminded of the danger into which he'd put himself.

Ignoring the woman's unmistakable gestures to stay put, Tara continued to ease her way across the floor until she could peek around the edge of the counter. His Stetson lay discarded on the floor. Her foot crunched on a piece of glass. With her skirts gathered in one hand and her other hand pressed against the wall to keep her balance, she quickly picked up the hat and placed it on her own bonnet before continuing carefully toward the broken window.

A splinter of glass pierced through the delicate material of her glove, leaving a crimson stain on the white surface. Ignoring the sting, she pulled out the offending fragment, determined to tread more carefully across the floor. She'd deal with the blemished article of clothing later.

Once she reached the corner, she pressed her back against the brick wall and strained her neck to make out what was going on. From her new vantage point, she could see out onto the street and to the other side of the boardwalk that had been abandoned by dozens of early afternoon shoppers.

A man dressed in black pointed his gun to the sky and took another shot. She scanned her limited view through the framed window for a sign of the lawman. There was movement to her left. Finally, she caught sight of him. He was crouching behind a display of vegetables out in front of the mercantile, waiting his next move. The gunman let out a string of profanities. Tara covered her ears, then froze as the lawman stealthily moved across the boardwalk toward the street. A plank of wood groaned beneath his weight. The gunman whirled around and aimed his weapon.

Tara screamed, then everything went black.

⊰≈⊱

Aaron flinched at the deafening scream that pierced the humid afternoon air. The barrel of the gun that had been aimed at him a moment ago jerked to the left as the man turned to find the source of the scream. Being convinced the gunman was as crazy as a loon and wouldn't hear his approach had been Aaron's first mistake. But the gunman's last move had just sealed his fate. All Aaron had needed was a two-second distraction to be able to restrain the man from injuring any innocent bystander. The scream had given him just that.

In four quick strides, Aaron reached the man. He secured the gun first, throwing it out of arm's reach, then tackled the felon to the ground before the man had the opportunity to react to what had hit him. The gunman twisted around and threw a punch, skimming his knuckles across Aaron's jaw. But Aaron had a good six inches on the man as well as extra muscle, and in a matter of seconds he had the man subdued.

With his knee against the man's back, Aaron pushed away the blue-eyed vision that appeared in front of him, wondering if it had been her ruse that had saved his life. Another second later, if the gunman had any sense of accuracy, the bullet would have hit its mark and gone straight through his heart.

"Why didn't you just shoot him?"

Aaron turned and looked up at the rider behind him. The sheriff dismounted from his stallion and folded his arms across his chest.

Aaron rubbed his jaw, thankful the man hadn't broken it. "I'm not the killing kind. Try to avoid it at all costs."

"Even at the cost of your own life?" The lawman stepped forward and rolled the gunman over onto his back. "Either way, it looks as if I'm in your debt once again, Mr. Jefferson."

"I just happened to be at the right place at the right time."

"If I'm not mistaken, I've got a wanted poster for this rogue." The man tried to sit up, but the sheriff pushed him back down with the heel of his boot. "I appreciate your quick thinking. Any chance you might be looking for a job as deputy? My new one just quit on me."

Aaron shook his head. "Thanks kindly for the offer, but I believe I've got enough on my plate at the moment."

"Working for the government, I suppose you would."

Aaron hauled the gunman to his feet. "But I would be happy to escort this man to the jail for you."

The front of Aaron's plaid shirt and denim jeans were covered with dust, and he'd lost his Stetson somewhere in the process. Glancing at the wooden sign hanging above the jail across the street, he had to wonder what kind of sheriff ran such an unruly town.

If he hadn't known better, he might have thought he'd missed his mark and showed up in the lawless town of Abilene. Not that gunfights were uncommon. In decades past, learned men might have been excused for taking part in duels, but he drew the line at ruffians shooting innocent citizens in the streets.

He turned back to the post office and caught a flash of gray material through the broken window. He wondered if it was her. He still smelled the soft fragrance of her perfume, remembered every detail of her face, and could, even now, feel the softness of her skin when he'd briefly touched her jawline. And he didn't even know her name.

Part of him longed to go after her. To properly introduce himself and discover more about her. He had a dozen questions he wanted to ask. . . But now was not the time to go chasing after some beautiful woman who'd somehow managed to capture a corner of his heart. She'd be fine, and he'd be gone from this lawless town soon. There was no reason to concern himself over her anymore.

He picked up the prisoner's gun, then shoved it under his belt. With the prisoner firmly in his grasp, he made his way toward the jail. Once inside, he waited for the sheriff to secure the offender in one of the cells while he sat down and caught his breath.

The sheriff returned with two cups of hot coffee in his hands and passed Aaron one. "Thought you might need some. Your face is going to be sore. That felon gave you quite a punch."

Aaron rubbed his jaw and nodded. "I need to go and clean up, but before I go there is one thing you can help me with, Sheriff."

"Of course." The sheriff ripped the wanted poster off the wall and dropped it onto his desk. "The citizens of this town owe you our deepest gratitude, not to mention a hundred dollars in reward money for the capture of this Sean Roberts. What is it that I can do for you?"

Aaron leaned forward and decided to get right to the point. "Verified reports have been recovered that point to the fact that the gold stolen from the Union army is located in this area. I was sent to find it."

"Whoa, slow down." The sheriff shook his head as he slid into his chair. "You're not the first person to come charging into town with some grandiose idea that they are going to find the government's gold in these here parts and walk away with some hefty reward money."

"This isn't about the reward money. The government wants back what was stolen from them."

The sheriff tapped his pencil against the desk. "You probably won't believe this, but you're the second person today to walk in and tell me that they have information on where to find the gold."

Aaron sat up straight in his chair. "Who?"

"Another dreamer who thinks they can find fame and fortune by digging up some rumored pot of gold at the end of the rainbow." The sheriff's belly jiggled as he laughed. "I sent 'em to the land agent's office on another wild goose chase."

"What's his name?"

The sheriff shook his head. "Oh no. I shouldn't have even given you that much information. I thought it was bad enough to have one busybody poking around my town. Can't you see? This rumor has been circulating for years, and there's never been a sliver of proof that the gold even exists."

Aaron slapped his hands against the desk. "But I told you, I have documented sources who claim—"

"Who's making the claims, and what does that really mean? That someone's grandmother's cousin's uncle thought he saw a chest of gold being transported across his farm back during the war? Things like this don't just vanish. If there really was a trunk of the government's gold lying around, you can be sure that it's been spent by now." The man took off his glasses and held them up. "Now that I think of it, there's a man in Des Moines who recently built himself quite a house. It's rumored to have ten bedrooms, seven fireplaces, and an entire wing for the servants. Of course, I ain't never seen it, so I can't say for sure. Maybe you should rush over there and see if he knows anything about the gold."

Ten minutes later, Aaron unlocked the door to his hotel room and slipped inside the cramped space. He didn't particularly like the sheriff, but he was glad for the tidbit of information he'd managed to procure from him. He might not have gotten a name, but one thing was certain. After cleaning up, he was going to pay a visit to the land agent, and find out just exactly who was after his gold.

Chapter 5

Tara's head throbbed as she hurried down the boardwalk, leaving behind the embarrassing scene where she'd managed not only to slice her finger open, ruining one of her brand-new gloves, but also to faint dead away like some swooning female. When she'd come to, she'd managed to catch a glimpse of the sheriff and her lawman escorting the felon toward the jail.

Her lawman?

Her stomach tensed. The very thought was ridiculous. While she was relieved that the man had not been shot and killed, he wasn't hers—nor did she want him. Not that she could have him or had any intentions of going after him, because, undoubtedly, he felt the same way. He hadn't even come looking for her to make sure she was all right. No, the man had much better things to do than rescue her every time she managed to find herself in yet another embarrassing quandary.

Tara picked up her pace, determined to put an end to her rambling thoughts of a man she didn't even know. She was here for one reason and one reason only. To follow her aunt's leads and track down the government's gold. Period. No handsome strangers, no thoughts of love and romance. Too much was at stake.

Passing the barbershop, she noted that, once again, the street was filled with shoppers and businessmen carrying out their affairs as if nothing out of the ordinary had happened on this particular sunny July day. There were, in fact, no signs of the life-and-death situation that had, only moments before, given rise to panic in a number of the townspeople—herself included.

She passed a group of young girls, all wearing similar calico-print dresses and broad straw hats to block the summer sun. They eyed her curiously as they strolled by. Tara frowned and smoothed the front of her dress. Certainly, she looked a bit rumpled after scooting along the floor of the post office, where shards of glass had scattered across the dusty flooring. Ignoring the gaping stares, she pulled her bag closer and held her head high.

On the other hand, perhaps their curiosity had more to do with the fact that her dress, with its duchesse lace at the sleeves and silk edging, offered a peek at the very latest style from back east. Something one certainly wouldn't find in this part of the country.

A mother and child stepped out of the dry goods store in front of her. The child gave her a broad grin and waved before pointing at Tara and giggling. Suddenly, Tara wasn't so sure that the stares and gawking had anything to do with her tastes in fashion. The mother quickly whisked the young girl past Tara and toward the mercantile.

Tara frowned and put a hand to her head, wondering what could be so bad that. . . A hot blush scorched her face as she quickly pulled off the Stetson that still perched on her head.

How she'd managed to make such an obvious social blunder she had no idea. Tara glanced around, but everyone else seemed more concerned with his or her business at hand than the fact that she'd actually donned a man's hat in town. And a black Stetson at that. She felt her own hat to make certain it was still in place, then let out a deep breath as she continued on at a brisk pace for the land office. After taking care of her business there, she'd have to stop by the hotel and leave the offending article with Mrs. Meddler, assuming that was where the man was staying.

A bell jingled in the doorway of the land agent's office as Tara stepped inside.

"Can I help you, miss?" A tall, thin man with spectacles and curly tufts of blond hair poking out above his ears appeared from behind a tall stack of ledgers.

She held the black Stetson behind her back and smiled. "I'm interested in a particular piece of land, and wondered if you could possibly help me."

"Name's Horst Lehrer. At your service, ma'am." The man held out a bony hand and shook hers with more force than she expected.

"I'm Tara Young."

"If you're looking to buy a piece of property, Miss Young, then you've come to the right place."

Tara shook her head. "Actually, I'm looking for a piece of land that once belonged to a Mr. Richart Schlosser. From what I understand, he doesn't live in the area anymore, but I need to know which farm he owned. Possibly during the time of the War Between the States?"

"Mr. Schlosser. I recognize that name." The man rested his forefinger against his chin. "Give me just one moment. My wife says I have a memory that rivals that of anyone in the state when it comes to names. Never forget a name, no siree. Never forget a name."

The man began digging through the piles of ledgers while Tara stood patiently. Hopefully, there was some truth to the man's claims at never forgetting a name, but it was going to take more than a good memory to sort through the jumble of papers in this office. The odds of actually finding information on Mr. Schlosser seemed, well. . .she had her doubts such a miracle was even possible.

"Schlosser. . .S. . .Richart. . ." He picked up another ledger. "Let's see. Schlosser. It's a German name. Did you know that?"

"Interesting." Tara forced a smile. "I didn't know that."

"I like names." He glanced up at her. "And you're right, they are interesting. Take, for instance, my name. My last name is Lehrer, and it's German, as well. Means my father's grandfather, or perhaps his grandfather's father, was a teacher. That's where surnames originally come from, you know. Occupations, where one stays, or perhaps some unique physical characteristic. And my first name, Horst, means a thick grove. Always found that fascinating."

"I suppose, but—"

"My wife and I are expecting our first child in three months' time." He moved on to another stack of ledgers and flipped through the unorganized pile. "Having a tough time, though, trying to agree on the child's name. I want to pay close attention to the meaning behind the name, while my wife only cares about how the name sounds. You agree, don't you? That the meaning behind a name is just as important as the actual name."

Tara sneezed at the particles of dust that filled the room. "I. . .I suppose, though I can't say that I ever thought about it."

He pointed his hand at her. "Now, Tara. That's a lovely name. Do you know what it means—"

"I'm sorry, but I don't." She held up her gloved hand. "What about Mr. Schlosser?"

"Yes. . .yes. . .just one more place to look. . .Yes! Here it is. Mr. Richart Schlosser." He pulled a dusty file from the bottom of the stack and plopped it on the table in front of her.

A cloud of dust enveloped the stack of paper.

Tara sneezed again. "What does it say?"

"It looks to me as if Mr. Schlosser moved away after the war in sixty-six. Sold it to a man by the name of. . ." Mr. Lehrer turned his head to the right and squinted. "I can't quite read the writing."

Tara tapped her foot. "Who took notes on the transaction?"

"I did, but unfortunately my handwriting isn't nearly as clear as my memory."

Tara fiddled with the rim of the Stetson behind her back and prayed that he would come up with some sort of lead for her to follow up on.

"Yes, yes, now it's clear." Mr. Lehrer beamed. "It looks as if Mr. James Martin now owns that piece of land. Isn't far out, either. I'd say no more than five miles out of town to the west. You shouldn't have any trouble finding it. Now Jim isn't always the most hospitable man, but hopefully he'll know something about the whereabouts of Mr. Schlosser."

"So you have no idea what happened to the man?"

The land agent shook his head. "I remember the transaction between the two men. Met right here in my office to sign the deed papers. Mr. Schlosser seemed to be in a hurry to get out of town."

"What else can you remember? Anything that might have seemed insignificant at the time might prove important to finding him."

He shrugged a shoulder. "I'm sorry, but that was four years ago, and I've had a lot of people go through this office."

"But your memory for names. . .details."

"Names." Mr. Lehrer shot her a weak grin. "Mr. Martin might know something. They appeared to be friends, though I can't say that for sure. I know that Mr. Schlosser planned to include the majority of his furniture in the sale of the property."

"Is that a common thing to do?"

"Happens from time to time. All depends on the circumstances, I'd say."

Tara gripped the back of a wooden chair with her hand. "So that's all you remember?"

"I'm afraid so, but if you're interested in a nice piece of land—"

"Thank you very much, Mr. Lehrer. You've been a big help."

Tara strolled into the bright afternoon sunlight, glad to be out of the dusty office, and hurried to the hotel. She hoped to find Mrs. Meddler before returning to the Carpenters' farm. While the woman's attire had been rather plain and, frankly, out of date, the lobby of the hotel exhibited a bit more taste with its warm terra-cotta walls and walnut furniture. Not that it could begin to compare with Boston's Parker House or any of the other luxurious East Coast hotels, but for someone needing a place to stay overnight, it would surely be a welcome sight.

Much to Tara's relief, Mrs. Meddler sat behind the front desk of the empty lobby reading a dime novel with its recognizable orange cover.

"Why, Miss Young." The older woman greeted her with a broad smile. "I was hoping you'd stop by for a cup of tea. I've been wanting to know how you were faring in your new place."

"It's good to see you, as well, Mrs. Meddler." Tara set the Stetson on the counter, debating what she should do. "And while I greatly appreciate the invitation, I ought to get back to the Carpenters. They sent me to town with a letter to mail after lunch, and I'm afraid I've taken advantage of their time. What I really need—"

"Nonsense. There's always time for tea." Mrs. Meddler snapped the book shut and hopped down from the wooden stool. "Don't tell my husband I'm reading this. I keep my stack of dime novels hidden away, because he's always telling me what a waste of time and money they are."

"Don't worry. My lips are sealed." Tara echoed the jolly woman's laugh, realizing just how nice it was to see a familiar face even if she barely knew the woman.

Mrs. Meddler shoved her book beneath the counter and waved her hand. "Come. You must stay for tea. We have so much to talk about, such as the shoot-out this afternoon. Were you in town at the time?"

"Yes." Hat in hand, Tara followed her into the large, airy kitchen where Mrs. Meddler began filling the kettle with water.

The older woman placed her hands against her heart. "Such a fright that gave me. I hid behind the front desk until my husband assured me it was once again safe to come out. What is this world coming to is my question."

"I have to agree." Tara leaned against a wooden cupboard and shuddered. "I was in the post office and found the whole experience quite terrifying."

Mrs. Meddler set the kettle on the stove and motioned for Tara to sit at a small table in the corner of the room. "Then trust me when I say that a cup of tea will help soothe both our nerves. Most appropriate, if you ask me. It will be ready in just a minute."

Tara placed the hat on a table covered with a white lace cloth, then made herself comfortable in the padded chair. Mrs. Meddler was right. She needed some time to recover from the ordeal. She took in a deep breath and made herself relax. Her stomach growled as her senses filled with the fragrant scent of meat and spices mingling with rising yeast bread.

"Perhaps I need to stay until dinner." Tara laughed. "Whatever you're preparing smells wonderful."

Mrs. Meddler pulled a sugar jar from the cupboard, as well as a small container of cream. "It's my own mother's recipe for gumbo. She was French and lived in New Orleans for most of her life. Believe it or not, it tastes even better than it smells."

Tara's mouth watered, and she couldn't help but wonder if she'd be offered yet another jar of pickles tonight.

Mrs. Meddler set two floral-patterned china cups on a tray. "Isn't Mrs. Carpenter a decent cook?"

Tara cocked her head. "Yes, though I have a feeling that I will have eaten my share of homemade pickles before I leave."

"Every social, picnic, and holiday isn't complete without a jar of Mrs. Carpenter's infamous pickles." Mrs. Meddler placed her hands on her hips and chuckled. "But don't you worry. Most of us have found various ways to avoid actually eating them."

"Then I suppose I'm going to have to get creative on this one."

Mrs. Meddler picked up the black Stetson. "Whose hat is this, by the way?

You seem far too stylish to don one of these with your outfit."

Tara noticed the older woman's wink and laughed. "That's why I stopped by. You see, I'm not sure whose it is. A man left it behind at the post office during the shootout, and all I know about him is that he just arrived in town last night. He's tall with dark hair—"

"I know exactly who you are referring to." Mrs. Meddler spun the hat with a wide grin on her face. "Tall, solidly built with eyes the color of—"

"Toffee?" Tara felt a warm blush cover her cheeks. Something that was beginning to occur far too frequently.

"Exactly." Mrs. Meddler placed the hat back down and hurried to take the whistling kettle off the stove. "If I wasn't married, I'd consider snatching him up myself. Such a gentleman he is, too."

Tara giggled. "So you'll give him the hat, then. I don't even know his name."

"At a slight disadvantage then, aren't you?" Mrs. Meddler folded her hands across her chest and shook her head. "His name is Mr. Jefferson. Aaron Jefferson."

"Aaron Jefferson," Tara repeated.

"Now, have some tea. And who knows, perhaps Mr. Jefferson will come downstairs while you're here, and I can make the proper introductions."

❧

Aaron opened his eyes with a start. Sunlight shone through the small window of his hotel room, casting a golden glow across the worn bedspread. He'd have to hurry if he was going to make it to the land agent's office before it closed.

His joints complained as he sat up. His own father had died when he was thirty-five, a seemingly ancient age for a boy of six. Now thirty-five didn't seem near as old as he'd once thought, but even though he still felt young at heart, that didn't mean he was as agile as he used to be. Slamming a ruffian into the mud and getting swiped across the jaw wasn't something he wanted to do for a living anymore. A gunshot in the shoulder two years ago had cured him of that. This latest assignment was supposed to be straightforward detective work. Not a stint in capturing criminals in the streets.

Aaron searched for his Stetson, then remembered he'd lost it at some point. Maybe *she* had found it and had left it with the postmaster in case he stopped by looking for it. Feelings of guilt rushed over him. He should have gone back and made sure she was all right. The sheriff hadn't really needed his help escorting the prisoner to the jail, and their conversation could have waited.

You're a coward when it comes to women, Aaron Jefferson.

Shaking his head, he locked his room and headed downstairs. How could he have spent half his life fighting crime, taking down criminals, and risking everything to make this country a better place to live, yet become tongue-tied when standing next to a beautiful woman?

When standing next to *her*.

There was something about this particular blue-eyed woman with the auburn hair that left him feeling like an inadequate greenhorn instead of seasoned lawman. He couldn't help it. Her soft voice. . .the sincerity in her eyes. . .the way she smiled at him. . .had him completely captivated. Part of him hoped he ran into her again before he left town, while the other part of him preferred to finish his work as quickly as he could and avoid any such encounter.

He headed outside, pausing only to nod his greetings at the young woman working the front desk.

"Mr. Jefferson?"

Aaron stopped near the entrance to the hotel. "Yes?"

"Is this yours?"

Aaron retraced his steps across the carpet, this time stopping at the desk where he picked up his Stetson. "Where did you find it?"

"Mrs. Meddler had wanted to give it to you herself, but she went to help with the delivery of Mrs. Acker's new baby. Anyway, before she left she said that a woman brought it by who thought you might be staying here."

Aaron fiddled with the brim. The faint scent of roses mingled with his own shaving soap. *She* had brought it by.

He had to know who she was. "Do you know the name of the woman?"

"No. Mrs. Meddler just said to be sure to give you the hat and tell you that the woman's name was. . ." The young woman's smile faded. "Perhaps she did tell me the lady's name, but. . .I can't remember."

"Was she young or old—"

"All I know for sure is that Mrs. Meddler said that a woman brought it by. I never saw her." She shrugged and turned back to her magazine. "Sorry."

"Thanks, anyway." Aaron set the hat on his head and started outside.

He was disappointed that he'd been so close to finding out who she was, just to come up against another brick wall. He'd have to speak to Mrs. Meddler once she returned. He shook his head. Whoever this woman was, she'd become a distraction. And he couldn't afford that. The government was counting on him to find the money. Which brought him back to his real concern.

Aaron crossed the street and headed toward the land agent's office. Truth was, rumors were always plentiful, especially when a large amount of money was involved. He had no doubt that there would always be others looking for the lost gold, but this person seemed to have information that was keeping him a step ahead. How could this person potentially know more than he did?

Unless the person had somehow uncovered specific information leading to the location of the missing gold.

Chapter 6

Aaron glanced down the street, looking for the woman who'd delivered his hat. It had to have been her. Who else would have known where to find him? It appeared that she'd done a bit of detective work herself—but not a difficult assumption considering he was new to town and would most likely be staying at the hotel.

He tipped his hat at an older woman coming out of the mercantile and smiled in passing. Truth was, if he wanted to, he could do the same kind of investigation. In a small town like Browning City, it would be easy to find out where the Carpenters lived and, in turn, learn where she was staying.

Aaron pressed his hand against his front pocket and felt the crinkling letter of introduction signed by the chief himself. In his chosen career, when lives often hung in the balance, duty had to come before pleasure. In turn, thoughts of love and a family kept getting put off until after the next assignment came along.

Or until I prove I can live up to my own family's expectations for me.

Aaron pushed aside the thought and quickened his steps. This wasn't about his family. He simply didn't need the distraction from his work, especially when he had competition. The government would prefer not to pay the hefty reward money, but that could only be done if he found the gold first. And they were counting on him to do just that.

He stepped into the land agent's office and held back a sneeze. A layer of dust covered a desk piled high with papers and ledger books. The only two chairs in the small office were also covered with stacks of papers. He couldn't imagine how anyone could work in such an environment. Even the windows appeared as if they hadn't been cleaned for months, with their accumulation of grime from outside.

"Good afternoon. I'm Mr. Lehrer." A thin man appeared from the back of the room, held out his hand, and offered a broad smile. "How can I be of service to you today?"

"Name's Aaron Jefferson and I need some information." Aaron decided to get right to the point. "The sheriff said he sent someone to see you as they were tracking down either a person or perhaps the owner of a piece of land?"

The man shoved his wire spectacles up the bridge of his nose. "Today certainly is turning out to be quite a busy day for information."

"So someone did stop by?"

"About an hour or so ago. I answered a few questions, and we had a nice chat."

Aaron worked to conceal his interest. Finding this man might not be the ticket to finding the gold, but he wasn't going to ignore any leads.

"I need to know exactly what this person wanted."

Mr. Lehrer sat down at his desk and took out a steel nib pen as he shook his head. "I am sorry, but all transactions are private. You have to understand—"

"Not when it comes to the law." Andrew withdrew his badge from the front pocket of his vest and held it where Mr. Lehrer could see it.

Mr. Lehrer dropped his pen. "Who exactly are you?"

"I work for the United States government." Aaron shoved the badge back into his pocket. "I need to contact the person who was in here asking questions. He has some information I need."

"She—"

"She?" Aaron dipped his head. "I was under the impression that it was a man."

"Then you obviously haven't seen this woman. She was beautiful. Wide eyes, smooth skin, hair pinned up neatly, smartly dressed. . ."

An image of *her* filled his mind at the description. Aaron closed his eyes and tried unsuccessfully to push away the vision of the lovely stranger. The whole thing was ridiculous. How could he have become so enamored of someone he'd never properly met? He knew as much about Mr. Lehrer as he did about the woman. He had to forget her. Time to focus on this lead, not on a woman he very well might never see again.

"What else about her description?" Aaron leaned against the side of the desk. "What color was her hair?"

The land agent held up his pen and winced. "That, I'm afraid, I can't tell you. I'm color-blind."

"You're color-blind?" Aaron let out a sigh. All he needed were a few details, and he couldn't even get those. "Certainly you can tell me what she was looking for."

"Of course." Mr. Lehrer nodded. "A man by the name of Richart Schlosser."

Aaron worked to keep his frustration in check. In an office this unorganized, he wasn't sure he could trust the man's memory. "Are you sure that was the name?"

"I'm quite sure. I might be color-blind, but I never forget a name."

"And what did you tell her?"

Mr. Lehrer tapped his pen against the desk. "The man moved away about four years ago. James Martin now owns the farm."

Aaron stood up straight and tapped his Stetson against the palm of his hand. There was only one more thing he needed to know before he left. "Last question. What was the woman's name?"

"Her name is Tara Young. And if you're looking to find her, she was pretty persistent. I wouldn't be surprised if she heads out to Mr. Martin's the first chance she gets."

Tara finished reading aloud the last few verses from Psalms, chapter nineteen, then paused to take a peek at Mrs. Carpenter. The older woman sat sound asleep in her slat-back rocker. Tara yawned and wondered if she could sneak a few minutes of sleep, as well. Getting up at five thirty for the second day in a row, followed by boiling a new batch of brine for the pickles, had her longing for the quiet mornings back home where no one ever wakened her until the decent hour of eight or nine. And pickles were something they purchased from the shelves of the local grocer, never sweated over in the kitchen.

Her gaze rested once again on the weathered Bible with its thin pages. Her father had often read to her from the Psalms and other books of the Bible, but she didn't remember this particular one and its pronouncement that the Word of God was far more precious than gold. An interesting comparison, considering her own quest. While the thought was convicting, and she believed it to be true, her desire to track down the missing government gold had only intensified. Surely God would overlook her search for earthly treasures if He knew that her motives were in the right place.

How she was going to find the gold, though, was proving to be more difficult than she'd first imagined. Even now, she debated whether or not she should borrow the wagon this morning and pay a call on Mr. Martin. Not only did she worry about shirking her duties with the Carpenters, but obviously, a single woman such as herself paying a visit to a man she didn't know would never be considered appropriate. She wondered what Aunt Rachel would have done. There had to be a way to achieve her objective without tarnishing her reputation.

She pulled her copy of *Harper's Bazaar* out from under the edge of the serpentine-back sofa, determined to work on a plan as she flipped through the pages. While she'd read the magazine from cover to cover at least a dozen times on the trip here, she never tired of looking at the latest fashions. Skirts of pink coral trimmed with matching flounces and pink roses for the hair. Fawn-colored silk parasol, and a gorgeous lilac silk walking suit with a violet tunic.

Tara turned another page, stopping at a drawing of a beautiful parlor set made of black walnut and a contrasting trim. She read through the description of the grand room with its bold Chinese red walls. Included in the drawing was an Italian inlaid table with matching mirror, heavy curtains, and even a sidewall arrangement of shelves where daguerreotypes and prints were elegantly displayed.

She eyed the Carpenters' old-fashioned sitting room with its worn fabrics and out-of-date furnishings and wondered if Mrs. Carpenter would be opposed to a few minor alterations of the room. A bit of paint, stylish fabric, and rearranging of the furniture would do wonders for the room's mood. And it would certainly beat the pickling process.

Tara looked up at the sound of Mr. Carpenter's booted footsteps on the wooden floor. He stopped at the doorway and nodded in the direction of his wife. "She often falls asleep this time of morning if she didn't rest well at night, but she couldn't wait for you to read to her. Like mine, her eyes aren't strong anymore, and she has been missing her daily devotionals from the Word of God."

"I'm glad she enjoyed it."

Tara smiled, surprised at the feeling of contentment that washed over her. Though not quite as laborious as making pickles, reading aloud wasn't her favorite pastime. Knowing Mrs. Carpenter enjoyed hearing her read from the Bible shed a different light on things. While Tara had come to enjoy her years of education, it hadn't given her the chance to feel as though she were making a difference in anyone's life. And she liked the feeling.

"Why don't you go take a rest yourself?" Mr. Carpenter picked up a newspaper from his rocker and folded it under his arm before leaving the room. "You must be tired. With the pickles soaking and lunch simmering on the stove, I don't suppose there is anything else for you to do right now."

"I'm fine, really. I thought I would just read a bit."

He paused in the doorway. "It's a shame for you to have to stay cooped up inside. It's such a lovely day, but after your experience in town yesterday, me and the missus are a bit concerned about your safety. Granted, such a barrage of gunfire isn't a common occurrence, but all the same. . ."

Tara flicked at the edges of the magazine as his voice trailed off. If she could convince Mr. Carpenter to accompany her, she wouldn't have to worry about her reputation or her safety.

She cleared her throat. "While I understand your apprehension, I would love to go for a ride. I've always enjoyed exploring, and I wouldn't go far."

Mr. Carpenter pressed his lips together. "I just hate the idea of you out alone, but. . ."

Tara held her breath. A quick trip to town was one thing, barring another episode with a crazed gunman. Exploring the surrounding isolated farmland was different, and she knew it.

He tapped the newspaper against the wall. "I wouldn't mind at all going with you, though we'd have to take the wagon. I'm not much for riding horseback these days."

Tara glanced at his sleeping wife, remembering her words of caution, and wondered if she'd spoken out of turn. "I thought the wagon and your joints—"

"Don't you worry about me. The missus does enough of that. And besides, I need to get out of the house every now and then. Keeps me young."

Tara laughed. "Then I'll fetch my shawl and parasol and meet you outside."

Fifteen minutes later, they made their way up a grassy ridge. From this vantage point on the buckboard, Tara could see the surrounding landscape with its groves of oak trees and wildflowers nestled between cornfields that stretched as far as the eye could see. Sampson waved at them from the edge of one of the fields, his ever-present smile in place.

She waved back, then twirled her silk parasol between her fingers. "I hadn't expected Iowa to be so beautiful."

Mr. Carpenter nodded. "I agree with you now, but when Ginny and I first arrived, I wasn't sure I'd stay. Life was harder back then."

"Tell me about it."

Mr. Carpenter pulled back on the reins and slowed the horses to an easy trot. "The surroundings were quite different from what we were used to back east. Timber was limited, so we had to find alternative materials for building our homes and for fuel and fencing. We used things like Osage orange hedges for fencing, and our first house was made of sod. And there were other concerns. Not only did we have to build our own homes and our furniture, we also had to watch for signs of fires that could wipe out everything we'd built. It was lonely, and sickness was prevalent."

A frown covered the older man's normally jovial expression. Tara pushed a strand of her hair out of her face, struck by the hard life this couple had faced. "What made you decide to stay?"

"Besides being too stubborn to admit defeat?" Mr. Carpenter shook his head and laughed. "Things eventually began to change. The soil is rich and fertile, and as the population grew, we found ourselves connected to people again."

Tara couldn't help but notice the irony in the situation. "While you were longing for contact with people, we often complain that the city is too full of people."

"That, my dear, is one of the main reasons I left." Mr. Carpenter stopped at the top of another rise, showing her the beauty of the prairie that extended for miles. "Any place in particular you'd like to go?"

"Yes, actually." Tara paused, wondering how she should broach the subject. She didn't want Mr. Carpenter to find out about her search for the gold, but she needed his help to find Mr. Martin's farm. "I've been reading my aunt's journal, and she mentions a man by the name of Richart Schlosser. Did you know him?"

"Schlosser." Mr. Carpenter shook his head. "Can't say that I do, though that doesn't mean much. The railroad has brought scores of immigrants who have settled into the area."

"I found out in town that Mr. Schlosser moved away about four years ago, and James Martin bought his farm."

"Now there's a name I recognize. Lost his wife last year and hasn't ever been quite the same."

Tara leaned forward. "Do you know where he lives?"

Mr. Carpenter's eyes twinkled. "It's not far from here, if you'd like to stop by, though the man isn't extremely friendly."

"It's worth a try, if you don't mind."

With Mr. Carpenter's entertaining spin on stories from his past, it didn't take long before they reached the farmhouse that, at one time, must have been lovely. Wind, rain, and neglect, though, seemed to have worn away most of the character of the saltbox house. She wasn't even sure anyone still lived there.

Mr. Carpenter stopped the wagon in front of the house and called out, but his voice was quickly carried off by the wind.

Tara strained to look through the small glass panes in the front of the house, wondering if she should get down from the wagon and knock on the front door. "It looks empty to me."

The golden ball of the sun rose toward its zenith behind the farmhouse, leaving behind a trail of white light that pierced through the cloudy sky. The silhouette of a man on horseback appeared from the east and made its way toward the wagon.

She sat up straight and tried to block the sun with her hand so she could see the rider. "Is that him?"

"Could be, but I'm not sure. As I recall, Mr. Martin's rather small in stature."

Tall figure, broad shoulders, black Stetson. . . Tara's eyes widened as the figure came into view. Surely it wasn't Mr. Jefferson himself. She felt a blush cover her cheeks. She'd spent far too much time daydreaming about a man she knew nothing about, and now her heart raced at the mere thought of him.

The man on horseback bridged the gap between them, and a few moments later, she knew it was him.

"That's him," she whispered, grasping the seat to steady herself.

Mr. Carpenter gave her a sideways glance. "Who?"

"The man who rescued me at the station."

Aaron felt a surge of unwelcome anticipation run through him as he approached the wagon near the farmhouse. It couldn't be her. . .but it was.

He dismounted from his horse and tipped his hat. "I see we meet again."

Clear blue eyes stared back at him, and he wondered if she felt the same unexplained emotions he was experiencing. Today she wore a yellow dress and a straw hat that looked striking on her, but he couldn't remove his gaze from her face. Fair skin, rosy cheeks with perhaps a hint of a blush, long dark lashes. . .

She pressed her gloved fingers to her lips before responding. "We. . .Mr. Carpenter and I were just out for a morning ride."

Remembering his manners, Aaron turned and nodded at the older gentleman. "It's nice to see you again, sir. This young lady and I have met twice in rather unusual circumstances yet have never been properly introduced."

"And I am afraid that I have the advantage." She closed her parasol and set it in her lap, while he waited for her response with great interest. "Mrs. Meddler from the hotel told me your name when I left your hat."

She smiled at him, and he feared his heart might burst from his chest.

He cleared his throat. "Which, by the way, was very kind of you. I'm glad to see, as well, that you are all right after that frightening incident in town yesterday. I apologize for not returning to find you, but I needed to help the sheriff—"

"Please don't worry about me." She shook her head. "I was a bit shaken after the episode, naturally, but I have recovered completely from the incident."

"I am very glad to hear that."

Mr. Carpenter coughed beside her. "No wonder the two of you have never introduced yourselves. How could you when you spend your entire time exchanging such sugary pleasantries?"

Aaron caught the surprised look on her face before turning to Mr. Carpenter. A look that no doubt mirrored his own. Surely his attraction toward the woman wasn't that apparent.

Mr. Carpenter gave them both a toothless grin. "Mr. Jefferson, I'd like to introduce you to my cousin's granddaughter, Miss Tara Young."

Chapter 7

Aaron automatically reached out to shake her hand while his mind fought to make the connection. "I'm very happy to make your acquaintance, Miss Young."

Tara Young?

Aaron felt the muscles in his jaw tense. Surely he had misunderstood the elderly gentleman.

He caught her gaze. "It is Miss Young, isn't it?"

She pulled back her hand. "Yes. Why do you ask?"

Aaron frowned. This couldn't be Tara Young, fortune hunter and gold digger. This woman was too beautiful and cultured to have traveled to Iowa simply to track down the government's lost gold. It just didn't make any sense.

"Is something the matter?" Her eyes darkened, seemingly as unsure at his reaction as he was by the news he'd just been handed.

"Of course not, it's just that—"

"You'll come back to the farm for lunch now, won't you, lad?" Mr. Carpenter saved Aaron from having to come up with a response. "It's the least we can do for your having saved Miss Young's life."

"Twice." A smile lit up her face, causing his pulse to hammer.

Aaron forced a smile in return. He had no desire to deceive her, but the only way he was going to find out her source of information was to learn what he could about her. There was no time like the present to follow this unexpected lead, and he'd just been given the perfect opportunity. It also didn't hurt that the woman of his current inquiry happened to be beautiful and engaging. A far more interesting task than the majority of his assignments.

"Lunch would be nice. Thank you." Aaron nodded and followed beside the wagon at a slow pace.

He also wouldn't mind a home-cooked meal. Not that the meals at the hotel under the watchful eye of Mrs. Meddler hadn't been acceptable, but nothing surpassed a real home-cooked meal.

Aaron rested his hands on the leather pommel and let the rhythmic motion of the saddle take away some of the tension that had formed in his shoulder muscles. "Do you know the owner of this farmhouse? I'm assuming you had planned to pay a visit on the proprietor."

She flashed him a coy smile. "I admit I thought the same about you. Strange we would happen to visit the same farmhouse on the same day. It's too bad no one was home."

"It is quite a coincidence, isn't it?" Aaron adjusted the brim of his Stetson, wondering how to explain why he was here if asked directly.

Miss Young swatted at an insect buzzing around her head. "I was intending to speak to the owner. A Mr. James Martin. Do you know him?"

"No, but I was hoping to meet him. Why did you need to speak to him?"

"It's a bit of an involved story, since I've never actually met the man." She leaned back against the buckboard and let the parasol block the sun from her face. "My aunt knew the previous owner of this land, and I was hoping Mr. Martin might know where he lived now. I'd like to find the man."

"A close friend of your aunt's, I assume then?"

"They were. . .acquaintances."

He watched out of the corner of his eye as she pressed her lips together. Obviously the woman had some secrets to hide. He turned his attention to the horizon as they headed west toward the Carpenter farm. She didn't trust him. Yet. And rightly so, because he was a complete stranger. The fact he carried a badge might help, but he needed something more. Something that would help shed light into his character of being one who was both sympathetic and trustworthy. Not simply a tough, rugged lawman.

"And what about you, Mr. Jefferson?" She eyed him skeptically. "Why did you need to see Mr. Martin this morning?"

"I'm considering buying a farm in the area." The words tumbled out before Aaron had considered the consequences.

Her eyes widened. "This land's for sale?"

"I'm not sure about this farm, to be honest." Aaron stumbled over his words, wishing he could erase his previous statement.

The muscles in his back tensed. Something happened to him when he was around this woman, and now he'd gone from tongue-tied to sharing private matters better left unsaid.

He offered her a weak smile. "I know there are several farms for sale in the area, and I've found in life that it never hurts to ask."

"You're certainly right, young man." Mr. Carpenter flicked the reins to pick up the horse's pace and nodded. "Martin's property would need a lot of work, but you have a good eye for land. Fertile soil with a number of streams going through it. I've often thought it a pity that this piece of land has been neglected for the past few years."

Miss Young cocked her head. "Still, I must say that I'm surprised because I had assumed that you were from back east and only here temporarily. Somehow as a lawman you don't seem the type to settle down and run a farm."

"It's true that I've lived most of my life in the saddle, traveling from place to place, but. . ."

Aaron dug the heels of his boots into the sides of the mare. He was managing to dig himself a hole, and if he wasn't careful, he'd end up burying himself alive. He hadn't planned to talk about his plans for the future. These were dreams he hadn't intended to share with anyone.

He cleared his throat. "My grandparents moved to Iowa in the forties, and I lived about fifty miles from here until I was twelve."

While he rarely allowed himself to dwell on the idea, he had always dreamed of buying his own piece of land along the Mississippi River, or perhaps a large farm in the middle of the state. He would raise cattle and hogs and watch the corn grow.

He drew in a deep breath and savored the familiar smells of the land. The sweet aroma of wild roses mingled with the earthy scent of the fertile ground. Somehow she'd managed to remind him how much he loved the land. Along with a John Deere plow, he'd form straight furrows in the dirt that would then nourish the seeds of a crop.

Not that he didn't enjoy what he did. He'd spent his entire life working hard to get ahead and live up to his family name. His grandparents and his parents had passed away years ago, but that didn't change the fact that being a lawman was in his blood, and there was nothing he found more satisfying than bringing an outlaw to justice, and, in turn, making the country a safer place.

For seven months now, he'd stayed in hotels night after night while chasing down leads for the government on a cache of gold that many believed didn't even exist. From Washington DC through Virginia and a corner of Pennsylvania, he'd followed every piece of information his superiors had passed down to him. But these days, he was tired of traveling. He was tired of being alone.

He glanced at Miss Young with her frilly dress and silk parasol. She belonged in an elegant parlor back east, not riding on a decrepit wagon across the endless Iowa prairie. Which brought back to mind the question as to why she was here. It was time to find a way to move the focus of the conversation from himself to her. Not only did he need to avoid starting any rumors about why he was here, he needed to find out everything she knew.

He cleared his throat. "So what really brought you to Iowa, Miss Young?"

❧

Tara swatted at a mosquito and paused before answering the question. From the resolute expression on Mr. Jefferson's face, she was certain there was something more to his inquiry than simply a way to fill the minutes until they arrived at the Carpenter farm. A few moments ago, she would have assumed that he had posed his question in order to get to know her better. She'd seen the look of interest in his eyes the first time they met at the station, then again outside the post office when his hand had brushed across hers, causing shivers to run up her spine. And she was certain he'd felt it, as well.

Something, though, had changed. She'd felt it the moment Mr. Carpenter introduced her and said her name. Though he tried to hide it, the surprise on Mr. Jefferson's face had been clear. But why? Perhaps she was only fearful about someone finding out why she was here. Rumors regarding the gold had circulated for years, but she was certain the information she held could easily start a stampede across the state if she wasn't careful.

But he couldn't know why she was really here. Her conversation with the sheriff had been made in the strictest of confidences. While she wasn't so naive to believe that he might not share the information she'd given him with another lawman, what reason did the sheriff have to even mention the gold? He'd told her himself that searching for the gold was a ridiculous waste of time, and she had no reason to doubt he believed that.

She'd also been careful when speaking with the land agent, cautioning him never to mention the gold. Even Mr. Carpenter had no reason to suspect why she had come to Iowa. So what was it?

She looked down at her attire and frowned. The yellow crepe dress with its overskirt of the same fabric wasn't exactly an appropriate choice for a ride through the cornfields. Wide ribbon sashes and lace edgings were more suited for an afternoon visit to one of her parents' neighbors. She fiddled with the silk trim of her sleeve. She couldn't help it. The very thought of wearing a simple calico garment made her skin crawl.

Tara stared at the soft fabric until her eyes crossed. Perhaps Mr. Jefferson, like her own parents, didn't believe she belonged on a farm, living in the middle of Iowa. And perhaps they were right. But wasn't that exactly what she had set out to prove? If she failed to go ahead with her quest, she'd never know if she was capable of more than speaking a few witty phrases of conversation at a party and looking pretty.

"Miss Young? Are you all right?"

Tara looked up at Mr. Jefferson, surprised that the farm was already in view. She nodded. "Of course. I'm sorry. I suppose your question made me think about home."

"Do you miss Boston?"

"Not as much as I thought I would." She didn't want her answer to sound shallow. "Even with its conveniences, the city is dirty, noisy, and overcrowded. Still, I miss my friends, the architecture, artwork, and even the church we attend every Sunday."

"To ease a bit of your concern. Pastor Reeves's preaching can rival what any big city has to offer," Mr. Carpenter said reassuringly. "He's a man of God who preaches straight from the Word."

"I'm sure you're right. I just. . ."

Tara's voice trailed. Mr. Jefferson looked at her as they approached the farmhouse, and her pulse started to race. She turned away, determined to find a way to discover the gold while at the same time keeping her heart intact.

Chapter 8

Aaron crunched down on another pickle and smiled. It had been a long time since he'd sat at a family table and shared a meal, albeit one with such an interesting family, to say the least. Mr. Carpenter, with his denim overalls and toothless grin, was proving to have an unlimited reservoir of comical tales from his adventurous past. He sat at the end of the table and kept them entertained with story after story while Mrs. Carpenter, when she wasn't bustling around and making sure everyone had what they needed, sat beside him, listening as though she were hearing the narratives for the first time.

Aaron's gaze turned to Miss Young, something he'd found himself doing far too often during the meal. She sat forward slightly, her eyes wide with interest, and her food seemingly forgotten as she listened to the story Mr. Carpenter told of a cattle stampede that almost killed him when he worked as a cowhand in his younger days. While she looked somewhat out of place with her fancy dress and impeccable manners against the worn furnishings of the dining room, one thing was notable. She didn't seem to possess the arrogant attitudes he'd observed in most young women of means. Such a realization was refreshing.

Not that her manners and propriety mattered to him, because they didn't. Not in the least. And just because she happened to be both beautiful and modest was no cause for him to get distracted from the real reason he was here. His duty was to find out what information Miss Young had regarding the gold. Starting with, perhaps, the obvious question as to why a woman of noticeable means had traveled across several states to work as the caregiver for two elderly relatives. Were the Carpenters a key to finding the gold? Or did Miss Young's information lay solely with her aunt's acquaintance, Mr. Schlosser?

No matter how many times he tried to convince himself that he was only sitting at the Carpenters' table and eating stew and sour pickles because he needed to learn why she was here, he found himself lost in her smile and the soft lilt of her laugh. Aaron frowned. Perhaps it was too bad that she wasn't homely. It would certainly have made the job easier for him and given him fewer distractions to face.

Seemingly unaware of the effect she had on him, Miss Young pushed back an unruly curl that had fallen across her cheek. "So what made you leave the life of a cowboy, Mr. Carpenter?"

161

The older man squeezed his wife's hand. "I met this beauty and decided there was more to life than earning a living in a saddle."

Aaron took a bite of stew. Looking at the older couple, he realized that all their years of marriage hadn't faded the love between them. He couldn't help but wonder if he'd ever be so blessed to find a woman willing to share a life with him through whatever the future held.

He frowned again. Since when did he allow thoughts of love and marriage to run so rampant through his thoughts? He'd settle down one day and buy that farm, facts he'd impetuously shared with Miss Young, but there were other things that had to be done first. He gripped the edges of his chair and, for the moment, couldn't remember any of his excuses. . .couldn't remember why he shouldn't let his heart lead the way for once in his life.

He finished off his pickle, determined to change the subject. "When did you settle in Iowa, Mr. Carpenter?"

"Eighteen thirty-six. Seems like yesterday in so many ways."

"My husband is right. I still remember those first few years when all we could do was try to survive." Mrs. Carpenter passed Aaron the bowl of pickles and laughed. "Didn't even have a good cucumber patch back then. Which reminds me. You mustn't let me forget to send you home with a jar or two of my pickles, young man."

Aaron smiled and took another one. If making a good impression meant eating yet another sour pickle, he was happy to do it. There was a lull in the conversation as they finished the thick stew and homemade bread. It seemed the perfect opportunity to ask about the gold without anyone perceiving his real intentions. Who knew better what had happened in this territory the past few decades than Mr. Carpenter? And if the man had information. . . Aaron decided to take a chance.

He buttered a slice of bread. "You've lived in this state for a good many years, Mr. Carpenter. I've heard rumors that the government lost a cache of gold in these parts. Have you ever heard such a claim?"

While Aaron addressed Mr. Carpenter, he watched Miss Young out of the corner of his eye. He saw the flicker of something in her expression as her brow lowered. Surprise? Worry?

Mr. Carpenter waved his hand in the air, shaking his head. "Son, there've been rumors of gold in this country for as long as I can remember, from lost gold to gold mines. Look at Illinois and Georgia back in the twenties, California in the forties, Colorado, Nevada. . .why not Iowa? If you ask me, the rumors are usually nothing more than a bunch of nonsense."

"I suppose you do have a point." Aaron set his spoon down and wondered if the man could be right.

It wasn't a new thought. The government had supplied him with confirmation that the gold still existed. He'd interviewed dozens of sources from Washington DC to the banks of the Mississippi, and many of them had led him a step further, but to what? To the truth that the gold was nothing more than a rumor? His superiors denied such a charge, but after months of searching, there were times when even he was beginning to doubt. No gold meant that everything he'd invested in this assignment had been for nothing. And that, in his mind, was unacceptable.

"If one looks closely at history, there are always very few men who actually make it rich in the gold runs." Mr. Carpenter held up his spoon. "The Good Book tells us that the Lord and His decrees are far more precious than gold. It's a shame a few more people don't believe that. The world might be a better place if we did."

Aaron nodded his head. "Another good point, sir."

But the Good Book also said, "Whatsoever ye do, do it heartily, as to the Lord, and not unto men." Which was exactly what he was trying to do. And if his quest ended up proving nothing one way or the other? Did his hard work make up for his failure in God's eyes?

Mr. Carpenter wiped his face with his napkin, then scooted back the chair. "Miss Young has yet to have seen much of the beauty of this area, including the stream that runs through the edge of our property. Perhaps the two of you would enjoy a bit of exercise. It's lovely this time of year."

Aaron shook off the dismal questions that troubled him, and instead, looked at Miss Young and tried to read her expression. There was nothing he'd rather do at the moment than spend the afternoon with her, and he'd just been given the perfect opportunity.

He pushed his plate away. "Miss Young, I believe I could spare an hour or so if you'd enjoy a short ride."

He was certain he saw a tint of blush color her cheeks before she responded. "That would be nice, Mr. Jefferson, but I need to first clear the table and wash the dishes."

"Nonsense." Mrs. Carpenter stood and took a plate out of Miss Young's hands. "You already worked half the morning on my pickles. I'd say you deserve a bit of time for yourself."

Miss Young rose to protest. "But—"

"Just enjoy yourselves. I'll let you prepare dinner once you return."

⌘

Tara rode beside Mr. Jefferson on one of Mr. Carpenter's horses as they made their way toward the creek east of the property. From the rise in the terrain, she could see the far bank of the stream that flowed through the edge of the

Carpenters' property. Yellow rays of afternoon sun hit the clear water, leaving behind tiny diamonds that danced in the ripples. Beyond the stream, instead of cornfields, lay acres of tall prairie grass, yet to be plowed.

Mr. Carpenter was right. It was a perfect day for riding, and the landscape, as she'd already come to discover, was beautiful. Only she could hardly concentrate on the view with Mr. Jefferson riding beside her. They'd discussed a number of intriguing political topics from President Grant's recent defeat against the Senate in his attempt to annex the Dominican Republic to the appointment of the first black to congress.

She stole a peek at the handsome lawman. Their discussions had soon moved to a spiritual thread, but as much as she enjoyed their conversation, she realized she still didn't know what had brought him to Browning City. Vivid images of adventure and romance filled her mind, like something out of one of Mrs. Meddler's dime novels. Maybe he was on the trail of a notorious desperado, or perhaps an entire gang of outlaws. Surely the fact that he'd saved her twice ranked fairly insignificant against the dashing heroics he'd accomplished in his career.

Mr. Jefferson turned and noticed her gaze. She dipped her head, embarrassed he'd caught her staring at him. The knowledge that she was blushing again infuriated her. She'd spent her entire life learning how to be a proper lady who strove to be dignified and elegant at all times. Why, then, did one look at Mr. Jefferson melt every sense of decorum she could muster and leave her feeling vulnerable and defenseless?

He cleared his throat. "May I be so bold as to ask you a question?"

"I suppose." She adjusted the fabric of her russet-colored riding costume against the coat of her dappled mare.

Mr. Jefferson's eyes had turned a pale shade of caramel in the sunlight. "I'm curious as to why a beautiful and cultured young woman, such as yourself, chose to come to Iowa. From your dress and manners, I'm assuming you don't need the income."

Tara frowned.

"I'm sorry, if my question is at all offensive—"

"No, it's just that. . ." That what?

She played with the brim of her wide straw hat, wanting to believe that his question was not a barb intended to prick her conscience. But what if he saw her as a shallow individual looking for a bit of adventure at the expense of an elderly couple's generosity? Or even worse, being a man of the law, he might wonder if she had lost her financial position and was only here to prey on the financial assets of her remaining family.

Before arriving in Iowa, she'd never stopped to consider the fact that her attire would be out of place amongst the rolling hills of Iowa. But what was she to do? Toss her stylish wardrobe in exchange for a closet filled with hand-sewn clothes made from gingham fabric from the mercantile? She'd always taken pride in her appearance, but here it seemed to be a constant disadvantage rather than an asset.

Tara pulled back on the reins to slow the mare as the bank of the creek appeared before them. She wondered what she should say. She certainly couldn't mention the gold, but not stating her real reason for coming might prove just as suspicious.

"While I've only been here a short while, I believe the arrangements with my distant relatives is working out well. They needed someone to help around the house, read to them from the Bible and such, and I wanted to see a bit more of this part of the country." She didn't give him time to respond before posing her own question. "What about you? Besides the fact that you are a lawman, I know little about why you are here."

She watched as he pressed his lips together and turned his head slightly. It seemed that she wasn't the only one with a secret. Of course, being a lawman, he had the right, she supposed, to keep his mission undisclosed, but that didn't squelch her sense of curiosity.

He clicked his tongue and pulled the horse to a stop before dismounting. "I'm doing some work for the government. Most of it is confidential, though, I'm afraid."

And undoubtedly important.

Suddenly her dreams seemed very shallow and insignificant. How was chasing down a rumored pot of gold any better than pursuing clothes, fashion, and parties back east? Not that her entire life had been full of such shallow objectives. A good portion of her time had been spent in charity work. Her small offerings, though, never seemed enough to make a difference in anyone's life. The poor continued to funnel into the church for food twice a week, and the children in the orphanage always needed new clothes and shoes. There never seemed to be enough time or resources to meet all the needs.

Searching for the gold had been a way for her to do something important. Her one chance to do something beyond the mundane tasks of everyday life. But her quest to aid the government seemed insignificant. Her parents had saved dozens, if not hundreds, of lives by being a part of the Underground Railroad during the war. She'd seen glimpses of wide-eyed children with their ebony skin as they scurried with their parents into the cellar below the house. The same heroics had been true for her aunt Rachel. Slipping messages to key people had made a small yet significant difference in the outcome of the war.

What good was ladling soup into the bowls of the poor twice a week when those same individuals would go hungry the next night? It wasn't a solution; it was simply postponing the inevitable. And what good was a pair of shoes to a small child who needed the love of a mother and father?

"Can I help you down?" He stood beside her horse with a ready hand to aid her.

Tara pushed aside the unwelcome thoughts and swallowed hard at his nearness. "Please."

She felt the strength in his arms when he lifted her off the horse as if she were no heavier than a sack of goose feathers. Not wanting to meet his gaze, she studied the tip of his chin and its small dimple. Once her feet hit the ground, she couldn't stop herself from looking up briefly and smiling to thank him.

His Stetson blocked the sun that had begun its descent in the western sky. Everything around her faded, and for a moment, she couldn't breathe. No longer could she hear the song of the goldfinch, or smell the scent of the wildflowers blowing in the soft summer breeze. It was just the two of them and a strange connection she couldn't explain. Her horse stamped and nudged her in the back. She clasped her hands and turned away, breaking the suspended moment.

Aaron took a step back. Something had passed between them, but he wasn't sure what. All he knew was that there had been something in her eyes as she'd looked at him that had reached all the way to the depths of his heart. It was something unexpected, something he couldn't explain. And he didn't know if he wanted to.

He reached down and picked up a couple of smooth pebbles. There was too much at stake. His superiors were beginning to pressure him. Finding the gold was not only a governmental priority, his career hung in the balance, as well. He had no time for distractions. And he needed to find out what she knew.

He walked toward the stream edge and skipped a stone across the glassy water. He wouldn't lie to her, but telling her the truth would no doubt push her away. It would turn him into the opponent instead of a potential suitor. Not that he had any chances of actually becoming her suitor.

"There is something I need to tell you." He tossed another pebble into the creek and watched it skip across the water.

Miss Young leaned against the trunk of a tall tree beside him with a lazy smile across her face. He wondered what would happen if he bridged the distance between them and kissed her. He shook his head and pushed away the ridiculous thought. Confronting her might be the last thing he wanted to do, but it was what he had to do.

He stared at the water flowing slowly toward the south. "I know why you're here."

"Excuse me?"

"I know that you're not really here to take care of the Carpenters." He turned to face her. "I know about the gold."

She took a step forward and raised her chin. "The gold?"

"Gold stolen from the US government at the end of the war. That's why you're here. To find it."

"How did you. . . ? I don't understand."

Aaron clasped his hands behind his back. "It's a small town, Miss Young. One really can't trust anyone to keep a secret, especially when it comes to gold."

"Sheriff Morton." She shook her head and looked up at him. "So what do you want from me?"

He scuffed the toe of his boot against the ground, wishing things could have been different between them. "I want you to give me the information you have and stop looking for the gold. I will pay you for any tip you give me that leads to the finding of the cache."

"You can't be serious." Any feelings of attraction that had glimmered in her eyes a few moments ago were gone. "Why should I do that?"

"Because I'm a lawman who's qualified to track down the information and who's working for the government."

"I don't see how your qualifications have gotten you anywhere so far." She shoved her fists against her hips and frowned. "Otherwise, you wouldn't still be chasing down the rumored gold or trying to extract information from me."

Aaron felt the veins in his neck pulse. "I'm not—"

"And let me tell you something, Mr. Jefferson." Her fists balled at her sides. "I have no intention of telling you, or anyone else, the information I have. Do you think I left the comforts of my home in Boston to come to this place and simply give up?"

He shook his head. "You don't understand what's at stake here—or the danger your life could be in if the wrong people get involved."

"No, I don't think you understand." Miss Young crossed the grassy knoll to where they had tethered the horses and attempted to mount the mare.

He hurried to her side to help her, but she held up her hand to stop him. "Thank you, but I don't need your help, Mr. Jefferson. Not now. Not ever. I have proof that the gold exists. Mark my words. It's only a matter of time before I find it."

Chapter 9

*T*ara swallowed hard and forced her horse to sprint faster. She could feel her heart pounding in her chest, but she refused to give in to fear. Fear was the enemy, and time was running out. It had taken two weeks, but she'd finally managed to unravel the majority of the clues in her aunt's journal. She'd also discovered that there were others searching for the gold. Others who would do anything to get their hands on the journal she possessed.

But that was something she'd never allow.

The house loomed before her in the distance. The shabby saltbox structure her aunt had written of was the key to the gold. That she knew for sure. All she needed was to unlock the last few paragraphs and her service to her country would be complete. If her assumptions were correct, she'd be able to secure the gold before the others.

"The masked bullion my comrade holds, remains forever secluded beneath the ring of woody perennials, there to be confined until the adversary is trounced."

She repeated aloud the phrase from the journal. Masked meant hidden. Bullion referred to the gold. My comrade—

A gunshot ripped through the morning air. She slid to the ground, bringing the horse to an abrupt halt. Then she clutched the journal beneath her arm as she ran to the side of the house for cover. Another shot pierced the morning stillness. The enemy had arrived before her. She caught sight of his black Stetson as he rounded the corner, and her breath caught in her throat.

It wasn't the adversary from Aunt Rachel's journal.

It was Mr. Jefferson.

Tara sat up with a start, then lay back down too quickly, whacking her head against the headboard. A rooster crowed outside. The sun had yet to wrap its warm fingers across the acres of farmland and prairies, but already she could hear Mrs. Carpenter bustling downstairs. In a few moments, she'd knock on Tara's door and announce the start of yet another day.

Tara let out a long sigh. For two weeks now, she'd risen before dawn. Today, she wanted to sleep in. Between morning Bible readings, farm chores, and evening prayers, they'd spent the time cleaning every nook and cranny of the house, an undertaking Tara was convinced hadn't transpired for at least half a decade. And while she hadn't been able to talk Mrs. Carpenter into making any major changes in the antiquated furnishings, she had to admit that she was amazed at the transformation that had occurred.

Mrs. Carpenter continued to sing her praises, claiming that she'd never have had the energy to accomplish such a feat without Tara's help. But for a city girl who'd never placed one foot on a farm before arriving in Iowa, the housework hadn't been the only challenge. From milking the cows to collecting the eggs to ensuring the new lambs didn't escape from their pen, she'd fallen into bed exhausted at night. Even the last of the pickles had been sealed in mason jars yesterday afternoon and lined up in neat rows in the cellar until the next church social. And all of this had given her little time to pursue the gold.

Tara reached over and lit the kerosene lamp beside her bed before pulling out her aunt's journal from beneath her pillow. Stifling a yawn, she opened the pages to the one she'd marked. Aunt Rachel's handwriting was easy to read, but the meaning behind it was often coded. In her dreams the meaning seemed clear, but in real life the answers were far less easy to interpret. She was sure she was missing something important in her aunt's writings, but exactly what, she didn't know.

One thing was certain, however. Mr. Jefferson was not mentioned in her aunt's journal. But that didn't stop him from plaguing her dreams. She'd seen him twice since his insistence that she stop her search. Both times had been at church, which wasn't a setting where she could openly speak her mind. So, instead, like any proper lady, she'd made sure that she was well mannered and cordial as she greeted him. But that was it. She refused to be taken in by his enchanting eyes or his smile that set her heart to racing, not once forgetting that he had become her opponent.

She pulled her robe closer around her shoulders. She hadn't forgotten Pastor Reeves's words, either. His convicting sermon from the book of Colossians had lingered with her, reminding her that she wasn't to serve men, but God. And once again, her motives for coming to Iowa came into question. Trying to please others while proving she could do something valuable with her life perhaps wasn't as noble as she'd once thought.

Shoving aside feelings of guilt, Tara fingered the edge of the journal and read once again the entry for April 17, 1864.

"Received word from MS today. Further contact unsafe."

Tara squeezed her eyes shut, wishing her aunt Rachel were here to explain the words she'd penned. Tara missed her so much. But crying certainly wouldn't accomplish anything. From an earlier entry, she knew that MS stood for Mr. Schlosser, and that he had been one of her aunt's contacts. Aunt Rachel herself had once confided some of the secret code that had been used and had told her that the bullion referred to the government's gold. But secured where?

She needed to speak to Mr. Schlosser. Mr. Martin, her only connection to

Mr. Schlosser, had been away for the past month and was planning to return today. Somehow, in the middle of laundering the bedding and washing the feathers from the mattresses and whatever else Mrs. Carpenter had planned, she was determined to slip out of the house and find a way to pay a call on the man.

She'd made several friends in town, including Constance Van de Kieft and the pastor's wife, Mary, but telling the Carpenters she was going visiting at one place while actually calling on Mr. Martin wasn't an option. Neither was taking Mr. Carpenter with her this time. The older man was feeling somewhat under the weather, and Mrs. Carpenter was insisting he stayed at home until he felt better.

Tara quickly changed her clothes. Then she tugged on the bottom of her short cape with determination. She would just have to take a chance and go by herself, and hopefully, she'd be able to find answers to her questions.

She opened the door to Mrs. Carpenter's cheery grin. "Good morning, Miss Young. I was just about to knock. You're up bright and early."

Tara forced a smile, feeling anything but chipper at the older woman's greeting. "Good morning, Mrs. Carpenter."

"I've brought you something more suitable to wear."

Tara's brows rose in question as she took the calico garment that was thrust into her hands. For the past few weeks, she'd donned two of her own simpler dresses while working. Neither was fit to wear in public anymore, but they'd been suitable for the work they had done.

Tara held up the plain dress that had to have been made decades earlier. "What am I to do with this?"

"I wanted to surprise you." Mrs. Carpenter held up a worn cookbook.

Tara frowned. A calico dress, a dog-eared cookbook. . .and a surprise? Something worse than making pickles? Tara wasn't sure she was ready for one of Mrs. Carpenter's surprises.

The older woman hugged the book to her chest. "I've been wanting to make a wool sweater for Mr. Carpenter, and thought what better time now that you are here. You can help me with the dye bath and the spinning—"

"Excuse me, Mrs. Carpenter." Tara held up her hand in protest. "I have never spun wool let alone dyed wool—"

"You mustn't worry." She shot Tara a broad smile. "I'm going to teach you."

❧

Tara set the gallon pot full of the used dye bath on one of the porch steps, then headed toward the clothesline with the wool. After a morning of washing and rinsing the wool, then making a dye bath and coloring the wool, she was ready to crawl back into bed. Still, she had to admit that the rich plum color of the yarn would make a stunning sweater. If she only knew how to make such an item—which she didn't.

Of course, that was bound to change. Mrs. Carpenter planned to teach her not only the dyeing process of the wool that she'd learned today, but also the spinning and actual crafting of the garment. While she could embroider and do other simple forms of needlework, such a task was not something she'd ever attempted. Nor had wanted to. That was the very reason she enjoyed the ease of readymade fashions from the city where she could purchase the costumes featured in *Harper's Bazaar* with little effort.

While Mrs. Carpenter went to start lunch, Tara had simple instructions to hang the dyed wool out to dry in the shade before fetching a few potatoes from the cellar. She was hoping that as soon as lunch was over, she'd be able to pay Mr. Martin a visit.

One of the lambs bleated behind her, and Tara spun around to shoo the young animal back into its pen. How it managed to escape from the confines of its enclosure she had no idea, but it wasn't the first time she'd had to chase the little animal back to its mother.

"Now, Cotton Ball." She placed her hands on her hips and spoke sternly to the lamb. "I don't have time for any nonsense today. I've got to finish up here so I can go and meet with Mr. Martin." She leaned down to whisper the last sentence. "He's going to help me find the gold."

Cotton Ball skittered to the right. Tara lunged for the lamb and missed. He went to the left, and she followed his move, before he made a quick maneuver toward the house. . .and the tub of dye.

"No. . .no. . .no." Tara's eyes widened in horror. "The dye is for after you've been sheared, not before. . ."

She picked up her skirts and ran after the lamb. All she needed was a plum-colored lamb in the sheep pen. What would Mr. and Mrs. Carpenter say to that? The lamb continued toward the tub at a brisk pace with Tara right behind. If she could stop the lamb before it tried to run up the stairs. . .

Tara didn't see the stump until it was too late. Tripping across the lawn, she fell flat on her face at the bottom of the staircase. Frightened by her scream, the lamb tried to run up the stairs and landed in the pot of dye.

Tara looked up in horror. The tub teetered on the edge of the stair while the lamb struggled to get its footing. Tara tried to get up, but she was too slow. Cotton Ball moved forward, and the entire contents of the tub, sheep and all, dumped on top of Tara's head.

❧

Aaron stuffed the telegram into the pocket of his denim pants and frowned as he walked down the crowded boardwalk toward the livery. For two weeks now he'd followed every lead he had, and his superiors were not going to be pleased with his findings. His discrete conversations with three suspect people in the area, had, like the rest of his efforts, turned up no new leads. His opinion now was that there was no proof left the gold ever existed. And if it did, no doubt it had been broken up into smaller lots and spent years ago.

Now they wanted him back in Washington by the end of the month. With answers. One would think that the government, with its recent establishment of the Department of Justice and other political concerns, would be less inclined to worry about a cache of lost gold. But apparently that wasn't the case.

Wiping the sweat off the back of his neck with his hand, he longed for a tall glass of lemonade to quench his thirst from the hot and humid afternoon. Maybe when he returned from Mr. Martin's, he'd stop by the hotel restaurant. But because his superiors wanted answers, he was determined to follow through on the assignment until he found the gold—or until he uncovered solid evidence that the gold was gone.

He'd spent his entire life working to get ahead, trying to live up to the name his parents had bestowed on him, Aaron Thomas Jefferson, and to the high standards of his family lineage. This assignment was no different. He might not have forgotten his grandfather's spiritual nurturing, which tried to teach him to rely on Christ alone, but those words had faded as the years progressed and had been replaced by a determination to forge ahead on his own.

"Mr. Jefferson?"

Aaron stopped in front of the barbershop. He'd almost walked by Pastor Reeves without even seeing him. "It's good to see you again, Pastor."

The man stood before him with a few pieces of mail in his hand. "My wife wanted to invite you to supper, but you always slip out of church so quickly, we haven't had a chance to ask you."

"I'm sorry, sir." Aaron tipped the brim of his Stetson to block the sun. "I'm not planning to stay in town much longer, I'm afraid."

The friendly preacher laughed. "Hope it isn't my sermons that are running you off."

Aaron couldn't help but like the man and his sense of humor. "Not at all. In fact, your lessons have been quite timely."

Enough to prick his conscience and to cause him to reevaluate his life and the motives behind what he did. The man had a point when he pressed that service to God had to come before trying to please man. It wasn't a thought he planned to brush off without some serious consideration.

Pastor Reeves tapped the mail against the palm of his hand, seemingly in no hurry to end their conversation. "I heard you were interested in buying a farm in the area. Does that mean you might return soon?"

"Buying a farm? I. . .I'm honestly not sure at this point."

Aaron frowned. Perhaps it was time to go back to Washington. There was no telling what other rumors regarding why he was here were circulating in this small town. News that he was searching for the gold was the last thing he needed right now. And if Miss Young had been involved—

"Either way, I hope to see you at church on Sunday." Pastor Reeves reached out to shake his hand. "And don't forget, you're more than welcome to stay for lunch afterward. My wife makes the best dumplings this side of the Mississippi."

Aaron forced a smile and shook the man's hand. "I appreciate your kindness, Pastor Reeves."

Aaron watched the man of God make his way toward the small church building that sat on the edge of town. While he honestly did value the man's kindness, thoughts of food, no matter how delicious, were low on his priorities right now as he strived to stay focused on the job at hand.

He'd even managed to forget about Miss Young. At least most of the time.

She, though, was the reason he was in such a hurry today. Rumor had it that Mr. Martin had arrived home late last night from a trip to see family members. And Aaron was determined to talk to Mr. Martin before Miss Young had a chance to show up and ruin everything.

Securing the feisty stallion he'd rented from the livery while he was in town, Aaron followed the road until Mr. Martin's worn saltbox house came into view. Little had changed since his first visit two weeks ago when he'd encountered not only an empty house, but had also learned the identity of Miss Young. He scanned the horizon and the unspoiled land, thankful there was no sign of the woman today. Luck must be on his side. Mr. Martin sat out on the front steps.

He stopped in front of the house and dismounted. "Mr. Martin? Name's Aaron Jefferson. I was wondering if I could speak to you for a moment."

"What do you want?" The balding man took a swig of whatever he was drinking.

"I won't take much of your time, but I'm trying to find out about the—"

Mr. Martin turned away at the squeaky wheel of an approaching wagon.

Aaron followed his gaze, his heart plummeting when he realized who was driving the wagon. "You've got to be kidding."

"Why? You know the woman?"

"Yes, in fact, I do." Aaron dipped his head to block the sun. Miss Tara Young sat erect in the wagon, heading straight for Mr. Martin's house. "It would seem as if you have quite a number of visitors today."

The man set his drink down and stood. "Strange. I'm not used to company."

"Mr. Martin, I really would like to speak to you, but would you excuse me for one moment, please?"

Mr. Martin shrugged. "Don't make any difference to me. I ain't going anywhere."

Aaron rushed across the dusty drive toward the wagon, determined to speak to her in private before she ruined any chance he might have at an interview with Mr. Martin. She pulled on the reins to stop the horses and eyed him skeptically without saying a word.

He folded his arms across his chest and let out a deep sigh. "Miss Young. It appears we meet again."

Chapter 10

Aaron opened his mouth, but everything he wanted to tell Miss Young vanished. Why was it that one look at her auburn hair and bright blue eyes left him completely enchanted to the point that he wanted to forget she was the opposition? He'd worked hard to erase her from his daydreams, but nighttime had been another story. She'd occupied his dreams, and seeing her again only reinforced the unpleasant truth that she'd completely captured his attention.

He shoved his thumbs in his belt loops. "I. . .I wasn't expecting to see you again."

Her cautious smile didn't reach her eyes. "We are after the same pot of gold, are we not?"

Aaron took a step closer to the wagon. Something wasn't quite right with her appearance. While she was impeccably dressed as always with her pink dress and matching parasol, something had changed. A jumble of curls was held neatly beneath a straw bonnet, but her hair seemed to be a shade or two darker. Almost a. . .a plum color? And her fair cheeks had splotches of purple. If she'd come down with something. . .

"Are you feeling all right, Miss Young?"

She fiddled with the ribbons that held her bonnet in place beneath her chin and looked away. "Of course I'm all right. Why do you ask?"

Aaron cocked his head, wondering if it would be better to simply drop the subject, but curiosity got the better of him. "Your face is a bit—"

"Purple?" She looked him straight in the eye. "Then may I suggest that you should never fall into a dye bath, especially one that has been made with very potent berries? It tends to stain the skin temporarily. Or at least it did to me, and I assume that explanation will satisfy your curiosity regarding the slight change in my appearance."

He pressed his lips together and suppressed a laugh. He should have never brought up the issue, but now that she had acknowledged something had happened, he had to know more. The subsequent images she'd invoked were far too amusing. "You fell into a dye bath?"

"It was the lamb, actually, but that doesn't matter." She held up her hand as if to stop him from asking any more questions. "Mr. Jefferson, may we please return to the topic at hand?"

He paused. "The topic at hand?"

"Mr. Martin and the gold. I'm assuming that you are here for that reason."

"But the lamb—"

"The gold, Mr. Jefferson."

"You're quite right. And Mr. Martin's connection." Aaron eyed a small spot near her chin that he imagined to be in the shape of a heart and cleared his throat. She must have been in quite a hurry to beat him here to have failed to remedy her appearance. "I know I cannot force you to leave, but I want to make it clear that I will be the one who will conduct this interview."

She held her head high. "I suppose you believe that would be to my advantage, considering you are the one qualified in the areas of investigations and interviews."

"I. . .well. . . Of course I am." Aaron shook his head. She was doing it again. Here he was in a professional capacity, and she was leaving him tongue-tied. He needed this lead and couldn't afford for her to ruin it for him.

Miss Young picked up her parasol and held out her hand. "Would you mind helping me down, Mr. Jefferson?"

Aaron paused. He didn't want to feel the softness of her gloved hand. He didn't want to wonder what it would be like to kiss her, or—

"Mr. Jefferson?"

"Of course. I'm sorry." He took a step forward and grasped her hand to help her descend, but he didn't let go after she'd stepped on the ground. "Do we have a deal, Miss Young?"

"That I remain silent during the interview?"

"Exactly."

She bit the edge of her bottom lip and didn't respond for a moment. Aaron's jaw tightened. He knew he had a fine line to walk. He needed Miss Young for this investigation more than she needed him. Mr. Martin might hold the key to finding Mr. Schlosser, but if Miss Young held further information that might lead to the discovery of the gold, he couldn't afford to make her angry. Winning her trust again might be the best method, but that didn't change the fact that he needed to be in charge of this investigation and, in particular, the interview with Mr. Martin. She might be able to charm her way into the lives of those involved, but he was the one experienced in the interviewing process.

"Knowing that you are a professional," she finally offered, "I will do my best not to interfere, but—"

"Miss Young." He wondered if his request for her to remain silent was possible. "I need more than an *I'll do my best* from you."

"Please do not worry. This is just as important to me as it is to you." She opened her parasol to block the sun. "But let me remind you that I was the one who secured this information for you in the first place. Without it, I believe, you are out of leads."

"I wouldn't go that far, Miss Young."

"We shall see, but for now, I think we have a job to do. Mr. Martin is waiting."

⬠

Tara followed Mr. Jefferson, willing her hands not to shake. She couldn't believe that she hadn't managed to beat the man here. If it hadn't been for the unfortunate incident with Cotton Ball and the dye. . . She let out a long sigh, determined to forget the fact that, in her rush to beat Mr. Jefferson to the farm, she'd failed to completely get rid of all the signs of the purple dye.

There was no telling what the man thought of her now, but she didn't care. Or at least she didn't want to care. All she needed to do was focus on getting the information she needed, regardless of the fact that *he* was walking beside her, close enough that she could smell the spicy scent of his shaving soap and see the solid form of his stature. She shook her head. She still held her aunt's diary, which meant she had the upper hand. A fact that Mr. Jefferson no doubt found extremely annoying.

They stopped in front of the porch, and Mr. Jefferson addressed the owner of the farmhouse. "I am sorry for the interruption."

Mr. Martin took off his hat and scratched his head. "You never told me why you were here, Mr. . . ?"

"Mr. Jefferson. Aaron Jefferson." Aaron reached out to shake the man's hand.

"And my name is Miss Young." Tara stepped forward, determined not to be pushed aside by Mr. Jefferson. "We're here to find out some information regarding the man you bought this property from. A Mr. S—"

Tara felt the insistent jab of Mr. Jefferson's elbow against her upper arm, then caught his piercing stare. She frowned. Keeping her word was not going to be easy.

Mr. Jefferson grasped her elbow. "Would you mind if we came in for a moment, Mr. Martin? I promise we won't take up much of your time."

Mr. Martin rubbed his chin. "For a minute, I suppose."

Tara walked beside Mr. Jefferson up the stairs, trying to ignore the fact that his touch made her pulse race and forget why she was here. Distraction was the last thing she needed at this moment. Ignoring his presence, she instead took in the details of the weathered saltbox house. Inside, the sitting room was sparsely furnished with little more than a sofa, three chairs, and a table. Lace curtains, a shade of dull grey, hung on the wall, obviously not having been washed for some time. A handmade quilt lay on the back of the sofa, but its faded colors showed only a hint of what it once must have looked like with stunning reds, yellows, and purples. A daguerreotype of a woman sat on a small table beside the sofa, but beyond a few throw pillows and books, there were no other personal articles.

Mr. Martin motioned to the worn sofa, and Tara sat down beside Mr. Jefferson. "I'd offer you both something to drink, but I've just arrived home. Not much left in the pantry."

"Please, don't concern yourself." Tara set her parasol beside her, then folded her hands in her lap. "We didn't come to take advantage of your hospitality."

"Allow me get straight to the point, Mr. Martin." Mr. Jefferson sat forward and rested his elbows against his thighs. "We are looking for the previous owner of this house, a Mr. Schlosser. We were hoping you might know of his whereabouts."

"Mr. Schlosser? I have no idea." Mr. Martin sat down in the rocking chair and shook his head. "Ain't seen the man since I moved into this house a good four years ago."

Tara didn't try to stop the flood of disappointment that swept over her. Without Mr. Schlosser, unless she could interpret more of the journal on her own, she was out of leads with nothing further to go on. Which in turn meant she was no closer to finding the gold than Mr. Jefferson was, a thought that brought with it a large amount of frustration.

Not wanting to waste any more of the man's time, she rose to leave, but Mr. Jefferson motioned for her to sit back down before he spoke. "During the transaction, Mr. Schlosser must have given you some indication as to where he was going."

"Said he was headed west. Montana. . .South Dakota?" Mr. Martin shrugged a shoulder. "Can't say that I rightly remember. Besides, don't think the man ever stayed anywhere long enough to put down roots. He'd only lived here about two years when he up and sold the lot. Always wondered where he got his money. Never seemed to work much but traveled all the time."

"A traveling salesman perhaps?" Tara struggled to take deep breaths and slow her pulse. What if Mr. Schlosser had taken a part of the government's gold to fund his own undertakings? She had to know more.

"A salesman's got to have a product. And as I recall, there were no goods."

Mr. Jefferson wasn't finished. "We understand that when Mr. Schlosser sold you the property, you also bought all the furnishings."

Mr. Martin nodded. "I did, but if you look around you can see that none of it was worth much. Tables and chairs, the sofa, a bed, and an old chest were all he had to offer."

Tara's brows rose. She hadn't thought of that angle. Perhaps there was a spark of hope after all. What if Mr. Schlosser had left some of the letters behind in the chest? Some clue to the location of the gold that could be interpreted only by someone who knew him or her aunt Rachel. . .like herself.

Mr. Jefferson cleared his throat. "You mentioned a chest. Did there happen to be any papers inside?"

Mr. Martin rocked back in his chair, his eyes narrowing at the question. "Why exactly do you need to find Mr. Schlosser?"

Tara shot Mr. Jefferson a worried look, afraid they'd pushed the man too far. They arrived as complete strangers and were now asking him to make a search of his house for possible missing articles.

"My aunt—"

Mr. Jefferson whacked the heel of her shoe with the toe of his boot. She clenched her hands together. The man was without a doubt completely exasperating. Granted, she had to admit that he was quite good at extracting information, but that didn't mean that she had no right to participate in the interview at all. Surely she came across as less of a threat than the tall, rugged lawman beside her.

Mr. Jefferson avoided her gaze. "Miss Young's aunt knew Mr. Schlosser. They exchanged letters throughout the years, and as a sentimental gesture, Miss Young is trying to track them down."

"Mr. Schlosser wasn't married, but I—"

"They were only friends, but it's very important we track down these letters."

Mr. Martin rubbed the stubble on his chin, then rose from his chair. "I'll be right back."

Mr. Jefferson waited until Mr. Martin had disappeared down the hallway before speaking. "You're not doing a good job of keeping your part of the deal."

"I'm sorry, it's just that—"

"There's a lot at stake here, Miss Young."

"For both of us."

Tara picked up the daguerreotype beside her. Fighting with Mr. Jefferson wasn't the answer. What was it about him that made her want to scream with frustration while at the same time made her desire to know everything he was thinking? If it weren't for the missing gold that had managed to wedge its way between them and their opposing goals to find it, she would have liked for their relationship to turn in another direction altogether. She'd seen the interest in his eyes, despite the fact that he now saw her as the opponent and not a lady to call upon.

She took a peek at him, knowing he was praying right now that when Mr. Martin returned, he'd carry with him the answer to their search. His lips were pressed together, and his hands were clasped tightly in his lap. He was determined to track down this gold with or without her. And something told her that his resolve had a personal meaning to it. Perhaps they both were looking at things wrong. Unwavering from their quest as they sought to prove themselves. Or maybe he didn't have anything to prove. Maybe it was just a job to him.

She studied the photo of the young woman in her hand. While her dress was plain and she wasn't smiling, there was a softness in her expression.

Tara looked up as Mr. Martin stepped back into the room. "She's beautiful. Who is she?"

"Is that why you're here?" Mr. Martin's face reddened as he crossed the room in three long steps.

While he hadn't actually welcomed them warmly into his home, any signs of friendliness had vanished from his expression. He reached to grab the photo from her. The frame slipped out of her hands, and glass shattered against the floor.

"I'm sorry." Tara covered her mouth with her hand.

Mr. Jefferson stood. "Mr. Martin—"

"Now look what you've done." The man's eyes flashed as he glared at them. "Mr. Schlosser was just an excuse, wasn't he? A reason for you to come into my home without my knowin' your true intentions."

Tara pressed her back against the sofa, feeling the rise of panic fill her stomach. "Of course not, but I—"

"My wife is none of your business." Mr. Martin pulled a rifle off the fireplace mantel and pointed it at them. "Now get out. Both of you. You've done enough damage for one day."

Mr. Jefferson grasped Tara's elbow and pulled her up from the couch. "Mr. Martin, I promise you, we had no intentions to—"

Mr. Martin fired a shot into the ceiling. Bits of dust filtered through the afternoon sunlight that streamed through the window. "I said, get out."

With Mr. Jefferson at her elbow, Tara tripped across the wooden floor, praying with each step that it wouldn't be her last.

Chapter 11

Aaron kept his hand on Miss Young's elbow as they hurried down the wooden porch steps toward the wagon. How was it that he'd come to ask a few simple questions and ended up almost getting shot? He didn't know what there was about this woman, but she certainly seemed to be a target for trouble. The attack at the station, the incident at the post office, and now this. . .even her new violet shade of hair seemed to be a sign that the woman couldn't avoid getting herself into a mess. And with a sheep and a pot of dye bath no less.

Grabbing the reins of his horse in his free hand, he escorted them both across the hard ground outside Mr. Martin's house toward her wagon.

Miss Young bustled beside him to keep up. "Mr. Jefferson, I am sorry. I never intended—"

"If you would just be quiet for a moment, please." Without stopping, Aaron turned to check on the whereabouts of Mr. Martin. The last thing he wanted was a bullet in his back.

The middle-aged man stood in the doorway watching them, but thankfully, he'd set the gun down beside him. Mr. Martin might not seem to be mentally stable, but that didn't change the fact that Miss Young's presence could have cost him not only a lead in his case but also his life. There was no telling how much more he might have uncovered on his own. Mr. Martin had gone to look for something, and now Aaron was quite certain that he'd never know what it was.

"It looks as if he's not going to shoot us." Aaron gritted his teeth. "Though I'd say that's the only good thing about this morning."

"I hate guns." Miss Young stumbled on the uneven ground, and he tightened his grip to steady her. "Mr. Jefferson, I said I was sorry. I thought my presence could help, my being a woman and all. One would think that he would prefer to open up and talk to me over a lawman like yourself."

"Your charm might do wonders at a church picnic, parties, and other social gatherings, but as you can see, it had little effect in a professional capacity." Aaron frowned. His words might hold a dash of truth, but hadn't she managed to work her way straight into his heart? "Besides, sorry won't change the fact that Mr. Martin will never want to speak to either of us again."

He stared out across the fertile pastureland toward the west, where a decent-sized herd of cattle grazed, and scowled. While his words held truth, he'd seen the compassion in her eyes as she'd asked Mr. Martin about the woman in the picture and heard the gentle way she'd talked to him. In truth, it wasn't her fault that the man got upset. But all of that didn't change the fact that they'd lost a valuable lead, and unless he wanted to take another chance at getting shot, he was going to have to come up with another way to find Mr. Schlosser.

Working on an alternative solution, Aaron stopped at the wagon to help her onto the buckboard. She lifted the hem of her skirt and pulled herself up into the wagon, ignoring his outstretched hand. He dropped his arms to his sides and grunted. He'd never met a more stubborn woman.

"I'm going to accompany you home." He scratched the back of his neck and wondered if he were simply a glutton for punishment as her blue eyes widened.

Tara picked up the reins and clicked her tongue at the horse. "I don't need an escort, Mr. Jefferson."

Aaron raised his brow as he mounted his horse. "Considering the fact that you can't seem to stay out of trouble, I believe an escort would be most appropriate."

She reached up to touch the back of her hair, and despite the seriousness of the situation, Aaron found himself wanting to laugh. The shade of purple was actually quite becoming on her. There was little doubt in his mind that life around Miss Young would never be dull.

Which was exactly what was bothering him. Aaron stared straight ahead as they left Mr. Martin's house and tried to avoid the temptation to sneak another peek at her. She was beautiful, intelligent, compassionate. . .why then couldn't she drop this ridiculous quest to find the gold?

And then what? Did he really think that would change things between them? That he would find a way to court her? He was leaving soon and would most likely never see her again. Even if he did buy a farm and settle down somewhere nearby, Miss Young wasn't the kind of woman who would be content living the rest of her days on a secluded farm in Iowa. He was quite certain that she wouldn't last six months here. Once the cold hit and the snow began to fall, she'd no doubt miss her upscale Boston home with its piped-in gas and plush furnishings. Besides that, Browning City boasted little shopping or parties or. . .

He looked at her and willed his heart to not care. While her cheeks were rosy and her eyes bright, her jaw was set in determination. She was just as determined as he was to find the gold. But that wasn't all. The gold had just been an excuse as to why things wouldn't work between them. The truth was, even without the quest, they'd never be able to make a relationship work. They were simply too different. Their relationship would prove to be more difficult to achieve than inding the government's lost cache.

He would accompany her to the Carpenters' farm, then say his farewells. He still had a chance to find Mr. Schlosser—on his own. But first he owed her an apology.

He tipped the brim of his Stetson. "I'm truly sorry for my harsh words, Miss Young. While the situation was strained, you didn't deserve such a reprimand."

Tara's eyes widened at the apology. She had expected a lecture, not a confession from the man riding beside her. He was turning out to be quite an anomaly. Practiced lawman on one hand yet willing to ask for forgiveness when the situation warranted such an action. She found the gesture not only surprising but also refreshing.

"I do appreciate the apology, but. . ."

She hesitated. Apology or not, it was obvious that his own determination to find the gold hadn't wavered. And she'd just lost her last lead. Until she could either interpret the rest of her aunt's journal or find Mr. Schlosser through another means, instead of returning home a hero, she was stuck in Iowa eating pickles, carding wool, and whatever other messy project Mrs. Carpenter asked her to do.

She looked to her right at the endless sea of corn planted by one of Mr. Martin's neighbors. At first, she'd found the setting monotonous, but she had to admit that there was something about the open space of the land and lush rolling hills that gave her a sense of peace she'd never felt before. She loved the sincerity of the people and the quiet surroundings after the constant rush of life in Boston. Even the fresh scent of the summer air was a welcome relief from the congestion of the city. But that didn't mean she wanted to stay.

Mr. Jefferson's plan to buy a farm had briefly caused her to entertain the idea of staying in Iowa. But it would be presumptuous to even imagine that he would ever want to share his piece of land with her. That he'd want to share his life with her.

"Were you going to say something?"

She glanced up at him as he spoke and bit her lip. He was handsome, intelligent, even compassionate at times. Why then couldn't he allow her to continue her quest to find the gold? In the end, both she and the government would be happy, albeit the government would be out the hefty reward money. No. She was determined not to let Mr. Jefferson's handsome profile and undeniable charm get in the way of her proving her worth to her family.

"It doesn't change anything, you know." She braced herself as the wagon went over a slight dip in the road.

"What doesn't change anything?"

"Your apology. While I do very much appreciate your kindness in the situation, I'm still determined to find the gold."

Mr. Jefferson's lips curled into a slight smile. "I hadn't expected anything less from you, Miss Young. I believe that in the past few weeks of our acquaintance, I've come to recognize that your determination matches your beauty."

"I. . ." She closed her jaw, now knowing what to say in response.

If he was trying to sweet-talk her, he was doing a fine job. But she wasn't going to let him manipulate the situation. His profile, tall and well built while sitting high on the back of a black stallion, was one that took her breath away. But she wouldn't allow such thoughts to fill her mind any longer. There was certainly more to life than good looks, and all the charm in the world wasn't going to remedy the situation between them. No, she would return to the Carpenters' home, do her best to manage all the jobs Mrs. Carpenter asked her to accomplish. . .and find the gold.

"The judgments of the Lord are true and righteous altogether. More to be desired are they than gold. . ."

The passage from Psalm nineteen fluttered through her mind. She gripped the reins tighter and frowned.

But I don't actually want the gold, Lord. Just the. . .

Just the what? The recognition? The chance to prove herself to her country in an important fashion? The honor that would come with finding something the government hadn't been able to track down for years? Something that even Mr. Jefferson hadn't been able to track down.

"Where your treasure is, My child, there will your heart be also."

Tara rode in silence beside Mr. Jefferson, her heart suddenly heavy with the Lord's clear reminder from His Word. She couldn't deny the truth. She'd been so wrapped up in following the treasures of this earth that she'd stopped focusing on storing up treasures in heaven.

Can't I do both, Lord?

There had to be a way. The Carpenters' farmhouse came into view, and while she couldn't ignore the pointed words, neither was she ready to let go of her search.

I need to do this, Lord.

She was tired of living in the shadow of her parents and aunt. While there might be little she could ever hope to achieve in her life that would come close to their noble accomplishments, she'd never forgive herself if she didn't at least try. The last thing she wanted was to wake up one day, old and unhappy, because she'd failed to do something important with her life. Surely the good Lord understood how she felt.

Tara brought the wagon to a stop in the front yard. Clothes fluttered in the breeze on the clothesline. A sheep bleated in the pen, and she caught sight of the violet colored lamb. Turning away, she sighed. Good looks and charm had never proved to be enough. She'd always managed to bungle what was important.

She turned and caught Mr. Jefferson's gaze, hoping he hadn't noticed the tangible results of her morning escapades running through the sheep pen. "You know I'm going to do this on my own."

He shot her a grin. "And so am I."

"I wouldn't expect anything less from you."

What does God expect?

She tried to push aside the words, but they lingered in the back of her mind.

"Then may the best man, or woman as the case may be, win." Mr. Jefferson tipped his hat, then with the nudge of his boots against the side of the stallion, he raced across the fertile farmland and out of sight.

Aaron wanted to hit his head against the wall. He'd spent a week tracking down Mr. Schlosser, but every lead had come up empty. Except the last one. The rumors were plentiful, but the final piece of proof had just confirmed that Mr. Schlosser had died in a mineshaft somewhere in South Dakota eighteen months ago.

He glanced around the hotel restaurant that was empty except for an older couple sitting at a corner table. Sunlight streamed through windows that overlooked the main street of town. At least today, all seemed quiet as shoppers hurried about their business. With red tablecloths, a stone fireplace, and a few simple paintings, the atmosphere was as pleasant as the meal. But today he could barely taste the food.

He dropped the telegram onto the table and took another bite of the roast beef and potatoes he'd ordered for lunch, frustrated. Another dead end. And perhaps his last. There was only one thing left for him to do before returning to Washington with nothing more to show for his efforts than a handful of hotel bills.

He was going to have to speak to Miss Young. If he didn't, he would have to admit that he'd run this investigation as far as it would go, and it was over. He wasn't yet ready for that. Not when there was a chance for one last lead.

Aaron picked up the pencil and piece of paper he'd borrowed from Mrs. Meddler and began to scrawl out a message. It wasn't as if he didn't want to see Miss Young again. Because he did. Every day, as he walked the streets of town, he watched for her, but there had been no sign of the beauty. He'd even considered stopping by the Carpenters' farm, knowing the elderly couple would welcome a visit from him. But he hadn't. He was ashamed to think that his pride had gotten in the way of seeing her again, but there seemed little other explanation.

Instead of that line of thought, he focused on the note he was writing.

Dear Miss Young,
*   I have new information and a proposition you might find interesting. Please meet me for coffee at the hotel restaurant tomorrow at two if it is possible.*

*   Sincerely,*
*   Aaron Jefferson*

He tapped the pencil against the table. He wasn't sure his plan was going to work and that she'd actually agree to see him, but he didn't have much choice. Aaron reread the note one last time. A young boy who worked at the hotel walked into the restaurant, and Aaron called him over to his table. The boy had promised Aaron he'd deliver the message to Miss Young for a small fee. Aaron pulled out some change from his pocket and set it on the table beside the note.

It was time to call a truce.

Chapter 12

Tara fingered the note, surprised at Mr. Jefferson's desire to meet with her. Of course, the request was strictly business, but that didn't stop her pulse from quickening at the thought of seeing him again. For the past week, she had attempted to put him and his piercing toffee-colored eyes out of her mind, but her efforts were in vain. He'd managed to leave an imprint on her heart that she couldn't erase. And no matter how irritated he made her with his determination to find the gold single-handedly, she hadn't been able to ignore his other, more gallant, characteristics. His apology, for one, had shattered any remaining impressions that he was simply a tough lawman compelled only by his assignment. The man had a heart.

She stuffed the request into the pocket of her apron, then finished drying the last of the dishes. With both new information and a proposition, she couldn't help but wonder exactly what it was that he had discovered. Her attempts to locate Mr. Schlosser had resulted in nothing. No one in town seemed to remember much about the man, and she didn't have the resources Mr. Jefferson had. With no leads to follow, she'd stayed up late at night reading her aunt's journal by the smoky light of a kerosene lamp, trying to uncover any additional clues that might lead to the gold. But the result had only left her frustrated—and tired.

Mrs. Carpenter bustled into the kitchen with two jars of pickles in her hands. "You've done a fine job, Tara. Thank you so much for your help. With my joints seemingly stiffer by the day, I don't know what I would do without you."

Tara smiled at the comment. For the first time in her life, she was finding satisfaction in hard work. "Are you sure you don't mind my going into town this afternoon?"

"Not at all, dear." Mrs. Carpenter set the pickles on the kitchen counter and dug through a drawer until she pulled out a thin red ribbon. "The fresh air will do you good. I told Mr. Carpenter last night that you've been working far too hard this past week. Between farm chores, the garden, and knitting, you've had little time for yourself."

Tara placed the stack of dry plates on the shelf, then wiped her hands on a towel. She was surprised at how much she was beginning to enjoy life on the farm. While the Carpenters had primarily retired and now rented out the majority of their land to tenant farmers, there was still plenty of work.

Certainly, she missed her mornings of sleeping in and never relished the early crow of the rooster, but she'd found a sense of pride in seeing the results of her efforts on the breakfast table or in a batch of jam to be given away to the tenants' wives. There had even been enough of the purple wool for her to start her own shawl. Something she'd never imagined herself doing.

Mrs. Carpenter tied the ribbon around one of the jars and made a neat bow. "Can I ask you to do a favor for me?"

"Of course."

"Dr. Harding's wife, Wilma, is a bit under the weather. If you wouldn't mind taking her one of these jars. My mother always believed good homegrown food to be good for the constitution, so I figure why not my pickles? And the other jar is for that handsome lawman, Mr. Jefferson."

Tara felt a blush creep up her cheeks at the mention of his name. "You know, of course, that our meeting is strictly for business. He has some information on an old friend of my aunt's that he wants to pass on to me."

Mrs. Carpenter rested her hands on her hips and smiled. "It's a shame he won't be stopping by the farmhouse. Feel free to invite the gentleman over for lunch. Perhaps Sunday after church, if he isn't too busy."

"I will." Tara slipped the yellow apron over her head and folded it.

Thoughts of church left her feeling somber. While her quest for the gold had uncovered few, if any, answers regarding its location, the pursuit had exposed a vast number of spiritual questions. And like the gold, the answers seemed out of reach.

She placed her apron on the counter, then tapped her fingers against the wood. "Mrs. Carpenter, would you mind if I asked you a question?"

The older woman worked to tie the second ribbon. "Of course not. I may not have all the solutions, but I do have a listening ear."

"Is it wrong to want to do something important?" Tara fiddled with the hemmed edge of the apron and tried to rework her question so she said what her heart really felt. "I guess what I'm trying to say is, is it wrong to want to something that perhaps would. . .would prove one's self to the world? To prove that one is. . ."

". . .Worth something?"

Tara winced. "That sounds shallow, but yes."

Wasn't that exactly what she was trying to do? Prove her worth to herself, her family, and even God?

Mrs. Carpenter cocked her head. "I suppose whether or not it's shallow would depend on the situation and one's heart."

"It always goes back to the motives of the heart." Tara remembered the words that had stuck with her all week. " 'Where your treasure is, there will your heart be also.' "

"Jesus did say that, and there is a lot of truth to it." Mrs. Carpenter poured herself a cup of hot coffee from the stove, then sat at the table. "I've worked on this farm for almost forty years, and while I can't begin to do what I did when I was younger, for a long time I believed what I did was completely unimportant. What good is milking a cow every morning or the endless gathering of eggs from the chickens?"

Tara grinned. "Believe it or not, I've started to find satisfaction in such chores, but I see your point. That's exactly how I've been feeling. As though nothing I do is enough."

The older woman took a sip of her coffee before adding a spoonful of sugar. "I spent years longing to accomplish something heroic for God, and I was never happy with who I was. Then I learned something from a dear friend of mine that has stuck with me for years. I might long to accomplish something big that the world sees as impressive, but what's even more important is that I approach every day's household tasks and duties as if they were indeed just as valuable. To spend each day as if I were doing everything for Christ Himself."

Tara leaned back against the counter. "That's quite a profound statement."

"Jesus said as much when He told us to seek first His kingdom and His righteousness, and all these things shall be added unto us. It's always been a matter of the heart."

Tara knew Mrs. Carpenter was right. She'd been so obsessed with her mission that she'd neglected her own relationship with God. And, as hard as it was to admit it, she knew she needed to work on getting her heart right with God and get her treasure in the right place. But surely, that didn't make what she was doing wrong.

Or did it?

"God looks at our heart," the older woman continued. "The motives behind our actions, whether it's a big task like Moses leading the Israelites across the Red Sea or a simple one like cleaning out a horse stall for God's glory. If you've ever read through the Old Testament, it's amazing at how God looks on the inside before He ever looks at what we have accomplished."

Tara pressed her fingertips together. "It reminds me of Sampson. Always whistling a cheerful tune even when he's mucking a stall."

She knew there was nothing innately wrong with her quest for gold. But her motives had become self-seeking. That's where the problem lay. Now all she had to do was figure out how to set things right with God.

❧

Aaron watched as Miss Young entered the hotel restaurant; then he breathed out a sigh of relief. He stood as she approached his table, trying to ignore how lovely she looked. Her blue dress, with its contrasting white trim, highlighted her eyes, and her hair, pinned up neatly beneath one of her fancy hats, was now back to its normal shade of auburn.

He pulled out her chair and waited for her to be seated. "I wasn't sure you'd come."

She gave him a shy grin. "You made it a bit hard for me to refuse. New information and a proposition? Sounds like a bit of a truce."

"You could say that."

Aaron sat down and laid his Stetson on the table. He shouldn't feel so pleased that she was sitting across from him at one of the restaurant's corner tables, or that he was about to ask her for assistance in a government matter. But he couldn't help it. He'd wanted to see her again. Wanted to continue their conversations on farming, art, and spiritual matters. To simply spend the afternoon getting to know her better without the gold coming between them.

However, that wasn't why he was here. Nothing had really changed. He planned to ask for her help—beg, if need be, to get his job done. And once he found the gold, or some sort of proof that it couldn't be recovered, then he'd take on the next assignment. Or retire to some rolling hillside near the banks of the Mississippi. Alone.

"I. . .thanks for coming." He pressed his lips together, determined not to get tongue-tied today. "What would you like to drink?"

Miss Young set her light wrap on the chair behind her. "Lemonade would be wonderful."

Aaron motioned for the waitress and ordered them each a glass before continuing their conversation. "It's hot today, isn't it?"

"Very." She smiled and his heart tripped. "But I still enjoyed the drive here. The fields are sprinkled with Queen Anne's lace and the perfume of wild roses."

"And there are clouds in the horizon." He tugged on his collar, longing for relief from the stifling heat. A light breeze filtered in from the open front door but did little to alleviate the humid air. "I believe we're in for some wet weather. Might help cool things down."

"Mr. Carpenter said the crops could use another good rain. He's afraid production will be down this year."

The waitress put tall glasses of lemonade in front of them, then headed back to the kitchen. At two o'clock in the afternoon the place was quiet with no other patrons, which was exactly what he'd counted on. What they had to discuss had to be kept between them.

"For a city girl, you've learned a lot since your arrival in Iowa." He caught her gaze, grateful for the few minutes of small talk before things between them got serious. "You need to be careful, though."

"And why is that?"

"For instance, wild parsnip is often mistaken for Queen Anne's lace, but the wild parsnip is a rather toxic plant that can actually burn the skin if one isn't careful. Things aren't always what they appear to be."

"Apparently, I have much to learn." She cocked her head. "Does that apply to people, as well?"

"In my line of work, I've found that one must always be cautious."

Aaron toyed with the cloth napkin. Looking at her heart-shaped face and full lips, it was easy to forget the real reason he was here. He shifted his gaze to the decorative wallpaper behind her. Swirls of lavender blurred before him as he tried to refocus on the matter at hand. He wasn't here because the woman sitting across from him made him want to retire and settle down. He was here to make a deal and find the gold.

"Is there anything else I should watch out for?"

He blinked at her question and turned back to her. Was there anything else to watch out for? Here was a woman who'd been attacked, shot at, threatened, and had somehow even managed to color her hair purple. If anything, people needed to watch out when they were around *her*.

He shook his head. But she'd been talking about plants. Queen Anne's lace. . .roses. . . "To watch out for what?"

"You mentioned wild parsnip."

"Oh. I don't know. . ." He shook his head and tried to think. "Poison ivy, stinging nettle, and the black locust tree, I suppose, for starters."

She smiled at him. "I didn't know you were interested in such matters."

"My grandfather taught me a love and a respect for the land."

"But we're not here to discuss plants, are we?" She looked around the empty room then leaned forward. "I'm anxious to know what information you have to share with me."

Aaron cleared his throat. She was right. It was time to get to the issue at hand. "I found out yesterday that Mr. Schlosser is dead."

Miss Young drew in a sharp breath, and he cringed. He hadn't meant to be so blunt. He'd found himself so wrapped up in her presence that he knew he needed to forge past all the small talk or he'd find the afternoon spent with no progress made. But what happened to his skills of diplomacy and discretion? If he had any hope of getting what he wanted, then he would have to be careful how he said things.

"I'm sorry." He picked up his lemonade and let the small chunks of ice swirl in the glass. "It came as quite a shock to me, as well. I was hoping that your lead would pay off."

"I'm just surprised." She took a sip of her drink. "This changes things substantially."

"It means that we are both out of leads. Unless. . ." He let his voice trail off. He had to sound convincing. "Unless we work together."

Her eyes widened. "You want me to help you?"

"You have information. I have the resources. Together, we might actually be able to recover the gold."

He liked the thought of them working together. He couldn't help it. A lonely retirement wasn't an appealing future. As hard as he'd tried not to, she was the one he saw sitting beside him on a porch swing watching the sunrise or on a cold winter evening in front of the fireplace.

"What about the reward money?" She eyed him cautiously. "Would you still be willing to make good on it?"

"Of course."

She lowered her gaze. "I know what you're thinking, and I don't want you to believe that I'm completely self-centered."

He wasn't sure what she meant. "I don't."

She frowned "It's really not about the money."

"Then what is it about?"

She stared at her glass and began wiping away the condensation. "It's about proving I can do something worthwhile in life."

"I don't understand."

Miss Young folded her hands on the table and looked at him. "My aunt was a spy for the Union in the war. She made a difference, risking her life while passing important information to key people. My parents were a part of the Underground Railroad. They helped countless people escaping from slavery. And as for myself. . ." She shrugged. "I've failed to do anything of value."

Aaron shook his head, wondering how a beautiful and intelligent woman could think such a thing about herself. "But you told me about your charity work and—"

"What good is giving a child a blanket or a pair of shoes, when you can't assure him that he will one day have a home where he is loved?" An underlying passion resonated through her voice as she gripped the edge of the table. "What assurance is it to give a cup of soup to someone one day when the next day she'll still be hungry? Everything I've done is small. Insignificant. I want to do something. . .something big with my life."

Aaron was surprised at her display of honesty, but he also understood exactly where she was coming from. Hadn't he spent his whole life searching for the same things? Yearning to find a way to measure up to someone else's standard. There was one thing, though, that wasn't clear in his mind.

He longed to understand completely what was in her heart. "You say you want to make a difference to people, but how does finding the gold accomplish that?"

"I don't know." She fidgeted in her chair. "I read my aunt's journals after hearing her stories while she was still living. Finding the gold seemed like something tangible I could do to help my country. A silly idea, wasn't it—"

"No." He reached out and squeezed her hand, then pulled back at the intimate gesture. He had no right to bridge that gap between them. And he mustn't forget that their relationship was strictly business. "I'm sorry, but no. I don't think your actions were foolish. Not at all."

Miss Young's gaze rested on the hand that he had touched. "They were foolish, and you know it."

He folded his arms across his chest. "I think you're wrong."

"How can you understand how I feel?" She shook her head, and he didn't miss the tears that pooled in the corners of her eyes. "You've spent your life making this country a better place by bringing criminals to justice and stopping evil men from following through with their plans. You've made a difference."

Aaron winced. Her words might seem true to someone looking at his life from the outside, but to him, his actions had never been enough. At least not enough in the eyes of some.

"Have you ever thought about what God sees as success and failure?"

He stopped to consider her question, though it wasn't something he hadn't thought of before. He'd wondered the very same thing a dozen times. Did his hard work make up for his failures in God's eyes? It was a question to which he'd never found the answer.

"I'm not sure, but I doubt He sees things the way we do."

"Do you have an example?"

He wasn't following her train of thought. "An example?"

"From the Bible. I just thought of the widow who gave her last two coins to the offering. Man saw that as foolish, but Jesus held her up as an example because He saw how her motives were pure compared to the rich and their large offerings." She leaned forward, intent. "Jesus saw the motivations of the woman's heart, not how much she gave."

"You're right."

He'd spent his whole life worrying about the external results and far too little time examining his heart and what really mattered. The significance of what she said was sobering. An image of Jesus on the cross flashed before him. Christ was the one Man who'd never concerned Himself with what the world said or thought about Him. Instead, He'd spent His time on earth teaching the truth. And none of it had been what the people expected.

"What about the life of Jesus?" he offered. "To the world, don't you think His life was a failure? Not only did all His followers leave Him, the mob had Him crucified. But God saw success in Christ's sufferings on the cross even when everyone else heralded the event as a complete failure."

She nodded. "God knew the final outcome. And the fact that Jesus would conquer death. And that's why He looks at our hearts. It doesn't matter if we're parting the Red Sea or cleaning out a horse stall."

"What?"

She laughed for the first time all afternoon. "Or shall I say that whether we're chasing a pot of gold or a band of outlaws for a living, it isn't as important as whether or not we are following Him with our whole heart."

He matched her broad grin. "I'd say you're exactly right."

"I have the journal. I suppose you'd like to look at it."

"You wouldn't mind?"

She shook her head. "And besides, our conversation has given me an idea."

Chapter 13

Tara read through the last few verses of Romans chapter eight, then laid her Bible on the small table beside the rocking chair. She took a deep breath. From the front porch of the Carpenters' home, the air was fragrant with the sweet-smelling honeysuckle that grew along the side of the house. It had rained all night, bringing a renewed freshness to the morning temperature. For the first time in months, she felt surrounded by a warm blanket of contentment.

She ran her fingers across the leather-bound Bible her parents had given her on her sixteenth birthday. Verse thirty-seven in particular had stood out during her devotional. Paul had written that in all things we are more than conquerors through Him that loved us. The straightforward words were significant, especially in the light of her conversation with Mr. Jefferson yesterday.

Aaron Jefferson.

Just the thought of his name made her smile. The man continued to amaze her. Rarely had she met someone willing to discuss spiritual matters in such a forthright and honest way. And while he seemed to be grappling with his own uncertainties, his sincerity in discovering God's will for his life was evident. And his example of Christ's death as the ultimate victory out of perceived failure was key.

It was a situation that didn't make sense to the world. Life through death. Success through sacrifice. Storing up treasures in heaven and not on this world. But God's Word was clear. Only through Christ would she be able to find her worth. The reminder was freeing. And one she regretted not grasping sooner. When she'd made the decision to give her life to Christ, she had confessed He was Lord and had been baptized into His death in order to live a new life. It was time she started fully living that position as the daughter of the King. Time she stopped worrying about how the world saw her.

She knew now that she didn't have to find the gold to be worth something in God's eyes. Christ wanted her to daily live for Him, no matter what she was doing. He'd accepted the widow's small gift as if it were all of Solomon's wealth. And He would accept all her offerings, gifts, and talents as she used them for His glory. He just wanted her undivided heart.

A horse and rider galloping down the dusty lane toward the Carpenters' home caught her attention. Tara stood and put her hand above her eyes to shield the morning sun. The older couple hadn't mentioned that they were expecting company, though an occasional visit from the pastor or one of the other members of the church wasn't uncommon.

Or maybe Mr. Jefferson had decided to call on her this morning instead of waiting to meet again at the hotel restaurant with her aunt's journal as he'd suggested. The thought of seeing him now made her heart flutter, and she strained for a view of his ever-present Stetson.

The rider slowed as he approached the house, but this man wasn't wearing a black hat. She wrapped her hand around the porch's solid post. Faded denim jeans paired with a worn plaid shirt. . .

It wasn't Mr. Jefferson. It was Mr. Martin.

The man stopped in front of the house and slid off his chestnut mount. He tipped his hat, but his expression was far from friendly. "Good day, Miss Young."

"Mr. Martin." Tara clasped her hands together. "I wasn't expecting to see you today."

"I'm sure you weren't." The man's gaze scanned the front of the house while his hand rested on his sidearm. Either he had news regarding their quest for papers Mr. Schlosser had left behind, or the man was here on other business. From his somber expression, something made her fear the latter.

She attempted to keep a smile in her voice. "Is there something I can do for you today?"

He stopped at the bottom of the staircase. "Where are the Carpenters?"

"Inside, finishing their morning coffee." Tara felt her lip twitch. "Why—"

"Is anyone else around?"

Sampson had gone into town for supplies. Even the nearest tenant farmer was likely to be out of earshot.

"I can't say for sure."

He pulled a gun out of his holster and marched up the stairs. "I want you to take me to the Carpenters. Now."

Tara couldn't move. She stared at the gun and tried to breathe slowly so she wouldn't faint. What had the scripture said this morning?

"Who shall separate us from the love of Christ? Shall tribulation, or distress—"

"I believe I gave you an order, Miss Young."

Tara moved to open the front door, praying each step of the way. The verse continued to flow through her mind. *"Or persecution, or famine, or nakedness, or peril, or sword"*—or gun. . .*"Nay, in all these things we are more than conquerors through him that loved us."*

Through Christ.

"Where are they?" Mr. Martin's voice reverberated through the quiet house.

Repeating the verse in her mind, she led him through the kitchen and into the dining area with the large window overlooking the back pasture.

"Tara?" Mr. Carpenter's smile vanished as he moved to stand, but Mr. Martin shoved him back in the chair.

Tara sat across from the Carpenters as ordered. "I'm sorry. He has a gun."

The cozy dining room, where they had shared dozens of meals over the past few weeks, seemed suddenly cold. Even the warming summer sun couldn't take away the chill she felt. Mrs. Carpenter grabbed onto her husband's arm, her eyes widening in fear.

He set his coffee mug on the table and clasped his wife's hand. "What do you want?"

"Where's Mr. Jefferson?"

Tara tried to speak, but fear seeped through every pore of her body. Mr. Jefferson had been right. She seemed to have a knack for attracting trouble. Except this time, she had no idea what she'd just gotten herself into.

"I asked you a question, Miss Young." Mr. Martin smacked his hand against the table.

Tara jumped. "He's. . .I don't know. In town somewhere, I suppose. I haven't seen him today."

She squeezed her eyes shut for a moment. *"We are more than conquerors. We are more than conquerors."* She repeated the words over and over and tried to get a grip on the panic enveloping her.

Mr. Martin pointed the gun out the window as he paced the room and scanned the horizon.

"Neither death, nor life. . .nor height, nor death. . .shall be able to separate us from the love of God."

Scenes flashed through Tara's mind of times she'd longed to do something bold and heroic. This time, she knew she didn't have to prove anything. Inside her being, as a child of God, was a far greater source of strength than anything she could ever have on her own. Silently, she began to pray, until the fear faded into a dim image of what it had been before.

"Mr. Martin?"

He turned to face her. "What?"

She sat up straight and looked him in the eye. "I'm sorry our visit the other day upset you. I'm assuming that's what this is about?"

He took a step toward her and shook his head. "How can you act as if you have no idea? You came into my house with the pretense of finding a stack of letters that belonged to your aunt, when what you really wanted to do was to set a trap for me. I'm not stupid."

"Of course you're not." Tara worked to keep her voice calm. "This is about your wife, isn't it?"

"Matilda." For an instant his face softened. "Matilda Grace Martin. I loved her so much."

"I'm sure you did." Tara measured each word she spoke. "I saw her picture. She was beautiful."

The man let out a forced laugh. "She never thought so. She was thin and never had the energy to do very much. No one understood except for me. I told her that I didn't care if she couldn't work the farm like the other women. I would just work twice as hard."

Tara nodded slowly. "She was sick?"

He turned to her, obviously surprised by her comment. But Tara knew her words were not her own. And the peace she was experiencing at the moment could come only from God and not her own wisdom.

"I never should have brought her here." He rubbed his chin and walked back to the window. "I thought a change might help. A place of our own where she could breathe fresh air like the doctors back east told us. Nothing I did helped her. She just kept getting weaker and weaker until one day she couldn't even get out of bed."

Tara watched the slight changes in Mr. Martin as the sadness of losing his wife began to replace his focused anger. "I'm so sorry."

Mrs. Carpenter leaned forward. "But you said she went back east to stay with her mother."

Mr. Martin's jaw tensed. "You were just like the others. You never cared—"

"That's not true."

Tara held up her hand. "Where is your wife, Mr. Martin?"

He shook his head and began pacing along the window. "I won't go to jail. My land is the only thing I have left of her, and I can't leave."

"No one is asking you to leave, Mr. Martin."

"Don't lie to me." He waved the gun in the air, and the hard lines returned to his face. "That's why you came. I know it. You and Mr. Jefferson. Snooping around, asking questions. You came to take me to jail."

"No, we came looking for Mr. Schlosser. That's the truth. I'm terribly sorry about your wife. I know it must hurt so much to be away from her."

Mr. Martin's hand began to shake. "I killed her."

Tara felt a wave of shock rush through here. "You killed your wife?"

"I didn't mean to, but I killed her."

"She was sick, Mr. Martin, and she died. Isn't that right?"

"She was so sick. But I couldn't save her. I tried. I wanted to make her better, but one day didn't wake up." He pressed the side of the gun against his forehead and groaned. "I buried her on my land so I could be close to her. But I couldn't tell anyone. They would think that I was a bad man. That I belonged in jail like my father."

"No one thinks you killed your wife. It's going to be all right." Tara stood up slowly. "Give me the gun, Mr. Martin. We don't want anyone to accidentally get hurt. I know you don't want that. You're not that kind of man."

His lowered his hand, but he didn't let go of the gun. His gaze shifted toward the front door. "No. I can't. It's a trap."

His expression hardened as he turned to her, held up the gun, and pointed it at her heart.

Chapter 14

Aaron paced the hotel lobby, waiting for Miss Young's arrival. She was an hour late, and if his fears were correct, she'd just stood him up. Rotating the brim of his Stetson between his fingers, he stopped in front of the narrow plate of glass that overlooked the street. The boardwalk was busy with morning shoppers, but there was no sign of the impulsive young woman with auburn hair who'd stepped into his life and managed to turn it upside down.

One thing in particular had him worried. What if she had found something in her aunt's journal after their discussion and decided to proceed with the search on her own? The very idea made his stomach turn. Knowing Miss Young, she'd end up in yet another fix. And this time, he might not be there to save her.

He pulled his watch from his trouser pocket and opened the case to check the time once more. She was now an hour and five minutes late.

"Constantly checking the time rarely makes it pass any faster, Mr. Jefferson."

Aaron spun around on the heels of his boots. Mrs. Meddler, the hotel owner's wife, stood there, observing him with her typical inquisitive gaze. Far from attractive, with her narrow face and too-thin nose, the woman's one pleasant feature was her jovial personality, but even that quality, he'd discovered at their first meeting, was overbearing at times.

"Is she late?" Mrs. Meddler folded her hands across her well-endowed form and smiled.

He scratched the back of his head. "Who?"

"Miss Young, of course."

It would seem that nothing got past the woman. Aaron cleared his throat. "I. . .well. . .yes, but we were only meeting for business."

Mrs. Meddler nodded, the grin never leaving her face. "I'm sure from what I witnessed yesterday in the restaurant that you are correct. Strictly business. Of course, that doesn't explain the slight blush that stained her face every time you looked at her, or the way you stuttered whenever she asked you a question."

Aaron's eyes widened at the unsolicited observation. The woman seemed to be everywhere. Perhaps she should be the one working for the government. He was obviously losing his touch.

He closed his eyes for a moment and struggled to gain back his composure. "Mrs. Meddler—"

"It's all right to admit it." Her eyes held a hint of amusement.

"Admit what?" If it was possible, the woman exasperated him more than Miss Young did. He'd never been one to avoid the issue at hand. He wanted the facts presented up front, but she had him running in circles like a decapitated rooster in a barnyard.

"Admit that you're attracted to her." Mrs. Meddler waved her finger at him. "That perhaps you even have feelings for her. Miss Young is a lovely young woman, with a heart for God and others. You couldn't do any better."

He slapped his hat against his trouser leg and pressed his lips together before speaking. "You've forgotten one small detail, Mrs. Meddler. I don't even know her. Every time I've seen her has been surrounded by mayhem and disaster. Not exactly the environment for courtship. . .if that was what I was looking for, which I'm not."

"Oh? I didn't hear any gunshots or see any signs of trouble in the restaurant yesterday while the two of you were here." Mrs. Meddler let out a soft sigh and shook her head. "No, on the contrary, the atmosphere was quite ideal. But perhaps my husband is correct when he tells me that I read far too many dime novels and have my head in the clouds, but I can tell love when I see it—"

"Love?" Aaron coughed. Now her comments had crossed the line from inquisitive to intrusive.

He bit down on his tongue so he wouldn't say something foolish. He didn't have feelings for the young woman, let alone feelings of love. Why, the very idea was preposterous. The woman got herself into trouble every time she turned around. She needed a bodyguard, not a husband, because she was impulsive, rash, and reckless.

No. He had no intentions of falling for Miss Young, or even discussing her for that matter.

Mrs. Meddler stepped forward. Apparently she wasn't finished. "I did have to laugh the day I saw her wearing your black Stetson on her head as she strode down the boardwalk. It was yours, wasn't it?"

"My Stetson?" He glanced at his hat and frowned.

What was the woman referring to now? His mind went back to the day they'd been shot at outside the post office. He'd lost his hat, and Miss Young had been the one to return it, but he couldn't imagine her wearing it. Mrs. Meddler was obviously incorrect. Too many of those made-up tales not only had her head in the clouds, they'd also clouded her eyesight.

He shook his head. He would never figure out the reason Miss Young would have been wearing his Stetson, so there was no use trying. "Mrs. Meddler, I must protest. I am simply meeting Miss Young to discuss business relating to my work for the government. She has some information for me. . ."

Aaron sucked in a deep breath. Splendid. Not only was he coming close to losing his temper, he was giving away too much information, as well.

Because the woman's right.

She's right? He shoved the thought aside. The woman was certainly not correct in her assessment. He was going to go straight to the Carpenter farm to find Miss Young so he could finish his business and leave town. And the sooner he left the better.

He took a step toward the door. "Mrs. Meddler, if you will excuse me, I need to go now."

She smiled again as he turned to leave. "Please give my regards to Miss Young and have her stop by for tea at her earliest convenience. I do so enjoy her company."

Aaron gave her a curt nod, then strode down the boardwalk toward the livery. He normally wasn't one to get frustrated so easily, but that woman was intent on putting ideas in his head. Ideas that he had no time for analyzing.

Because it's the truth and you know it.

He grunted and shoved his hat onto his head. There was no way around it. He had to concede defeat. As much as he longed to admit that Mrs. Meddler was only an interfering busybody with her pointed words and attempts at matchmaking, his heart knew that she was at least partially correct. Love might be too strong a word, but what was the use denying the truth? Miss Tara Young had waltzed into his life like an unexpected afternoon rain shower and left everything a bit brighter. He couldn't deny it. Despite the trouble that seemed to follow wherever she went, she'd managed to work her way right into the middle of his heart.

Swiftly saddling his stallion at the livery, he made his way toward the Carpenter farmhouse, his thoughts in a muddled jumble. Why was it, when dealing with a woman—when dealing with Miss Young—logic and rational thinking seemed to vanish? He had no idea what he was going to say to her, or even if he should say something to her. He had no time for courting even if his heart was intent on winning this round.

As he approached the Carpenters' house, he could already see the subtle changes that had transformed the double-story dwelling. The flower beds in the front had been trimmed and weeded, and the front porch now sported a brand-new coat of white paint. He was quite certain that the improvements had all been made under the watchful eye of Miss Young.

A horse was tethered beside the porch, and if he wasn't mistaken, it didn't belong to the Carpenters. An uneasy feeling tried to surface, but he pushed aside the worrisome thought. Just because Miss Young had a knack for trouble didn't mean there was anything wrong this morning. The Carpenters simply had a visitor.

Dismounting from his stallion, he started up the front porch steps, then stopped. After years of being a lawman he couldn't ignore the warning signs. Surely his overcautious feelings were nothing more than an acknowledgement of the fact that Miss Young was involved. That alone should make him more cautious. But the fact remained. Something wasn't right. A visitor would mean tea and coffee in the front parlor, or perhaps on the front porch, and what he saw through the sitting room windows confirmed that the area was empty.

Aaron made his way along the front porch. Even if he was wrong, erring on the side of caution had rarely left him off target. He moved silently toward the side of the house. The scent of honeysuckle filled his senses, and he struggled not to sneeze. He held his breath until the unsettled feeling passed, then stepped up alongside the dining room.

A man stood with his back to the window. . .and he held a gun. A stab of fear pierced through Aaron's gut. The balding man turned his head slightly, giving Aaron a clear view of the man's profile.

James Martin.

Making sure he stayed as close to the house as possible, Aaron pushed aside the panic and took another side step to confirm who else was in the room. Miss Young stood across from the gunman. He caught her gaze through the window. He saw the subtle shake of her head and frowned. He wasn't sure what she meant, but there was no way he wasn't getting involved in the situation. It was too late for that. Especially when the person Mr. Martin was holding the gun on the woman he loved.

Loved?

Aaron grunted. Mrs. Meddler had apparently been right on all accounts. He, with all his strong notions of finishing his job without any further distractions, had fallen in love with Miss Young. But before he let plans of courting fill his mind, he needed a plan. He was going to have to be careful, for one false move and he was certain Mr. Martin was unstable enough that he would pull the trigger. And Miss Young certainly wasn't skilled enough in the art of negotiation so that she could remedy the situation on her own.

But if anything happened to her. . .

Aaron moved swiftly toward the back of the house and, feeling completely out of control for the first time in his life, he began to pray.

⌘

Tara's heart pounded at the sight of Mr. Jefferson. Thankfully, Mr. Martin hadn't seemed to have noticed her attempts to convey a message. All she needed was Mr. Jefferson to burst his way into the room and spook Mr. Martin. She was quite certain that with one false move, Mr. Martin would fire his pistol. And it was aimed straight at her.

Mr. Martin had spent the past hour talking about his wife, her sickness, and how no one had seemed to care about their situation. Knowing many of the good people of Browning City, Tara was quite certain that wasn't true, but it was clearly his interpretation of the situation. The Carpenters had said little during the ordeal, which was best. There was no use aggravating the man further.

Tara glanced again at the window, but Mr. Jefferson had disappeared. Undoubtedly, he'd assumed that she had stood him up and had come after her to make sure she didn't further pursue the gold without him. He had nothing to worry about. With a gun pointed at her for the past hour, she wasn't going anywhere.

She was also quite certain that he was, right now, coming up with a plan to rescue her and the Carpenters. With a gun in Mr. Martin's hand, though, there was little chance that such an action could succeed without someone getting hurt. It was time to put an end to this.

Sending up another prayer, she stood slowly, her gaze never leaving her captor's. "I can't change the past, Mr. Martin, but I can help you change the future."

❧

Aaron opened the back door and tried to remember the layout of the rectangular farmhouse. His options were limited. The sitting room and the Carpenters' bedroom were in the front of the house, while the kitchen and dining area made up the back half. A partial wall separated the dining area from the kitchen, giving him cover until he had to make his presence known. But from experience he knew the setup wouldn't allow a surprise attack.

Setting his Stetson on the counter, he crouched on the wooden floor planks and prayed for an answer. He needed a distraction, but what? With Mr. Martin holding the gun less than six feet from Miss Young, he couldn't take a chance of startling the man. Even if he had bad aim, the chances were still too great that he would hit her.

He needed control of the situation. But that was the one thing he didn't have. And he didn't foresee any changes right away. He heard voices in the next room. Miss Young's soft, soothing voice and Mr. Martin's raspy responses.

He was out of options.

What do I do, God?

Aaron waited for a response, an idea, anything that would get her and the Carpenters out. . .alive. His brow began to sweat. His stomach churned. He was used to pushing his way in and taking charge of a situation, not waiting around for the situation to diffuse on its own. Or in this case, explode from the barrel of a gun.

That was the option he couldn't handle. He couldn't stand by and do nothing, yet rushing in would only bring disaster.

Aaron cried out again to God. *I need your help, Lord. I need You. What do I do?*

The question struck him. He balanced on the heels of his boots and studied a knot in the grain on the floor. Its texture was rough and jagged. Like the edges of his heart. When was the last time he'd stopped and asked God for guidance? When was the last time he hadn't simply forged ahead on his own and instead sat quietly listening for his Savior's answer? He'd been so wrapped up in proving himself and trying to live up to his name that he'd failed to let his relationship with Christ guide him.

Miss Young's question at the restaurant struck him again. *"Have you ever thought about what God sees as success and failure?"*

He'd wanted success, and had worked hard at it until the desire permeated every aspect of his life. He knew there was nothing wrong with his chosen profession, except that he'd put it above his relationship with Christ. The fact that Jesus Himself had given up success in order to bring the world salvation convicted him. Christ had worked to please only one person in life. His heavenly Father. Even to the point of taking on the sins of the world and allowing Himself to be sacrificed for the sake of a lost world.

Everything led back to the cross, and what his Savior had done for him.

Oh Lord, I've wandered so far from Your presence in search of my own success and earthly treasures. Help me to find You again.

"Mr. Jefferson? You can come in here now."

Aaron froze. Miss Young's voice sounded shaky as she called from the other room. He hesitated. What if it was a trap, and Mr. Martin was forcing her to call him into the room?

"Really, everything's all right now." She stepped into the kitchen with the gun in her hand pointing toward the floor.

He walked toward her. "How'd you know I was here? And the gun. . ."

Her voice was shaky and her face pale, but the relief in her eyes was clear. "I knew you'd come to my rescue, but there weren't many options in this situation. I also knew that I was the one who was going to have to talk Mr. Martin into giving me the gun. Somehow, God gave me the words to say."

She dropped the weapon into his hand and leaned against the counter. He wrapped his arms around her waist, afraid she might collapse. Something told him, though, that she was stronger than he'd ever imagined.

The Carpenters entered the kitchen behind her. Mr. Carpenter's hand rested possessively around his wife's shoulder.

Aaron held Miss Young steady as he addressed the older couple. "Are you both all right?"

"Yes." Mr. Carpenter shook Aaron's free hand. "But we'd be obliged if you would take Mr. Martin in to the sheriff. If it hadn't been for Tara and her well-spoken words, well, I don't know what would have happened."

Miss Young shook her head. "Today, they were God's words. Never mine."

"Then God was speaking mighty powerfully. You saved our lives." He nodded his head in thanks. "I'm going to take the missus here to go sit down. It was quite a scare for us both."

As the Carpenters left the room, Aaron glanced at Mr. Martin. He sat in a chair in the corner of the room, a glazed expression on his face. The man wasn't going anywhere for the moment.

Aaron turned back to Miss Young. A rosy blush had returned to her cheeks, and he wasn't certain if it was from the relief that the situation was over or from his nearness. He hoped it was because she shared the same feelings toward him he felt toward her.

"Mr. Jefferson—"

He pushed back an errant curl that hung across her cheek. "I think after all we've been through together, it's time you called me by my first name. Do you mind?"

"Not at all. . .Aaron."

He liked the sound of her voice when she said his name. And liked the feel of her in his arms.

"And please, call me Tara."

He nodded. There was so much he wanted to tell her, but he was going to first have to get Mr. Martin to the sheriff's office and give her a chance to catch her breath after the ordeal.

"There's one other thing you might want to know." Tara looked up at him, her eyes wide with anticipation. "While we were talking, Mr. Martin showed me letters he'd found belonging to Mr. Schlosser. They were from my aunt."

Chapter 15

Tara felt her knees tremble, but this time it wasn't from fear. She grabbed onto the counter to steady herself. Mr. Jefferson—Aaron's—gaze hadn't left her face, and there was something in his eyes she couldn't ignore. From their first few encounters, she'd noted his interest in her despite their opposing goals, but there was something different lurking in the depths of his eyes today. Something deeper and more intense.

Could it be true that his feelings went further than mere attraction?

He fumbled with his hat between his hands. "I need to take Mr. Martin into town. Are you going to be all right?"

She nodded, not sure if she could speak anymore. "I. . .yes. I'll be fine."

He raised his hand toward her face as if he was going to stroke her cheek, then pulled his arm down. "I'd best be going."

"Are you coming back?" She followed him into the dining area, conscious of the desperation in her voice, but unable to control it.

"Give me time to get him to the sheriff's office, and I'll return." He rested his Stetson on his head. "We can look over the letters together."

From the Carpenters' front porch, she watched as he escorted Mr. Martin along the edge of the cornfield until they disappeared into the hazy horizon. She swallowed her disappointment. Part of her had longed for Aaron to stay and pull her back into his arms where she'd felt safe. To tell her how relieved he was she hadn't been hurt.

Instead he'd promised to return. . .to see the letters.

Tara leaned against the wooden banister and tugged on the edge of her jacket. The endless fields of corn and apple orchards that had grown tiresome during the journey to Iowa and the first weeks that followed seemed to have taken on a richer hue. She took in a deep breath of the fresh air that brought with it the fragrance of honeysuckle and the rich scent of the fertile earth that made this land a farmer's dream. A recent letter from her parents had urged her to return home to the ease of city life, but thoughts of what she had in Boston were coming fewer and further between. Just as Aaron had somehow stolen a corner of her heart, the vast state of Iowa had managed to do the same thing.

She could imagine staying. . .with him.

Tara shook her head and crossed the wide porch toward the front door.

Truth was, it didn't matter what the handsome lawman felt toward her. She might have noted a change in his expression, but something else, far more important, had just changed in her own life.

For the first time, she'd managed to completely trust in God and had faced her fears. The result had been greater than finding a stash of gold. What she'd experienced might not have had as far-reaching consequences as her aunt spying for the North or her parents' involvement with the Underground Railroad, but nevertheless, her own actions had made a difference in the lives of three other people. Most importantly, she was struck with God's faithfulness in the situation. Her words to Mr. Martin had not come from her own wisdom and understanding. God had given her the grace and courage she had needed for the moment.

"Tara?"

She stepped inside the house where the Carpenters sat side by side on the sofa. Mr. Carpenter's arm was wrapped protectively around his wife, whose face was still paler than a winter's snowfall.

Tara paused in the entryway, her hands clasped tightly in front of her. She was worried. While she knew the couple to be resilient, such an ordeal, especially at their age, couldn't be good for their well-being. "Are you both all right?"

Mr. Carpenter held his gold watch between the fingers of his free hand and continued to click the cover open and shut. "Only time I've been this scared is when Sam Barnett burst into our Sunday night prayer meeting with a rifle in his hands and whiskey on his breath. Poor Virginia. I thought the woman was going to faint over her husband's scandalous behavior. Turned out, all he wanted was supper on the table. A few too many drinks had wrecked his thinkin'."

Mrs. Carpenter frowned and nudged her husband with her elbow. "Gossip aside, we need to thank the good Lord it's over."

"You're right." Tara sat across from them on a worn chair. And at least no one had been shot. . .or fainted during today's arduous situation. Including herself. "Mr. Jefferson is taking Mr. Martin to the sheriff's office. I thought I'd make you both a cup of tea if you'd like. It might help you to relax."

"That would be wonderful, dear." Mrs. Carpenter leaned into her husband's shoulder. "Looks to me as if today turned out to be a bit more exciting than collecting the eggs, wouldn't you think?"

Tara placed her hand against her chest and let out a low chuckle, thankful for the lighter turn of the conversation. "I've decided that if I end up spending the rest of my life collecting eggs and milking cows, that will be thrill enough for me."

Color began to come back into the older woman's face. "Sometimes being heroic in God's eyes simply means listening quietly and following His voice. Which is precisely what I saw you do with Mr. Martin."

Tara shrugged a shoulder. "I don't feel heroic by any means, but I can't help but be reminded of the passage I read last night when God appeared to Elijah. The prophet waited through the violent wind, earthquakes, and even a fire to find God, yet He wasn't in any of those."

Mr. Carpenter nodded. "Instead He was in the gentle whisper many of us miss."

"I've always believed that I had to do something big to serve God." Pieces of the puzzle Tara had been struggling with for weeks began to come together. "I don't know if I feel heroic, but I did hear God's quiet whisper today."

Mrs. Carpenter reached out to squeeze Tara's hand. "Then you've learned a wise lesson that many fail to ever realize."

Tara stood to start toward the kitchen, her thoughts still focused on their discussion. "I'll go and make some tea now."

"Tara?"

She turned back to face Mrs. Carpenter. "Yes?"

"Thank you for what you did today."

Aaron approached the Carpenters' farm, hopeful that his entire life was about to change. No longer did he care what the letters contained. True, he would soon find out whether Miss Young—Tara's—information regarding the gold would pan out or not, but his mind was focused on other things. He smiled at the thought of her name. Tara. The name was beautiful, but not nearly as beautiful as the woman who wore it. For the first time in months, he'd found something worthwhile to pursue. Something far greater than the gold that he had chased after for so long.

Tara sat on the front porch, engrossed in something.

The letters.

His heart plummeted for an instant. What if her involvement with him reached no further than the gold? He'd know soon enough. Her face lit up when she saw him, bringing with it a sigh of relief on his part. No, he couldn't be wrong. He'd seen the way she looked at him. It wasn't simply about the gold.

Aaron dismounted from his horse, tethered the reins, then took the porch stairs two at a time. "Hi."

"Hi." She looked up at him and smiled.

He balanced his Stetson on one of the porch posts. Color once again tinged her cheeks. The fear that had edged her eyes had disappeared, leaving them bright and hopeful. She looked beautiful.

He shoved his hands into his pockets and rocked back on his heels. "You'll be glad to know that Mr. Martin is behind bars and will no doubt go to trial at some point."

"I feel sorry for the man." His assurances hadn't brought about the continued smile he expected from her. "I think he's overcome by the loss of his wife. He must have loved her so much. It's heartbreaking, really."

"True." Aaron sat down beside her on one of the rocking chairs. "But the fact remains that we can't take a chance that he does something like that again and shoots someone."

"I suppose you're right." She held up the stack of letters. "I read through them."

"And. . ."

No matter how hard his pulse pounded at the sight of her, or how much her presence distracted him, he still was anxious to find out the truth.

Tara flipped through the pages. "I'm certain that all four letters were penned by my aunt, and they weren't sent through the mail. They were hand delivered by a private source. And as alluded to in her journal, Mr. Schlosser was one of my aunt's trusted contacts."

He scooted closer to her. "Do the letters talk about the gold?"

"Yes, and I think I've read enough of my aunt's journal to put most of it together. But it's not at all what I expected."

"Really?" Aaron tried to read her expression, but he couldn't. Disappointment? Loss? Relief?

He stared at the letters in her hands. They were the last link he had to the gold, and if they didn't come through with a new lead, he was heading back to Washington to report to his superiors. His last trip back to the capitol if things went his way today.

She handed him the first page from the short stack of communication. "In early 1865, Mr. Schlosser was fighting against the South in Virginia. One of the prisoners started bragging about his part in stealing a large amount of gold from the US Army. Whatever the man said apparently was enough to convince Mr. Schlosser that he was telling the truth about the stolen cache." She pointed to the bottom of the letter he held. "When my aunt found out about the gold from Mr. Schlosser, she believed that the money would aid the North in the war and decided to take it upon herself to find it."

"She must have been quite a woman. She was working for her country during a dangerous time." He scanned through the flowery-written letter before catching Tara's gaze. "So what happened to the gold?"

"Following Mr. Schlosser's information, she tracked the stolen cache to a farm outside Browning City, but when she got there it was too late."

"Too late? What do you mean?"

She offered him the second letter. "The details are scant at this point. All I can figure out is that someone got wind of the fact that she was looking for the gold. In any case, when she arrived at the farmhouse, three men, dressed in black, were in the process of removing the gold from the premises. She hid in a hayloft, then tried to follow, but ended up losing them. She wasn't ever able to pick up their trail again. She even told the local authorities, but they never came up with a solid lead to find the men, either. It was as if the gold vanished into thin air."

"Wow." Aaron slapped the letters against his leg.

Her lips curled into a solemn frown. "It's another dead end, Aaron."

This time, he didn't miss the disappointment in her eyes. He longed to reach out and hold her hands. To pull her into his arms and assure her that he didn't care if she was a spy, a farmhand, or the president of the United States, for that matter. To him, she was everything he'd ever dreamed of in a woman. . .in a wife.

But the timing wasn't right yet.

Instead, he gripped the armrests of the rocker instead. "Are you disappointed?"

"To be honest?" She looked up at him from beneath her long, dark lashes. "I don't think I care about the gold anymore."

"I thought you had your heart set on finding it."

"I did. At one time, anyway." She brushed a stray lock of hair away from her face. "In reading these letters, I had to wonder why my aunt never mentioned any of the details of her coming to Browning City and searching for the gold in her journal."

"Maybe she stopped writing for a while."

"Maybe, but what really surprised me was her last letter." She ran her hand across one of the worn pages, then outlined her aunt's signature with the tip of her finger. "She expressed feelings that her role as a courier wasn't making an impact in the outcome of the war. That was why she wanted to find the gold." Her eyes darkened. "I can't understand how she could ever feel that way. She was one of the heroes of the war in my eyes."

"She was a hero." Aaron searched for an answer that didn't sound pat. "Maybe, in her mind, she felt that passing information wasn't important enough, and she wanted to do something bigger."

Tara laughed, but he didn't miss the frustration behind the gesture. "If you're right, then what about me? I've spent my whole life trying to live up to her. And she didn't think that what she did was enough?"

He shook his head. "You don't have to pass messages behind enemy lines or find a missing cache of gold to be of value."

"I know." For the first time since his arrival, her face brightened into a smile. "The truth is, while I may not have found what I was after, I have found something far more priceless. I've finally been able to realize that I don't have to prove myself to be of value. I just need to serve God with my whole heart. Nothing more is required of me. Big or small, I just need to do it for Him."

Aaron let out a low whistle. "You're not the only one who needs to confess, then. I've lived my life seeking the wrong things. Did I ever tell you what my whole name is?"

Tara shook her head.

"Aaron Thomas Jefferson. My parents named me after one of their heroes, President Jefferson."

She arched her brow. "A big name to live up to."

"And in turn, I've spent every moment working to live up to my family's expectations. I've done the same things spiritually, as well, in trying to work for my salvation. It struck me when we talked about what Christ did on the cross that I don't have to do that. The cost has already been paid. I've spent far too long trying to show that I'm someone—something I never needed to do. Aren't we all already someone in God's eyes just being His creation made in His image?"

"You'd think that it would be an easy lesson to learn, wouldn't it?"

Aaron set the letters he held on the small table beside him and moved to stand by the porch railing. "There is another thing I've realized these past few days, as well."

❦

Tara caught that same look in his eyes that made her heart stand still and the rest of her want to swoon. She rose to join him. "What is that?"

"I thought I should wait until we knew each other longer, but I'm not going to." He reached out to grasp her hands, then pulled them toward his chest. "I've realized that I don't want to spend the rest of my life without you, Tara. I want you to marry me."

"Marry you? I. . ." For a moment, she was lost in his gaze and couldn't speak. So much had changed since she'd left Boston. She'd believed that coming to Iowa would strengthen her worth. Instead, she'd found that the strength she'd longed to find was already within her—through Christ.

And now Aaron wanted to marry her!

He moved away from her. "I'm sorry. I have spoken too soon and out of turn. I know we haven't known each other long, but—"

"No. It's not that at all." She took a step forward into his arms. "Have you ever had a dream, and when it came true, you couldn't believe it was actually happening?"

He held her hands and rubbed the backs of her fingers with his thumbs. "I guess I've felt that way with you since the day we met. I had a hard time believing you were real."

"What do you mean?"

He lowered his face until she could feel his breath tickling her cheek. "I've spent my life waiting for God to send me someone who would make my life complete. Once I found you. . .well, it's sufficient to say that I don't ever want to lose you."

His kiss left her breathless. For once, something out of her dreams measured up in real life. After a lingering moment, he pulled away and ran his thumb down her cheek.

"You're beautiful."

"I never answered your question." She laughed as he matched her smile.

"Will you?"

"Yes. Of course I'll marry you." Her gaze swept across the picturesque landscape surrounding the farmhouse that had come to feel like home. "Does that mean I get to live in Iowa the rest of my life?"

"Not necessarily. I'll move to Boston if it means being with you."

She shook her head and wrapped her arms around his neck. "I might be a city girl, but if you have your heart set on a farm in Iowa, then I don't want to be any other place."

There was no denying the joy in his expression. "So you're becoming a country girl?"

She grabbed his hat from the post beside her and shoved it on top of her bonnet. "What do you think?"

"Now all you need is a pair of denim overalls." Laughing, he pulled down the brim until it covered her eyes. "I have to ask you one thing, or it's going to nag at me forever."

She pushed the hat back out of her face. "What's that?"

"Mrs. Meddler said she saw you wearing my Stetson one afternoon—"

"What?" Tara covered her mouth and giggled. "She actually saw me?"

"That's what she said, but you're always so impeccably dressed, I simply couldn't think of a reason for you to be walking down Main Street wearing my hat."

Tara eyed him from beneath the wide brim. "I must confess. In all the confusion during the shootout, I picked your hat up off the floor and, since I was crawling, I set it on my head for safekeeping. Then I completely forgot what I had done until I was greeted along the boardwalk with a few odd looks."

"I imagine you looked rather stunning. Like right now." Aaron hung the Stetson back on the post rail before bending over and brushing her lips gently with his. "What are your parents going to say about me?"

Tara felt her stomach tense, but she was determined not to worry about a reaction from them that had yet to take place. "They weren't happy about my excursion to Iowa, as they call it. My mother especially. She has a heart of gold but can be rather difficult at times. They believe I'm simply going through a phase and expect me to come running home to the ease of city life after a few weeks on the farm."

He pulled her toward him and nodded. "So now that I've managed to convince you to marry this besotted lawman, I'm going to have to try my hand at convincing your parents?"

"Exactly."

Chapter 16

I simply won't allow you to marry him, Tara Rachel Young. There is nothing more to discuss." Tara's mother leaned forward in the walnut-framed settee that had recently been reupholstered and took a nibble of chocolate-dipped shortbread.

Tara sat across from her in the parlor of her parents' fashionable Boston residence and bit her lip. Somewhere in the Bible there was a verse on being slow to speak and slow to anger. If ever there had been a time to heed such advice, it was now.

She ran her hand across the polished armrest. She'd always loved the room with its ruby colored walls, fringed swag window coverings, and ornate furniture. But today even the whatnot cabinet that displayed her mother's china, daguerreotypes, and prized Staffordshire dogs and figurines seemed overdone and made her long for the simplicity of the farm.

She watched her mother calmly pour a cup of tea as if they were discussing this year's weather or what play was currently running at the Boston Theatre. Two topics about which Tara cared nothing at the moment. Smoothing down the fabric of her violet chambray gauze dress, she didn't miss the irony of how completely unfit the new gown would be on the farm. She was certain her mother had meant the gesture as a peace offering, but to Tara it had become a reminder of what she missed. Gathering the eggs in the morning while watching the sun make its daily appearance, making jam for the tenants' wives, or knitting on the front porch while chatting about what was happening in town. She missed the Carpenters, Sampson, Mrs. Meddler, and especially she missed Aaron.

"Have a cup of tea." Her mother waved her hand at the table laden not only with the hot drink, cream, and sugar, but a large assortment of sandwiches, cakes, and scones, as well.

Tara eyed the tempting array placed artistically on the doily-lined platter. "Father and Aaron haven't arrived yet."

Her heart trembled as she spoke Aaron's name. With Mrs. Meddler's oldest daughter agreeing to take over her employment at the Carpenters', Tara had arrived home two weeks ago, believing that the only way to share the news of her engagement was in person. After setting a wedding date for late November, Aaron had promised to join her as soon as he completed his work for the government. Now all that was left to do was convince her parents, her mother in particular, that marrying Aaron was the right thing to do.

"They're late, and the tea is getting cold." Her mother reached out a pudgy hand and poured a second cup from the Chinese porcelain pot that had belonged to her great-grandmother. That one item was worth more than all the Carpenters' serving dishes put together.

Tara took the still-steamy drink that perched on the edge of the side table and managed a sip. Her mother believed in tea at four and wanted no excuses for tardiness. But there was more to today's bad-temperedness than simply a delayed guest. Her mother's testy moods were getting more and more difficult to handle, and Tara knew the source to be her unexpected engagement to a man her parents had never met.

Tara breathed in the orange fragrance of the tea and frowned. "So that's it? Subject closed?"

Her mother added a scone topped with Devonshire cream to her plate. "You can't be serious about marrying a man from Iowa of all places—"

"He's not from Iowa." Tara leaned forward. "He's from Philadelphia, he works for the government, and—"

"—he wants to run a farm. I know." Her mother settled back into the sofa. "Tara, please. How many times do I have to tell you that the idea is absolutely ridiculous? It's one thing to be a guest on a farm for a few weeks and perhaps help with some of the simple tasks, but running a farm is an entirely different matter."

Tara set down her teacup, afraid she might throw it across the room. She was tired of all the questions and nagging she'd endured since her return home. She needed her mother to understand that she had fallen in love with Aaron Jefferson, and such a sentiment was not a passing phase.

She glanced at the carved clock that hung on the wall. Her father and Aaron were thirty minutes late. Tardiness was an intolerable offense to her mother, despite the fact that one had little control over trains and other public sources of transportation. Still, Tara needed Aaron to arrive before things progressed from a one-sided battle of words to something more lethal where she said something she'd regret.

Determined to keep her mouth shut, she took a bite of a cucumber basil sandwich. The savory hors d'oeuvre the cook made used to be her favorite, but today the dainty snack tasted as dry as a pile of hay. No doubt her father was giving Aaron a similar lecture right now on why his daughter, who had been educated to live among Boston's society, would never adjust to life on a farm.

How to prove her parents were wrong was the question.

Tara couldn't help but try again. "Mother, all I ask is that before you pass judgment on someone you've never met, please just wait until you meet Aaron. I don't want to argue with you, but I came to love Iowa. And it's true that farming is not for everyone, but it's for us. For Aaron and me."

Her mother patted the back of her coiffed hair that had been tastefully dyed to cover the gray she would never admit existed. "I raised you to marry someone in a position of influence and authority. This trip to Iowa was supposed to be a short stint to show you a bit of the world and prepare you to settle down." Her mother's teacup clanked inside the saucer as she placed it on the side table. Her eyes, rimmed in black kohl, widened in anger. "But instead you agreed to marry, without our permission, the first ruffian who shows the least bit of interest in you."

Tara scrunched up her cloth napkin between her fingers. It was no use. She would never convince her mother that marrying Aaron was what was best for her life. She'd have to wait until he arrived and pray that he could somehow charm his way into her mother's heart the same way he'd won her over.

The door in the front hall opened, and Tara felt her stomach clench. She had no plans to disrespect her parents, but she was nineteen and certainly old enough to make her own decisions. Why, she was practically an old maid!

A moment later, Aaron stood in the doorway. It had seemed like forever since she'd seen him, but his presence in the room only made her more certain of her decision.

His eyes brightened at the sight of her, and he offered her a broad smile. "Tara. It's so good to see you—"

"You all are late." Her mother stood and pushed her skirts behind her. "Come and sit down before your tea turns stone cold."

Her father set his hat on the back of a chair. "Darling, I want to first introduce you to Mr. Aaron Jefferson from Philadelphia."

Tara rose slowly to stand beside her mother, wishing she could have a moment alone with Aaron before facing her parents. His face was freshly shaved and as handsome as ever. Black hair lay curled against his collar, and his white shirt showed off his tanned skin. After a moment, she managed to tear her gaze from Aaron to look at her father who was smiling as he rubbed the edges of his mustache. Her gaze went back to Aaron. He was smiling, as well. Something had obviously transpired between the two men on the route from the train station to the house.

Aaron stepped up to greet her mother. "Mrs. Young. I'm pleased to finally make your acquaintance."

"Likewise, Mr. Jefferson." Her mother's frown had yet to vanish. "I've heard so many things about you."

"All good, I hope." Aaron laughed. "And I must say, if I didn't know better, I would have thought the two of you were sisters, Mrs. Young."

From her mother's expression, Aaron's words did little to ease the tension in the room.

Her mother sat back down. "Flattery and smooth talk should be left at the door, Mr. Jefferson. Neither are welcome in this house."

"Mother." Tara's eyes widened as the four of them sat down in silence. The rhythmic ticking of the clock became the only sound piercing the heavy mood that circulated though the room.

⌘

Aaron stole a glance at Tara perched beside him on the edge of the sofa. Her expression had paled at her mother's comment, but he didn't miss the determination in her eyes. Somehow, he'd forgotten how beautiful she was. Her hair was swept up under a new hat with purple flowers on top and velvet ribbons hanging down the back. Her matching dress was just as stunning. But that's not what he had missed. He'd missed her laugh, her conversation, and the way she always managed to make him smile. He longed for a moment of privacy to take her into his arms and tell her how much he loved her.

With her mother's piercing gaze fixed on him, he instead studied the painted wall that was covered with framed floral drawings and struggled with how best to approach the woman. While Mr. Young had seemed agreeable with the proposed wedding, he had told Aaron quite plainly that he was going to have to find a way to charm his wife if she was ever to agree to the marriage. The older man had given him two hints. Flowers and politics.

Aaron cleared his throat and managed a smile. "I understand you have a passion for gardening, Mrs. Young."

"I do, in fact." Mrs. Young's words were clipped as she stirred her tea. "Azaleas, roses, violets, morning glories, orchids. . ."

Aaron clasped his hands together in front of him and leaned forward. "I don't think I ever mentioned this to Tara, but my uncle was an orchid hunter. He was sent to South America to find a particular rare species for a wealthy Englishman."

Mrs. Young quirked an eyebrow. "Really?"

"Yes, and let me tell you, such a job was not for the faint of heart." He waved his arms in an exaggerated gesture. "When my uncle was twenty years old, the demand by the wealthy for orchids had grown to such frenzy that it was necessary for those wishing to acquire different varieties of the rare flower to send well-chosen gardeners and other such qualified men on a remote quest to find them. To many, money was no object, so they offered a huge reward to those who would risk their lives in search of a new breed of orchid."

He allowed the intensity in his voice to grow. "Their travels took them around the world to places like the Far East and South America, and through it all they had to deal with the ever-present dangers of disease, venomous snakes, wild animals, and savages."

"Savages?" Mrs. Young jumped back.

"Oh yes, and the competition was fierce. These men were often corrupt and had no qualms about stooping to spying, an assortment of unlawful activities. . . and even murder."

Tara stifled a giggle beside him, while Mrs. Young sat speechless. Even Mr. Young seemed intrigued by the tale.

"Whoever managed to survive these perils," Aaron continued, "and bring the plants back safely to Europe were bestowed with riches, and at times the orchids were even named for the one who found them."

"I've always had an interest in growing things." Tara's mother didn't try to hide the excitement on her face. "And the orchids. I've seen a few rare samples myself. They have such breathtaking colors."

"I, too, have an interest in horticulture." Aaron picked up a bite-sized crab puff off his plate and popped it into his mouth.

"You do?"

He nodded and swallowed. "I know Tara has told you about out plans."

"She spoke of farming." The smile on Mrs. Young's face disappeared. "I must say quite honestly, Mr. Jefferson, that a farm in Iowa is not what I had in mind for my only daughter."

Aaron sampled a slice of cake next, forcing himself to stay calm and focused. "Have you ever been to Iowa, Mrs. Young?"

The woman's expression hardened. "No."

"This is delicious, by the way." He held up the marbled sweet. "Imagine this, if you will. While the country might not have all the conveniences of the city, one awakes each morning to a sunrise unlike anything you've ever seen before. And that's just the beginning. Quiet prairies, dotted by wildflowers, stretch on mile after mile. The soil is fertile enough to grow an ear of corn twice the size of my hand."

"Really?" Mrs. Young glanced at her husband. "What kind of farm are you proposing?"

"We have many different options, really. Cattle, horses, pigs, and of course, corn, to name a few."

"From what I've gathered, Mr. Jefferson is quite a lawman." Mr. Young spoke up for the first time since their arrival. "Worked on government cases in Washington until more recently when he was commissioned to work an important field assignment for them. And there's one other fact that might interest you, darling. Did Tara ever mention to you that Mr. Jefferson is related to former President Thomas Jefferson?"

"President Jefferson." Mrs. Young set down her teacup and pressed her hand against her chest. "Why, I do believe you have a bit of political blood running through your veins, then, after all."

The smile on Mrs. Young's face was subtle, but he didn't miss it. She rose from her chair and strode to the bookshelf located on the far side of the room. "I just happen to have a book on the man in my collection, and to think that you're related to him."

While Mrs. Young searched the bookshelf, Tara turned to Aaron. "You never told me you were related to President Jefferson."

"You never asked." He reached out and boldly squeezed her hand. "I didn't think that fact would matter to you."

"It doesn't, but. . ."

He leaned forward to whisper. "Your father told me that we were going to have to pull out every trump card I had to offer."

Mr. Young cleared his throat. "I think there's really only one question left to ask the young man, darling."

Mrs. Young turned with the book in her hand. "And what would that be?"

Mr. Young caught his gaze. "Mr. Jefferson, do you love my daughter?"

There was no doubt in Aaron's mind. "Yes, sir, I do. And I'm willing to spend the rest of my life making her happy."

"Tara, why didn't you tell me that your Mr. Jefferson was such a charming man? I'm pleasantly surprised." Mrs. Young waltzed back across the room. "And Mr. Jefferson, I do hope you're planning to stay for dinner so we will have a chance to further discuss your. . .and my daughter's plans for the future. November, you said?"

Tara nodded.

"Then there's no time to lose. We have a wedding to plan."

Epilogue

Two months later

Tara stood in front of the full-length beveled mirror, admiring the exquisite pattern of her wedding dress. Rays of morning sunlight broke through the stained glass window in the small room of the church, catching the silvery glint of the hand-sewn sequins that ornately lined the edges of the silky material. Following the style set three decades earlier by Queen Victoria's marriage, the white dress was a work of art. There was one thing she couldn't argue with. Her mother's tastes were impeccable.

From the moment Aaron first spoke of his uncle's adventures as an orchid hunter and his being related to President Jefferson, he'd managed to work his way straight into her mother's world. It had been nothing short of a miracle in Tara's eyes. Not that the planning of their wedding had been completely void of arguments, but Tara had learned early on that the best way for them all to get along was simply to let her mother work out the majority of the details. Whether lavender ham tea sandwiches or sage cheese wafers were served after the ceremony or which flowers adorned the bridal bouquet mattered little to her. All that she really cared about was the fact that she was about to become Mrs. Aaron Thomas Jefferson.

Even now, with the ceremony in less than thirty minutes, her mother had run off to discuss some grave concern with the minister. Tara wasn't even sure what the issue was. She pinched her cheeks to add a touch of extra color to her complexion. Aaron had been right when suggesting they should have eloped, but they both realized that such an act would have robbed her parents of the joy of seeing their only daughter marry. And that was something Tara was unwilling to do, as much as the idea of the two of them escaping the frenzy of the wedding appealed to her. In any case, she and Aaron planned to board a train for Iowa where they would begin their life together this very day.

A sharp knock on the door drew her out of her reverie.

"Mother?" She opened the door partway, then sucked in a deep breath. "Aaron?"

"Hi."

Her breathing quickened at the sight of him. "What are you doing here? Tradition forbids you to see me until the ceremony—"

"You look beautiful."

Tara felt a blush creep up her cheeks, and her knees threatened to give way beneath her. She regarded his colorful attire and his freshly shaved face, and she breathed in the fresh scent of his shaving soap. His mulberry frock coat and gray trousers made him look far more dashing than any other gentleman she'd ever seen.

Who really cared about tradition, anyway?

He leaned against the doorframe, his gaze never leaving her face. "Between formal teas in your honor and a constant array of wedding plans, I've missed you."

She was certain he'd still be able to make her blush fifty years from now. "We'll be married within the hour—"

"After which I must endure the five-course meal your mother planned, along with hours of socializing and other such formalities." He shot her a lopsided grin before leaning forward and brushing his lips across hers. "I just needed five minutes with you. Alone."

His words brought a smile to her lips. "We should have eloped."

He eyed the empty hallway. "There's still time. We could be on the next train to Iowa. . ."

"My mother would send a pack of lawmen after us."

"I know." He laughed as he took her hand and rubbed her fingers. "I promise I'll leave, but I've been thinking about something."

"What's that?"

"The missing gold might have only have been a rumor, but—"

"Someone will find the gold one day." She flashed him a smile. "I'm certain of that."

"Maybe, but I think there's one thing we can both agree on."

"And what is that?"

He leaned down for a second kiss. "The gold doesn't matter anymore, because I've found something far better than any hidden treasure. I love you, Tara soon-to-be Mrs. Jefferson."

She reached up to kiss him back. "And I love you, Mr. Jefferson."

Tara stepped into his warm embrace and sent up a prayer of thanks. They'd both found treasure—not only in the rewards of their spiritual journey but also in each other. And that, in itself, was worth far more than any riches of this world.

LISA HARRIS

Lisa and her husband, Scott, along with their three children, live in northern South Africa, where they work as missionaries. When she's not spending time with her family, her ministry, or writing, she enjoys traveling, learning how to cook different ethnic foods, and going on game drives through the Africa bush with her husband and kids. Find more about her latest books at www.lisaharriswrites.com.

BETTER THAN GOLD

Chapter 1

1876

VALENTINE PARTY PERFECT *STOP* F PROPOSED *STOP* ACCEPTED *STOP* MARRYING IN JUNE *STOP*

Lily Reese keyed in the telegram that had originated in Philadelphia and would speed along the wires from station to station until it reached its destination somewhere in Kansas. With each click of the code she knew well enough to produce in her sleep after three years as an operator, this kind of news never failed to thrill her.

Nor make her daydream.

Shivering in her tiny office to one side of the Browning City, Iowa, railway station, Lily imagined herself as the recipient of a proposal on Valentine's Day. She would wear a red silk dress, though it wasn't the best color for her blond hair, blue eyes, and fair complexion. Pink looked better. And Matt Campbell would walk her home through a frosty night with stars blazing above like crystal beads. He would go down on one knee. . . .

All right, she didn't know him quite well enough to be in love with him or for him to be in love with her. Yet Valentine's Day had spoken of romance for so long, it might put the notion of working toward a proposal in his head.

The clacking of the machine yanked her back to the present. Since the last of her family had died three years earlier, leaving her completely alone and causing her to lose the farm, she had to earn her living, and that meant sending and receiving telegrams, not fussing over what had not happened on February 14.

This was February 15, and those crystal beads had not been stars. They proved to be frozen rain descending as ice so thick no one had attended the party Lily planned as an excuse to invite Matt to the house where she boarded. She wanted to impress him with her applesauce cake and excellent coffee. And her new dress. It was wool, not silk. It did, however, boast falls of fine, white lace she had crocheted herself. Yet one more Iowa storm prevented her entertainment and a chance to make progress with her romantic intentions. Now Matt had departed on the morning train and would not return for several days since he worked for the railroad and traveled a great deal.

"Lucky Matt." She sighed then concentrated on another message coming through.

ARRIVING AFTERNOON TRAIN *STOP* LOOK FORWARD TO
MEETING YOU *STOP* YOUR LONG-LOST GREAT-NEPHEW BEN
PURCELL *STOP*

Lily blinked. No, she was not mistaken. The message was indeed meant for Deborah Twining, the elderly lady with whom Lily lived. Mrs. Twining allowed Lily to stay in her small home's only spare bedroom free of charge in exchange for Lily performing most of the household tasks of cooking and cleaning. Lily owed Mrs. Twining so much, from providing her a place to live to the older woman using her influence in town to get Lily hired at Western Union—first as a messenger and then as a telegraph operator, despite her lack of experience. She wanted nothing to upset her landlady and friend. But this message could, coming so abruptly. The train to which the telegram referred was due to arrive within the next five minutes.

"Someone was asleep on the job." Lily frowned at the message. She could never get it delivered before the train pulled into the station. She should have received the message at her telegraph hours earlier.

"Why are you frowning, Miss Lily?" Theo Forsling, the ticket agent who also served as the porter, poked his grizzled head around the edge of the door. "Someone send you bad news?"

"No." At least she hoped it would not prove to be bad news. "Someone in Davenport must have been asleep at his station. This message was supposed to arrive this morning."

"Better late than never." The old man chuckled.

"I'm not sure that's true with this." Lily waved the flimsy piece of paper in the air. "It's about a passenger arriving—" The blast of a whistle interrupted her. "On this train."

"Good. Good. If someone is actu'ly arriving to stay a piece, they may need a porter." Grinning, he closed the door. Through the window, she saw him heading for the platform.

She also noticed Tom Bailyn, the owner of the new mercantile; Lars Gilchrist, owner of the other mercantile and the livery; and Jake Doerfel, the newspaper owner and editor. The store owners were likely there to pick up supplies from the train. Jake met every train hoping for a story.

"And I have one for you." She jumped off her stool and dashed out the door. "Jake? Mr. Gilchrist?"

At her call, all four men on the platform turned around.

"I need someone to deliver this to Mrs. Twining immediately." She waved the slip of yellow paper in the icy wind pouring through the open-sided depot. "It's about her nephew arriving."

The train chugged around the corner at that moment, the squeal of brakes and *hiss* of steam drowning out her words. Apparently, however, she had said enough. All the men except for the porter jogged back to her.

"He's my new livery manager, you know." Mr. Gilchrist took the telegram into his sausage-sized fingers. "Didn't expect him until next week but makes sense he'd come before starting work. Things aren't quite ready for him, I'm afraid."

"But he's the new man in town?" Jake, not much taller than Lily, bobbed up and down on his toes, as though trying to make himself as tall as the two store owners. They towered over him by at least a full head. "Single? Do you know if he's single? Is it true Mrs. Twining only learned of his whereabouts two weeks ago? Why didn't he ever contact her?"

"Please," Lily said between giggles. "They knew one another when Mr. Purcell was a child, but for the rest, you'll have to ask him or Mrs. Twining."

"You mean you live with her and don't know the answers?" Jake shook his head. "Don't believe that for a minute, Miss Lily."

"Maybe," Tom drawled in his rumbling baritone, "she doesn't think it's right to tell you private information about someone else."

"You're right, Tom." Lily gave him a smile. "I learned most of what I know from telegrams and from Mrs. Twining, so I can't breathe a word about it to anyone except her. And now that I mention telegrams, I must get back to my machine. Will one of you gentlemen be so kind?"

The station needed a regular messenger, as she had been when she first started working for the company, but no one had replaced the lad who had run off to hunt for gold in Colorado the year before.

"I'll be happy to deliver it, Miss Lily." Mr. Gilchrist patted her on the shoulder. "Don't you worry about that. I walk right past her house on the way to the store."

"But if I take it, I can get some answers out of her." Jake reached for the telegram. "She's been a bit closemouthed about this nephew of hers."

"She told me enough to convince me to hire him." Mr. Gilchrist raised it out of the smaller man's reach.

Laughing, Lily retreated to her office. Through the window, she saw the three men still talking—or perhaps arguing—as they moved out of her line of sight.

She wished she could see the platform from where she sat. Although more freight unloaded from the trains than passengers, sometimes the travelers stepped from the cars and milled about to get some fresh air. On the occasions she was able to be outside and see them, Lily took in every detail of the ladies' fashions, from their hats to their gowns to their shoes. Occasionally she peeked at the gentlemen, too. If a handsome prince existed, he would have to step off that train to see her, sweep her off her feet, and carry her away to the bright lights and lively company of Chicago, Philadelphia, or even New York. Which city didn't matter so long as it had pavement, bright lights, and lots and lots of people.

She possessed high standards for the gentleman with whom she would someday share her life. He needed to be more than handsome; he needed to be entertaining, energetic, and a Christian.

Matt fit all those requirements except the entertaining part. He remained a bit too quiet around her. Maybe he was shy. No matter. She could fix that, and among others, one quiet person mattered less. He was fine to look at, and when he sang hymns in church, her heart just melted.

She glanced toward the window, again wishing she could see the platform. She wanted a glimpse of Mrs. Twining's nephew before he got into town and everyone else saw him first. If Toby, the young man who took the next shift, arrived a few minutes early instead of his usual few minutes late, she would be outside and on her way home in time to catch a glimpse of Ben Purcell, if not meet him outright. Meet the man whose existence could change her life and not for the better.

"Miss Lily?" someone spoke as he opened the door.

Lily glanced up at one of the railroad engineers. "Something wrong, sir?"

"Nothing serious. Just some bad track between here and Davenport. Probably ice damage. Will you send that back to Davenport?"

"Yes, sir, of course." Lily began to key in the message with the further specifics the engineer gave her.

"Thank you." He tipped his hat and headed back to the train.

Lily followed his progress. She saw no one in the depot.

She sighed. "Must have missed him. Now Becky and Eva will likely see him first." She frowned at her machine.

"Hey, and I'm even on time tonight." Toby shuffled in on feet that always appeared far too big for his spindly legs. "So what's the long face about?"

"I wanted to see someone is all." Lily hopped off her stool and snatched up her coat and hat.

"Mrs. Twining's nephew?" Toby took his place before the telegraph machine.

"How did you know?"

"Got hooked into delivering that telegram to her." He began to write his time of arrival in the log. "But you haven't missed him. He's still on the platform talking to Theo."

"Thank you." Lily settled her hat on her head with the aid of her reflection in the window, bade Toby good night, then left the office.

Toby was right. The stranger still stood on the platform with Theo. She thought going up to him would be too forward, since he wasn't her relative. At the same time, she could hardly stay around the depot waiting for him to walk past.

She would simply head home at a leisurely pace and hope he caught up with her.

She must know how readily Mrs. Twining would accept him. Or prefer his company over Lily's.

❧

Ben Purcell strode down the platform toward the baggage car. Stretching his legs after the daylong trip in the crowded railway coach felt wonderful. So did being in the fresh air. He inhaled. Despite the sting of coal smoke, the wind blowing off Iowa's rolling hills surrounded him with the crisp aromas of wet earth, animals, and open space. He smiled and stepped to the side of the baggage car, where a stocky older man prepared to heave Ben's heavy trunk onto the platform.

"Let me." Ben set down his valise and grabbed one end of the trunk to help the porter ease it onto the platform.

"What ya got in there? Gold?" The porter cackled. "Not that anyone brings gold into Browning City. Some have come huntin' for gold over the years, though."

"No gold for me." Ben retrieved his valise from the platform, since it, not the trunk, held his worldly wealth in greenbacks, not gold. "I've come here to work."

"Yep. Thought so." The porter jumped from the railroad car and sauntered over to a handcart. "Need me to take that to the hotel for you? Your room at the livery isn't ready yet 'cause you're early. And Miz Twining ain't got room for you with Miss Lily living there."

Ben stared at him. "You know who I am?"

"Ben Purcell, right?" This time, the porter threw back his head and emitted a bellow of mirth.

Everyone on the platform turned to stare. Two big, blond men laughed, too, before turning away, carrying yard-high crates as though they were no larger than matchboxes.

Ben grinned. "You got me there, sir. How did you know who I am?"

"Everyone in town knows you're expected."

"I suppose they would."

If Great-Aunt Deborah told everyone about his imminent arrival, of course they would know. Ben hoped she had—and with as much excitement as he'd experienced every day since finding her address and then the advertisement for a manager needed at the livery. It was more than an answer to prayer.

It was a sign that the Lord said, "It's time for you to find your permanent place in the world."

"So is it the hotel?" The porter repeated his earlier question.

Ben still hesitated. He wished to meet his great-aunt as soon as possible—reacquaint himself, to be truthful. But twenty years' separation was a long time.

"You'll want to freshen up a mite before meeting Miz Twining." The porter gave Ben a sidelong glance.

"You're right." Ben headed down the platform. "The hotel, then."

"Mrs. Meddler will take good care of you." The handcart trundled in Ben's wake. "She'll—"

A *hiss* of steam and increased engine power drowned out the rest of the porter's words as the train accelerated. Railway cars slid past. People stared out the windows. A few people to whom Ben had spoken during the trip waved to him. He paused to wave back until the train picked up speed and the faces became blurs then disappeared altogether. Baggage and freight cars followed, speeding the passengers and goods farther west to more open and inexpensive land.

But Ben had family in Browning City.

Family!

"How far is it to the hotel?" He turned to the porter. "Can you push that all the way?"

"I most certainly can." The man straightened his shoulders and jutted out his chin. "Been known to push two at once when necessary. You ask anyone about Theo Forsling. Strongest man in Iowa." He grinned. "Once upon a time. Won the plowing contest three years running before the rheumatism got into my knees. Mr. John Deere himself was here in seventy-one."

"John Deere himself, eh?" Ben held out his hand. "Then I'm honored to have you meet me at the train, Mr. Forsling."

"Ah, shucks, no mister to me." Forsling fairly glowed as he gripped Ben's hand in a powerful clasp. "I'm Theo to everybody in these parts. And speaking of these parts. . ." He released Ben's hand and shoved the cart to the end of the platform. "Better get a move on before we freeze where we stand."

"It is a powerful wind." Ben paced forward, his free hand shoved into his pocket.

With the train gone, fresh air swirled around him. He flared his nostrils to take in as much as he could. With every breath, he felt a little more of the city stink leaving his body. He had walked on Iowa soil for less than a quarter hour and already he could not understand why his father had traded the prairie for the road and city.

Actually for many cities, each dirtier and more crowded than the last.

"Like it?" Theo trotted beside Ben despite his claim to having bad knees.

"So far."

They left the depot. A skinny youth hunched over the telegraph machine waved to them. Ben waved back.

"Looks like Miss Lily has gone on home." Theo increased his pace on the road that headed into town. "But maybe we'll catch her up yet. Prettiest girl in Browning City."

"Lily." The name sounded familiar to Ben, but he couldn't place it at the moment. The one letter from his aunt had been full of names.

"Yep. Lily Reese, the daytime telegraph op—ah, there she is." Theo shot up his left arm to indicate a diminutive figure gliding along the road as though she stepped over a boardwalk rather than an icy street. Between a jaunty wool bonnet and heavy coat, blond hair gleamed in the twilight. Pale gold hair. Wheat gold hair.

"I see what you mean about hunting gold here," Ben murmured.

"Haw, haw, haw," Theo bellowed, slapping his leg.

The young woman stopped and turned. Her delicate features went well with her shining hair and fine form. She stood too far away for Ben to catch the color of her eyes in the fading light, but he guessed they would be blue. Sky blue.

"That yeller hair of hers ain't what I meant by folks hunting gold around here." Theo grinned. "But it'll do for a start. Step it up, boy; I'll introduce you."

"Yes, sir." Ben stepped it up.

Their footfalls crunched on the icy gravel. The cart trundled like distant thunder. A *crack* like a tree branch breaking under a load of ice echoed above the deeper tones of wheels and heels.

The last thing Ben remembered was feeling something slam into the side of his head.

Chapter 2

With a shriek of horror, Lily raced back to the newcomer. She slipped in the frozen mud on the road. Her knee twisted, sending pain shooting up her leg. She ignored it and sprinted the last dozen feet to where the man lay.

"What happened?" She dropped to her knees beside him, wincing. "Did he miss his footing?"

"No, Miss Lily." Theo sank to the ground across from her with a creaking and popping of joints. "He was shot."

She gasped. "Shot? With what?"

"Rifle."

"Nonsense. We're too close to town." Her own heart racing, Lily touched the side of the stranger's neck, feeling for a pulse. "That was only a tree branch cracking under the weight of ice. Oh, praise God, his heartbeat is strong. He only stunned himself—" She broke off as warm stickiness soaked through her mittens. "Theo?" Her voice felt strangled in her throat. "He's bleeding."

"How badly?" Theo raised the man's head in one broad palm and probed with his fingers.

"Is he—did a bullet. . ." Lily couldn't form the right question in her mind, let alone speak it aloud. Despite her own misgivings regarding Ben Purcell threatening her role as the closest thing to family Mrs. Twining had, Lily didn't want him to suffer. Nor did she wish to be the one to tell the elderly lady that her sole blood kin was. . .dying. It would break Mrs. Twining's heart after so many weeks of hope and anticipation.

Tears began to course down Lily's face. The wind chilled them against her skin. "Theo—" She stopped again. She closed her eyes, deciding she was better off praying for the Lord to help.

"Cut a furrow right across his scalp." Theo gave his report in a soothing tone. "Stunned him, but he's not going to die on us."

Thank You, Lord.

Lily opened her eyes. "He'll die if we don't get him someplace warm and have the doctor see to him—sew him up or whatever is necessary."

She knew nothing of gunshot wounds. Browning City was not the Wild West. Occasionally a farmhand drank too much and fired his gun, but that was more in high spirits than anything. Rifles were for hunting.

"We need to stop the bleeding." It was the only thing she could think to do. She yanked off her mittens and tossed them on the ground; then she opened her pocketbook and drew out her handkerchief—a scrap of linen and crocheted lace. It was an inadequate bandage at best, but it was all she had.

"I'll do it." Theo snatched the cloth from her and pressed it to the gash above the man's right ear.

So close. Another half an inch. . .

Lily swallowed a bitter taste in her throat. "I—I guess I can go run for help, but I hate leaving you here with some crazy man shooting off a gun."

"I'll be all right, and you can go faster than I can."

She could, and they needed help at once. Still she hesitated. She glanced from Theo's craggy face, a crease cutting between his bushy eyebrows like a river valley, to the stranger's smooth, strong features.

Her mouth went dry. She had seen some handsome men in her life, but even in repose, this man topped them all.

"Get going, child." Theo's voice held a chuckle as though he understood the reason for her hesitation did not stem entirely from her concern about leaving him alone with the unconscious man. "Mr. Purcell here will be catching an ague."

"So it is Ben Purcell." Lily sprang to her feet. Her knee threatened to buckle, and she grabbed the handle of the cart for support.

The cart.

"Theo, we can take him to town on this. I'm sure the two of us can lift him that high. Of course, we'll have to leave his trunk behind, but don't you think getting him to help is more important than possessions?"

Not that she would want her worldly goods left in the middle of the road.

"Good thinking." Theo rose. "Now you let me get that trunk down. It's mighty heavy."

Despite his protests, Lily assisted the older man in lowering the trunk to the road. Lifting Ben Purcell onto the handcart would be easy after the weight of his luggage.

She was wrong. He was a big man and a dead weight. No, not dead—limp. He would not be dead. Mrs. Twining had lost too many family members in her lifetime, including her children. Learning of Ben's whereabouts had brought her so much joy, it simply could not vanish before she had a chance to get to know him and appreciate him. *Not appreciate him to the exclusion of you, my girl.* Lily squashed the uncharitable thought, but it hung in her heart like a lead weight.

She must help him. Yet neither she nor Theo possessed the strength to get him off the ground high enough to set him on the cart bed even with a unified effort. On their second try, she thought she heard him moan. The third time, an outright groan emanated from his lips.

Perspiring inside her wool dress and coat, Lily set Mr. Purcell's feet back onto the road. If this were a big city, she could ask a dozen passersby for aid. Not here among the warehouses and silos between Browning City and the depot. At nightfall in the winter, with another train not due for hours, no one would pass by them soon enough to be of help.

"I'll have to run for help after all." She gritted her teeth in frustration. "We're hurting him. We can cover him with this." She unbuttoned her coat.

"No." The soft word from the wounded man cut through the air.

Lily jumped. "Mr. Purcell?"

"Not your coat." His speech sounded a little blurry. "Such a tiny thing. You'll freeze."

"Sir, I. . ." Lily felt her cheeks heat.

Theo guffawed. "Run along, girl. I think he'll do fine."

The buttons unfastened, Lily pulled off her coat and started to drape it over Mr. Purcell despite his protest.

He held up one hand and pushed it away. "I said no." His voice came out stronger, and he raised himself on one elbow. "Where's the mule?"

"Mule?" Theo and Lily asked together.

"The one that kicked me in the head."

"No mule, sir." Lily shook her head. "It was—"

Theo stooped again to slip his hands beneath Mr. Purcell's shoulders. "If I give you a hand, do you think you can get yourself into the cart?"

"If you can help me work out which way is up."

"That way." Lily pointed at the sky now growing darker by the minute.

"Funny." Mr. Purcell gave Lily a crooked, if somewhat thin-lipped, grin and pointed one finger at her. "Thought I saw an angel over thatta way."

Lily's cheeks heated. She didn't want this man to flirt with her. She wanted Matt to flirt with her, so she could care about him, not this stranger, this interloper.

Theo chuckled. "She is purty enough to be an angel."

"You're both full of nonsense." Lily pressed her cold hands against her hot cheeks. "I'm going to run ahead and warn the doctor to expect you."

"Why don't we take him straight to Mrs. Twining?" Theo eased Mr. Purcell to a sitting position. "She will be expecting him by now."

"Was going to the hotel." Mr. Purcell raised his hands to his head. When his fingers touched the gash, he grimaced. "Guess I do need a doc."

"He has an extra room if it's available." Lily feared it might not be with the cold weather bringing on the influenza. "Mrs. Twining doesn't have any space."

He could use your room, and you could stay with Rebecca.

Lily's conscience pricked her as she watched Mr. Purcell struggle to rise high enough for Theo to help him onto the cart bed.

"Of course he should stay with Mrs. Twining," Lily said. "She wouldn't want it any other way."

Hoping neither man guessed her momentary selfishness, Lily turned and dashed down the road toward town.

Although no more than a quarter mile away, Browning City might go unnoticed to a nighttime traveler save for the scents of coal and wood smoke and cooking dinners in the air and the occasional flash of a lantern as someone performed outdoor chores. Businesses closed at supper time. In the winter, Lily arrived at work in the dark. If she had to stay late, she went home in the darkness, too. So she knew the road well. This evening, the wind drove the clouds from the sky, leaving it full of stars as she had longed for the previous night.

She welcomed them, too, though for a far different reason. She moved faster. In a few minutes, she reached the doctor's house on the edge of town. As she feared, someone with influenza and no family to take care of him slept in the physician's spare room.

"But if he's been shot, he needs more care than he'll get at the hotel, good as Mrs. Meddler can be." Doc Smythe shook his head. His glasses winked in the lamplight. "Shot indeed. Do they think we're in the territories or something?"

"I don't know. I guess I should tell the sheriff, too." Lily shoved her icy fingers into the pockets of her coat. "But I'd better get to Mrs. Twining's first."

"You do that. I'll let the sheriff know when I'm done with the lad." Doc Smythe grabbed up his bag. "I'll just go out to meet Theo. Shot indeed."

Lily heard him muttering as he headed in the opposite direction from her. "Shot indeed," she said herself. "Nonsense."

Yet Ben Purcell bore a gash on the side of his head where something had furrowed across his scalp. Nothing but a bullet could do so much damage from far enough away that the perpetrator remained hidden from the road.

Lily suddenly grew aware of how the cottonwoods and warehouses made excellent cover along the road and increased her pace. Her knee throbbed. She bit down on the pain, lifted her skirts into her hands, and raced up the road until it turned into Main Street. Past Pine Street, then Oak; past the Gilchrist Mercantile, newspaper office, and the office side of the livery. When she reached Maple Street, she turned and fairly galloped the last block to Mrs. Twining's cottage. Breathless, she leaped up the two front steps, pounded across the porch, and yanked open the front door. "Mrs. Twining?"

Her words emerged between gasps for breath. "Missus—oh, there you are." She stopped in the center of the parlor, her hand to her heaving chest. "There's. . . been. . .an accident."

At least she hoped it had been an accident and not some lunatic taking target practice on newcomers.

"Then catch your breath and tell me." Mrs. Twining's quavery voice and faded blue eyes conveyed calm and peace.

Lily wanted to sink down at the older woman's feet and let her talk of God's mercy and love until the panic departed.

"But there isn't time." She spoke her protest and regret aloud. "They'll be here any minute now."

"If you're referring to Ben's early arrival, that nice young man from the telegraph dropped off the telegram." Mrs. Twining smiled. "How glad I will be to see him."

"I'm not so certain of that." Lily bit her lip, reorganized her thoughts. "The accident—the incident involves Mr. Purcell."

"It does?" Mrs. Twining leaned forward in her straight-backed chair. Her lined face paled. "Is he—what happened?"

"We think someone was out shooting and hit him." Afraid the elderly lady would have an apoplexy, Lily grasped her shoulders. "But it's only a flesh wound. Theo Forsling is bringing him with the handcart. And the doctor has gone out to meet them."

"Shooting, you say?" Mrs. Twining stared at the window with its covering of white lace curtains. "Shot?"

"Yes. He should be all right, but he couldn't go to the hotel. . . . Mrs. Twining, should I get you a glass of water? Some tea?"

"No, no, thank you." Mrs. Twining shifted her shoulders, allowing them to settle in their normal, erect pose, and raised her chin. "Then we must see to things here. You won't mind giving up your room to him, will you?"

"They're already bringing him here." Lily headed down the short hallway from which one reached both bedrooms. "I'll clear out some of my things for him and pack some stuff to take to Rebecca's."

"It won't do. She lives all the way across town." Mrs. Twining followed Lily into the bedroom, leaning heavily on her cane. "You can stay next door with Mildred Willoughby."

"But. . ." Lily would not argue about how "all the way across town" was only six blocks and Mildred Willoughby next door would keep her up talking all night. Not to mention that Mrs. Willoughby would expect payment if Lily needed to stay more than a single night. Of course, she could not impose on Becky's family, either.

Oh, the depletion of her savings!

But it couldn't be helped. Mr. Purcell needed to stay with his aunt until the livery was ready for him. And Mrs. Twining would still need her around to help with the cooking and cleaning, which Lily already did to earn her room and board. The arrangement worked well for both ladies. Lily could save most of her earnings, and Mrs. Twining could remain in the house her husband had built for her more than thirty years earlier, before Iowa was even a state. Otherwise, she would have to go back east and live with her late husband's sister in Philadelphia.

Lily knew her choice in a similar situation would be Philadelphia. She knew no other land than Iowa, but how she wanted to.

Someday. . .if she didn't have to deplete her savings paying someone rent.

Her conscience pricked her again, and she returned her attention to Mrs. Twining.

"As soon as they get here," she said, "I'll go ask Mrs. Willoughby. Right now, I should get some hot water going."

She stepped back into the tiny entryway in time to hear the rumble of the cart's two wheels on frozen mud and the murmur of men's voices. She opened the door. Thin streams of light from lamps in the parlor illuminated Theo, Doc, and Mr. Purcell. With the aid of the two Browning City men, Ben Purcell climbed off the cart and headed up the front steps. Blood streaked the side of his face and lay in a dark patch over his shoulder.

Not a good way to meet a long-lost relative.

"Will you go heat the water?" Lily asked, hoping Mrs. Twining would go straightaway and not see her nephew in such a condition.

"You can do that, child. I haven't seen this lad since he was knee-high to a grasshopper, and I'm not going to let a little blood scare me off now."

It was a lot, not a little. Still, Lily would not argue with her elder.

"Yes, ma'am." She backed toward the kitchen, not wanting to miss the reunion.

Ben Purcell stepped across the threshold to his great-aunt's house under his own power. Though he appeared to waver a bit and braced himself with one palm against the door frame, he held open his arms. So tiny she stood no higher than his chest, Mrs. Twining rushed to him, cane thudding, and threw her arms around his waist.

"My dear boy."

"Great-Aunt Deborah." He curved one arm around her shoulders and bowed his head.

Lily noticed his scalp now bore a white bandage. He still supported himself with his free hand against the door frame. She thought he needed to be lying down. Yet who would interrupt this moment? Certainly not she, despite the frigid air swirling through the house and chilling her face.

Her wet face.

She dashed the tears away with the back of her hand and spun toward the kitchen. She would not, not, not allow her own pain to cloud Mrs. Twining's happy meeting with her great-nephew. The death of Lily's remaining family three years earlier gave her no cause to feel hurt that the closest person to her had found a real relation.

Work. She must make herself busy. Occupation with her hands helped keep her mind away from thoughts she did not wish to entertain.

"I am not jealous." She set the pan atop the stove with more force than necessary. "Jealousy is a sin."

She dipped water from the bucket beside the back door and poured it into the pan. She needed more wood for the stove and would now need to pump more water from the well in the yard.

"Miss Lily?" Theo banged open the kitchen door. "Doc needs some hot water."

"Soon." Lily emptied another dipperful into the pan. "Is he—will he be all right?"

"In a few days. Here, let me fetch you some more wood." He slipped out the back door and returned in a moment with an armful of short logs. "Doc wants him to rest here for a few days."

Only a few. Paying someone rent for a few days wouldn't set her back too far in her plans for escape from Iowa before the year was out.

But what would happen if Mrs. Twining liked having her nephew around instead of Lily? The older woman owed Lily nothing. She wasn't family.

Lily gnawed her lower lip as she poured hot water into a bowl for Theo to carry in to the doctor; then she set a pot on the stove for coffee. She disliked the idea of being stranded in Iowa any longer than necessary. Browning City was not home—was not where she belonged. It was merely a depot on her journey. . . . She hoped.

Her heart began to race as it had on the road earlier, and she opened the kitchen window for fresh air to breathe.

Room and board would take all of her wages if it came to that. She wouldn't be able to save any more, or so little she would be old before she got to the city. She would be too old to attract the kind of husband she truly wanted, a man who enjoyed social activity and bright lights. A man who enjoyed travel, like Matt. . . A man who could provide her with a fine house. . . A home to call her own.

But Ben Purcell didn't have a home of his own, either. He had intended to go to the hotel, since the room behind the livery wasn't yet fit for anyone's habitation.

"If it were ready. . ."

Able to breathe without effort, Lily closed the window and bustled around the kitchen, cutting slices of cake, setting out cups for coffee, checking the larder for something with which she could prepare soup for the invalid. Now her heart raced with excitement and purpose.

Tomorrow she would offer her services to Mr. Gilchrist to make the room behind the livery so inviting that Ben Purcell would want to live there instead of with his aunt.

Chapter 3

The joy in Ben's heart proved powerful enough to counteract the pounding in his head. The latter, he knew, would go away in a day or two, though the scar would remain with him for all his mortal life. The former, however, felt as if it grew each time he saw his great-aunt.

"Family."

The six letters tasted sweet on his tongue—

Unlike the bitter medicine the doctor insisted he take for the pain.

One aunt wasn't much family to most folk, Ben supposed. It wasn't the wife and children for whom he daily prayed to come into his life. Yet one aunt in the form of Deborah Twining, whose faith in God seemed to be as powerful as she appeared to be frail, was enough for Ben's happiness to bubble up each time she thumped her cane into his room for an hour or two of talking about his mother and other relatives and discussing how he wished to settle in a small town like Browning City and get his own land.

Judging from the angle of pallid sunlight creeping through a gap in the curtains, Great-Aunt Deborah would arrive any minute with an afternoon cup of tea for each of them. Despite disliking the brew, he drank it to please her. Sometimes, Lily Reese arrived in time to prepare the tea. She never came into his room with his aunt, but he heard her voice through the door. The pleasure of remembering every word he heard her say occupied him during his waking hours of recovering from the gunshot.

Even as he thought about her, he heard her light, quick steps crunch up the front walk and click across the porch. He knew they belonged to her. None of his aunt's friends moved with so much speed and grace. Over the three days the doctor insisted he remain in bed, he learned each caller by her footfalls. He also knew Lily by her rhythmic rap upon the door. But he recalled little of her face, as he had not seen it clearly. He remembered golden hair.

"Golden hair and a silver laugh." Ben chuckled at his fanciful words, words much like those in the poetry books that had sometimes made their way into his father's peddler cart.

Listening to her speaking with Great-Aunt Deborah, however, he believed his thoughts weren't too farfetched. Light and clear, her voice reminded him of sleigh bells. Perhaps she sang. . . .

"What does the doctor say?" Lily's voice came through with clarity as she stepped from entryway to kitchen.

"He'll be with us another forty years or so." Great-Aunt Deborah laughed. "But he can't go to work until the headache and double vision leave him. Which is more than all right by me. I do enjoy his company."

"That's unfortunate. I—I mean about him not being able to start work. Does Mr. Gilchrist. . ." Lily's voice grew muffled behind the kitchen door.

Ben closed his eyes. The mention of Mr. Gilchrist's name intensified the headache. He was supposed to start work in six days. Laid up as he was, he could not prepare his living quarters nor get to know the town. He had also missed church on Sunday. No matter what the doctor said, he would be in a pew on the upcoming Sunday and at the livery the following Monday.

He would be at the sheriff's office sooner. The first day he got out of the house, he intended to pay the lawman a call and learn what he had discovered about the shooting.

"I won't let him in to see you," Great-Aunt Deborah had insisted in her cracked yet still firm voice. "He's come by twice, but Doc and I agree you need rest."

Ben wished he could disagree with her and get out of bed anyway. Weeks of working extra hard to pay for his move to Browning City and, before that, the grief over losing his father so suddenly seemed to be taking their toll on him. Not to mention the bullet across his skull and the rock on which he had hit his head when he fell. He had needed the rest.

With the rattle of the approaching tea service, he determined to remain out of bed all day tomorrow and be out of the house the day after that. If nothing else, he wanted to be well enough for his aunt to serve him the strong, dark coffee he smelled when Lily made it, instead of that bland brew from leaves.

He smelled coffee at that moment.

Do you prefer it, too, Miss Reese? He smiled at the notion and continued to smile as Great-Aunt Deborah entered the room with a teapot, cups, and slices of cake on a tray.

"It'll spoil your supper, but Lily insisted." She grinned at him. "Lily likes to feed people."

"A fine thing in a body." Ben rose and took the tray from his aunt. "Does she ever eat anything herself?"

"Yes, she does. She's been eating in the kitchen while I join you here." Great-Aunt Deborah lowered herself onto a straight-backed chair. "She'll join us when you're well enough to come to the table. But I think this respite from all she does for me is good. With her work at the telegraph office and caring for me, I think she doesn't have enough time to be as sociable as a girl her age should be."

Ben was still a bit bewildered about Lily's role in his aunt's household. "What all does she do for you?"

"All those things these old joints of mine won't let me do anymore." Great-Aunt Deborah chuckled. "Which means just about everything but read. She cooks and cleans and does the shopping in exchange for her room and board."

Ben straightened, blinking against a bit of dizziness. "Then I should get out of here as soon as possible so she can have her room back. I have displaced your boarder, and it must be costing her something to stay—"

"Don't fret about that, lad." Great-Aunt Deborah shook her head. "She isn't suffering. And where would you go? The hotel?"

"The livery has a room, I believe."

"I understand it isn't yet fit for anybody to live there. Now eat some cake, or Lily will be disappointed."

"I wouldn't want to disappoint her." Ben took a slice of cake, though his conscience dampened his appetite.

He didn't like the idea of taking from Lily. Yet he enjoyed Great-Aunt Deborah so much, he didn't want to leave if she didn't insist. Despite her assurances, however, he decided that he had better get well immediately and set the quarters at the livery to rights so he could move in and give Lily back her room.

He could start this evening.

"I'm well enough to sit to dinner at the table now," he said, "if my staying in bed means she's been eating alone."

"Uh-uh." Great-Aunt Deborah leaned forward and poked him with the tip of her cane. "No getting up until Doc says it's all right."

Ben grimaced.

"None of that. You want to start work next week, don't you?"

"Yes, ma'am. But I'll be as weak as a baby if I don't get moving around soon."

"Eat some more of this cake. Lily made it for a party we didn't have because of the weather." Great-Aunt Deborah slid another slice of cake onto his plate and set down her cane to pour tea.

He choked down the applesauce cake, which he knew should taste good, and the tea. All the while, he smelled coffee, and his mouth watered.

"Can I have coffee tomorrow, ma'am?" He felt like a child begging for a treat.

"May you." Her eyes twinkled.

He started to respond but stopped, his eyes widening. "You always did that to me, didn't you? Corrected me from saying *can* to *may*."

"I did." Her face softened like crumpled tissue paper. "You were such a sweet but mischievous child that your mother never knew whether to hug you or punish you when you were naughty."

They sat in silence for a moment, Great-Aunt Deborah blinking away tears, Ben seeking memories.

"I was already six years old when she died, but I don't remember nearly enough of her." He shook his head, winced from a stab of pain, and sighed. "I never found so much as a picture."

"She was pretty. She looked like her grandmother—my sister—and you."

That made Ben laugh. "I hope I'm not pretty."

She laughed, too. "No, lad, you're handsome, and you probably know it. Why is it you aren't married yet?"

"No home for a wife yet."

"Mr. Twining and I didn't have one, either. We started our life together in a wagon."

"I can't wish that on a wife. Not after spending the past twenty years in one."

He wanted to ask her if she knew why his father had taken to the road for good after Momma died but kept it to himself. He wanted to talk of the happy times he couldn't remember of his childhood when he had family around him.

"You always were good with animals." Great-Aunt Deborah spoke as though she read his thoughts. "You spent a lot of time in the livery with your uncle."

"I seem to always remember horses around." He hesitated. "Why did he sell the livery?"

She smiled. "We were getting old, lad. Then some unsavory folk came through causing trouble around the end of the war, and Mr. Twining just didn't like the place anymore. He sold it to Charlie Jones, who turned around and sold it to Lars Gilchrist a few years after that."

"Why—"

"I'll go see how Lily is making out with dinner. She brought a nice piece of venison from Mr. Bailyn and is planning on a stew."

Ben's stomach rumbled despite the cake and tea.

"It won't be ready for another two hours." Chuckling, she headed toward the door, cane supporting her, she supporting the tray.

Ben sprang up faster than his head wanted him to and opened the door. He hoped for a glimpse of Lily, but the kitchen door stood closed.

"Maybe tomorrow," he murmured.

❧

When Lily had to work late at the telegraph office the next day, Ben experienced a stab of disappointment. Great-Aunt Deborah and he ate leftover stew. Doc, however, gave him permission to begin going about his life: "If you take it easy."

The medical man sounded so stern that Ben said, "Yes, sir," and felt like saluting.

The doctor's instructions made little impact on Ben's actions. Immediately after Doc Smythe left, Ben donned his coat—washed and pressed, he noted—his hat, apparently retrieved from the road, and his boots. Protected against the cold, snowy weather, he departed for the sheriff's office. Despite the chilly air, several persons moved about their business. Some of them spoke to him. Many tipped hats in greeting. All of them gave him a second glance.

Ben smiled. He had spent too many days of his life as the stranger in a small town where everyone knew everyone else to mind about the looks of curiosity.

"Soon I won't be a stranger."

He expected they all knew who he was. The fact of someone shooting at him upon his arrival would make him even more of an oddity than the average stranger strolling through town.

His head clearing for the first time since he stepped into that flying lead, Ben paused in the middle of the Main Street boardwalk and frowned. He'd known the sheriff wanted to speak with him about the shooting but figured the lawman simply wanted to know if Ben had seen anything that could identify the gunman.

Ben didn't believe for a minute that he had been the intended target of the shooting. He hoped the sheriff and others didn't think that of him, either. The notion would make life uncomfortable for Great-Aunt Deborah. People might even think he should leave town.

His quick prayer failed to lighten his heavy heart before he reached the sheriff's office. Taking a deep breath, Ben opened the thick wooden door and stepped inside.

Heat, the aroma of wood smoke and strong coffee, and a tuneless humming somewhere in another room met him inside. So did the surprisingly young man wearing the sheriff's badge and seated with his feet propped on the desk.

"How may I help you?" He had a deep, rich voice that seemed at odds with his cherubic countenance.

"I'm Ben Purcell." Ben held out his hand.

"About time." The sheriff swung his feet to the floor and rose. "You should have been in here four days ago."

Ben did not respond and withdrew his hand. The man knew why he hadn't been.

"Name's Dodd. Billy Dodd. Have a seat. Coffee?"

"Yes, thank you."

Deciding the man was friendlier than his words had first implied, Ben lowered himself onto the other chair. "I suppose you don't have much crime here, do you?"

It seemed a good topic for conversing with a lawman.

"No, sir." Dodd chuckled. "I work at a saddler half my time. That's why old Sheriff Morton moved on. Bored here." He poured coffee from a pot simmering on the stove into two thick mugs and carried them to the desk. "That's why I wanted to talk to you. People just don't get shot around here."

"I don't get shot around anywhere." Ben smiled.

"Humph." Dodd slid onto his chair and propped his elbows on the desk. "Funny thing that, you coming into town and getting hit straight off. Sure you didn't bring an enemy along?"

"Sheriff Dodd, sir. . ." Ben paused, choosing his words with care. "I don't have many friends. Never stayed in one place long enough to make and keep them. But the same goes for enemies. As far as I know, I don't have any of those."

"I can only take your word for that." Dodd blew across the top of his coffee. "But in these parts, we're inclined to take a man's word. And you are Miz Twining's nephew or something, aren't you?"

"Great-nephew, yes."

"Mm-hmm." Dodd nodded. "That counts for something. We all think the world of her. So if she vouches for you, you stay."

Ben raised his eyebrows. "And if she didn't?"

"We don't want crime in this town. Hasn't been any since those train robbers rode in here and tried to settle right after the war."

Gold. Ben recalled Great-Aunt Deborah mentioning trouble coming to town and having something to do with the livery.

"I mean," Dodd added, "sometimes a youth gets a hold of some rotgut and kicks up a ruckus, and we have an occasional stealing of a horse or cow, but that's all it is. Boring, but we like it that way."

"I can understand why."

Ben had experienced too many weeks in cities where one never left so much as an apple unattended or it disappeared.

"So we want to catch the man who did this to Miz Twining's nephew." Dodd's forehead creased with his frown. "Any ideas?"

Ben shook his head. A few stars floated before his eyes. "No idea. I didn't see a thing. It was getting dark and. . ."

At the memory of seeing the small, female form ahead of him, he felt his neck grow warm under his collar.

"I wasn't looking for anyone. Just talking to Theo and—boom." He touched the side of his head.

"Hmm." Dodd's badge rose and fell with his sigh. "Thought maybe you'd remember something. It's just such a strange thing."

"Yes, sir, it is." Ben reckoned his coffee was cool enough to drink and took a sip. It was as thick as mud and tasted as rich as molasses after all the tea he'd had lately. "Sorry I can't be of more help."

"Not your fault. But maybe you can tell me where you're from and why it took you so long to come to Miz Twining after she was widowed."

"I'm from here." Ben settled back in his chair, coffee cup in hand. "My parents had a farm a long time ago; then Momma died and Pa took to the roads and me along with him. I didn't remember much about my family until Pa died and I went through his papers. I found some old letters from Deborah Twining and thought she might be my mother's aunt, so I sent a telegram here to see if she was still around."

"Such a pity. My folks have been here for over thirty years, and my wife's folks have been here nearly as long. Iowa wasn't even a state yet, and they had it rough, but it's paid off. We're settled for good."

"I'd like that."

"If you're telling me the truth about not having enemies here, then you're welcome to stay. We still need folks to settle and help this town prosper."

"I'm telling the truth." Ben took care not to let his annoyance show in his voice.

Although Dodd continued in a friendly manner, Ben finished his coffee and departed from the office as quickly as he could without being impolite, for he couldn't shake the notion that the sheriff didn't quite believe him.

Thoughtful about why the man would doubt him despite saying that the town would accept Deborah Twining's great-nephew, Ben stepped from the heat to the cold and came face-to-face with Lily Reese.

Seeing her by the light of day, even the gray light from the clouds, Ben knew he wouldn't forget any detail now. With eyes the color of an October sky and hair the color of wheat, smooth, creamy skin, and a straight, slim nose, she appeared as delicate as the flower for which she was named. His mouth went dry, and words clogged his throat.

"Good afternoon, Mr. Purcell." She gave him a smile that curled his toes up inside his boots. "I'm glad to see you about."

"I am, too. I mean, I'm glad to be about."

Now his ears burned.

"May I walk you somewhere, Miss Reese?"

The offer was bold, since they hadn't been properly introduced, but he had listened to her voice for days and felt like he knew her.

"Thank you for asking, but I need to rush off." She began to move away from him as she spoke. "I begged Toby to come in and work at the telegraph office for an hour so I could reach the mercantile. It always closes before I finish work."

"I should be on my way to the mercantile myself." Ben fell into step beside her. "I need to tell Mr. Gilchrist that I can start work on Monday."

"I'm pleased to hear that." She glanced over her shoulder. "I see you finally met the sheriff."

"Yes, ma'am, I did."

Lily laughed. "You expected someone older and wiser?"

"I think I did."

Ben wanted to change the subject. He didn't want to speak of how the sheriff seemed not to believe him regarding his lack of enemies. He glanced about, seeking another topic of conversation, and caught sight of a patch of ice right in front of them from where a shop's eaves had dripped onto the walk.

"Have a care." He slipped one hand beneath her elbow to support her.

She pulled her arm away so fast she slid on the frozen patch.

He grasped her arm again, steadying her. "I warned you to have a care." He made his tone light and teasing and smiled down at her.

She stood motionless, looking up at him with alarm clouding her eyes and turning down the corners of her mouth.

He felt like she looked—dazed.

"I need to hurry." Her voice sounded hoarse, not at all her usual clear tones.

He nodded and released her. "I'd better let you. I'm not as quick as I'd like to be quite yet. We can talk some tonight at my aunt's house."

But Lily didn't arrive at Great-Aunt Deborah's house that night.

"She sent a note saying she was working late, that Theo would walk her home and she would eat with her friend Becky," Great-Aunt Deborah explained. "Will you get that chicken off the stove? I can put it into the pot, but I can't lift it once it's filled with meat and stock."

Ben moved the stewed chicken from the stove. "You sit down. I'll serve up."

Once they were seated with plates of fragrant chicken and biscuits and he had asked the blessing over the food, Ben brought up the subject of Miss Lily Reese again.

"I ran into her today when I came out of the sheriff's office."

"In the middle of the day?" Great-Aunt Deborah forked up some peas but didn't eat them. "That's odd."

Nothing was as odd or disturbing to his heart as the jolt he'd felt when he held her arm tightly enough to keep her from falling. Before, he had only experienced that sensation when he'd found himself too close to a lightning strike.

And Lily had felt it, too. At least Ben presumed she did from that expression of dismay on her face.

"I wonder why she wasn't working," Great-Aunt Deborah said.

"She was headed to the mercantile. Someone named Toby was working for her for an hour, she said."

"Ah." His aunt still looked thoughtful as she resumed eating. "Did you go see Mr. Gilchrist?"

"I'll go tomorrow. Miss Lily was headed there, so I thought I'd wait."

Great-Aunt Deborah's snowy eyebrows arched. "Didn't you want to walk with her?"

"More than anything. I mean"—he laughed—"yes, ma'am, I thought it would be a fine thing to do, especially since the walk was icy. But she seemed in a hurry."

"Lily is always in a hurry. You need to run to keep up with her. But. . ." She paused for several bites, so long that Ben could barely stop himself from demanding she continue. At last, she set down her fork and folded her hands on the edge of the table. "Lily is the kindest and prettiest girl around. She is a hard worker and is always thinking up ways to help people out. She can cook and sew and loves the Lord when she remembers she is supposed to put Him first in her life, but she isn't a girl you should fall for. Becky Bates is a much better prospect."

"Oh?" Ben's appetite slackened. "Why do you say that after saying all those fine things about Miss Lily?"

"Because she doesn't want a man who wants to stay in a small town like you do." Great-Aunt Deborah sighed heavily enough to make her body tremble. "Lily was left alone on her family farm for months. Now she wants nothing more than to move to a big city as fast as possible."

Chapter 4

Lily shivered, though she felt no cold even in her drafty telegraph office. She experienced the sensation of Ben's hand firm on her arm, and it made her warm all over. A terrible predicament.

"I don't want to find him attractive." She spoke aloud in the empty office. "Mrs. Twining says he wants to stay here, and he works in a livery."

It was a good job. Many ladies would be happy to catch a husband like him. Lily didn't happen to be one of those females who were satisfied with a man who merely had a good job. She didn't need to be rich; she simply wanted to be more than a girl from a farm or a small town.

Now she had even more motivation for wanting to get Ben's room behind the livery fixed up nice so he could move in. Mrs. Willoughby wasn't charging her much rent in exchange for help around the house, and she still took her meals at Mrs. Twining's in exchange for cooking and shopping and housework. Still, even a few bits a week depleted Lily's savings.

"And Mrs. Twining wants him to stay with her." Lily rubbed her eyes.

She had scarcely slept since her encounter with Ben the day before. All night, she'd tossed and turned, remembering, touching her arm, trying to rub away the tingle, trying not to see his face, which looked as dazed as she'd felt.

Good. Maybe he didn't want to like her, either. He needed a nice, quiet girl. Becky would be perfect for him. She wanted nothing more than a home and family and maybe a trip into Davenport for shopping once a year.

Lily shuddered again and took a message off the telegraph regarding a robbery in Des Moines; she would pass it along to the sheriff in case the thieves came to Browning City.

Jake would want the news, too. He was always looking for sensational news for his paper. Today's issue had a long article about Ben Purcell arriving and getting shot. It ended with a plea for someone to confess to the crime or give information about the gunman.

If only the incident had scared Ben off—

Lily interrupted her thought before she finished it. "Please forgive me, Lord. I am being so unkind to him, and he is making Mrs. Twining so happy."

Miserable about her uncharitable attitude toward Ben Purcell, Lily escaped from the telegraph office the minute Toby arrived and said little to Theo as they trotted straight to Becky's house.

"Will you come help me with the livery living quarters?" she greeted her friend.

Becky jumped back and flung up her hands. "Help! I think I've been run over by a locomotive. Where did it come from?"

"I'm only a freight wagon." Lily laughed and dropped her hat and coat onto a chest inside the Bateses' front door.

"Headed downhill. Come have some coffee or something and tell me what this is all about." Becky turned and directed her steps toward the kitchen. "I haven't seen you long enough this week to talk, and you were the first person to meet Ben Purcell."

"Theo met him at the train, but we never had a proper introduction." With the familiarity of many visits, Lily began to take cups and saucers out of the cupboard while Becky set a coffeepot on the stove. "And he was kind of crazy in the head when I first spoke with him. Kept talking about seeing angels."

"Was he that close to death?" Becky turned her face to show her eyes wide with horror. "I thought it was just a scalp wound."

"It was." Lily set down the cups and hugged her friend. "He thought I was an angel is all. Silly man."

"I think that is terribly romantic." Becky sighed. "Do you think it was love at first sight?"

"No such thing." Lily remembered the jolt at his touch on her arm and turned away in case she blushed. "Now, if he'd seen you, I'd believe it."

"Ha. I'm too dark to be mistaken for an angel."

Becky did have dark hair and eyes, and the roses in her cheeks made her complexion glow with good health. In Lily's opinion, Becky was the prettiest girl in Browning City.

"I went to the mercantile today, and Mr. Gilchrist said he would send over all the things we need to make that room behind the livery fine to live in." Lily spoke too fast in her desire to change the subject away from talk of romance and Ben Purcell.

She could talk about Ben Purcell and his having a nice place to live besides Mrs. Twining's.

"It needs to be cleaned and some rugs put on the floor and curtains and things. But the walls are solid. Will you help me?"

"You know I will." Becky left the coffee simmering and lifted the lid on a pot of rice and beans.

Spicy steam drifted into the room.

"I thought red beans and rice were for Mondays." Lily inhaled the exotic aroma.

Becky's parents were from Louisiana and ate things not common in Browning City.

"It is, but Momma was sick on Monday, so we put off the washing." Becky lowered her voice. "I think she's increasing. Imagine that. Me with another brother or sister when I'm nineteen."

"You're so lucky." Lily's tone was wistful.

She never stopped missing her family.

"We are blessed, but you will be one day, too. God will give you a family again."

Lily said nothing. She wasn't so sure Becky was right.

"Do you want a dish of this rice before the hordes come in to eat it all?" Becky asked.

"I'll wait for the hordes."

Lily enjoyed the tumult around the Bateses' dinner table. She never failed to leave smiling.

"We can talk about how to fix up that room until they come. Mr. Purcell needs a place of his own to live."

Becky nodded. "Especially since everyone says he intends to stay here for good."

⁜

Saturday afternoon, Lily and Becky stood in the middle of the living quarters behind the livery barn and grimaced at each other.

"It's gloomy," Becky pronounced.

"It is." Lily glanced from the small, grimy window to the floor littered with crushed leaves, dirt, and she didn't want to guess what else, to the stove so caked with grease it would catch fire if anyone struck a match near it, let alone inside it. "The last man who lived here must have been a vagabond," Lily said.

"Since Mr. Jones sold it to Mr. Gilchrist, no one's lived here for long." Becky hefted a bristle brush from the supplies Mr. Gilchrist had sent over for them to use. "The last man said he didn't like the sounds the place makes."

"How could he work in a livery and not like the sound of horses?"

Lily thought that the best part. Horses were such beautiful creatures, and she liked the sound of them munching hay and grain.

Becky giggled. "He said people walked around in the livery at night. But he never saw anyone, and we know ghosts don't exist."

"Some folk don't take to being alone."

Lily had imagined all sorts of awful things when she was alone on her family farm, before the bank men came to send her away because she couldn't pay the mortgage.

"But a body isn't really alone here." Becky handed Lily a bucket and picked one up herself. "I mean, there are all sorts of people close by, and I don't know a soul here who wouldn't let you in for a talk and cup of coffee."

"Me, either." Lily headed for the pump in the yard. Hot water would be better than the icy stuff that would come out of the well, but she dared not light the stove. "We'll clean that stove first. The rest will be easy after that."

It was. After four hours of hard work that left their hands red, dresses soiled, and hearts satisfied with the labor, Lily and Becky found the stove dried out enough for a fire. They lit it and two lanterns then stood back to survey their handiwork.

"It looks nice now," Becky declared.

"It does. I think he'll be comfortable here."

Yellows and oranges might not be the colors a man would choose, but they brightened the dark wood walls with curtains, rag rugs, and a bedspread provided from Mrs. Twining's attic. With the fire warming up the room and a few kitchen utensils inviting a body to cook a simple meal, the room was habitable.

"It's just not as nice as living at Mrs. Twining's." Lily didn't mean to speak her thoughts aloud, but once they were out, she was glad she had. "I know she wants him to stay."

"But you've lived with her for three years." Becky dropped onto the room's only chair, now cushioned with pillows Lily had sewn between messages at the telegraph office. "It's your room."

"It's Mrs. Twining's room."

"And doesn't living with Mrs. Willoughby cost you money?"

"Not much if I do some work for her." Lily leaned against the door leading from the room to the livery—and it opened behind her.

"Yie!" Lily staggered back. Strong hands caught her by the elbows. Ben's hands. She knew it without glancing up.

And she looked a fright with her hair tied up in a kerchief, her face likely smudged, since Becky's was, and her gown soiled. She cared and wondered why she should. She didn't care what Ben thought of her looks. Now, if Matt walked in. . .

"I beg your pardon." Ben still held her elbows. "I didn't expect. . .this." His voice grew husky. "Did you ladies do all this for me?"

"Mrs. Twining and Mr. Gilchrist provided the supplies." Becky, her cheeks rosier than usual, drew her skirt together over a streak of dirt down the front. "We just provided the elbow grease. I'm Becky Bates, Lily's friend, by the way."

"Pleased to meet you, Miss Bates. And thank you." Ben let go. "I thought— I was expecting. . ." He cleared his throat. "How can I thank you?"

"No thanks necessary." Becky spoke to him, but she stared at Lily.

Lily knew why. She wasn't usually tongue-tied. Between embarrassment over Ben's seeing her so grubby and her guilty conscience, words escaped her.

"I feel like I should do something to repay you," Ben continued.

"Don't, please." Lily scampered to the far side of the room and began to fuss with the fall of a curtain. "It was nothing."

"Not to me." Ben's boot heels clicked on the floorboards. "It's the closest thing to a home I've had since I can remember. And I know you gave up a day off to do this for me."

Lily shrugged. She couldn't say that she had nothing better to do; she did. She had lace to crochet and sew on her dress before church the next day, as Matt should be back from his travels. He would be at church, and she could talk to him during the fellowship time afterward.

"Would that be acceptable to you, too, Miss Lily?"

Ben's speaking her name brought Lily back to the present.

She faced him. "I'm sorry. I was thinking of something else."

Good. That would convince him that her work on his room meant nothing to her.

Except it does.

She gulped. "What did you ask?"

Becky's eyes widened, and her mouth formed an O of confusion.

"I asked if I could take you two ladies to dinner at the hotel as a thank-you for your work." Ben smiled at her in a tight-lipped way that told her he was unsure of himself.

She wanted to refuse.

She wanted to cry.

She could do neither.

"You need not thank us," she said.

"But. . ." Becky pressed the back of her hand to her lips.

Lily knew Becky would love to go to dinner at the hotel as a guest, because she worked there on the occasions when it was full, such as for a wedding dinner. If Lily refused, Becky couldn't accept.

"We need to clean up," Lily hedged.

"There's time for that." Ben gave her an encouraging smile.

"It won't take either of us long." Becky's face brightened. "It can't be much later than four o'clock."

"All right, then." Lily made herself smile. "Should we meet you there?"

"No, I'll collect both of you. Miss Becky, where do you live?"

Becky gave him directions to her house. "It's on the far side of town but won't take you a minute to get there."

"Then I'll collect you first. Miss Lily, we will see you about six o'clock if that will do."

"It'll do fine." Lily added quietly, "Thank you. Here's the key Mr. Gilchrist gave me when I offered to clean."

"We'd better hurry." Becky headed for the outside door.

"Good day." Lily gathered up bristle brushes and buckets.

Ben opened the door for them. "I still can't get over all this work you two did. Now I can move in here, and you can come back and stay in your own room."

Lily nodded. She would be a hypocrite if she said he need not do that. Yet she felt as though that were the right thing to say. So she said nothing as she and Becky departed.

"What's wrong?" Becky posed the question the instant they were out of earshot.

"I feel terrible." Lily glanced over her shoulder.

Ben couldn't see them once they were on the street.

"You should have said something. If you're ill, we shouldn't go to dinner."

"Not that kind of terrible. In here." Lily tapped her chest with a bristle brush handle.

"Why? Using your day off to fix that place up should make you feel good. It is a fine example of service to another."

Lily walked several paces in silence then blurted out, "It wasn't a service. It was completely selfish."

"What are you talking about? You aren't at all selfish. I remember the time we all had the influenza—"

"Stop." Lily waved the brush in the air. "Yes, I know I helped your family. You all welcomed me the minute I moved here and didn't know a soul. What else would I do but repay you for your kindness? But this wasn't a repayment."

"Which makes it all that much more special."

"No, it's not special. I did this for me."

"You, but—oh!" The exclamation emerged as though someone had punched Becky in the middle. "You did it so he will move there, and you can return to Mrs. Twining's and not pay rent anymore, right?"

"Right. And that's wrong. And now he wants to take us out to dinner to thank us. And I don't deserve it." Breathless from her speech, Lily fell silent.

Becky said nothing, either. Their footfalls crunched on gravel, and their breath puffed white in the dusk gray air. Around them, lights winked on in the houses and the aromas of cooking suppers wafted into the evening.

Lily's stomach growled. "I guess dinner will be good. Mrs. Meddler sets a fine table. But I don't deserve it."

"Well, I do." Becky stuck her nose in the air pertly, minced a few steps, then laughed. "You know, Lil, sometimes people do nice things for themselves. Your reason for fixing up the room might not be charitable, but I think he wants to take us to dinner because he's sweet on you."

"Nonsense. He doesn't know me."

But he'd looked as stunned as she'd felt when he first touched her arm.

She shook off the memory. "I think he would be a perfect match for you."

"Now who's talking nonsense?" Becky laughed. "Didn't you see how he couldn't stop looking at you?"

"No, I did not."

She'd had her back to him most of the time.

"Well, it's true. He did. That's why I say he's sweet on you."

"If you're right—and I'm not saying you are—he can have his mind changed." Lily smiled, her spirits lightening at the prospect of playing matchmaker. "It's perfect. You want to be a wife and mother here in Browning City. And he says he wants to stay here. He has an excellent position there at the livery, and—stop laughing. People will come out and stare at us. I am serious."

"I know." Becky wiped her eyes on her sleeve. "That's what's so funny." She sobered. "And a little frightening. You usually make things happen like you want them to."

⟨◦⟩

Dinner proved to be a success. Determined now to make a match between Becky and Ben, Lily smiled a great deal and said little unless it was to promote her friend in Ben's eyes. He responded to her sallies with a marked interest in Becky, smiling at her, asking her about her family. He had been to Louisiana not long after the war, about the time Becky's family moved north to Iowa, so they had something to talk about that did not include Lily. When they apologized for not including her, she admitted that she would rather listen and learn.

"You know I want to learn all I can about interesting places," she said.

Her plans worked just fine all the way to Becky's. Then she found herself alone with Ben. They strolled through a night cleared of clouds.

This should be Matt beside me! Lily cried out inside her head.

They could talk of all the places the railroad took a body, all the places it would take a body once it expanded even farther around the country. They could discuss moving away to one of those places where people wanted more excitement than a plowing contest and the spring bazaar, sewing bees and an Easter egg hunt.

"I love the peace here." Ben inhaled a lungful of fresh air. "And everything smells so good."

"Does it?" Lily sniffed. "It smells like snow to me."

"Is that what the freshness is? How right are you about that?"

"I've lived in this state all my life. I know how to read the weather."

"In one state all your life." Ben nodded to a lone man stepping out of the hotel. "What's that like? I mean, was it here in Browning City?"

"No, I lived more north. My family had a farm." Lily hugged her arms across her middle.

"Had?" Ben's tone gently probed.

"We lost it."

She didn't want to talk about her family on such a perfect night, even a perfect night with the wrong man.

"I'm sorry. That must have been rough on you."

"Browning City isn't as lonely as the farm got to be, and I like my work."

"But don't you want land?" Ben tilted his head back. "I want land. I want to stand out in a field and stare at a sky like this without a single light to dim the stars."

"I like lights. I like people and noise. It's just the opposite of being left alone like I was."

"Music?"

"Yes. I mean, I like to listen to it. I'm not talented. What about you?"

"Can't carry a tune in a bucket." He laughed.

Lily joined him in the humor, yet she thought maybe he exaggerated. She could not believe a man with the rich timbre of his speaking voice couldn't sing.

"Becky has a lovely singing voice." Lily spoke one more accolade of her friend.

"Becky is a lovely lady."

Lily skipped around the corner leading to Mrs. Willoughby's house. He liked Becky. Wonderful. He thought she was lovely.

Ben paused at the end of Mrs. Willoughby's front walk. "And so are you, Miss Lily. That simple dinner at the hotel wasn't nearly enough to thank the two of you for the time you took to get my room ready for me. I'll have to do—"

"Nothing, please." Lily's tone held desperation. "I—I wasn't being in the least selfless when I cleaned up that room. I was thinking of myself, not you."

A burden lifted from her heart at the confession.

Except Ben laughed. He threw back his head and let the rolling sound drift to the stars.

Lily faced him, shaking her head. "I just admitted that I am a selfish creature, and you laugh at me."

"I'm sorry. I'm not laughing at you. I am laughing because I am so happy to be around a lady who is so refreshingly honest." He touched her cheek with his fingertips. "Of course you did all that work to get your room back. But, to me, that doesn't at all lessen the importance of having my own place to stay, a place that doesn't roll on wheels. And you did that for me, whatever the reason."

"So—" Lily's mouth felt dry. "So did Becky."

"She sure did, and I'm grateful to her, too."

Good. He wasn't singling Lily out. Still. . .that touch on her cheek. . .

"I must get inside." Lily turned away. "I'm freezing. Enjoy your quarters, and thank you again for dinner."

"See you in church?"

"Of course." Lily dashed up the walk and front stoop.

Inside Mrs. Willoughby's house, which always smelled of camphor, Lily paused to listen to Ben's retreating footfalls. He had an easy stride that diminished quickly into the distance. A fine man who was all wrong for her. She must continue her efforts to match him up with Becky.

"How do I get them together?"

Church was impossible. Becky sat with her family to help keep her siblings in line. After the service, her mother needed Becky to corral the children into coats and a line to herd them home. No, Lily needed to get Becky away from her family so she would be free to show Ben more of her charm.

Thinking about an opportunity to play matchmaker, Lily slept little that night. The next day, her head swam with rejected ideas and too little sleep until Mary, the pastor's wife, reminded the congregation of the Easter egg hunt coming up in six weeks.

"We will have a separate party for the adults afterward."

No entertainment for six weeks? Too long. Lily would plan a party, a "welcome to Browning City" party for Ben. Mrs. Twining would be in favor of the idea. Best of all, she'd make certain he met everyone in town he should, as well as get to better know his future wife. It was the least she could do to repay him for being so gracious about her selfish motives for fixing up his chamber.

Chapter 5

Y ou should come into the parlor and join us." Ben stood in the doorway to the overheated kitchen and smiled down at Lily. "The kitchen won't fly away if you aren't here to hold it down."

"But the coffee may boil over." Lily picked up a knife. "And if people want more cake—"

"They can come get it themselves. Now come along. You haven't sat down for a minute since the guests arrived." Ben held out his hand to her.

As she did anytime they met, and shaking hands or even giving an object like a plate or cup to one another that might result in his touching her, Lily skittered away like a frightened rabbit. She busied herself with something, even unnecessary tasks, to avoid being near him.

The reaction made Ben smile. If she were indifferent to him, she wouldn't work so hard to keep out of his way.

"Or I could just take the rest of this food into the parlor for you." He started to lift the heavy tray of cake and sandwiches. "Will that do?"

"No, no, I need to keep them covered." Lily flicked a tea towel over the lot. "They'll go stale if I don't keep them moist, and we can't have a towel over them out there. People wouldn't eat anything. So I must stay here and fill plates."

"Everyone here, even my rather infirm great-aunt, can fill his own plate." Ben stepped forward and took Lily's hand.

Despite the heat in the kitchen, her fingers were freezing.

"You need to be near a fire." He glanced at the stove and grinned at her.

That coaxed a slow smile out of her. "Maybe I'm tired."

"But these people are your friends, your neighbors. You've known them for years."

"Only three. They're more your aunt's friends and neighbors. My friends haven't come." She looked so disappointed that he squeezed her hand and gently drew her forward.

"I'm your friend, and I'm here."

"But Becky and Matt aren't, and I particularly wanted them here." She blinked, glanced down, and drew her hand free. "Maybe they'll come later."

"If they do, you'll be closer to the door to greet them."

Lily looked up at him and laughed. "Did you sell things with your father?"

"I did. I was especially good at selling pretty ribbons to the ladies."

"I can imagine you were." She set the last sandwich on the tray. "Now, do you think anyone in the parlor wants anything?"

"Your presence." Ben opened the door again. "At least I do, and I'm the guest of honor. So come along."

"Yes, sir." Lily headed for the doorway, stopped, and yanked off her apron.

Ben decided not to tell her that a loose curl bobbed on the back of her neck. It looked so sweet he wanted to touch it to see if it felt as silky as it looked.

He followed her and the bouncing curl from the kitchen.

In the parlor, a blazing fire and a dozen voices greeted them with warmth. Listening to everyone greet Lily, watching their faces light as she entered the room, Ben wondered how she could say that they were not her friends and neighbors. Every man and woman in the parlor received joy from her arrival in their midst.

So did he. The parlor looked complete with her present, as though someone had restored a missing link to a chain. More like the clasp holding it all together.

"Come sit here, Miss Lily." Jake Doerfel, the newspaperman, shifted to sit on the arm of the sofa and left an empty place on the cushion beside Mrs. Reeves, the pastor's wife.

Lily shook her head. "Ben should sit down. He's the guest of honor."

"My great-nephew is too much a gentleman to sit down and leave you standing." Great-Aunt Deborah thumped her cane on the floor. "You should know that by now, Lily. Now sit so we can get back to talking about Ben with him here instead of behind his back."

"Were you really talking about me behind my back?" Ben crossed the room to perch on the edge of the windowsill beside Great-Aunt Deborah. "What were you saying?"

"That you had the good sense not to keep on leading the life your father led." Great-Aunt Deborah scowled. "It's no way to raise a family."

"Or even find a wife," said Jackson Reeves, the pastor, "so you can raise that family."

"Hold up." Ben held up one hand in a staying gesture, palm forward. "I have to establish myself first."

"And meet the young ladies who aren't taken," Jake put in. "Kind of like Miss Lily here." He poked a pencil-thin finger into her shoulder.

She turned the color of a ripe strawberry.

Ben grinned. "She'll do for a start, but I'm sure Browning City has someone else to give me a choice."

"There's Becky Bates and Emma Kirkpatrick and Eva Gilchrist when she's in town, and. . ." Lily rattled off a list of female names a yard long.

She spoke each name so quickly and precisely that Ben wondered if she had them memorized. Since the night he took her and Becky out to dinner at the hotel, Ben suspected that Lily intended to play matchmaker between Becky and him. With everyone watching them, he couldn't resist teasing her a bit more about giving him a selection of young ladies from which to choose.

"I thought maybe this party was going to be a parade of ladies. I'm so disappointed."

Everyone laughed. Everyone except Lily. She looked hurt. Ben thought her lower lip quivered a bit before she drew it between her teeth and ducked her head.

"I guess I scared them off at church last week," Ben said, regretting having teased Lily.

"Not from what I heard." Jackson guffawed.

"Nor I." Jake began to sketch in the air. "I think I sold a paper to every single female in Browning City. They wanted that drawing I made of you, Ben. If I had a camera and could have taken a photograph, I could have sold those for ten times the cost of a paper."

Laughter broke out again. With the tables turned on him, Ben joined in. He was glad to see Lily smiling.

"I did invite a few more people." Lily glanced toward the door. "I don't know why they haven't come."

"He'll have a chance to meet everyone as the weather improves." Mary Reeves patted Lily's hand.

"This is quite enough of a crowd for this house for now." Great-Aunt Deborah reached for her cup of coffee. "But you'd better take the leftover cake and pie to the church tomorrow, or we'll both get as round as pumpkins."

"So are you glad you settled here even without a bevy of females lined up?" Mr. Gilchrist asked.

"Quite glad." Ben couldn't stop himself from glancing in Lily's direction.

She was talking with Jake Doerfel. The newspaperman was amusing her. How pretty she was when she laughed.

"Aye, she is a fine-looking girl." Mr. Gilchrist nodded his head, his white hair catching the lamplight and glowing. "But it makes me weary to watch her. Never sits still. If this town doesn't offer her enough excitement, she stirs it up."

Ben grinned. "I can't imagine this town ever having excitement, which is fine with me."

"Oh no, we've had our share of thrills. Mostly because of the gold."

"Lars, please." Great-Aunt Deborah groaned. "Don't bring up that subject again."

But the others had ceased talking and turned to stare at Lars Gilchrist.

"Now, Deborah, you know it's true about the gold being the most excitement we've had here in years." Mr. Gilchrist nodded his head. "Three times now it's brought us a thrill, first when the thieves rode through—"

"Allegedly rode through," Great-Aunt Deborah interrupted.

"Or stayed, I understand." Jake stood as though intending to give a speech.

"No evidence of that." Jackson Reeves looked as thin-lipped as Great-Aunt Deborah did.

"But we have had government men and young women alike seeking that gold." Mary smiled. "Andrew and Tara Jefferson and Constance and Hans Van de Kieft looked. None of them found it, but they found their life mates."

"A much richer haul than gold no one is sure exists." Great-Aunt Deborah sounded positively sharp-tongued.

"I don't know much about it." Despite his aunt's disapproval of the subject, Ben wanted details.

He wanted gold. Gold would buy him land, provide him with permanence—a house, a wife, children—far sooner than would working and saving every penny possible.

"Theo did mention something about it when I arrived," he added.

"Theo talks too much." Great-Aunt Deborah held out her coffee cup. "Lily, may I have some more?"

"Of course." Lily sprang to her feet.

"I'll get it," Ben offered.

Lily fetched the cup. "No, Ben, I'll get it. You stay here and talk with your guests."

"It was stolen from the Union at the end of the war." Jake shifted his weight from foot to foot. "Taken right out from under the noses of some Pinkertons, or so the story goes. They were identified, and some folk in these parts swore they recognized them from drawings. Some said one of the farmers in these parts was involved. But nothing was ever proved or found, and that farmer skedaddled out of here not too long after."

"How much gold?" Ben persisted.

"Too much for a couple of men on horseback to carry," Great-Aunt Deborah snapped.

"Most folk think Jim Mitchell buried it on his farm," Gilchrist said. "But if he did, don't know why he'd've sold all his equipment to me before he left town."

"Constance and Hans live there now," Mary added. "They've never found a thing, and not for lack of trying."

"But the government is still offering a reward for it," Jake said. "A big reward. So the story must be true at least in part, and getting the reward would be worth the try."

"But how does one try in this vast land?" Ben glanced toward the windows, where darkness and the town curtained millions of acres possibly concealing his key to having everything for which he had yearned and prayed since a child.

I'm going to find it, Lord.

Great-Aunt Deborah would not talk about the gold. Ben tried to get more information out of her after the party, but she gave him the same answer every time. "Concentrate on working hard and seeking the Lord's will for your life."

Ben thought, but refrained from saying, that he saw nothing wrong with God wanting him to find the gold. At least he didn't think seeking it would do any harm.

So Monday, with the horses, mule, and both buggies rented out, he left a sign on the livery door that said he would be back shortly. Mr. Gilchrist had told him he could take breaks during the day, especially if everything was rented or if the weather made business slow. Taking advantage of this generosity, Ben strode down Main Street and entered the newspaper office.

"Not surprised to see you." Jake Doerfel grinned at him. "You seemed mighty interested in that gold. Just getting around to sorting out the old issues."

"Did the previous editor keep back issues?" Ben asked.

"Not very regular, and some are water damaged. You're welcome to look." Jake opened a door behind his paper-strewn desk. "Wish I could make copies of those pages. I could sell them for ten times what a paper costs and make my fortune."

"Do you think that many people would be interested?"

The instant he asked the question, Ben knew it was foolish. From what he had learned, over the past ten years, two young women had come hundreds of miles to find the gold because they had read of it somewhere.

"I'll see what I can learn." Ben circled the desk and entered the back room.

It smelled of mice and dampness, ink and paper. For several moments, he simply stood and stared at the papers stacked from floor to ceiling. Years' worth. Sometimes several copies from the same week, he realized on closer inspection. It appeared as though no one ever threw out an extra paper. He plucked a stack of papers from the pile Jake indicated. War news of the gold disappearing. He began to hunt through the stacks in search of more information. Dust and mildew rose like swamp gas. He began to sneeze. At the end of the half hour he had allowed himself, however, he knew that two men rode through town, put their horses up at the livery, rode on to Jim Mitchell's farm, then disappeared. Only suspicion and speculation tied the men to the vanished gold, especially when Jim Mitchell sold out and disappeared himself. Other than mentions of Miss Constance Miller and Miss Tara Young coming to town to seek the gold at two different times after the war, the story vanished from the news. Locating further information about the gold appeared as difficult as discovering the treasure itself.

Extremely dirty and a little discouraged, Ben thanked the newspaperman and strode back to the livery in time to collect one buggy and horse and have a cup of coffee before the rest of the animals came in. Feeding, watering, and rubbing them down took up the rest of the day. By dark, he had finished his work. Weary, he wanted to fix his supper and rest. At the same time, he experienced a restlessness he knew stemmed from his pursuit of information about the stolen gold.

"Perhaps this is wrong, Lord?" He shrugged on his coat.

A brisk walk in the frosty air would do him good. But he didn't know where to go until he heard a train whistle blast its mournful tune across the countryside.

According to the clock in the Scott's Bank window, the train was late. He hoped nothing was wrong. Lily would know if something were.

He turned his feet toward the train station. If nothing else, he could escort her home. She shouldn't be walking through the dark anyway. Of course, she might already be home, but no one could blame a body for trying.

He met Lily halfway between the railway station and town, recognizing her quick, light steps crunching on the frozen gravel.

"Lily?"

She gasped. "Oh, Ben, it's you."

"Who did you expect?" He fell into step beside her.

"No one, but since you got shot. . .I admit it. I am a bit nervous on this road now whenever Theo can't walk me home after dark."

"Then I'm glad I'm here to walk you home." He hesitated. "I'm always glad to walk you home if I can get away on time."

He held his breath, waiting for her response.

"Thank you."

Since he expected a rejection of his offer, her simple thanks felt like a blessing.

"I noticed the train was late." He took the first item of conversation that came to him.

"Nearly half an hour. Toby was late, too. Toby is almost always late. Some ice on track slowed the train out of Davenport. The land is low there near the river, and ice is a problem."

"Or for the engineer to have a cup of coffee?" he joked.

She smiled. "Something like that. Speaking of ice, it's getting cold again." She shivered. "I think we're going to get more snow."

"Do you smell it?"

"No."

"Then I say we won't. It's March."

"It's also Iowa." She wrapped her arms around herself. "We can get snow in April."

"Thank you for the warning. I'll keep supplies in as much as I can."

"We always do."

They covered a hundred yards or so without speaking.

Then Lily took an audible breath. "I saw you met all the people at church who didn't come on Saturday."

"Yes, they were all generous enough to introduce themselves and apologize for not attending."

"That was good of them, but I still wish they had been able to come."

"It was only a handful."

"But I like lots of people around." Lily sighed. "Twelve does not make a respectable number for a party. And it was just too bad that Becky had a cold in her head. And the others had other commitments. Young people, I mean," she finished in a rush.

"Lily, I enjoyed every minute." He wanted to touch her hand, reassure her that the gathering in his honor pleased him more than mere words could express. He would try, though. "I might have had parties when I was a child, but I don't recall. So as far as I am concerned, Saturday was the first one meant for me I've ever had. And that makes it perfect."

"Thank you." In the faint light drifting from the houses, he caught her shy smile slanted in his direction.

His heart contracted. His breath caught in his throat. Great-Aunt Deborah's words came to him, reminding him that Lily wasn't for him. Yet no amount of words could stop a body from caring about another.

He needed to change the subject, make it less personal before he said something that would scare her off. He needed time to convince her to stay—if she was supposed to.

If she was meant for him.

Until he knew one way or the other, he saw nothing wrong with capturing her attention.

"I thought the discussion of the gold was interesting."

"It was." Lily looked thoughtful for a moment as they approached Great-Aunt Deborah's house.

"Did I say something wrong?" he asked.

266

"Not wrong. . ." She stepped onto the bottom tread of the porch stairs. "It's a never-ending source of fascination to all of us here in Browning City."

"Except for Great-Aunt Deborah."

"Except for Mrs. Twining." Lily clasped her gloved hands together beneath her chin and gazed at him. "You see, she doesn't like the talk because one of the legends surrounding the gold is that the last place anyone ever saw one of the robbers or his saddlebags was in the livery."

"And her husband, my great-uncle, owned it then."

Chapter 6

Lily knew of only one way to divert a man's interest from her—make matters clear to him that her interests lay elsewhere. That was exactly what she must do where Ben was concerned. She knew he liked her more than she wanted him to. So she must show him that she would have a man like Matt Campbell or nobody at all in Browning City.

Matt wouldn't stay in Browning City any longer than she would. His work with the railroad would carry him away as soon as a promotion came his way.

Typing in a message for the Davenport station regarding Matt, Lily thought a promotion was likely to come his way sooner than later. Good for her sake if she could engage his interest in her. She had not yet managed to get herself out of this back of beyond town through promotion. All the city jobs went to operators with more seniority. She would get out through marriage or money.

Money. Strange how Ben wanted to find the gold as much as anyone else did. Lily thought he was above that sort of hankering after wealth. Perhaps he possessed more ambition than she suspected. If only those ambitions didn't still seem to turn toward this outpost of Iowa civilization, she would find his attentions pleasing. Disturbing.

His touch on her cheek the other night had blurred her mind. Such a reaction seemed wrong to her, and she considered discussing it with Mary Reeves. Surely she should not find Ben attractive while setting her sights on another man.

And that other man was on his way home to Browning City. His train would come in too late for Lily to still be at work, but now Becky could include him in the planning committee for the Easter egg hunt. Since his parents' house, where he stayed when in town, lay only a block from Mrs. Twining's, he could walk her over to Becky's house. Lily knew she could get Becky to manage that for her.

So she dressed with care the night of the committee meeting. Nothing too fancy. She didn't have an extensive wardrobe. But she pinned a crocheted collar to her blue wool dress and another fall of lace around the knot of her hair. Pleased that she looked as good as she could, she listened for approaching footfalls and a knock on the door.

She heard whistling first. Tuneless whistling. Odd. Matt never whistled to her knowledge.

At the first *crunch* of a step on the front walk, Lily began to suspect the worst. When the knock sounded, she knew she was right.

With a sinking heart, she opened the door. "Good evening, Ben. You came out of your way to fetch me."

"Only two blocks." He removed his hat and stepped into the entryway. "Good evening, Great-Aunt Deborah. What are you reading?"

"Judges, lad." Mrs. Twining held up her Bible, a finger marking her place between the pages. "What scripture have you read lately, Ben?"

"The Gospel of Matthew." He looked at Lily.

She knew they wanted her to share what she, too, was reading. Except she hadn't read her Bible recently. She had been too busy making lace and working either at the telegraph office or for Mrs. Twining. She was too tired at night and too rushed in the morning.

"I've been neglectful." At least she knew enough to confess her sin to other Christians.

"You can't know God's will for your life without reading His Word." Mrs. Twining appeared sad rather than reproving.

Lily nodded and turned to pluck her coat from a hook by the door. "I always intend to read it. . . . I know that's not good enough. I'll start tomorrow."

"I'll look in on you." Ben's smile took the sting out of his words, but Lily still felt chastised.

"We should go." She opened the front door. "We can walk over with Matt Campbell. He should be on his way here any minute."

"He's already gone to Becky's house," Ben said. "He carried some things home from the mercantile for her."

"I see."

Lily did see and didn't like the picture. Becky and Matt? No, that wouldn't do at all.

He was probably just being kind.

While neglecting me.

Ben closed the front door behind them. "He asked me to come fetch you."

So he hadn't neglected her. That helped a bit.

But not enough.

"Were you all in the mercantile?" Lily set off at a brisk pace. "Or did he go to the livery to ask you?"

"We were all at the mercantile." Ben's voice held a note of amusement. "He did have to run back to ask me to come by for you, if that helps."

"Helps with what?"

"Your feeling like he forgot about you in favor of Becky."

"I—" Lily's cheeks stung with the flush of embarrassment.

"I expect that's interesting work as a railroad engineer." Ben slipped his hand beneath her elbow. "Takes him all sorts of places."

Lily tensed herself against liking Ben's fingers cupping her arm. "It is. He's interesting. When a body can get him to talk, he'll tell you about all those mountains and cities and lonely plains. . . ." Her voice choked up on her. The lights from the houses blurred before her eyes. Her longing for what seemed impossible to get became a physical ache.

"It's not all good, Lily." Ben's tone was gentle. "It's lonely and cold and wearying to the soul to always be moving."

"Matt doesn't think so."

"Of course he does."

"How do you know? Do you know him as well as I do?"

"Maybe—ah, there are Eva Gilchrist and Tom Bailyn. Now that's an interesting pair, with her daddy owning one mercantile and Tom owning the other."

"I haven't talked to her since she got home." Lily wanted to run up to Eva and bombard her with questions about Philadelphia, but she held back. "She's been visiting her mother's folks."

Eva and Tom waited for Lily and Ben. When a wagon rumbled past, Lily managed to fall into step beside Eva, forcing the men behind them.

"I can't wait to see what you're wearing. Is it very smart and new?"

"Of course." Eva let out her low chuckle of a laugh. "And yes, I will be happy to let you copy the pattern. But it does feel good to be home. I am fatigued to death with all the social calls they arranged for me while trying to find me a husband."

"Did they succeed?" Lily tried to think how to extract every detail of Eva's journey from her. "Are you engaged?"

"No. None of them had any intention of coming west to take over Daddy's business or the farm with me."

"With—" Lily stopped so abruptly, Ben stepped on the back of her heel.

"I beg your pardon," he apologized.

"My fault." Lily wriggled her heel back into her shoe. "I was just so surprised I forgot to keep walking. Eva, you didn't really want to come back here, did you?"

"I did." Eva linked her arm with Lily's and got the party moving again. "I love Iowa in the spring. And I missed church. My relatives hardly ever go."

The instant they reached the bottom of the front walk to Becky's house, four children burst from the front door and raced out to surround them with excited chatter regarding their likes and dislikes for the Easter egg hunt.

"Did you say you want a real chicken instead of an egg?" Lily scooped up the youngest child and carried her to the house. "That could be kind of hard to catch."

"I'd do it." Molly, a four-year-old cherub in looks and imp in behavior, hooked her arm around Lily's neck. " 'Cause then we would always have eggs to bake cakes."

"Ah, is that why?" Smiling, Lily entered the warmth of the Bateses' house.

Several minutes of confusion reigned while Mrs. Bates hustled the children off to bed, Mr. Bates collected coats and hats, and Becky asked people's preference for coffee or tea.

Lily loved every minute of the hubbub. She wished it would continue or that she lived in a household like Becky's—one that rarely knew peace and quiet. She knew she would be alone in the city if she didn't have a husband with whom she could move there, but she believed she would never feel alone with hundreds of people within shouting distance.

At last, the six of them sat around the Bateses' kitchen table, and Matt lifted a sheet of foolscap off the top of a block of writing paper. "Becky and I already made a list of things we need to accomplish." He flashed his wide grin at her. "She was just full of ideas. Good ones."

Becky blushed and grinned back.

Lily stared. Coffee burned in her stomach.

She must be mistaken. Surely Matt and Becky weren't courting. Surely he would find her dull.

But how could anyone find Becky dull? She was lively and pretty and smart. Lily adored her. That Matt adored her, too, seemed inevitable.

But I wanted Ben to fall for her.

Ben scarcely noted Becky's presence. He danced attendance on Eva and Lily, leaving Matt to fetch and carry anything Becky needed and Tom to crack jokes about having nothing to do and putting his feet up.

Lily admitted—grudgingly—that Becky and Matt looked good together. They both had fine, dark eyes and curly dark hair. They both shared brilliant, white smiles.

But they didn't share anything else. Lily knew it. Becky wanted to stay put. Matt traveled. Becky would never like that.

Lord, can't they see that this will be disastrous for them?

Lily was so engrossed in her concerns that she didn't notice the conversation turning away from the Easter egg hunt party to a charitable event to start a library in Browning City—due to Eva's sojourn to the East.

"I did enjoy going," she said. "I enjoy coming home even more."

"I feel the same way." Matt nodded. "When I see the Browning City depot coming into view, I want to pile on steam and get here faster."

"You don't want to shoot out of here faster?" Lily asked before she could stop herself.

"Not any faster than necessary." Matt picked up his coffee cup and held it between his hands. A dreamy expression came over his face. "I pass farm after farm with each trip, and I can't help but wonder what it would be like to stay put year after year."

"Tedious," Lily murmured.

"Traveling is tedious." Ben looked straight at her, though he addressed the group. "I did it for nearly twenty years. When I gave my heart to the Lord, the first thing He had to work on with me was not envying all those folks I passed who had real houses to live in."

"A real house is good." Lily agreed with him on that. "We had a snug one on our family farm. But it went the same way as the land—to the bank. So a body may as well not have one."

"Unless you can pay for it outright," Tom put in. "I waited to buy the mercantile from Evan Cooper until I could own it outright and have living quarters above."

"I intend to do the same thing," Ben said. "I may be old and gray before I can afford a farm, but I'll own it."

"I just worked out today that I can buy the farm I want." Matt made the announcement in a quiet voice that rang with joy.

And he gazed at Becky when he said it.

Lily stared at him. "You are giving up the railroad? Travel? All those places you talk about?"

"Yes, ma'am, I am." Matt looked like he would burst with joy. "I turned in my notice today."

"But just the other day. . ." Lily stopped.

She couldn't say what the telegram about him contained, the praise for his skill and recommendation for promotion to more regular routes. But if he knew, surely he would change his mind.

"I was offered a better position." Matt spoke as though reading her mind. "You probably knew that, Lily."

She nodded.

"I'd have been traveling between Des Moines and Chicago and home regularly. More pay, too. But I turned it down. I'm thirty-two. It's time I settled down."

Lily felt as though someone had yanked a chair out from beneath her. If she were able to find work elsewhere, especially work with more pay, she wouldn't turn it down. For months, she had pinned her hopes of getting out of Browning City on her savings growing and on Matt Campbell taking a serious interest in combining their futures at the altar. Now all she could count on were her savings, and they looked too pitiful for any kind of life in the city. Yet she counted herself fortunate that he had fallen for Becky instead of her.

"Lily?" Ben laid his hand on the back of her chair. "You look a bit peaked. Do you want to go home?"

She did feel unwell.

"Yes, please." She gave everyone a bright smile. "Good night, everyone. May I call on you Sunday afternoon to look at your Eastern clothes, Eva?"

"Right after church. Come to dinner." Eva kissed Lily's cheek. "It'll be fun because I am going to get a lace collar out of you yet."

Lily said her good-byes to the others and allowed Ben to usher her from the house.

Neither of them spoke for the first three blocks. Around them, the night lay still save for the *hiss* of wind through bare tree branches and a banging shutter somewhere in the distance. Clouds obscured the sky, and though they didn't have a lantern to brighten the streets, Lily knew every hollow and rut well enough not to trip in the poor light as long as she concentrated. If Ben remained silent, she could pay attention to her feet.

"Why do you think the city is so grand?" He broke the stillness with a question that made Lily stumble.

She set her chin. "It has more people and more lights and more things going on. A body doesn't get lonely there."

"You're mistaken in that, Lily." He took her gloved hand in his. "I was lonely all the time when I was in the city."

"You were lonely all the time you were traveling, from what you said."

She knew she should withdraw her hand from his, but she liked the strength of his fingers around hers.

"I was until I met the Lord face-to-face, so to speak." His voice held a smile. "I talked to Him after that whenever Pa didn't have much to say. He didn't have much to say very often unless he was selling one of his goods from the wagon. He sure could make friends then."

"He must have met a trainload of people over the years." Lily knew she sounded wistful as she gazed into the distance. "Lots of people to be friends with at any time."

"Lily." Ben stopped and faced her. "When my father died, not one person he had met over the years was there. He collapsed in the street in Chicago, and not one person came to his aid."

"That's. . .terrible." Lily shook her head to clear it. "I mean, you'd think someone would stop."

"You would." Ben tightened his hand on hers. "I found him myself about the time a policeman got there."

"So someone did summon help." Lily felt relief lightening her mood.

"Someone complained about him blocking their shop doorway."

Lily flinched. "That must have hurt you terribly."

"You know what hurt worse?" Ben resumed walking, urging Lily along with him. "No one came to his funeral. I sent notices to the paper. I thought a few of his regular customers would come or a few people he'd helped along the way would take a minute to pay their respects. But no one did."

"I'm so sorry. But if he had stayed in that one place for years, it would have been different."

"Possibly for the funeral, yes, but not the other. No one can live in a city long enough to know everybody."

"But that's part of what must be interesting about it. I mean, someone new is always around the corner, unlike here." Lily waved her hand to the silent, near-dark town. "Other than Jake Doerfel buying the old newspaper last month, you were the first person to come here to stay permanently in an age."

"And you and Theo stopped to help this stranger."

"We knew who you were. Of course we helped Mrs. Twining's great-nephew."

"And you helped me because you both knew her."

Lily wanted to argue with him, but words escaped her until they reached Mrs. Twining's street.

"Ben, life isn't all good in a small town. We have people here, and that means we have bad things happen. People get into fights and steal things. Someone stole my pocketbook right out of the telegraph office one day. I'd just gotten paid and didn't have time to get to the bank. When I ran out to give a message to Theo to deliver, my money vanished."

"That must have been rough on you."

"More than rough. I had to eat into my savings to get by until my next pay. And I'm not a stranger here. I've lived in Browning City for three years. Everyone knows me because of the telegraph."

"I think everyone knows you because of everything you do here."

"Which is just what I'm saying." Lily yanked her hand from his at last and curled her fingers into fists. "I am always organizing one function or another to make this town more entertaining, and I find ways to raise money for the school and church. . .and then someone steals from me."

"Could it have been someone from the train and not a Browning City resident at all?"

"It. . ." Lily thought a moment. "I suppose it could have been."

"And maybe they really needed that money. I'm not saying their action was right, but considering that money as a gift to the Lord instead of something taken from you helps."

Lily took in his words and nodded. "It does. Ben, I. . ." She gazed up at him and wished she could see his face clearly. "I truly admire your faith in God. I could never have thought of things that way."

He chuckled. "It's easy to give others advice. I'd probably feel about the same as you if someone stole my pay."

"Just put it in the bank immediately. The bankers are trustworthy here."

"I know, but they're both customers, so I don't know which one to use."

"Half to each?"

They laughed as they headed onto the porch.

Lily rested her hand on the doorknob. "Good night, Ben. Thank you."

Ben brushed the knuckles of his gloved hand across her cheekbone. "Thank you, Lily."

Before she could ask him for what he'd thanked her, he turned and strode down the walk to the street.

Lily slipped inside and locked the door behind her. But that was as far as she moved toward readying herself for sleep. Instead, she leaned against the door and listened to his footfalls dwindle into the distance.

When she no longer heard him, she tilted her face to heaven. "I know now that I am a poor Christian, Lord. I don't know what to do about it yet, but I have a feeling I'm going to find out."

She suspected that Ben would continue to play a role in showing her. Such a pity he wasn't the right man to play a far different role in her life.

Chapter 7

No matter how many times Ben examined the livery, he could not figure out how anyone could have hidden so much as a half eagle in the building, let alone an entire cache of stolen gold. Walls, floor, and roof consisted of boards fitted together with near seamless perfection. When his great-uncle built the livery, he'd constructed it to last through generations of Iowa winds and weather. Even Ben's little room in the back demonstrated craftsmanship meant for longevity. If legend of the thieves having cached their illicit loot in the livery bore any fragment of truth, someone far more clever than Ben would have to work out how they'd accomplished the task.

He thought perhaps the thieves stowed it amid a collection of farm equipment gathering dust in one corner of the building. Mr. Gilchrist had said that soon after purchasing the livery he'd bought the equipment from Jim Mitchell, a farmer leaving the district. It was of little to no interest to Ben, so he turned his attention to the hayloft, but only briefly. One look around told him that nothing stashed up there would go unnoticed for months, let alone years.

No, the gold was not in the livery any more than it had been in any other location treasure hunters had explored over the eleven years since the war ended and the money disappeared. He had no more chance of finding easy wealth than had anyone else.

Disappointment lay heavy on his heart. He didn't long for a quick addition to his savings because he was lazy. He liked exerting himself, found great satisfaction in ending a day with the knowledge that he had wasted few to no minutes of his time. He liked the sensation of muscles fatigued from honest labor rather than aching from sitting still.

But he wanted to remain in Browning City. He had been here a month and knew he had found the place he had sought since growing old enough to realize that life on the road was not what most other folks experienced in their lives. Browning City was home. Perhaps he recalled something of the place from his childhood, though Great-Aunt Deborah pointed out how much the town had changed in twenty years. Two banks. Two general stores. A newspaper. Farmers had come and gone, prospered and failed, grown restless and settled down to build the next generation.

Ben wanted to settle down and build the next generation—with Lily at his side.

Except Lily didn't want to be at his side. She yearned for life beyond the rolling prairies of Iowa. She sought the faster pace of the city because it was as far from her homeland as a body could imagine.

Having spent much of his life moving from farmland to small town, from village to metropolis, Ben knew happiness did not lie in crowds and one entertainment after another. The pleasure was fleeting, leaving one emptier afterward than before. He suspected that Lily would learn this for herself once she had the experience. He feared she would suffer for insisting that she learned.

He didn't want her to suffer. Lily Reese had seen too much pain in her life already. Ben wanted to give her joy, make her laugh, meet life's challenges together.

"Thy will be done, Lord." He meant what he said at the end of each prayer for his future. Yet at the same time, visions of a reward for locating government gold glittered in the corners of his mind.

With gold, he could have his own land while he was still young enough to work it hard and make it prosper. He could do more. He could provide his wife with occasional journeys to Chicago, enough so she would appreciate the camaraderie and caring of a small town.

Without the miracle of finding gold, Ben resigned himself to waiting while he saved enough from his wages to purchase land and observing Lily's search for happiness in ceaseless activity.

Lily was involved in so many different activities Ben couldn't keep them all straight. Easter egg hunt for the children. Easter egg hunt and party for adults. Something she called the spring bazaar. Each planning meeting and preparation seemed to take up her time to the exclusion of walking with him. She didn't even stay in the parlor and visit when he called on Great-Aunt Deborah. After serving them coffee and cake or cookies, she escaped into the kitchen, her room, or to someone else's home.

Ben suspected she was avoiding him.

The idea of that made him smile. She had to have some kind of feelings for him to make herself scarce whenever he was around.

As March slipped into its latter half, Ben grew weary of fleeting glimpses of Lily and even more rare conversations, despite their paths crossing during church and at the homes of mutual acquaintances. He took matters into his own hands. On a day warm enough to promise spring in the near future, in spite of heavy rainfall, a day too wet for anyone to be interested in riding, Ben took out one of the buggies and drove it toward the train station. All the way, riding with the top up, he scanned the road for a diminutive figure trudging through the mud.

He caught up with her halfway between railroad and town.

"Climb in." He reined in beside her. "You're drenched."

She glanced up, and a stream of rain cascaded into her face. She wiped it away with a soaked sleeve. "Is something wrong? Mrs. Twining?"

"No, nothing's wrong."

She crossed her arms over her middle. "Then why are you here?"

"It's raining. Business was slow at the livery." He grinned at her. "I thought I could offer a pretty lady a ride under those circumstances."

"You can. . . ." She laughed. "You know I can't say no." She took his hand, gathered up her skirt, and swung herself aboard. "I think you're taking advantage of me, Mr. Purcell."

"Mr. Purcell?" He handed her a dry rug to place over her knees before getting the horse going again. "I know you've been a stranger lately, but surely not that much."

"I apologize." She settled back against the seat while he turned the buggy back toward Browning City. "Some inspectors from Western Union were here all day, so I've been calling everyone, even Theo, 'Mister.' "

"Is something wrong at the telegraph office?"

Ben's gut tightened. If the company discontinued Browning City's telegraph service, Lily would leave before he had a chance to change her mind about the town. Worse, it would confirm her belief that Browning City was too much of a backwater to endure any longer.

"I think all is well." Lily tucked her hands inside her coat sleeves. "They were nice to me, but they wanted to see how fast I can key in a message."

"Are you fast?"

"Compared to the other operators, yes, but I don't know about the ones in the city offices where they get more messages."

"Do you want to be faster than they are?" He held the horse to a slow, steady pace to make the drive last a handful of minutes longer.

"I like to be good at what I do." She shifted on the seat so she faced him. "If nothing is wrong, why did you come fetch me?"

"It's raining. And"—he gripped the reins—"I wanted a chance to see you."

"Why?"

"I never get to see you anymore."

She drew her golden brows together. "I saw you at church yesterday."

"Saw me, yes. But you didn't speak to me."

"No, I didn't." She repositioned herself to face the curtain of rain sluicing off the buggy top in a silvery curtain. "We're fortunate this isn't snow."

"And maybe you count yourself fortunate that this drive is so short." He spoke more harshly than he intended but didn't regret doing so.

He couldn't stop her from evading him in the street or at church, but she didn't need to switch the subject to the weather, something strangers might discuss in a railroad car, while riding in a buggy with him.

He tightened his hands on the reins and sent the horse careening around the last corner faster than prudent. A wheel slipped in the muddy street, and the buggy lurched.

Lily grasped the edge of the seat. "You're angry with me."

"I am annoyed." He slowed the vehicle to a halt before Great-Aunt Deborah's house. "I want to know what happened to the lady who was honest enough to admit she helped me out of selfishness."

"You want me to admit to some other wrong to you? Because I won't." She glared up at him for a moment then turned away. "I haven't done anything bad to you. I simply have other responsibilities and interests that don't include you."

"Is that the truth?"

She continued to gaze into the wet darkness.

"At least you aren't telling more than one lie."

She stiffened. "I never lied."

"You exaggerate the truth, then."

"I—maybe a little." Her tone held the tiniest hint of a laugh.

"Much better." He lifted a strand of damp hair from where it clung to her cheek. "May I ask why—in a warmer place than here?"

"Mrs. Twining has her ladies' prayer meeting tonight. I usually attend, but if you insist, I guess you can come into the kitchen."

"Don't sound so unhappy about the prospect of my calling."

"I don't want you to call." She flicked the rug aside, rose, and stepped down from the buggy without assistance. "I'm just being polite in letting you come by for coffee."

"Thank you." He tipped his hat. "I'll be there at seven o'clock."

"Seven thirty."

"Yes, ma'am."

He watched her until she disappeared into the house; then he drove around to the livery. Horse and buggy dried as best as he could, and the former fed, he entered his quarters to prepare his simple meal of bread, cheese, and a rather withered apple from the previous year's harvest. The two hours he had to wait dragged so long he took up one of the books that had gone with his father and him around the country. It was one of his mother's books, something more appealing to females, he supposed, so he'd never read it. But, while waiting until he could see Lily, he grew so engrossed in the tale of a young woman and her foolish choices he realized he was going to be late.

He dropped the book onto the table and jumped up from the chair so fast he knocked it over. Leaving it where it lay, he snatched his coat from its hook by the door and dashed into the night. Remembering he forgot to lock the door, he turned back, locked up, and sprinted through the rain.

At Great-Aunt Deborah's house, he saw the shadows of several ladies through the lace curtains, so he circled the house to the back door.

Lily opened it before he raised his hand to knock. "You're soaked, and the temperature is dropping. Come in and get warm by the fire."

He gazed at Lily, her hair tied back with a ribbon, her gown a faded calico, and felt warmed already.

"You look really pretty," he blurted out before he could stop himself.

"I look like a schoolgirl, but my hair was wet."

"You look like a pretty lady to me." He clasped his hands behind his back. "But you don't want compliments from me."

"I—" She compressed her lips. Then she raised her head and met his look with a twinkle in her eyes. "You already caught me nearly telling a fib tonight. I won't tell another one by saying I don't like compliments as much as the next female. But I will say that I'd rather you didn't give them to me."

"Why not?"

"I'm not staying here." She turned toward the stove and picked up the coffeepot. "I'd best make more with those ladies out there."

Without asking her, Ben began to take cups and saucers from the cupboard and set them on the table. He found spoons and set them beside the cups in perfect alignment with the coffee things. Did he have the correct side? Somewhere he had heard or read about a proper way to set things out. He didn't recall what the procedure was. He simply concentrated on each detail until he knew he could make his tone casual when he asked, "When?"

"I have no idea." She dipped water into the coffeepot. "Maybe as soon as May, after the plowing contest."

"After the what?"

"A plowing contest. We have it every year at the same time as the spring bazaar."

Something niggled at his mind.

"That's right. Theo mentioned it my first day here, I think." He drew out a chair. "Why don't you tell me about it while the coffee boils?"

"It's just what it sounds like." She took the proffered seat. "Men from all over come. They pay a small fee; then they take a plow and see who can plow the straightest and fastest furrow down a field. It's a cash prize."

"So it's a race while drawing a plow." He took a chair facing her. "Or does one get to use a horse or mule?"

"No, you pull it yourself." She picked up the spoon from beside her saucer, moving it about in circles against the pine surface. "It's a comfortable prize."

"A pity I don't have a plow. I have spent many springs plowing fields. My father and I hired ourselves out when money got tight. I got pretty good at it."

"I think it's a pity ladies aren't allowed to enter." She popped out of her chair and headed for the fragrant-smelling coffee. "I helped plow every year, too. Helped drive the mule until I was seventeen."

"Was that how old you were when your family lost the farm?" He posed the question in a soft voice.

She shook her head. "That was the year I lost my family. A fever came through, and they all died. Typhoid. It didn't kill me, but I was too sick to work. So I lost the farm the next year."

"Lily. . ." He started to rise.

She waved him back down. "I'll go fill up the ladies' cups and come right back." She vanished through the kitchen doorway.

Ben still saw her in his mind's eye, a slight figure. Too slight to have worked behind a plow. Too delicate for year after year of battering Iowa wind and rain, snow and sun. Maybe she was made for town life, not the life of a farmer's wife. Who was he to say she should want a different life from the one she wanted?

That hidden treasure sure could give her an easier life.

Winning the prize for the plowing contest seemed more likely a means of gaining extra money.

If he had a plow.

He was thinking of how he could borrow one from the farm equipment in the livery, when Lily returned and filled his cup without asking and reseated herself across from him.

"I think you want to talk to me about something." She avoided his gaze.

"I want to know why you're too busy to talk to me." He gave her an encouraging smile. She began to make circles with the spoon again. "It's too embarrassing to say."

"May I guess?"

She shrugged.

"You don't like me, but because I'm Deborah Twining's great-nephew, you don't want to say so."

She wrinkled her nose. "You know that's not it."

"You don't have time for one more friend."

"No one should be that busy."

"Hmm." He tapped a finger against his chin and stared past her shoulder. "You don't dislike me, and you like lots of friends, so–o–o. . ." He shifted his position and caught her gaze too fast for her to look away. "Maybe you think I like you too much, and you don't want me to."

"I—maybe—yes."

And she liked him too much. He read it in the way she tore her gaze from his and darted her glance around the room. Panic. Afraid he would confront her with that, too.

"I'll let it go at that, Lily." He rose, his coffee untouched. "But I'm praying for you and for myself, and I'd like you to give me a chance. Please. At least stop avoiding me when we're in the same room together. Agreed? It's just plain hurtful."

That was unfair. Ben suspected Lily couldn't hurt anyone intentionally.

She rose and held out her hand. "I promise to talk to you when our paths cross. But, Ben, please don't let that happen too often."

"It'll happen as often as the Lord is willing." Grinning, he took her hand, squeezed it, and slipped out the back door.

He whistled all the way to the livery. A man just had to whistle when he knew the lady fast taking hold of his heart wasn't indifferent to him.

Still whistling, he entered the livery through the front door and began his nightly rounds of the horses and mule. He passed by the corner with the discarded farm equipment, an area that should be cleaned out to make room for parking at least one buggy inside. He pulled back the tarpaulin and stared at the things with growing excitement.

The plow was a fine one.

Since the night wasn't far advanced, Ben sprinted across town to Mr. Gilchrist's house. He went to the back door in case the owner was occupied with guests.

Mr. Gilchrist himself stood at the kitchen stove making pancakes. "Come on in, lad. Hungry?"

"I wasn't."

"You are now. Sit down and tell me what brings you out in the rain. Nothing serious, I trust."

"No, sir. Everything is good, though business was slow today."

"Sure, it would be. Sit down. Sit down."

With only a little reluctance to have his boss serve him, Ben sat. Over the hotcakes, he explained about the contest and wanting to borrow the plow.

"I can practice on days off if the weather ever turns nice. If you say it's all right for me to use that old plow in the livery."

"Use it? Lad, you can have it. I have no use for it. No one has ever wanted to rent it."

"Well, thank you, sir. That's very generous, but not necessary."

"Sure it is. I wasn't making any money on that livery until you came along. You keep it making money, and I'll be generous."

As pleased as Ben was to have the plow given to him, he also recognized the gentle threat in Mr. Gilchrist's words—if the livery had a bad month or so, Ben could be out of work.

But the Lord just wouldn't hold up Ben's life like that, not for something so silly and unlikely.

Concern tossed aside, he trotted home through rain that was growing to feel more like ice than water and slipped the key into the lock of his quarters.

The key didn't need to turn.

The door had already been unlocked.

Chapter 8

The sound of the closing back door echoing in her ears, Lily propped her elbows on the table and covered her face with her hands. "Lord, I need to leave here. I need to leave here soon."

She needed to leave before she fell in love with Ben Purcell.

If it wasn't already too late.

She shivered despite the warmth of the stove behind her. She couldn't be in love with Ben. It was the most ridiculous notion she had ever had. He wasn't right for her, with his desire to stay put in this small, poky town, where even hat styles were a year or more out-of-date.

Yet not so long ago—so short a time ago, she blushed to remember—she'd thought Matt Campbell was right for her. Maybe she simply knew nothing about love.

That was it. She wasn't falling for Ben Purcell. She just didn't understand what her heart wanted—except to leave Browning City.

The spring bazaar was her biggest hope for earning enough money to seek her fortune in the city. She and some of her friends had rented a booth. Lily intended to sell her handmade lace, the art of which she had learned from her French grandmother. Becky, Eva, and some others intended to sell sweets they made themselves. Lily figured the combination of lace and candy went well together because the children would pull their mothers over to the booth to purchase the treats and the mothers would buy pieces of the lace. On Saturday, they all intended to get together to begin planning how they would decorate the booth and to pore over sweets recipes, possibly even experiment with a few, like the toffee.

They would meet if the weather cooperated. She'd learned never to count on Iowa weather to behave in March. One could have sunshine and blue skies one day and be planning a picnic. The next, a foot of snow might fall and all activity would come to a halt.

Listening to the *tap, tap, tap* of rain against the kitchen window, Lily considered the other offering of an Iowa March—ice.

She rose from the table and slipped into the parlor. "Ladies, I'm sorry to interrupt, but it sounds as though the rain has turned to sleet."

Groans met her announcement.

"If any of you wishes, I can walk you home."

"No, no."

"You can't do that and come back by yourself."

"You're too little to support a woman my size."

Protest rained as thick as the ice crystals outside. Ignoring the objections, Lily retrieved her coat and hat and returned to the parlor.

"Take my walking cane, child." Mrs. Twining held it out to her. "It'll give you balance if the streets are slippery."

"Thank you, ma'am, but what will you do?"

"Sit here and stay warm." Mrs. Twining smiled. "And pray you all safely to your doors."

None of the ladies lived far away. Glancing over the three of them, Lily chose the frailest appearing of them and offered her arm. She doubted she could hold the other two up if they fell, but at least she would be there to fetch help.

With much laughter and some genteel shrieks when a foot slipped, the ladies headed through the night. Within a quarter hour, Lily delivered each safely to her door then returned home. Already a glaze of ice coated the wooden front steps. Leaning heavily on Mrs. Twining's cane, Lily reached the door without incident and stepped into the warmth of the house with a prayer of thanksgiving.

"It's treacherous out there." She returned the cane to Mrs. Twining. "But at least this time of year, we know it won't last."

Except it did last. In the morning, Lily woke to an eerie stillness punctuated by the occasional *crack* of a branch breaking under its load of frozen water. She wondered how she would get to work across the slick landscape. Knowing that doing so would take more time than usual, she hurried to dress and prepare a small breakfast.

She was setting a tray of coffee and toast out to carry into Mrs. Twining when someone pounded on the back door.

"Miss Lily?" Toby stood on the other side of the door, shivering. "The lines are down. There aren't any messages getting through in either direction."

"So should I go into the office or not?" Lily backed away from the door so Toby could step into the kitchen.

"No, ma'am. Theo says to stay home." Toby glanced at the coffeepot. "May I—"

"Of course. Let me deliver this tray to Mrs. Twining first."

And take a few minutes to compose myself.

She wanted to cry. At least one day of missed wages. If damage to the wires was bad enough, she would miss more than one day of work.

Once again, she calculated her flagging savings.

She also saw days of boredom ahead. Going anywhere just wasn't safe with inches of ice coating the roads. Broken tree branches fell and struck people down. Wagons lost traction and careened into walkways. Feet slipped out from beneath a body, and the fall broke even the sturdiest legs.

She had to stay home and resign herself to no one calling.

When snow began to fall at noon, she accepted yet more time off work and confinement to the house with Mrs. Twining.

Not that Mrs. Twining was poor company. Lily never tired of hearing the older woman's tales of her early years as a society miss in Philadelphia, how she had fallen for adventurous Mr. Twining and how they had begun their trek west.

"We headed to Michigan first. Then things got too crowded around Detroit, so we moved down into southern Illinois. But Iowa was getting civilized enough for folks to settle and prosper, so we acquired land here and finished raising our children."

"My family did much the same." Lily slipped her hook through a loop of fine, white thread. "But you must have wanted people closer together. I mean, you helped found Browning City."

"We hoped to make this a stage stop so we didn't have to travel so far for goods. It worked, and now we have the train depot and a telegraph."

"But you chose to live in town after it was built up a bit."

"Yes, we did. After our son. . ." Mrs. Twining swallowed. "After our son died, we couldn't keep up with the farm, so we moved into town and bought the livery from the sale of the land."

"I'm sorry you had to give up your homestead." Lily bent over her lace making. "But I'm glad you're here."

"I am, too." Mrs. Twining's voice held a gentle smile. "I wouldn't have your company if we hadn't. Shall I read some scripture to you while you work?"

"Please."

Lily thought about her declaration to Mrs. Twining and Ben weeks ago about reading her Bible more. She hadn't done it much. She knew too many of the verses she might run across, things like not storing up riches and not worrying about the future. So easy for persons who knew what their lives would be to claim that was right. But since her family died, her life had felt unsettled, temporary, poised for the next leap to somewhere else.

She feared Mrs. Twining might choose one of those passages. Instead, she read from the Psalms, chapters of rejoicing in the Lord's love and goodness.

The afternoon wore on. Snowflakes the size of two-bit pieces fell from the sky in an endless barrage. At dusk, the wind kicked up, drifting the snow against trees, fences, and the back door.

Lily had to push with all her strength to open the door so she could fetch more firewood. Wind caught her hat and sent it sailing into the darkness then tore her hair from its pins and flung it across her face in heavy, wet strands.

"I hate this place!" She cried the words into the night, where she knew no one could hear her. "I want to run away."

The kitchen door slammed behind her. She staggered to the woodpile and grabbed up as many logs as she could hold. Fighting the wind like a beast caught in a locomotive's cowcatcher, she stumbled back to the door and reached for the handle with near-frozen fingers.

Another hand reached it first.

"Let me help you," Ben Purcell shouted over the blizzard's roar.

He opened the door. She toppled inside, dropping logs and gasping for breath. A moment later, he entered with more logs and his own bare head white with snow.

She wanted to hug him. She hadn't felt like hugging a man ever in her life. But the sight of Ben, tall and broad shouldered, sturdy and full of life, sent such a wave of joy through her that she knew she should run as fast and as far away from him as she could.

Except she couldn't run anywhere. The weather held her captive.

Ben's gaze held her captive.

"You—you shouldn't have come out in this," she said through a dry throat.

"I couldn't leave you ladies on your own once the storm grew worse." He set his load of logs in the wood box and stooped to gather up the ones she had dropped. "I think if I hadn't come along, you'd be in Kansas by now."

"Missouri."

"Hmm?"

"The wind is from the north. It would send me to Missouri."

"Right." He laughed up at her.

Lily wrapped her arms around herself.

She fell the rest of the way in love with Ben Purcell.

⤳⤳

She couldn't fall out of love with him while he stayed around for the rest of the storm.

"You ladies need someone to fetch and carry for you. It's too bad for either of you to go outside." He made his pronouncement with such authority that even his great-aunt didn't argue with him.

So he fixed himself a pallet on the kitchen floor and kept the stove supplied with wood. When Mrs. Twining and Lily woke the following morning, they found the house warm and breakfast nearly ready.

"Whatever your father did wrong in dragging you around the country," Mrs.

287

Twining told Ben, "he did right when he taught you your manners."

"He said Momma would want me to have them." Ben smiled. " 'Never disrespect a lady of any age or station' was what he told me from the time I was small."

"How is the weather?" Lily changed the subject with an abruptness she knew was rude. She had to. She couldn't tolerate an image of Ben as a small boy with curly dark hair that would forever be unruly and blue eyes that sparkled with mischief. The picture reminded her of children, marriage, life stranded in Iowa because her heart proved to be a foolish instrument.

"The snow is letting up, and the wind has died." Ben studied her face. "Do you need to get to the station?"

"Not if the lines are still down." She stood and began to gather the dishes. "Perhaps we should go out and see if anyone needs help."

Anything not to be confined in the same house with him.

"I did that all day yesterday." Ben lifted a pan of water to heat for dish washing. "Mrs. Willoughby, Miss Hansen, and Mrs. Longerbeam all have plenty of wood and supplies. I believe the others all have family, so I'm here to take care of mine."

"I'm not. . ." Lily stopped herself.

"Of course you're family." Mrs. Twining caught hold of Lily's hand as she reached for an empty coffee cup.

"Thank you." Lily didn't want to hurt the older woman by denying the truth of her words. "I'd better be a good girl and do my chores."

"I'll help." Ben picked up a tea towel.

While Mrs. Twining read to them, they washed up the breakfast dishes. After they finished with that, he insisted on helping Lily with peeling potatoes and carrots for a stew and kneading the bread dough. He brought in more wood, swept the floor, and always stayed far too close to her.

If I don't get away, Lord, Lily prayed when she managed a few private moments in her room, *I will simply burst. I'll come apart like a dropped cup and be useless.*

She parted the curtain to see if maybe she could hike over to Becky's house. All those children would make the hours fly past. But the wind had begun to howl and toss broken limbs about like leaves.

She smelled the bread baking and returned to the kitchen to assure herself it wasn't burning. It wasn't. Out of excuses for staying away, she joined Ben and Mrs. Twining in the parlor.

"We could play charades," Ben suggested.

"No fun with only three people." Lily shuddered. "I am no actress."

"Well," Mrs. Twining said. "We can play word-guessing games. I think up an object, and you ask questions to try to figure it out."

"Pa and I used to play this." Ben settled back on the sofa. "It passed hours on the road. You can say only yes or no to the questions."

"And maybe we should ask only a certain number of questions." Lily thought the game sounded like a good way to avoid talking about more personal matters with Ben. "Whoever guesses correctly, wins. You start, Mrs. Twining."

"I have it." She wrapped her cane on the floor like a starting gun for a race. "Ben, first question to you."

"Is it in this room?"

"Yes."

"Is it warm?" Lily asked.

"Yes."

"Can it ever be cold?" Ben tossed in his question.

"Yes."

"Fireplace!" Lily and Ben cried together.

Mrs. Twining laughed. "No."

They took turns asking questions, neither of them guessing again.

"Is it bigger than the ceiling?" from Ben.

"No."

"Smaller than the lamp?" from Lily.

"No."

"Does it ever leave this room?"

"Yes." Mrs. Twining gave one *bang* with the cane. "Your questions are up. Any guesses?"

Ben and Lily shook their heads.

"It's the two of you." Mrs. Twining smiled. "The two people I love best."

"Oh. Well. . . Thank you." Lily blinked, but fearing she might cry, she leaped from her chair and raced to the kitchen.

The bread was finished. She rolled up her cuffs to protect the sleeves of her second-best dress, removed the loaves from the oven, and gave the stew a stir. Fragrant steam wafted into the room. She tasted the concoction, added a pinch more salt and a dash of pepper. Voices drifted to her from the parlor, the words indistinct, their nearness a comfort.

She wouldn't have that in the city. She would be alone, which was why she had believed she could persuade Matt to move to the city, as well. She didn't want to be alone again as she had been on the farm after her family died.

"But you won't be." She gave herself a quiet scolding. "You will have people all around you all the time. It's what you want."

But Mrs. Twining was old and had lost all but one member of her real family. She had taken Lily in. Lily knew the older woman would not stop her, yet leaving her felt a little like betrayal. Mrs. Twining cared enough to understand

Lily's restlessness, her need for activities Browning City couldn't provide.

And Ben? He would keep her there because he cared about her.

Unable to face him across the parlor again, catch him gazing at her, smiling at her, reaching his hand out to her, Lily chose to remain in the kitchen. She could make a sweet to go with the stew and bread.

She entered the pantry to inspect the shelves. The previous autumn, she had preserved jars of wild berries. With those, she could make a cobbler or jellyrolls, or she could spread them warm on a plain cake. She would think of something to make from the ingredients at hand. No eggs. That meant a cobbler. Maybe she should use apples if they had any left.

Standing on tiptoe, she reached for the highest shelf where she had stowed last year's apples. Her fingertips brushed against the wrinkled side of a fruit. She could get a chair, but with a little more height, she could reach it now. . . .

She grasped the edge of the preserves shelf for balance.

And it collapsed.

Lily screamed. Wood cracked. Jars shattered, spraying the walls, floor, and Lily with shards of glass and rivers of sticky fruit. Blackberry juice ran down the front of her second-best dress, staining it, ruining it.

Lily burst into tears.

"Are you all right?" Ben bolted into the kitchen and drew Lily away from the glass. "Lily, are you hurt? Where? Oh, my dear, I can't see where you're cut."

"I'm not." Lily found herself sobbing against his chest, and his arms holding her close. "It's the mess. The fruit. My dress."

"Is that all?" He nudged her chin up and smiled down at her. "I was sure you received a mortal wound. But it's just some fruit and a dress."

"Just? Why you, you—oh."

Ben kissed her, driving distress, annoyance, and everything but love for him out of her head.

Chapter 9

I—I'm sorry." Ben leaped back a step but kept his gaze on Lily's face.

Her flushed face.

"I mean, I'm not sorry for my sake, but you—uh. . ." He shoved his hands into his pockets. "I shouldn't have done that."

"No." Lily pressed her fingers to her lips and closed her eyes. "We scarcely know each other. We—I. . . Oh." Her hand still against her mouth, she fled from the kitchen.

A moment later, a door closed with a decided *bang*.

"What was I thinking?" Ben raked his fingers through his hair.

He wasn't thinking. That was the problem. He'd let his natural instincts take over his good sense and given in to temptation. He would consider himself a blessed man if Lily so much as looked at him again, let alone talked to him.

Now that the storm had ceased save for the wind, he figured he should go home. Yet he didn't want to face Great-Aunt Deborah at the moment, and he couldn't fetch his coat without going through the parlor. Besides, he couldn't leave the mess on the floor. Cleaning it up would take some hard labor.

Just what he needed.

He stepped over the glass and preserves to fetch a broom. Behind him, he heard the *thump*, *thump*, *thump* of Great-Aunt Deborah's cane.

"What happened—aah."

Slowly Ben turned to face Great-Aunt Deborah. "It's worse than this." He felt his face heat. "I—uh—kissed her."

"Did you?" Great-Aunt Deborah's faded blue eyes brightened with a twinkle. "Imprudent, but understandable."

"She doesn't understand." Ben decided the mess was too sticky for the broom and stooped to gather glass fragments and dump them onto an old newspaper. "It's bound to push her away."

"It may." Great-Aunt Deborah lowered herself onto a kitchen chair. "And you'll have to let her go. But it might bring her back if things don't work out the way she wants them."

"Might." Ben flung a large chunk of glass onto the pile, scattering the smaller slivers. "It only took me five weeks to realize I'm in love with her. Why should it take another man longer?"

"She's lived here for three years without marrying."

"Because no one wanted her for his wife?"

Great-Aunt Deborah sighed. "Probably not. She's made it so clear all along that Browning City is merely a stopping place for a while that most young men keep their relationships with her as friendships."

"Wise of them." Ben gathered up the glass and stalked to the back door. "I should have listened to you about Lily. But I thought. . ." He allowed his words to die as he shoved into the frigid night and deposited the splintered jars in the trash bin.

He was a fool to think he could change Lily's mind. Of course he could not. He had too little to offer her. Yes, he worked in a good position, but he had no real home. Yes, in five years or so, he could save enough money to afford a farm and a few years after that, provided the harvests remained strong, a house worthy of a wife and family. In the event he won the plowing contest, he might shave off a year or two of that waiting time or build a house right away instead of waiting another half a decade after purchasing a farm. Either way, he could never give Lily the life she wanted, never provide her with pretty things and travel nor a host of people around her and occasional adventures.

All he had to offer her was his love.

Unless he found the gold.

He returned to the house to find Great-Aunt Deborah pouring water into a pot to heat.

"Only hot water and strong soap will get that up. I'll let you do the scrubbing. It's not men's work, and Lily made the mess, but it'll be good for you."

"It's the least I can do for her." Ben took the dipper from her. "I'll finish this up, and when I'm done, I'll return to the livery for good."

"As much as I appreciate your being here, I think that's wise." Great-Aunt Deborah returned to her chair. "The less you see of her for a while, the better."

"I'll do what I can to avoid her, but it won't be easy in this town." He thought about how the lack of a variety of people was one of Lily's objections to Browning City and laughed. "I'll wait for her to come to me, if she ever does."

He would also pray a great deal. A great deal more than he already had been praying about Lily, about obtaining money faster, about keeping safe.

He'd added the latter after finding his quarters unlocked. He knew he had locked them, yet wondered if the lock had failed. It was old, the wood around the hasp, worn. Possibly the mechanism sprang under pressure of rain and wind. Possibly.

But not likely.

He'd found an even more secure hiding place for his savings and planned to open an account at each bank the next day. Unfortunately the weather had prevented him from doing so. But it would also keep a thief out. Even so, he worried with the livery empty of his presence except for when he fed the animals. Upon reaching his quarters, he checked on his hiding place first. All appeared well, so he proceeded to feed the horses and mule.

After spending the past two nights with Lily, Great-Aunt Deborah, and himself gathered around the parlor or kitchen fires, he felt the stillness and quiet closing in on him like fog. Outside, the wind howled. Inside, even the animals seemed motionless.

"I used to like this." He spoke aloud to dispel the silence. "I could always feel Your presence better, Lord."

The four walls confined him, made him restless. He needed open air, a view, the smell of earth warmed from the sun or wet after rain.

Or maybe he simply missed companionship.

"Lord, give me the means by which I can win this woman as my wife."

If he could win her.

The latter thought crept unbidden into his head. He shoved it away. He didn't want to think about the possibility that Lily would never be a part of his life.

Yet that apprehension nagged at his mind in wakeful moments during the night and throughout a Sunday that saw few people attending church.

Lily and Great-Aunt Deborah were two of those who did not arrive at the service.

Concerned, Ben stopped at the house on his way home.

Lily answered the door. "I know. We weren't at church." She offered him a wan smile. "Mrs. Twining didn't think she could walk through this snow and ice, and I didn't want to leave her here alone. You know her. She would try to build up the fire and hurt herself carrying too many logs."

"Thank you for taking such good care of her." Ben glanced around him, seeking something else to say. "And you're all right?"

"Yes, thank you. I just want to get back to work." She gripped the edge of the door. "I'd invite you in, but Mrs. Twining is asleep."

"I understand. I'll pray the wires are up and running for you soon."

So she could earn more money that would take her away from him? What was he thinking?

"Thank you." She started to close the door. "The only good thing about a March storm is the snow doesn't last long."

"I hope not. This isn't good for the livery business, either." He grinned. "Maybe Mr. Gilchrist should buy a sleigh."

He left her smiling in the doorway. His heart rejoiced for that little blessing—he could still make her smile.

Taking Great-Aunt Deborah's advice, Ben steered clear of Lily. With all the businesses closed due to continued ice and snow on the streets in town and the roads leading to Browning City, as well as the railroad, he kept himself busy shoveling, scraping, and hacking ice away from walkways and roofs. In return, the residents kept him supplied with baked goods and dinner invitations.

He saw Lily once in the next three days. Bundled against the cold, she chopped at an icicle hanging from the eave of Great-Aunt Deborah's house.

"Lily." He removed the shovel from her gloved hand. "You're going to send that thing crashing down on your head."

"But it's making the eaves sag." She gestured upward. "Look. I'm afraid we'll get leaks inside."

"You should have asked me to help."

"I didn't know. . . ." She hugged herself. "You haven't been by to see us."

He looked into her eyes. "I thought maybe you didn't want to see me."

"I don't. I didn't. I mean. . ." She shoved her hands up her coat sleeves and stared past his shoulder. "We've missed you."

"We?" He grinned, unable to resist teasing her. "You don't look half big enough for one person, let alone big enough to be two or more."

"Oh, you." She let out a shaky laugh. "You know I meant Mrs. Twining and me."

"Yes, I did, but I wanted to hear you say it. . .Lily." Speaking her name made his insides quiver. Her sudden smile melted him.

"I value you, Ben."

"Thank you."

Not quite what he wanted from her, but a start.

"I heard you were entering the plowing contest and that someone broke into the livery last week." She blurted all the news in a rush. "Why didn't you tell us?"

He shrugged. "I only told one person—Lars Gilchrist. It didn't seem important enough, since nothing was taken."

"But it affected you, so—I mean, we're family." Color tinted her cheeks. "That is, Mrs. Twining is family."

"You were right the first time." He reached out his hand, stopped short of touching her. "Remember? We included you in our little family."

"That was kind of Mrs. Twining and you, but I'm afraid. . ." Her hands knotted inside her sleeves. "I need to get inside. My feet are freezing. May I offer you coffee?"

"No, thank you. I'm having dinner with the Gilchrists tonight and need to go get on some clean clothes."

"That's good of them to invite you." She turned toward the door, showing him only her profile. "Eva is as nice as she is pretty."

"Yes, she is."

Ben wanted to shout with joy at Lily's reaction to the news he was having dinner with Eva and Lars Gilchrist. Every tense line of her body proclaimed how little she liked the image of him across a table from the lovely blond.

She did care for him.

But he couldn't leave her thinking he and Eva might end up courting. Lily might leave town sooner.

"Tom Bailyn will be there, too," he added.

"Oh." Her shoulders relaxed. Her chin line softened. "I'm sure you will enjoy yourself. They have a housekeeper since Mrs. Gilchrist died last year. She's a wonderful cook."

"I doubt she makes bread as good as yours."

She smiled at him. It kept him warm on the walk home.

He would have jogged if ice didn't still create treacherous patches along the route.

Instead, he whistled while feeding and grooming the stock, hummed as he cleaned up and changed into fresh clothes, and sang aloud as he locked both doors of the livery and, lantern in hand, trudged through the night to the largest house in Browning City, that of Lars Gilchrist.

Fog rolled up from the river a mile away and across the land to meet him by the time he reached the Gilchrists'. Cold and damp, it was nonetheless a good sign.

"Temperature's rising," he said as he greeted his hostess.

"And by July, we'll be thinking fondly of this cold." Eva smiled. "Come on in, Ben. Rising temperatures or not, it's still chilly out there."

She led him into a parlor twice the size of Great-Aunt Deborah's and containing heavy mahogany furnishings and cushions in a dark red. To Ben, it looked like the lobby of a city hotel, not a home. For a moment, his mind snapped back to those hours spent with Lily and Great-Aunt Deborah, and he wanted to return there. Knowing that was impossible, he settled in to endure the evening.

Good food and dialogue helped. Mostly they discussed business. Being business rivals didn't seem to matter to Gilchrist and Bailyn. They shared frustrations over getting supplies, the quality of those goods they received, and a lack of variety in the products they could offer their customers.

"If I don't get more fabrics in," Bailyn confided, "every lady in Browning City will be wearing the same new spring dresses to the Easter egg hunt and spring bazaar."

"That's why I quit selling dry goods." Gilchrist forked up potatoes as fluffy as thistledown. "I was tired of the ladies complaining."

"And your daughter," Eva said as she handed Ben a plate of sliced bread still warm from the oven. "I think most of us send for fabrics ourselves."

"But it would be so much cheaper if we could purchase it in quantity," Bailyn said.

"Why don't you start selling more dry goods than grocery stuffs?" Ben suggested. "Then Mr. Gilchrist could carry the grocery stuffs."

The other three stared at him.

He gave them a sheepish grin. "My pa was a peddler. We only sold dry goods, so were able to carry a fair bit of choice for good prices."

"It's something to think about." Eva gazed into space and tapped her spoon on the table. "If you hired a seamstress, the ladies who can afford it wouldn't be going into Davenport or out to Des Moines to have their clothes made."

"And men their shirts," Gilchrist pointed out. "Nothing wrong with a seamstress making a man's shirts. I didn't know you had such business sense, Eva."

"I had you as a teacher, Papa."

Gilchrist blushed with obvious pleasure.

Everyone laughed.

"And we didn't know about Ben's knowledge of the dry goods business," Bailyn added in a moment. "You and I should have dinner at the hotel soon and talk more about it."

"Be glad to."

Ben's heart sang with the joy of finding a place where people wanted him, needed him.

His steps jaunty, he left the Gilchrists' house and strode home through fog so thick that moving through it felt like swimming. His lantern swung from his hand and set the mist sparkling like spangles on a circus costume. Despite the chill, he thought he smelled spring's approach in the air.

Like Lily smelling snow.

He smiled and reached for the doorknob to his quarters.

The door was unlocked.

"Lord, please let everything be all right."

Still clutching the lantern, he rushed through to the livery and inspected the horses and mule. They appeared quiet, even sleepy. The mule brayed in protest at being disturbed then turned to his hay. Assured the stock had not been harmed, Ben trudged to his own quarters, steps dragging, and held the light high.

The bed had been heaved aside, the floorboard torn up.

His savings were gone.

Chapter 10

Pounding on the kitchen door dragged Lily awake. With haste, she flung on a dress, fumbled the buttons closed up the front, and stumbled to the door in her bare feet.

"Who's there?"

"Lily, I'm sorry—"

"Ben?" She yanked open the door. "What in the world?"

"I'm so sorry to disturb you."

He avoided looking at her, and she realized her hair hung unbound down her back.

"What's wrong?" She stepped aside so he could enter the kitchen. "You look ghastly."

His face was white, his eyes dark hollows.

"Did you leave this for me?" He thrust a towel-wrapped bundle into her arms.

"Yes."

It was a loaf of bread.

"Maybe I was prideful to want you to compare my bread to the Gilchrists' hou—"

"Was the door unlocked when you arrived?"

She reeled under the impact of his harsh question. "Yes, it was. I couldn't have gotten in if—"

"What time was it?"

"What is this about?" She handed the bundle back to him and then snatched a shawl off a hook by the door and wrapped it around her shoulders.

"Please tell me." He dropped the parcel on the table.

The towel opened to reveal a crusty loaf of bread.

Lily's nostrils flared at the aroma.

"About six o'clock. Ben, what is wrong?"

He leaned on the table, breathing hard and staring at her. "The door was unlocked at six o'clock?"

"Yes." She grasped his arm. "Tell me what's wrong."

"I locked it when I left." He bunched his hands into fists. "The last time, I thought I could have been mistaken, but my quarters—Lily." His voice turned ragged. "They took all of my savings."

"Oh no! Oh, Ben." She slid her hand down to curve over one of his. "I didn't even notice the knob. The door was unlocked, but we don't usually lock our doors here, so I didn't think anything of it. I should have gone for the sheriff instead. I should have noticed something was wrong. I should have thought. But I just slipped in and dropped the bread on the table. I felt I was intruding anyway so I didn't look around."

She was babbling.

His hand relaxed beneath hers, though, so maybe the chatter helped him.

"We need to get to the sheriff." She turned to the hall. "Let me fetch my shoes and fix my hair and tell Mrs. Twining. I'll go over there with you."

He shouldn't be alone.

"Thank you."

She heard one of the chairs scrape across the floor as she turned toward Mrs. Twining's bedroom.

The older lady sat up in bed, her face lined with concern. "What has happened?"

Lily told her. "If you think it's all right, I'll go to the sheriff's with him. He's distressed."

"I can understand why he would be." Mrs. Twining shook her head. "All his savings. Why didn't the lad put them in a bank?"

"He didn't know which one to use, and nothing's been open since the last time he thinks he had an intruder." Lily paused in the doorway. "And this is Browning City. We don't have thieves here."

"Not often." Mrs. Twining sighed and looked all of her eighty or so years—old and sad.

"It's the gold," she said. "That rumor about it being in the livery has gone around again."

"But they took Ben's money." Lily cried out the words on a wave of pain. "He'll have to work most of his life to get that money back. He's such a good man; how could God let this happen to him?"

"God does nothing without a purpose, my dear. Now you run along and put some shoes on before you freeze, and go with Ben to see the sheriff, if you can wake him up this time of night. I'll stay here and pray."

"Thank you."

Lily scampered into her own room on lighter feet, the burden slipping from her heart. Yes, having his savings stolen was terrible, yet maybe God's plans didn't include Ben staying in Browning City and buying a farm. Maybe God wanted Ben and her together elsewhere.

She hastened to pull on stockings and shoes and braid her hair; then she dashed into the kitchen.

Ben sat at the table, his head bowed. She opened her mouth to tell him her new revelation, but he glanced up, smiled, and stopped the words at her lips.

His face was calm, peaceful. "I've been praying for the money to be restored."

"And you believe it will happen?" Lily shook her head. "I never got mine back."

"Did you ask God for it?"

"I think I did, but even He can't refill an empty purse."

"Lily, my dear, *God* and *can't* shouldn't be in the same sentence." Ben rose and took one of her hands between both of his. "He can do anything."

She shook her head, not in doubt but in confusion.

"We can talk about it later." He released her hand. "Where's your coat?"

She retrieved it, and they headed for the sheriff's office. Lily's thoughts spun so fast she couldn't think of anything to say. Ben didn't attempt to make conversation, either. She suspected he continued to pray.

She wanted his prayer to be answered for his sake, for the sake of such wonderful faith, such assurance that all would be well. Life never worked that way for her. In the past few years, God seemed to take from her, not give—her family, her pay, Ben.

She had been foolish to imagine he would move to the city now that he had lost his savings for the farm. He believed God would restore his money, and though Lily feared he was right, she couldn't imagine how.

Heart heavy, she reached the sheriff's office with Ben. The building, like the town, lay dark and still beneath a blanket of fog. Ben pounded on the door then took the lantern around back to the lawman's quarters. A few minutes later, a sleepy-eyed Sheriff Dodd pulled open the door and let them in.

"I don't know what I can do for you, Purcell." He began poking at embers glowing in the stove. "No way to find a thief tonight, not in this fog."

"You do need to be aware that we have a thief in Browning City."

Lily didn't miss how Ben said *we*, as though he already felt a part of the town.

"Never have done before you came." The sheriff rubbed his bristly chin, the rasp grating in the quiet. "Course, no one was ever shot until you came along, either. Not to my recollection anyhow."

"I had money stolen from the telegraph office." Lily jumped to Ben's defense. "So things do get stolen here from time to time."

"That was someone off the train." Dodd sighed. "But I'll make a note of it and ask around. Don't expect anyone saw anything. Clever man to use the fog to cover up his deeds."

"It happened before six o'clock," Lily persisted. "I delivered some bread to him, and the door wasn't locked."

"Been dark since about that time with this weather." Dodd shook his head. "Nobody was about, I'm sure."

"But—"

"Just thought you should know." Ben slipped his hand under Lily's elbow and guided her out of the office.

Once the door closed behind them, she turned toward Ben. "He thinks this is all your fault."

"Yes, he does. He thinks I brought an enemy with me." Ben set off at a brisk pace despite the low visibility, drawing Lily along with him. "But I never stayed anywhere long enough to make enemies."

"Or friends."

"Or friends."

"But you've only been here for a month and a half, and you've already made lots of friends."

He laughed without humor. "Lily, I never stayed anywhere for a month and a half. Three weeks for the spring plowing in farm country and four weeks in Chicago to settle up Pa's bills after he died."

"At least you were around lots of people."

"People, yes. Friends, no." Ben squeezed her arm. "But not all of them were unkind. I'd been attending a church. One of the men helped me sell our supplies, and a few of the ladies brought me food."

"So it wasn't all bad."

Lily found she needed to know the answer to that with an urgency that scared her. All she had been able to think about after her parents and then brother died and she sat alone on a farm miles from anyone was the notion of people, noise, light. The more the better. Browning City—as far as the stagecoach had brought her with the coin she could spare for travel—seemed like a haven. People had been kind, sympathetic, helpful in a practical way. But still too quiet, especially on nights like this when the weather kept everyone indoors. Since the deaths of her last family members left her alone and isolated on the farm, silence had frightened her, but now she wondered if being alone in a crowd could be just as bad.

"No, it wasn't all bad." Ben's voice sounded thoughtful. "I might have found a place there to settle if I hadn't run across Great-Aunt Deborah's name in Pa's papers. Leaving the city and coming here seemed the right thing to do after that."

Lily caught the edge of doubt in his tone.

"But now you're not sure?"

"It does seem someone doesn't want me here."

We all want you here.

Fortunately for Lily's sake, they reached Mrs. Twining's house before she gave in to temptation and spoke those words aloud.

Ben took her hand in his at the door. "Thank you for coming with me."

"It didn't do any good. He didn't want to hear about what time I was there or anything."

Ben chuckled. "I think he takes crime in his town as a personal offense against him. He'd rather ignore it."

Lily sighed, said good night, and slipped inside. When she told Mrs. Twining about what happened at the sheriff's office, she nodded in understanding and said about the same thing as Ben.

"If those gold thieves hadn't come through here after the war," the older woman concluded, "we probably wouldn't even pay a sheriff."

"Mrs. Twining, ma'am. . ." Lily hesitated, but since she had already begun, she couldn't back out now. "Do you think—I mean, I know you don't like to talk about it, but do you think this person could have been looking for the gold in the livery and just run across Ben's money and taken it instead?"

Mrs. Twining closed her eyes and nodded. "I'm afraid it could have happened that way." She held out one hand. "Will you pray with me that we are able to set these gold rumors to rest once and for all?"

Lily joined her in prayer but believed the only way to stop the legend and the gold seekers was to find the treasure.

⌘

"Mary Reeves is taking up a collection for Ben," Becky said as she greeted Lily at the door.

"A collection for Ben?" Lily shucked off her coat, almost too warm in the balmy spring weather that had descended on Browning City that Wednesday before Palm Sunday. "Why?"

The moment she asked the question, she realized it wasn't kind of her.

"You mean to replace what was stolen?" she concluded.

"Yes, and she has nearly enough to replace what was taken." Becky hugged Lily. "Isn't that wonderful? People here are so kind and generous. It's no wonder Matt decided to stay. And Ben, too."

Becky's announcement slammed into Lily.

"Yes, no wonder." Lily felt as flat, as colorless as she knew she sounded.

The town was replacing Ben's savings. Ben, who had been there for less than two months. Ben, who had a well-paying job and a place to live along with that job. Ben, who got invited everywhere to dinner because he was an eligible bachelor, so he didn't have to pay for much food. Ben, who had family.

Lily swallowed an enormous lump in her throat and forced herself to smile. "I guess he can stay here if he wants to and not have to wait a dozen years to buy a farm."

"I hope so." Becky grasped Lily's arm and drew her into the kitchen. "He's such a nice man. He must have shoveled out half this town after the storm. But you probably know more about him than the rest of us do." She winked.

Lily blushed and turned to the sound of running feet. She braced herself in time to meet the onslaught of two little girls with flying dark pigtails.

"My two favorite ragamuffins." She hugged them close. "I have presents for you."

"Goodie. Goodie."

The girls jumped up and down.

"It's 'Thank you.'" Becky smiled along with the reproof.

"But she hasn't given us anything yet," said Molly, the younger.

"That was rude, Moll," her elder sister by a year scolded.

Lily laughed and pulled tiny scraps of lace from her pocketbook. "Hats for your dolls. For Easter, of course."

"Yea!"

They started to rush from the room, halted as if caught up on strings, and raced back to hug Lily again.

"Thank you, Miss Lily."

Then they dashed off again.

"You spoil them." Becky began making coffee.

"I always wanted little sisters." Lily began to sort through materials they had collected to decorate the church hall for the Easter egg hunt. "I was the youngest and didn't like it."

Becky flashed a grin over her shoulder. "Maybe you should just have children."

"Becky, for shame." Lily felt her neck grow hot under her knot of hair. "I need a husband first."

"Of course you do." Becky started laughing. "I mean, the husband is easy from what I hear."

"Then you hear more than I do," Lily snapped.

"Calm yourself." Becky laid her hand on Lily's shoulder. "Has something upset you? I was only teasing about Ben. We all know he's head over heels for you."

"I don't want to stay here. He does. That's the end of it."

And people wanted him to stay.

"I can take a hint." Becky picked up a sheet of tissue paper and began to fashion a flower. "I'll talk about Matt instead. I never thought he'd look at me, not with you around, but he. . ."

Lily let Becky chatter on and on about Matt. It kept her from having to say anything as they made flowers and paper chains, drank coffee, and chuckled over eruptions of childish laughter from the other room.

At nine o'clock, Becky's oldest brother, a gangly youth of fifteen, sauntered into the kitchen. "Ma says I should walk you home, Miss Lily."

"Thank you, Devlin, but I may need to make a stop along the way."

Lily shrugged into her coat, hugged Becky good-bye, and stepped into the night, a silent Devlin beside her.

A heaven of stars arched overhead. Bright. Clear. Romantic. This was a night to share with a beloved.

Lily wrapped her arms across her body and trudged two streets over to the parsonage. She knew it was getting late to make a call. She also knew that Jackson and Mary never turned anyone from their door, regardless of the time.

Except they already had company. Lily spotted shadows through the curtains that indicated several adults in the parlor. She started to turn away.

The front door flew open on a cacophony of voices and laughter, light and movement.

"I'll remember that."

At the sound of Ben's voice, Lily missed a step then quickened her pace. "We'd better hurry, Dev."

"Lily? Lily Reese, is that you?" Footfalls pounded behind her. "Lily, wait up. I want to tell you the news." He caught up and ran around to face her. "The Lord did provide for returning my money. Isn't that wonderful?" He picked her up and swung her around.

Mirth erupted from Devlin and the house behind him.

Ben released her like the wrong end of a hot poker. "I apologize. I was so happy I forgot myself."

"I can understand why." Despite her aching heart, Lily laughed at his enthusiasm and antics. "You have amazing faith."

And she burst into tears.

"Lily. Lily, honey, what's wrong?" Ben slipped an arm around her shoulders and guided her to the house. "Come back here and sit down. Mary?"

"Yes, bring her in." Mary held the door wide.

The other guests and Devlin had discreetly gone on their way.

"What is it, sweetheart?" Mary pulled a handkerchief from her pocket and pressed it into Lily's hand. "Did something or someone hurt you?"

"Yes. No." Lily gulped and got herself under control. "I'm sorry. I'm sorry. I should go home now."

"I don't think you should." Ben pressed her hand. "But I'll leave you here with Mary and Jackson unless you want me to stay."

Lily did want him there. Nothing had felt better than his arm around her and him by her side, a bulwark of strength and comfort. Yet what she wanted to discuss with Mary concerned him.

"If Jackson doesn't care," Ben said, "I'll stay with him in his office so the two of you can talk alone. Then I'll be here to walk you home, Lily."

"Thank you." Lily gave him what she feared was a wan smile.

"Such a thoughtful man." Mary gave Ben a warmer smile. "I'll take Lily into my sewing room."

She led the way to a small chamber boasting more books than sewing supplies. It also contained two armchairs. She indicated one for Lily and took the other herself.

"Now tell me what has you so upset."

Lily bit her lip. Now that she had someone to whom she could express her reaction to Ben's good fortune, she realized how selfish she sounded. But who better to admit that to than the pastor's wife?

"I'm confused." Lily twisted her hands together on her lap. "This isn't nice."

Mary smiled. "I didn't think it would be. People don't usually get upset about nice things."

"No, but I mean—it makes me look. . .mean."

"I can't imagine you being mean, Lily." Mary reached forward and patted her hand. "Just talk."

"I'll try." Lily took a deep breath. "Last year, when I had my wages stolen, no one did anything to repay me. And I'd been here for two years. Ben is here for less than two months, and you organize a scheme to get donations."

"Aah."

Other than that one sound, Mary said nothing for so long, Lily wondered if she should leave, if the pastor's wife had given up on a poor-spirited and selfish woman like Lily Reese.

"Thank you for being honest with me," Mary said at last. "I can see why you might be hurt by that."

"It seems rather unfair." Lily heard the anger in her tone and bowed her head in shame.

"I think you're right. It does. But I'm going to be honest with you, my dear."

Lily looked up. "Why do you all deem him so much more important than you do me?"

Mary met and held Lily's gaze. "First of all, I didn't begin this collection. A few people came to me because Ben helped them out so much during the storm. People here aren't wealthy, but they're not poor, either, and they're generous with what they have. Ben was generous with his time and strength, and many people here, including businessmen, owed him for all the shoveling and scraping he did to clear the walkways and roads. He let people feed him, but he wouldn't take pay, even though we all know he wants to save enough money for a farm and settle here."

"I've done a great deal for this town, too. I organize the spring bazaar, the Christmas pageant, the harvest. . .any number of things."

"You do, and we appreciate all of them." Mary sighed. "But, Lily, you make it clear you do these things because you like entertainment, noise, and lots of people around you."

"And what's wrong—?" Lily caught her breath. Twin tears rolled down her cheeks. "You're saying that I am doing these things for myself and not others."

"Tell me if I'm wrong."

"I. . .can't."

Lily remembered her reasons for cleaning up Ben's quarters, making the room habitable. She had done it for herself, not for Ben.

She wanted to crawl under a table and hide. Better yet, take the next train out of Browning City before anyone learned how awful she was.

Except they already knew.

She wiped her eyes on her sleeve. "So you all didn't help me out when my wages were stolen because I'm selfish and you don't like me much."

"On the contrary, my dear." Mary's voice broke. "We love you very much, and we knew that the sooner you got enough money saved, the sooner you would leave us. If we had thought that loss was a true hardship, we would have helped and then some. But we don't want you to move east, where you don't know anyone and won't have a spiritual home and friends and family to support you. We want you here where we can love and protect you and give you the spiritual food you need to grow."

"But this isn't my home or my family. I lost those." She cried the words straight from her heart. "I was so alone, and everything was quiet. . . ." She began to sob.

"Oh, my dear." Mary knelt before Lily and clasped her hands in hers. "You weren't alone. God was with you. You simply needed to ask Him for help. Do you ever do that?"

Lily shook her head. "Not for myself. I pray for other people, but He doesn't want to help me."

"Of course He does." Mary snatched a piece of calico from the sewing table and handed it to Lily, who wiped her eyes on the colorful fabric. "He's with you every minute of every day. He wants to guide every step of your life and promises to see to all your needs. But He asks us to trust Him and give our hearts to Him. Have you done that, Lily? Have you given your heart to the Lord?"

"I asked Him to forgive my sins a long time ago."

Mary smiled. "That's a good start. But He wants you to give your heart to

Him, too. Give Him your life and all your desires and trust Him. Can you do that?"

"I. . ."

What if God wanted her to stay in Browning City?

Suddenly Lily couldn't breathe. She wanted to bolt from the room, run from the house, and keep on moving until she no longer felt trapped by that one thought.

"I don't know." She couldn't be anything but honest with Mary.

"Will you promise me to think about it?" Mary rose. "And read your Bible."

"Yes, ma'am."

Lily wiped her eyes again and wished she hadn't agreed to Ben's staying around to walk her home. She knew she must look a fright and didn't want him to see her that way.

But when she and Mary walked into the hallway and Ben and Pastor Jackson stepped from the office, Ben gave Lily such a warm smile she thought maybe she didn't look so bad after all.

"You ready to go home?" he asked.

She nodded. "Mrs. Twining will be worrying."

"Not Great-Aunt Deborah. She doesn't worry about anything. She just prays about it."

"She is a tower of spiritual strength in this town," Jackson said. "I have no doubts that her prayers brought you here, Ben. And will keep you here, too, the Lord willing."

"I'm praying He is." Ben shook the pastor's hand, nodded to Mary, and offered Lily his arm. "Shall we go?"

They walked into the night, arm in arm like a courting couple. Lily, however, felt anything but romantic despite the warmer air and chandelier of stars. Her heart felt as though someone had torn it free of its moorings and left it to drift about in her chest like an abandoned vessel in a whirlpool. She didn't know what to think and was far too frightened to pray for God's guidance.

Now that I know everyone here thinks I am a selfish beast, Lord, I really can't stay.

Yet she wished she possessed the kind of self-assurance Ben did, despite his vagabond lifestyle and lack of friends because of it.

Lack of friends before he arrived in Browning City.

"Ben," she burst out just moments before they reached Mrs. Twining's house, "will you tell me how you manage to trust that the Lord has the best for you in His plans?"

Chapter 11

Four days later, Ben sat on Mrs. Twining's hearth rug in the parlor, his Bible on his knee. "I learned to trust in the Lord when I had nothing else constant in my life. Yes, Pa was always there, but he didn't offer me much comfort when I became old enough to understand I didn't have the same kind of life as other boys."

Lily leaned toward him from her position on the sofa. "But how did you learn about giving your heart to God and trusting Him with your future?"

"We didn't travel on Sundays, and sometimes we were near a church." Ben tapped the battered Bible. "A pastor gave me this, and I just started reading. Eventually I started putting the Word together with what preachers said."

"So now you simply know that God will make everything right in your life?"

"I know it. I don't always feel like it."

Lily had struggled with this notion for the four days since her talk with Mary. Ben and she never seemed to have time to talk together, so Lily had picked up her Bible, dusted it off, and tried to read.

"It's just so big I don't know where to start."

"The Gospels are good. So is Romans." Ben began to flip through the worn pages of his Bible. "And Proverbs holds a great deal of wisdom. I like Proverbs chapter three, when I get concerned." He grinned. "*When*, Lily, not *if*. I worry all the time about what my future holds, that God won't do what I want Him to."

"But He restored your savings to you."

"Yes, but I don't know why. I know why I wanted Him to, but I don't know if it's what He wanted." Ben glanced toward the window, where rain streamed down the panes like a waterfall. "It's still not enough for what I truly want, and I may never have that."

Even with his face in profile, she read his longing. She understood it. Her heart hungered, too—and feared. She feared she would never have that which her heart desired.

She clasped her knees. "So how do you go on? I mean, I pray for things like Mrs. Twining's health and when you were hurt and for sunshine for the spring bazaar. But now I feel like those things were selfish prayers. Now I don't know what to pray."

"Two verses come to mind straightaway." Ben flattened the pages of his Bible and read. " 'Jesus said unto him, Thou shalt love the Lord thy God with all thy heart, and with all thy soul, and with all thy mind,' the twenty-second chapter of Matthew tells us. And Proverbs, chapter three, says, 'Trust in the Lord with all thine heart; and lean not unto thine own understanding. In all thy ways acknowledge him, and he shall direct thy paths.' "

"Those are tall orders." Lily spoke as she tucked scraps of yarn into her Bible to mark those passages. "I don't think I can do that."

"No one can. We need His strength to trust Him. That's really hard to do— admitting we can't do things ourselves."

"But you do," Lily protested.

"I don't all the time." Ben bowed his head. "I didn't when I discovered the theft of my savings. And I'm not sure now that I am trusting the Lord about other things in my heart, things I want that He may not want for me."

"I feel that way, too." Lily folded her hands on top of her Bible. "But even if we are afraid God wants something for us we don't want, should we pray about it? I mean, can we pray for what we want?"

"Yes, of course. He may just close the door on it." He reached out his hand. "What is it you want so badly, Lily, if you can share it with me?"

"A job in the city."

Pain flashed across his face.

"Why?" His voice was soft. "Why do you want to leave us?"

"I don't belong here." She laced her fingers together and held on tight, avoiding his gaze. "I didn't realize how much I was planning all these fetes and parties for my own sake. I said I was doing it for the town. Now I just can't face anyone. I could barely face anyone at church this morning."

"Was anyone unkind to you at church?"

"No. No one treated me any differently. But I feel different."

She felt like her sins had been exposed for all to see. Yet as she thought about it, she realized that her sins had been exposed only to herself. Everyone else already knew why she acted as she did.

"I just can't be a different person and stay here," she burst out. "No one will believe me."

"They will know." Ben gave her an encouraging smile. "But even if they don't, the Lord will, and He's the One who counts. Would you like to pray with me about it?"

"I can't." Lily rose. "Please, let me read and think about this some more. And it's time to get Mrs. Twining up from her nap."

"All right. Just let me or someone know when you want further guidance." Ben rose and went to the door. "I'm having dinner with the Gilchrists again, so

I can't stay. But I'll be praying for you. And I'd like your prayers for me, too. I have a number of things to give over to the Lord that I am hanging on to with all my might."

"I can do that."

Praying for him was easy. She didn't have to struggle over the things he desired if they might be in opposition to what God wanted for him. Praying for herself, however, proved difficult at best. During the next week, she read the third chapter of Proverbs several times, committing it to memory. She read the Gospel of Matthew all the way through and started on Romans. The words touched her, yet each time she dropped to her knees to ask the Lord to take her heart and her will, the words stuck in her throat. She could only pray about the fears running through her head.

"I want to find work in the city so I can go now. I want to go before I love Ben too much to leave."

Speaking the sentiment aloud, she knew she sounded silly. If she loved Ben, she would want to stay with him regardless of where he settled. Yet she knew she could not be happy remaining in Browning City, with or without Ben.

"I feel like I need to go now, Lord. Please provide me with the job I need to do this." She started to rise; then a thought struck her. "And I'm not sure how deeply this goes into my heart, but my head tells me to say, a job, if it is Thy will."

Feeling surprisingly better, she got up from her knees and went to bed. After a fine night's sleep, she woke to the cooing of a mourning dove and other less distinct birdsongs. Spring was on its way with daffodils poking their heads from the soil in yellow profusion and buds forming a green haze along the branches of trees.

It was a good time for a new start.

Her footfalls not as heavy as they had been the past few days, Lily headed to the telegraph office. Something good was going to happen today. She just knew it.

For the first half of the day, nothing out of the ordinary occurred. She sent and received messages. She worked on her crocheting in between those times. She welcomed Theo into the office while she ate her lunch.

Then the second half of her day began with the Morse-coded words:

IMPRESSED WITH YOUR WORK *STOP* WILL YOU COME WORK FOR US IN CHICAGO *STOP* NOTIFY BY MAY 1 *STOP* LETTER TO FOLLOW *STOP*

Lily said nothing of the job offer to anyone. She feared the knowledge would make people treat her differently at the Easter egg hunt on Saturday, and she didn't want a thing to spoil her joy in the knowledge that God had answered her prayer, that He had given her the desire of her heart.

"Maybe I am figuring this out, Lord, and giving You more of my life than I realize."

Bubbling with excitement, she dressed for the party with care. Although sunny, the mid-April day was too cool for a calico dress. She wore her blue wool frock, now with bands of ribbon to cover the preserve stains. While pulling it over her head, she couldn't help but remember the last time she had worn it. She had donned it to be pretty for Ben, and he had kissed her.

She pressed her fingers to her lips. She still believed he should not have done that. They weren't even courting. Yet for that moment, she felt secure and warm, feelings that proved as fleeting as the embrace.

"Put it aside." She gave herself a scolding for thinking of the incident with anything beyond embarrassment, as she fashioned a bow of ribbon for her hair. She was pinning a crocheted shawl around her shoulders when someone knocked on the front door.

"That'll be Becky and Matt," she called to Mrs. Twining. "I'll be right there."

She smoothed back the wings of hair over her ears and headed for the front door—where Ben stood on the porch with a handful of daffodils.

"They came up behind the livery this week." He held them out to her. "They were so bright and sunny, they reminded me of you."

"How—how sweet of you." Lily's heart did a foolish flip-flop. "Come in and talk to Mrs. Twining while I put these in water."

She buried her face in the sweet-smelling blossoms, loving them, wishing he hadn't brought them. Even more, she wished he hadn't said such a romantic thing to her.

Don't care about me, Ben. I'm leaving. I tell Western Union on Monday.

She tucked the flowers into a glass of water and returned to the parlor. "I have to wait for Becky and Matt."

"No, they went on to the hall." Ben kissed Mrs. Twining's cheek and crossed the room to open the front door. "I told them I'd come fetch you."

"But if we arrive together. . . Ben, you don't understand. That's the kind of thing courting couples do—attending a party like this together."

Ben grinned at her. "So Great-Aunt Deborah has informed me. And as I told her, Becky made the suggestion that I come fetch you."

"And I thought she was my friend." Lily's grumble held no rancor.

Ben laughed. "She's my friend, too." He held out his arm. "May I escort you, Miss Reese?"

"Since I don't want to go alone, I guess I'd better go along with this scheme of Becky's."

"That's not very gracious of you, Lily." Laughter crackled in Mrs. Twining's voice. "You run along and have a good time with my great-nephew."

Lily feared she would.

By the time the adults oversaw the Easter egg hunt and distribution of prizes for the children, she was having a good time. By the time the adult party began, she forgot she objected to attending the party with Ben as her beau. She forgot any grievances and experienced only the joy of playing games and singing with people she had known from two months to three years. People who invited her to be on their teams. . . People who teased her when she failed to score a point, and cheered her when she did. . .

People she realized were her friends.

"As always," Mary told her at the end of the festivities, "you and Becky did a fine job, and we have raised a respectable sum of money for books. Thank you."

"Everyone made it go on well." Lily lowered her eyes from Mary's penetrating gaze. "It's a good way to end a long, hard winter."

"And how are you doing?" Mary asked.

"Better. I'm praying a lot—or trying to—and reading my Bible."

She didn't tell Mary about the job offer.

"See you in church tomorrow."

In church the next day, Lily experienced the true joy of remembering the Resurrection. She always understood its significance, but for the first time, she sensed an uplifting of her heart, the lightening of a burden. She truly praised God with the rest of the congregation—people who cared about her, who hugged her or shook her hand, who sought her out. People who knew her shortcomings and appreciated her strengths.

Who will know me and still care about me in Chicago?

The question gave her pause as she composed her reply to the telegraph company on Monday morning.

And she held off on sending her acceptance.

On Friday afternoon, Lily noticed Ben amid the usual group of businessmen who came to meet the train. He waved at her through the window then turned to say something to Toby, who was racing to reach the office on schedule.

The youth laughed and yanked open the door. "Hurry, Miss Lily. There's someone here to see you."

"I can't leave until you're sitting on this stool." Lily rose and picked up her shawl.

The weather had warmed enough that a coat was no longer necessary except after dark or when the wind kicked up.

"I'm on it. I'm on it." Toby bounded over to the stool. "What time did the train get into the station?"

"Four twenty-six, and it's leaving now."

The whistle blasted through the depot.

"I'll send that on to Des Moines." Toby began turning the key. "Good night and enjoy your day off tomorrow."

"That's right. It is the third Saturday." Lily laughed at having forgotten she had a day off and exited the office.

Ben met her outside the door. "I was helping Mr. Gilchrist haul some goods down here and thought I'd wait to walk you home." He took her hand and tucked it into the crook of his arm. "I haven't seen you all week."

"I haven't gone anywhere." *Yet.*

"I know. I've been busy spading gardens for Great-Aunt Deborah's friends."

"But not for her?"

"Do you plant a garden?"

Not when I won't be around to tend it.

"I don't have the time for anything more than a few flowers to brighten the place up."

"Maybe she'll let me grow a few vegetables there." As they left the depot, Ben nodded to Tom Bailyn, Lars Gilchrist, and Jake Doerfel; the latter was talking to a stranger. "You can show me how to preserve them, and I'll reinforce that shelf before we put any more jars on it." He grinned down at her.

Lily melted inside at the memory of what occurred after the shelf broke. She shoved the memory away the best she knew how.

"Ben, I won't be here that long."

"You won't?" He halted in the center of the road and faced her. "How do you know that?"

"Because I've had a job offer in Chicago."

His face paled as though someone had shot him again. "When did that happen?"

"The Monday before Easter."

His obvious distress made her throat close.

"I should have known. The inspectors liked you, didn't they?"

She nodded.

"I see." He resumed walking, faster, too fast for her to keep up.

"Stop." She tugged on his arm.

"I'm sorry." He slowed. "I didn't want to hear about you going away. I thought. . . When do you leave?"

"I haven't accepted the position yet."

"No? Well, then." He paused and faced her, gripping both of her hands with his, a smile lighting his face in the evening sunshine. "What's holding you back?"

"I—I want to make sure it is what God wants for me."

There, she'd said it aloud.

"I think it's right. I prayed, and the offer came, but I can't bring myself to answer them. I'm not completely comfortable saying yes and making the move. Mrs. Twining needs someone to stay with her, and that'll take time to arrange. And there is the spring bazaar. I have commitments here. And—"

No, she wouldn't admit to him that she wasn't yet certain she could leave him behind.

"I just don't know how to know what the Lord wants for me," she concluded. "I read my Bible a lot now, but I still can't figure this out."

"Then will you come for a drive with me tomorrow?" He tucked her hand into the crook of his elbow again, and they resumed walking. "I asked Mr. Gilchrist if I could borrow one of the buggies and take you out for a drive if the weather is fine. Business is a little slow right now with the spring planting coming up, so he said yes. I know you're free tomorrow. Will you come? I'll provide the picnic, and I think you'll find it easier to seek God's will when you're not distracted by the noise and bustle of town."

"Ben, I. . ." A chill ran up her spine at the idea of going into the countryside, away from even a small town like Browning City. "I hate the quiet, with no people around."

"I'll be there." He covered her hand where it rested on his arm. "That will be enough for a few hours, won't it?"

She feared he was right.

"Can we come back if I don't like it?"

"Immediately."

"Then I'll go."

She regretted the acceptance the instant she said it. But she had agreed, so she would go. She tossed and turned all night, fearing that a few hours alone in Ben's company would tip the scale in favor of her staying in Browning City. But the quiet of the night around her told her she didn't want to stay. She wanted to leave and leave now. She didn't know why she was being so foolish and hadn't accepted the position in Chicago. Oh yes, because she had enjoyed herself so much at the Easter egg hunt and party. She had stayed because she felt responsible for the party arrangements. She stayed because she wanted to celebrate Easter in a church she knew. She stayed because. . .because. . .

She didn't have the courage to leave, just like she hadn't left the farm until the bank sent the sheriff's men to throw her things from the house. Only the things without value, of course. As she'd trudged to the stagecoach stop ten miles away, she vowed to never again live in the country and too far from neighbors to have help in times of need.

But what of the story Ben had told her regarding his father?

She remembered the tale as she readied herself to go driving with him. The city was full of people, yet no one had aided the older man.

Soon after Ben's arrival, she brought up the subject with him. "If people who live too far apart are strangers, then can people who are too close together be strangers, too?"

"I wouldn't think so over time." Ben assisted her into the buggy and leaped in after her.

A picnic basket took up a good third of the seat. Lily heaved it over her lap so it rested between them.

Ben grinned at her but said nothing about her action.

"Yes," he said as he got the horse moving, "I think one can make friends in the city, especially if you have a church. It just takes longer. People don't seem to be as trusting."

"That's a comfort to think about." Lily tilted her head back to feel the warmth of sunshine on her face. "When I was growing up, we didn't have many neighbors. They were far away, and we spent most of our time with just the family. Three generations of us."

"Did all of them die in the epidemic?" Ben asked in a quiet voice.

Lily shook her head. "No, Grandmomma just got old. Then Momma. . . I don't know what took her. She just got real tired and pale and slipped away from us about a year before the typhoid took Daddy and my brother. The other women in the area were older and busy with their own families. I didn't have any females my age to talk to until I came here."

"And gentlemen callers?" Ben flashed her a grin.

She ducked her head so the brim of her bonnet hid her face. "There were one or two of those. But I couldn't leave Daddy and Owen, my brother. And it's too nice a day to talk about those kinds of things. Where are you taking me?"

"To the piece of land I am going to buy."

"Oh." Lily shuddered.

"It's only six miles out of town."

"Too far to get in on a weeknight."

"I expect so."

Ben steered the buggy around a farm wagon filled with children. He waved to the man and woman on the seat. They and all of the children waved back.

"Who are they?" Lily asked.

"The people who own the farm next to the one I want." Ben rested one elbow on the picnic basket. "It's not large, but it runs along the river and has a good stream for water. There was a house there once, but it burned down a long time ago. It's uncultivated land except for grass, of course, and trees along the creek."

"It sounds pretty," Lily murmured.

"You sound dubious."

"Why are you taking me there?" she asked, changing the subject.

Ben laughed. "I understand—don't give me too much information about it and tell me what we're doing today. Well, Lily, we are going to enjoy the quiet, each other, this picnic, and the Lord."

Lily squirmed. "The last being first, of course."

"Only if you choose it to be."

She didn't know what she wanted to come first. She knew her enjoyment of Ben's company was the only reason she didn't tell him to turn the buggy around. Yet his certainty that he would purchase this particular piece of land made her wish she had stayed in town, spending her Saturday off browsing the shops or sitting in the sunshine on Mrs. Twining's front porch and working on lace to sell at the bazaar.

He was so committed to the life of a farmer that she should steer clear of him forever.

But sunshine, a warm breeze smelling of grass, damp earth, and their picnic fare, and later, when they reached their destination, the food itself left her drowsy and contented.

"It was kind of Mrs. Meddler at the hotel to make up that basket." Lily stood up from the rock she'd perched on and began to gather the papers in which chicken, rolls, and berry preserve tarts had been wrapped.

"I repaired one of the hanging wires on that chandelier in the dining room." Ben rose also and held out his hand. "Let's walk."

Lily slipped her hand into his and allowed him to guide her around the property. At the top of a rise, she caught sight of the road in one direction and the river in the other. The road looked empty as far as she could see in either direction. The river foamed in full spring flood between low bluffs. Its roar, muted by distance, and the song of half a dozen birds in the copse of trees by the stream feeding into the river were the only sounds she heard. Not even the ceaseless Iowa wind competed with the Mississippi for its voice to be heard.

"I need to talk." Lily spoke a little too loudly. "The silence makes me crazy. I was so alone on the farm for months. No one to talk to."

"I've been coming out here to talk to the Lord." Ben's tone was quiet. "My voice doesn't feel lost the way it does in the racket of town."

"I think the Lord can hear us no matter what is afoot around us."

"Of course He can." Ben smiled at her. "But can you hear Him?"

"I read my Bible. That's His words."

"Yes, but do His words come to you when you pray?"

"I. . .never thought about it."

"Will you now?" Ben faced her. "Let's take just a few minutes and pray. You have an important decision to make. You don't want to make a mistake."

Because she most certainly did not, Lily agreed. With Ben, she knelt on the grass, inhaled the sweetness from their crushing the tender stalks, and began to silently talk to God. *Lord, I can't live like this, yet I am not sure I have the courage to leave after all. I don't have an answer from You yet. Please give me an answer that makes sense to me. I can't live this far from people. This land is pretty, but I am so scared of the quiet. I don't like it. I can't—*

She stopped. She heard her voice in her head, and it wasn't a pleasant sound.

She sprang to her feet. "I want to leave—now."

"Now?" Ben blinked up at her. "It's early still, and I want to walk down to the river."

"Now. If you won't drive the buggy, I'll walk." With that, she turned and strode for the road.

Ben caught up with her. "Lily, what's wrong?"

"What's wrong? I sound whiny. I'm whining to God about what I can't do and don't want." She squeezed back tears. "I can't give up anything to Him—surrender."

"I understand." Ben clasped her shoulder as they reached the buggy. "I'm struggling with that myself."

"What can't you surrender to God?" Lily demanded.

Ben dropped his hand away. "You."

He left her side to fetch the hobbled horse. When he returned, Lily still had thought of no response. She trembled inside as though she had not eaten the hotel's delicious chicken and tarts. Emptiness gnawed at her.

Ben finished harnessing the horse to the buggy. "Need a hand up?"

She shook her head, stepped on the wheel, and swung herself into the buggy. It shook beneath her. She glanced down. The ground was soft, not too wet. Perfect for plowing. It was a fine place to farm.

Some lady would be happy to work the land at Ben's side.

Lily hugged herself and stared straight ahead.

Ben climbed in beside her, and the buggy rocked. "I should have found more stable earth to leave this on. We'd better get going."

They headed for the road. The buggy rattled and creaked beneath them. Ben frowned but said nothing. Lily remained silent, too. She felt ill in the badly sprung buggy on an even worse road.

Except the drive out hadn't felt so bad. Of course, they were traveling a bit faster now, perhaps. She suspected Ben wanted to be free of her as fast as she wanted to be away from him.

That was wrong, though. She didn't want to be apart—

The right wheel dropped into a rut.

"Ouch."

"I'm sorry. This isn't handling—"

A *crack* splintered the quiet.

"Hang on!" Ben shouted.

But she had nothing to hang on to as the right wheel broke loose. It spun away in one direction. Lily flew in another. Pain roared through her skull until blackness took over.

Chapter 12

Lily came to consciousness with a groan. If she hadn't heard herself, she would have believed she had lost her hearing. Silence lay over everything else like fog. She tried to open her eyes, but the lids remained too heavy, weighed down, she suspected, by smaller versions of the rock that had become her pillow.

Why did she have a rock for a pillow?

She tried to raise her left arm. Pain screamed along her shoulder. She lifted her right hand. Little discomfort. Much better. She touched her face. No stones on her eyelids. Just fatigue. She needed more sleep.

Another groan jerked her from her torpor. That wasn't her voice. Forcing her eyes open, she found she wasn't at Mrs. Twining's. She lay on the road. Remains of the wrecked buggy lay strewn a few yards away, with no sign of the horse in the shafts. Beyond that, she saw Ben crumpled like a heap of discarded laundry.

"Ben." She tried to stand.

Her legs collapsed beneath her. Barely, she caught herself from landing on her face.

"Please, Lord."

She didn't even know what to pray. One thought filled her head—get to Ben.

She crawled. Stones grinding into her hands and knees, she scuttled across the road to where Ben lay.

Where he lay too motionless and quiet to have groaned.

Her heart racing, Lily touched his neck. She found no pulse. His skin felt clammy.

Memory of a fetid room, cold skin, and silence swept through her. She was alone again. Ben had left her utterly alone with no one to help her. Everything, everyone she cared about had vanished once more.

She opened her mouth to scream.

"You weren't alone." Mary's words stopped Lily's cry. *"God was with you."*

"Are You there, God?" she called. "Ben really needs You right now."

Unless nothing could help him now.

Tensing, she moved her fingers on his neck and felt his pulse. It was weak, irregular, but it was there. She glanced around him, touched his scalp. She saw no blood, but she found a lump on the back of his head.

"Ben, can you hear me?" She ran her fingertips across his forehead. "Open your eyes for me."

He didn't move.

"Ben, you brought me out here. Don't leave me alone." She started to cry. "I don't know what to do out here. I can't call for help."

"God was with you."

"God is with you."

"How can I know that?" She covered her face with her hands. "I pray for answers, and You let this happen. You leave me alone out here with someone who's too quiet. You've left me."

Her voice grew hoarse, her sobs ragged. She was whimpering, accusing God of. . .

Doing something He had promised never to do—leave her.

Lily caught her breath and stared at a cloud drifting across the sky. Her head spun, so she rested it on her updrawn knees. She was reaching for something, a fullness, an understanding, an answer she knew she could reach if only her head didn't feel like an overripe melon.

God promised never to leave His people. Yet she felt abandoned. How could that be, since the Lord's Word was truth? Logic. . . Logic. . .

If God never left, and yet she never felt His presence even in her prayers, then she must have. . .must have. . .

Become absent from God.

"I've abandoned You." She hugged her knees tight to her chest. "I prayed, but I never really believed. I never truly gave up my heart to You."

As she had done with fixing up Ben's quarters and arranging parties to raise money for good causes, she had gone through the appropriate motions with God while her heart had been selfish. She filled up her life with work and play instead of devotion to the Lord.

"I need a whole lot of forgiveness, Lord," she whispered into the quiet. "I—"

"Lily?" Ben's voice interrupted her.

"Shh. I'm listening to my heart."

Ben chuckled then fell silent.

The world lay in stillness. Even the wind seemed to hold its breath while Lily stumbled through a prayer of surrender to the Lord. The quiet seeped into her mind, her heart, her soul. The shakiness vanished.

She raised her head and gazed into Ben's eyes.

"Good afternoon."

His voice sounded rough. His eyes weren't quite focused. Dirt smeared his face.

"Are you in pain?" she asked.

"Not when I look at both of your beautiful faces."

She giggled. "That isn't a good sign."

"Can you walk to town for help?"

"I can, but I won't leave you." She brushed his hair back from his brow. "It's Saturday. Someone will come by soon."

"You're not afraid of us being alone until they do?"

"We're not alone." She smiled down at him. "The Lord is with us."

Two days later, Ben straightened from his examination of the buggy wreckage. Some of the dizziness that had plagued him since the accident swept over him, and he swiped his sleeve across his brow.

"It was no accident." Ben frowned at Lars Gilchrist. "Someone tampered with the axle."

"How can you be certain?" Mr. Gilchrist looked old and tired. "Could it not have broken from age and poor repair?"

A twinge of anger plucked at Ben's gut.

"I keep everything in good repair, sir." He poked the pieces of axle with the toe of his boot. "It's been cut."

"It's not simply a flaw in the wood?"

"And a piece is missing."

Gilchrist scowled. "Why would someone take a piece of the axle?"

"It's a shorter piece from the wheel to the main shaft. This is long, but it's not long enough."

"It could have fallen somewhere else." Mr. Gilchrist glanced about the empty countryside where the accident had occurred. "The wheel rolled a good ways away."

"Yes, sir, and the piece had been cut from it by the time we all got back here. Two days is more than enough time."

"But why would someone want to do that to you and Miss Lily?" Gilchrist began to pace back and forth across the narrow road. "It makes no sense to me. You are two of the best young people I know. I can't imagine either of you having enemies."

"No, sir, whatever the sheriff might think." Ben tasted a hint of bitterness in his words and clamped his lips shut before he said more.

"Now, son, he's just trying to keep his town safe." Gilchrist laid a hand on Ben's shoulder. "And you know we had little crime to speak of before you came. It's a logical conclusion for him to draw."

"But I haven't done anything but move here and try to make a new life for myself." Ben shoved his hands into his pockets and headed for one of the two horses he and Gilchrist had ridden from town. "Before I came here to settle, I'd never stayed anywhere long enough to make enemies."

"So the problem lies somewhere else." Gilchrist joined him at the horses. "We just need to figure out where."

On the way back to Browning City, Ben wondered how to accomplish the task of learning who didn't want him in town and, just as important, why. The idea of Lily being the target was not something to consider. No one could think ill of her.

Of course, Ben didn't know why anyone would think ill of him, either. He didn't believe he was being self-centered to think such a thing. The town had welcomed him. He'd never had an enemy, and no one had ever asked him—or his father—to leave a place. When his father felt the need to move on, they had always gone of their own free will.

His father's free will. Ben had wanted to stay many times, but his father never did, and Ben couldn't let him go alone.

Yet someone didn't like Ben. Didn't like him and wanted to see him gone, maybe even permanently.

Heart heavy, Ben bade good day to Gilchrist in front of the general store; then he returned to the livery, leading the older man's horse. The stable appeared too empty with the buggy missing. The other one stood in its corner across from the plow and other farm equipment. After putting the horses into their stalls, Ben gave the second buggy a thorough inspection. Wheels, axle, singletree all looked undamaged.

"So how did whoever damaged the other one know I would take it instead of this one?" Ben rocked back on his heels and stared at the vehicle. "How did someone even know I would take out a buggy on Saturday instead of someone else?"

A quick recall told him any number of people could have known the latter. At least a dozen people had seen them drive out of town. Anyone could have followed them and cut the axle while Ben and Lily ate their picnic on the other side of the hill and out of sight of the road. In fact, the perpetrator would have had to carry out his deed in such a manner. Otherwise, the wheel would have broken off sooner, would have come off when they had barely left town.

"What is wrong here, Lord?" Ben spoke aloud in the empty stable.

Empty of people, that is. All but one horse still stood in their stalls. The one missing would be gone the entire week, rented out by a man who didn't like trains and needed to go to Des Moines. Business was slow. Far too slow. With feed and other supplies to purchase, Gilchrist hadn't made enough on the livery to pay Ben's wages.

A hint of fear crept up his spine. Slow business. Someone wanting to harm him or, at the least, scare him off.

"Am I wrong, Lord? Am I not to stay here after all?"

Wind blew the mourning wail of the afternoon train's whistle into town. Ben stood and glanced in the direction of the depot. He should go meet Lily. He hadn't seen her since Saturday. Doc Smythe had ordered both of them to stay in their homes and rest on Sunday, especially Ben, who had seen double for several hours after the buggy wreck. When Ben had stopped at Great-Aunt Deborah's house earlier in the day to ask after Lily, he learned she had gone to work.

"She looked well." Great-Aunt Deborah had smiled. "In truth, Ben, I've never seen her looking better. She looked peaceful."

Ben knew what Great-Aunt Deborah meant. Nothing was quite as beautiful as seeing Lily's face alight with peace and joy. Nothing sounded quite so sweet as hearing her say they were not alone because the Lord was with them.

As he strode toward the depot, Ben praised God for such good coming out of the accident. He hoped her newfound relationship with the Lord meant she would stay in Browning City.

If he was to stay there.

No. He pushed the nagging doubt aside. The attacks on him and the poor business at the livery were not signs from God that he should move on. Surely not. Business would pick up again once the weather stayed fine and planting ended.

As for the attacks on him. . . They must learn who was behind those, especially now that they had risked Lily's safety.

Thinking of Lily lightened his heart again, and he increased his stride. The depot came into sight. A few people headed toward him: some strangers, Tom Bailyn, Jake Doerfel. No sign of Lily.

Ben greeted Tom and Jake then crossed the station to the telegraph office. Lily sat at her machine keying in a message. When she finished, she glanced up at him, smiled, and waved.

"Waiting for Toby," she mouthed.

Ben nodded and leaned against the wall of the office to wait for her. What felt like much too much later, he heard footfalls running up the road and glanced around to see Toby galloping into the station.

"So sorry! So sorry!" he shouted in apology before he reached the office.

Lily shook her head but didn't look in the least upset as she slid off her stool and gathered up her things.

"To what do I owe the privilege of your escort?" she said as she greeted Ben and then spoke over her shoulder, "Toby, I forgot to tell you, the eastbound is running sixteen minutes late at the last report." She took Ben's arm without hesitation and looked up at him. "You didn't need to wait."

"Of course I did." He started walking toward town, thrilled to have Lily at his side.

Where he always wanted her.

"You're awfully patient with his being late all the time. If it's not rude of me to ask, do they pay you extra for waiting?"

"They do, but they've threatened to dismiss him several times." Lily sighed. "But I keep talking the supervisor from Davenport into keeping him on. Maybe I shouldn't let him get away with it, but he is the only wage earner for his mother and five younger brothers and sisters. Their father died in an accident last year. That's why he works a double shift."

Ben covered her hand with his. "I don't know how you could call yourself selfish, Lily." And for his own selfish reasons, he added, "Another operator wouldn't be so generous, staying on, more than likely."

"You mean if I leave."

"Yes."

"You truly want me to stay." She peered up at him from beneath the brim of her bonnet.

"Permanently." He took a deep breath. "I'd like to court you."

"Haven't you been already?" Her tone was light. "The picnic. Taking me to the Easter egg hunt. It looks like courting to everyone."

"Yes, and I want it to be official."

He wasn't being terribly clear, yet he suspected she understood what he meant—he wanted the kind of courting that led to engagement. He wanted, when they knew one another a bit longer—not too much longer—to marry her. He couldn't offer her everything he wanted to, but if she were willing to make do with the quarters behind the livery for a year or two—and if he won the plowing contest this year or next—they could have a fair life together.

No, a good life together.

His mouth dry, he took the next step. "I love you, Lily."

"Oh my." She tightened her hand on his arm. "Ben, I—"

"I understand if you don't feel the same way. I just had to say it and ask for a chance. But if you don't want to see me anymore now—"

"Shh." She drew her hand from under his and touched a gloved finger to his lips. "I want to spend time with you more than anyone. But at the same time, I—well, I'm afraid. I mean, I could so easily love you. But if I end up leaving, it would only hurt us both."

"Then don't leave." He took her hand in his, and they continued into town with fingers linked. "I thought you wouldn't want to go now. Saturday, you said you weren't afraid of being alone anymore."

"I wasn't. I'm not. But now I know I won't be alone in the city, either. It doesn't mean I have changed my mind about having to be alone, if you understand what I'm saying."

"I'm afraid I do." He sighed to relieve the pain around his heart. "But if you were to stay, I'd have a chance?"

"Better than a chance."

"Then why are you even thinking of leaving?" Stopping, he swung to face her and grasped her other hand. "Lily, if you care about me that much, why would you leave?"

She met his gaze. "You could come with me."

"I have no future in the city." Ben winced at the sadness in her eyes. "My future is here."

"And my future may be in the city." She turned away and resumed walking, Ben falling into step beside her. "I am still waiting to know what the Lord wants for me."

"Isn't time getting short to notify them?"

"Yes. But I have peace that I will know what to do when I need to."

Ben thought about the accident that could have seriously injured Lily, or worse, and had to give in. "I'll wait and pray for you."

"Thank you." She smiled. "And I'll pray that maybe you have a future in the city after all."

"It's not what I want." He glanced around at the houses and businesses beginning to line up on either side of them. "I was born here. My only family is here. But today—Lily, you need to know this. We didn't have an accident on Saturday."

"I beg your pardon? I have a headache that says we did."

"Me, too." Ben grimaced. "What I mean is that someone tampered with the buggy to make it crash."

Lily gasped. Her face paled. "How—I mean, why? I mean. . . Who would want to harm us?"

"Not us, my dear, me."

"But why—oh." A muscle ticked in Lily's jaw. "They're trying to scare you away from the livery."

"I can't help but think that." He knotted his free hand into a fist at anything that so much as appeared to upset Lily. "It's difficult to hunt for gold if I'm living there."

"But rumors of the gold have been around for years," Lily pointed out. "And no one has lived there for even longer than that."

"Someone who is new in town, who just learned of those rumors? Or someone from out of town?"

They turned the corner to Great-Aunt Deborah's street.

"I admit I looked around the livery myself." Ben gave an embarrassed laugh. "Who wouldn't want the reward money for finding that kind of treasure? It would help me buy my farm now instead of waiting several years. And I could make a wife more comfortable than I can now on what I earn. But that place is solidly built. I don't see how anyone could have hidden anything there."

"You had time to look." Lily paused at the end of Great-Aunt Deborah's walk. "No one else can do that." She held out her hands. "Be careful, Ben. I wish. . . Will you think about maybe this being the Lord's way of telling you that you shouldn't stay here?"

When she gazed up at him with her wide, blue eyes, Ben could deny her nothing.

"I'll pray about that, but I can't believe He would bring me here then send me away."

Except maybe to find her?

Now that was something to think about.

"May I see you tomorrow?"

"I think it would be better if we didn't see each other for a few days. Come to Sunday dinner."

"Sunday?" Ben protested so loudly the front curtain twitched back.

He waved to Great-Aunt Deborah then sighed. "You're probably right. Until Sunday." He touched her cheek and strode away at a near jog before he was tempted to do more.

He didn't understand what the Lord was doing to him. He'd prayed for family for years. He prayed for a stationary home and a godly wife. Now he had the former and a wonderful possibility for the latter, and she still talked about leaving.

She didn't love him enough to stay. That was all there was to it. If she loved him enough, she would give up notions of crowds and bright lights.

If you love her enough, maybe you would give up on open fields and a handful of people.

The thought jabbed him like a knife to his gut. Before falling in love with Lily, he had been so sure settling in Browning City was the right decision, the decision God wanted him to make. Now, he didn't know.

For the rest of the evening, he kept returning to the idea that he was supposed to leave town with Lily. He fought the notion and tried to think of ways he could make staying attractive to her. He knew he couldn't afford to support a wife in style as income matters stood. They wouldn't want for anything, but they would have little for extras, either. Extras like traveling. Lily would be unhappy. Yet in the city, she was the only one of them who would arrive with a job. He could find work, of course, but she couldn't work once they started a family.

"It seems impossible, Lord."

Those were his last words before he fell asleep. The aching place in his head resulting from the accident had spread across his brow and down his neck. He tossed and turned and woke in the middle of the night with his eyes and nose burning.

From smoke.

Chapter 13

Lily woke to a clanging bell and the sound of horses pounding along the street, shouts and the smell of smoke. Too much smoke for stove and hearth fires. More like. . .

She shot from bed and stumbled to the window. From her view of the side yard and Mrs. Willoughby's house, she could see nothing. She flung up the sash and leaned out, shivering in the chilly night air, then coughing as smoke billowed into her face on a gust of wind.

The fire was close, but she still couldn't tell where it was. She needed to find the location, carry buckets, help. Everyone in town who could help in a fire did so. They had no fire wagon.

She slammed the window and yanked a dress over her head. Not bothering with stockings, she shoved her feet into her shoes and laced them up. A shawl? No, too easy to catch sparks. Good for beating them out, though.

She tossed one around her shoulders and dashed into Mrs. Twining's room. The older lady sat up in bed, lighting a candle.

"Fire somewhere." Lily's words came out breathless. "I'm going out."

"Of course." Mrs. Twining coughed. "You be careful."

"I will."

"Do you know where the fire is?" Mrs. Twining's eyes filled with concern. "If we can smell this much smoke, it must be close."

"I know."

Lily worried their house might be in danger.

"But it's windy enough to blow the smoke to us."

And carry fire from building to building when they hadn't had rain in days.

"I'll come back if—if we need to leave here." Losing her things was not something to contemplate. All the lace she had made for the bazaar, clothes that were so expensive to replace, her hooks and needles, which cost even more. . .

But others might be losing their things right now. She must hurry, help save what she could.

Lily ran through the kitchen and grabbed two buckets from the pantry. Wind made the back door resist her push to open it. Wind reeking of smoke. Smoke stinging her nostrils and lungs. Too strong not to be a nearby fire.

She threw her shoulder against the door. Another gust of wind sent it crashing back into the door frame. Lily rushed into the night with a black sky overhead and an orange glow to the north.

As she headed toward that glow, she raced past the familiar homes and businesses that occupied that part of town. Dr. Smythe. Not far enough away. Gilchrist's. Still too near. Scott's Bank.

The livery.

Lily broke into a run, tripping and stumbling over uneven ground. "Not the livery. Lord, please, not the livery. Not Ben." More plea than prayer, words poured from Lily between gasps for air.

The livery was only a block away now. It felt like six blocks, like six miles. She crashed into the first line of a bucket brigade, trying to push past them.

"Lily, stop." Matt Campbell caught hold of her arm. "It's not safe."

"But Ben." She thrust her buckets into Matt's hands. "Take these. I have to help Ben."

"He doesn't need your help right now." Matt took her buckets.

Someone else thrust a full pail into her hands. "Pass it along, Lily." She did.

"Mary." Lily turned to the pastor's wife. "Where is Ben?"

"With the horses." Mary patted her shoulder then grasped another bucket.

"You're sure?" Lily scanned the scene around her.

Their line passed water from the well of the blacksmith's shop next to the livery. She couldn't see much around the bulk of the smithy shed. Not much more than flames licking up. Shouts, orders from the tone, proved indistinct above clanging pails, roaring flames, and the screams of frightened horses.

She hoped they were only frightened, not injured.

"I can't see anything." Her voice held a hysterical note, and she took a deep breath to calm herself. "Do you know what is happening?"

"Started in the roof, I heard," Matt said. "We're all too busy trying to keep it from spreading in this wind to pay much attention."

"But Ben is uninjured." Mary slid one more bucket into Lily's hand.

Lily took the bucket and the assurance with all the strength she could muster. She must. The town needed every able-bodied person to wet down other buildings and douse the main fire so nothing else caught. She recalled reading about what had happened in Chicago five years earlier. The city burned down—a city with fire equipment, a lake, and a river. The Mississippi was too far away to be of much help. Browning City's founders hadn't wanted to be right on the water in case of flood and to protect against river pirates. They should have thought of fire. Buckets seemed inadequate to subdue the flames. Each load of water seemed to enact no more good than a raindrop trying to put out a stove fire.

"Rain. Lord, we need rain."

She didn't realize she prayed aloud until Mary said, "Amen," in agreement.

"We have clouds," Matt put in. "But not—"

Cries of protest rang from the livery yard, louder than other shouts, a few words distinguishable.

"Stop."

"You can't."

"Leave it."

News rippled down the bucket line. When Lily heard, she wanted to break ranks and go after him, drag him away from the flames, away from danger.

"It's the money." Tears ran down her face like the water dripping down her skirt. "He needs the plow for the contest."

"He needs it badly enough to risk his life?" Mary sounded appalled. "I thought he had more sense than that."

"He does. I mean, he would. . ." Lily was sobbing. "He thinks if he has more money, I'll stay here and marry him. It's not the money. Doesn't he—"

Shouts of relief rang from the livery yard.

"He's safe out," someone at the head of the smithy shed called. "But risking his neck for a—"

A crash and roar of flames and human voices reverberated through the night. A column of sparks soared above the rooftops like upward-shooting stars.

"It's gone," many voices chorused. "Livery's gone."

Ben had just lost his livelihood, his living quarters, and probably everything he owned. Lily wanted to curl into a ball and cry. Yet she was too busy passing buckets of water to succumb to grief or to even think. Her group needed to extinguish the pinpoints of fire landing on the smithy.

Those pinpoints grew to tongues of flame.

"Faster on the water!" a man on a ladder shouted. "I need more water."

"We need rain," Mary said.

And it came; so light at first Lily didn't notice the extra dampness. Then the drops grew fatter and more frequent until she felt as though someone were pouring pails of water over her. Soon the smell of smoke turned into the stench of charred, wet wood. The last of the fires died in a gasp of steam.

"Coffee and food back at the church hall," Pastor Jackson Reeves announced from nearby.

Lily left the bucket line, knowing she could collect Mrs. Twining's pails in the morning, and began to hunt for Ben. With the fire out and rain falling, seeing faces grew impossible. She tried to call to him, but her throat was raw.

She would find him at the hall. He had nowhere else to go unless she found him and told him what she planned.

Along with dozens of other townsfolk, Lily trudged to the church hall.

There, with the stove warming the place and making everyone's clothes steam, several of the older ladies had prepared coffee and sandwiches. Not realizing she was cold until she began to grow warm, Lily accepted a cup of coffee and located Mrs. Willoughby.

"I'll need to stay with you again," she told the older lady. "I'll pay you, of course."

"You're such a sweet girl." Mrs. Willoughby beamed at her. "You know the best thing for that young man right now is to live with his aunt."

"Yes. I think family is where a body ought to be when everything else goes up in smoke." Lily sipped the bracing coffee. "Have you seen him?"

Mrs. Willoughby glanced past Lily's shoulder. "He just walked in."

"Thank you." Lily turned.

If Ben were not so tall, she never would have seen him for the crowd. As it was, she saw only his face, pale beneath a smudged layer of soot. A bruise marred his right cheekbone. His eyelids drooped, and his jaw looked taut. Too taut for a man given more to smiles than frowns. At that moment, he looked like someone who would never smile again.

Lily wove her way through the crowd of sooty townsfolk until she reached Ben. "Here." She gave him her coffee.

"Thank you." He took the cup from her.

His fingers brushed hers. His hand was cold, and he didn't smile at her.

"Don't you want this?" He held up the cup.

"I don't need it. I'm going back to Mrs. Twining's house right now to move my things out."

"Out?" Alarm flashed across his face. "But you can't leave yet."

Lily's heart twisted. "Not out of Browning City. I'm moving out of Mrs. Twining's house and into Mrs. Willoughby's so you can stay with family, where you belong."

"Oh, Lily. . ."

His throat worked. He reached out a reddened and blistered hand and laid his palm against her cheek.

"Thank you."

"You're welcome." Lily looked into his eyes, read tenderness replacing the distress, and knew she could never leave his side.

She didn't get any sleep that night. After clearing her things out of her room in Mrs. Twining's house and lugging what she could to Mrs. Willoughby's, she made the effort to bathe and wash her hair to rid herself of the reek of smoke. By the time she finished with drying her hair before the kitchen stove and making breakfast, she needed to go to work. She wanted to get to work. She had the most important telegram of her career to send.

Thank You for Offer *STOP* Decided to Stay In Browning
City *STOP*

The path seemed clear to Ben. With everything he owned except for the plow destroyed in the fire, without a livery to manage, with his heart certain Lily loved him, he would leave Browning City and hunt for work in Chicago.

"But I don't want you to just stay here and manage a new livery," Gilchrist protested at Ben's announcement. "I'd like you to manage my store, too. I think Tom and Eva are about to make a match of it, and I don't want to appear too much in competition with my son-in-law." He guffawed.

Ben nodded. "That would be awkward, but now that the two of you are starting to sell different things, it isn't so bad."

"No, but to tell you the truth, Ben, I would like to tend to my farm, make it pay before I'm too old."

The offer tempted Ben. For a moment, his heart felt torn in two different directions—stay with a town he had grown to love and what remained of his family or go to Chicago to be near Lily until he could ask her to marry him. He thought of how much he had prayed about his future and all the incidents leading to this moment and shook his head.

"I can't stay, but I am so honored you trust me after all that's happened."

"You didn't start that fire." Gilchrist leaned his hands on the store counter. "Have you talked with the sheriff today?"

"I'm on my way."

Ben wasn't looking forward to that interview.

"I thought I'd talk to you first, in case you wished to come with me."

"No need. You're an honest young man. You'll tell the truth to him just as you did to me."

"Thank you, sir." Ben turned toward the door. "I should get down there."

"If he gives you trouble, you send for—ah, here he comes now."

Sheriff Dodd stepped onto the boardwalk and yanked open the door. He brought the stench of charring with him, and ashes coated his shoes and lower pant legs.

"Saw you through the window, Purcell." Dodd drew his thin brows together. "Thought you were coming to the office first thing this morning."

"I had to find decent clothes first, sir." Ben discovered he had propped his fists on his hips, and he lowered his arms. "I was just on my way."

"Humph."

"Looks like you've been at the fire site," Gilchrist said.

"Sure have." Dodd glared at Ben. "You don't smoke?"

"No, sir."

"Leave a lantern on?" Dodd persisted.

"No, sir. And the stove was shut."

"Then how did it start?" Dodd's demand emerged like a challenge.

Ben took a deep, calming breath. "Sir, the fire started in the hayloft. I was asleep in my quarters in the back."

"Everyone saw the roof ablaze first." Gilchrist sounded as belligerent as the sheriff did. "If Ben had started it out of carelessness, it would have started below."

"True. True." Dodd sighed and mopped his brow. "I just don't like all these things happening in my town. It was peaceful until he"—he jabbed a finger toward Ben—"came along."

"Or other newcomers," Ben said.

Dodd and Gilchrist stared at him.

"Explain what you mean by that," Dodd commanded.

Ben explained what he and Lily had worked out about someone wanting to get him out of the livery so they could search it thoroughly for the gold.

"That's ridiculous." Dodd pinched his nostrils as though he smelled something foul.

"Not as ridiculous as you might think." Gilchrist rounded the counter and stood beside Ben. "Nearly ten years ago, a young lady tried shoveling up an entire field in search of that gold. Others have done crazy things to get at it."

"And a body would need to dismantle the place to find anything hidden there," Ben added. "If it is there."

"Hmm." Dodd hooked his thumbs into his belt and gazed at the ceiling as though contemplating the best of the garlic and onions hung there. "Are you suggesting somebody burned down that place to find gold?"

"A man desperate enough for treasure would stop at nothing to get it." Ben spoke softly so as not to break the sheriff's thoughtful mood.

"Hmm." Dodd scratched his chin. "Who else is new in town and started hearing stories of gold in the livery? Not too many folks move here in the middle of winter."

"I don't know," Ben admitted. "Lily Reese says that it's hard to say sometimes because we do get visitors."

We, Ben had said. As though he would remain a part of this town.

"Only three I know of since October." Gilchrist's lips thinned. "Tom Bailyn, a spinster lady come to live with her sister on a farm about ten miles away, and Jake Doerfel."

"I don't know of any more, really, when I think on it." Dodd laid a hand on his belt where most lawmen carried guns.

He sported a knife in a case and a short, thick club.

Dodd half faced the door. "Let me think on it, and I'll come back."

He strode from the store.

Ben turned to Gilchrist. "He didn't accuse me of burning down the livery to get to the gold that might be there."

"He wouldn't dare. I got him hired. I can get him unhired."

"Thank you."

Ben didn't know what else to say.

"We want you to stay here, lad. And Mrs. Twining sure could use family around in her last years."

"I know, but. . ." Ben hesitated then decided this kind man deserved the truth. "Lily has been offered a job in Chicago. I want to find work there and be close by her until I can support a wife."

"You have a job here and can support a wife just fine." Gilchrist's voice was a growl. "And if she doesn't love you enough to stay here, she isn't good enough for you."

"But she thinks God wants her to go."

"And you? Is it what the Lord wants for you?" Gilchrist gave him a penetrating look. "Or are you thinking of a heart for a woman instead of a heart for the Lord?"

Ben winced. "I wish I knew, sir. I was so sure I'd found the right place here, but everything points to me going. Lily and I wouldn't even have a place to live now if we married."

"You mean because some fool for gold tried scaring you off or killing you off? That doesn't sound like God's message to me, but then I'm not as versed in the Bible as Eva says I should be."

A tingle raced up Ben's spine—excitement, fear, anticipation.

"God uses anyone," he said. "Thank you for your wisdom. I'll think and pray about it."

He left the store to wander through the muddy streets of town. Although rain fell in intermittent bursts, he let himself get wet. He needed fresh air and space to think. Praying, he discovered, didn't work at the moment. No words would come to him any different from those he had spoken to God a thousand times or more. Yes, more.

He wanted a place where he belonged, a place for roots. Part of those roots should be a wife, children, and family. Yet God didn't seem to want him to have both.

No matter how hard he worked in the city, he could never earn enough to have the kind of home and land he could have here in Browning City, especially if he took Gilchrist's offer after all. If he won the plowing contest, too, he could buy the land before someone else snatched it up.

But he couldn't have these things and Lily, too. Indeed, nothing guaranteed he could have Lily at all.

"Everyone and everything I love gets taken from me." Words burst from him at the edge of town. "Just like Lily."

The earlier tearing of his heart seemed complete. A hollow space lay inside. He had tried to fill it with working hard with Pa, then making a home in Browning City, then the prospect of finding gold, and then the possibility of winning prize money, purchasing land, and winning Lily's heart.

Lily tried to banish her emptiness with noise and activity. He'd told her to fill it with the Lord, yet he hadn't truly done that himself. He yearned for solid things as much as she longed for crowds. He claimed he sought the Lord's direction, but he went in his own.

"Lord, I need Your forgiveness for my willfulness. Thy will be done, not mine."

He didn't know what else to pray, so he turned back toward town. Sheriff Dodd would want to talk with him again soon. He needed to see about getting some of his things replaced and tend to the livery horses in their temporary quarters at the blacksmith's. He would talk to Great-Aunt Deborah, too. She was his relation and possessed a godly spirit and kind heart. She would have advice for him.

Seeing Dodd ahead of him, Ben lengthened his stride and caught up with the lawman. "Have you come up with a plan?"

Dodd jumped. "Don't sneak up on a body like that." He faced Ben. "I was looking for you. I do have a plan. Some of us will stand guard over the livery and see if anyone comes to search the ashes."

"Not tonight."

Ben wanted to talk to Great-Aunt Deborah, and standing guard would prevent him doing so if he needed to be there at dusk.

"Yep, tonight."

"But the ashes will still be hot inside."

"All the more reason to stand guard. Stop any fires from starting again."

With the heavy rain that began in the afternoon, no fire had a chance. But Ben, Matt, and the sheriff hid in strategic locations around the site of the livery.

They got nothing during the vigil except cold and wet. Ben woke late the next day, sneezing and chilled. He let Great-Aunt Deborah cosset him through the morning, but as idleness made him uneasy, he prepared for another night's vigil.

"You shouldn't go out there again," Great-Aunt Deborah advised over dinner. "You haven't seen Lily since the fire."

Ben began to clear the table of dishes. "This has to be done and can't wait."

"Talking to Lily shouldn't wait, either."

Ben's stomach clenched. "So she did decide to go?"

"That's not for me to discuss with you." Great-Aunt Deborah compressed her lips, but her eyes twinkled.

Her reaction bemusing him, Ben said good night and left the house.

For the first three hours of a blessedly warm and dry night, nothing stirred in the ashes except the wind. Then the *crunch* of a footfall on the gravel of the stable yard alerted Ben to an intruder approaching. Ben stood motionless beneath the overhang of the blacksmith shop roof. Motionless and poised for action. Stars and a three-quarter moon illuminated the site enough for him to make out a shadow slipping to the edge of the burned timbers and walls.

Careful not to make any noise, Ben closed in on the man. From the corner of his eye, he caught movement indicating that Dodd moved in on the intruder, too.

"Now!" Dodd shouted.

He and Ben grabbed the man's arms.

"Yieeee!" He shrieked like an angry cat and lashed out with his feet.

"Don't move," Dodd commanded. "You're under arrest for trespassing and likely burning down the livery."

"No, no," squeaked Jake Doerfel. "I'm getting a story."

"In the middle of the night?"

For once, Ben appreciated the lawman's sarcasm.

"You could've gotten all the story you liked when you helped fight this blaze you started."

"I didn't start it." Jake tugged against Ben's hold. "I have no reason to do anything so foolish."

"Except look for gold," Ben said in the man's ear.

"Gold? What gold?" Jake's voice grew higher with each word. "I don't want anything to do with gold."

"You'd been reading all the back issues of the paper about the gold."

Jake kicked Ben's shin. "Shut your mouth about that."

"No matter," Dodd drawled. "We can all figure out you have all those old newspapers to read, too. You likely know more'n anyone else about the gold."

"No, no. I–I'm. . ." Suddenly he slumped in their hold. "It's my gold. Doerfel isn't my name. It's Mitchell. Jim Mitchell was my father, but he got himself killed without telling me where he hid the gold. But I'm going to find it. It's mine. It's mine." His voice broke on a sob.

"It belongs to the government," Dodd corrected. "And this livery belonged to Mr. Gilchrist. You destroyed it to find something that isn't yours."

"Or might not be there," Ben added.

"It is. It is. . . ."

Jake continued his protests all the way to the one cell the town called a jail.

"Do you think it really is in those ashes?" Matt asked.

"I don't know." Dodd rubbed a knuckle across his chin. "But we're gonna look."

The next day, they looked. Half the town turned out to help. Ben didn't see Lily, but she would be at the telegraph office. She would have enjoyed the festive atmosphere. People laughed and joked and gladly got their hands and clothes dirty moving ash-laden planks. The air crackled with excitement, and Ben's heart raced harder with each layer of the building they uncovered.

Each empty layer.

They found scraps of harness leather and canvas, twisted iron from buggy wheels and farm equipment. Nothing, right down to the earth below the foundation, resembled so much as the melted remains of gold.

Chapter 14

"I still can't believe someone would destroy his life over the chance at finding gold." Lily faced Ben across Mrs. Twining's kitchen table, seeing him for the first time since the fire. "Or worse, risk your life."

"The prospect of easy money makes people do strange and dangerous things." Ben rested his hands on the table. "But I'm safe."

"I am thankful for that." Lily smiled and fell silent.

Ben smiled back, but neither of them looked directly at one another. As the coffee steamed and the smell of a dried apple pie filled the kitchen, silence between them grew. Lily had so much to say to him that she didn't know where to start. She knew Ben wanted to talk to her, too. He had walked her home from the telegraph office, giving her that excuse, yet had said nothing of what lay on his mind. While she made dinner and the pie, he talked with his aunt. During the meal, the three of them discussed the fire and Jake Doerfel's attempts to find the gold. Now, alone for the first time since Saturday, they talked about Jake again, repeating what they had said earlier.

Lily wondered if she should speak up first. She'd always understood that the man brought up the subject of a relationship between a lady and himself, but maybe his odd upbringing hadn't taught him such things.

Maybe she should start, give him a nudge—or push—with her announcement. She clasped the edge of the table. "Ben, I want to tell you about my job—"

"Lily, I want to tell you about my decision," he said at the same time.

They looked at each other and laughed.

"You go first." They spoke at the same time again.

"Ladies first," Ben pronounced.

"All right." Lily took a deep breath. Her heart pounded against her ribs, tapping out a Morse code of apprehension. "I turned down the job offer."

"Lily." He swallowed. "You're staying?"

"Yes."

"Why?"

"Because. . ."

The words "I love you" stuck in her throat. She didn't think she was supposed to say so before he declared his intentions toward her.

"This is where I want to stay." She gave him another part of the answer.

337

"And where I believe the Lord wants me to stay. I was never at peace about taking the job in the city. I have peace about this decision. I don't need all the noise and people to be happy."

"I'm glad to hear it." He gave her a half smile, not an indication of joy at her announcement. "Though I've taken over your room."

"I can stay with Mrs. Willoughby or move to the boardinghouse."

Smelling a crust beginning to brown too much, Lily rose to remove the pie from the oven. She kept her back to him so he couldn't read her disappointment in his lack of enthusiasm for her remaining in Browning City.

"You should stay with family," she concluded.

"I wasn't going to continue living here in town." His voice was tight. "With everything that happened, things like my not having work at the livery now that it's burned down and not having a place to live made me think maybe the Lord wanted me to move on. I thought I had misunderstood what He wanted for me because I wanted it so much. But you seem to understand that."

"I do." She set the pie on the table, still without looking at him. "Sometimes I think we want something so much, we let ourselves believe it's what God wants for us." She picked up the coffeepot and faced him at last. "What will you do now that the livery is gone? Is Mr. Gilchrist going to rebuild?"

Am I any part of that life?

"He is. He still wants me to manage it, and he wants me to manage the store, too."

"Ben, that's wonderful! "

She wished she had the right to hug him.

She set down the coffeepot and reached for a knife to cut the pie.

He covered her hand with his. "Wait, please." He gazed into her eyes.

What she read there made her sink onto the nearest chair, her heart beating so hard she could scarcely breathe. Tenderness. Love. Longing. Everything she felt for him.

"Lily, may I be so bold as to ask if another reason you're staying here is because you care for me?"

"Yes. I mean, yes, you may ask, and yes, it's true." She reached for her coffee cup, realized it was still empty, and picked up his to wash the dryness from her throat. "I knew the night of the fire I wanted to stay near you."

"I was ready to leave here to be near you."

Then ask me to marry you.

She squeezed his hand, trying to convey the message to him without saying it.

"I would like—love—a future with you, Lily." A tremor ran through his fingers. "It's possible. That is, if you're interested enough, but. . ." He paused.

Lily bit back a shriek of frustration.

"I'm going to make good wages soon, and I have my savings." He continued his speech, avoiding her gaze again. "But I still don't feel I can ask you to marry me before I have a home for us."

She shouldn't have stayed in Browning City. Chicago would have offered them dozens of places to live once he had a job. But Browning City had nothing other than rooms to rent, not a good way to start married life.

Except. . .

"The livery?" Hope ran through her.

"When I accepted the job offer from Mr. Gilchrist this morning, I told him we shouldn't build quarters behind the livery. Too dangerous with needing to have a stove and all."

"You told him not to—" Lily stood and backed from the table. "He was going to? And you told him not to?"

"Yes, but—"

"We could have had a place to be together, but you prevented it?"

Ben sighed. "Lily, when I thought seriously about it, I knew I couldn't take my bride back to a room that forever smells like horses. You wouldn't like that."

"You didn't ask me if I would or would not." Tears stung her eyes. "Excuse me." She swung toward the door.

"No, wait." In a flash, he stood between her and the door. "I'm going about this all wrong. I'm trying to ask you if you'll wait for me."

"How long?" The flirtatious question slipped out before she could stop herself.

He frowned, but a twinkle sparked in his eyes. "Possibly for as long as you plan to love me."

"Is that all?" She touched her fingertips to his cheek. "Then it's only for as long as you plan to love me."

"That's a long time." He cradled her hand with his. "Something like forever."

❦

"Lily." Becky flung herself into Lily's arms before church on Sunday. "Matt asked me to marry him. I know we haven't been courting all that long, but we've known each other for ages, and he's so good and kind, and his parents are letting us have their house and—isn't it wonderful?"

"Truly."

Lily hugged her friend. She was happy for Becky, though the sight of Ben on the other side of the sanctuary, talking with Jackson Reeves, sent her heart into a confused spiral of joy and sorrow.

No matter what she said to him, he refused to propose to her until he could offer her a real home.

"So I need to buy yards and yards of lace from you." Becky linked her arm with Lily's. "Momma says I can have a whole new dress if I don't buy too much fabric for it, so I thought maybe lots of lace instead of a wide skirt."

"Make your skirt as wide as you like. I have yards of lace made. I'll give it to you."

"But what about the bazaar?"

Lily shrugged. "It's mostly just crocheted collars and cuffs I sell there."

Becky winked. "But what about your own wedding dress?"

"We don't have anywhere to live."

Although the fact hurt her, she experienced only a twinge of envy for her friend's blessing of a fiancé who could provide her with a proper home. The Lord knew what He wanted for her and Ben. He would provide. If He did not provide. . .

Lily didn't think that far. Her faith grew daily, but it still had its limitations. The prospect of a future without Ben as her husband hurt too much to contemplate.

"Someone in Browning City should build houses they can rent to people like you two and newcomers." Becky began tugging Lily toward Matt, who had joined Ben and Pastor Jackson. "Don't big cities have houses to rent?"

"Yes, I think they do. But we live here, and we plan to stay here."

"You can't believe how happy I am about that." Becky paused. "I couldn't imagine Browning City without you here stirring things up."

Lily frowned. "I hope I brought more than that to town."

"Browning City without you, Lily, would be like summer without sunshine." Becky grinned. "Is that good enough for you?"

"Better than good enough." Lily laughed, once again assured staying was right.

Even her frustration over the town having nowhere Ben and she could live made her doubt her decision only once or twice in the next week. Mostly, she was too busy finishing up preparations for the spring bazaar and anticipating the plowing contest. If Ben won, they could buy land and build a house. Yet she didn't know how he could win. Although he had rescued the plow from the fire, it had gotten scorched. It was also old and heavy, not like one of the improved John Deere plows some farmers had. Ben was young and strong, yet she wasn't certain he had as much experience as others did.

"God knows what He wants for us," she told herself each time she grew uncertain.

Part of her hoped it wasn't a farm miles from town. She doubted she would ever be satisfied with few to no neighbors near enough for anything from spontaneous dinners together to borrowing a cup of sugar. She felt her gift for organizing people to get things done could better be used in town than out, and she kept telling herself to let God have that talent for His glory, not her own.

Whatever her future, she employed every bit of her skill up to the minute the bazaar opened. Held outside town to have enough space and have a field for the contest close by, the fair of booths celebrated all the skills farm- and townsfolk employed during the more idle winter months. More barter than exchange of coin took place, but because everyone paid for a booth, the community received money. This year, everyone worked hard to raise funds for a library. The previous year, they had raised money for a church hall.

Lily had taken only cash the previous year, her first to participate. She didn't intend to carry on the same practice this year. She'd felt no need for antimacassars, quilts, and frilly aprons before. That had all changed.

She understood the meaning behind the words "hope chest."

By the end of the first day, she didn't have a crocheted collar or cuff left. Her box held some coins and numerous linens, exquisitely stitched by ladies who took pride in their work. She had even exchanged a length of lace for a colorful rag rug.

One day, she would have her own floor on which to spread it.

Without any goods to sell the next day, she helped Becky, Eva, and the others with their toffee; then she closed up shop and walked arm in arm with the other women to the edge of the field.

"Are Matt and Tom joining us?" she asked them.

"They're referees." Eva glanced at the line of plows across from them. "This field is stonier than I remember from when I came two years ago."

"I think Iowa grows as many stones as it does crops." Becky giggled. "One year, when Mr. Deere himself came, a man plowed up a rock so big his blade bent."

Eva made a face. "I hope it wasn't the blade of a John Deere plow."

"It wasn't, and he pointed that out, of—oh, there's Matt." Becky waved.

Even across a field, Lily saw Matt's face light up. She wondered how she had ever thought he would care for her, or she for him. She scarcely thought of him now.

She had scarcely thought of him since meeting Ben.

Ben stood a hundred feet or so from Matt. He squatted before his plow, tinkering with something she couldn't see from this distance.

She shaded her eyes with her hand. "Is everything all right?"

"You worry too much." Becky slipped her arm around Lily's waist. "He'll do fine. Even third place is good."

Eva held up her hand. "Hush, they're about to start."

Sheriff Dodd stepped forward and read from a sheet of paper. Lily couldn't hear the words, only his sonorous voice, but presumed he pronounced the rules. When he finished his speech, he stepped behind the line of men and plows, picked a rifle up from the ground, and fired into the air.

The three ladies jumped, laughed, and started to cheer Ben on. All around them, ladies called for their men to do well, and children ran about, shouting for their daddies.

Only in the Iowa countryside, Lily couldn't help thinking, *would an entire town turn out to watch grown men pull plows across a field. Never would city folk do something so silly.*

Or with so much togetherness and fun.

Even if Ben didn't win, the bazaar and contest were worth every minute with her friends.

Her family.

Filled with love for the women beside her, she hugged both of them.

"I know." Becky hugged her back. "I'm worried, too."

"About what?" Lily blinked, glanced back at the field, and understood.

Ben was faltering. No, not him, his plow.

"He hit a rock." Eva narrowed her eyes against the glare of the noonday sun. "The blade is uneven now."

"Oh no, that takes off points if the furrows aren't straight," Becky wailed. "It's just not fair."

"It's not." Lily's heart sank into her middle.

She started to pray.

Ben kept going, but he fell far behind half the other men. In no way could he win.

Lily clenched her hands and tried to pray. She was so sure the Lord wanted them together. She didn't know how He could give her peace about staying in Browning City, even make her happy about it, then keep her and Ben apart.

I can't bear to see him day after day and stay mere friends.

But of course she would if the Lord wanted her to.

I accept this, Lord.

"I wonder if the plow was damaged in the fire," Eva mused. "It just doesn't look right. See that crack?"

Lily and Becky shook their heads.

"You have remarkable eyesight." Lily leaned forward, squinting. "I can't see a—oh, yes, I can."

A groove formed along the side of the plow. She also noticed the crease between Ben's eyes and tightness of his chin.

"Another rock might break it."

As Becky spoke, the blade struck another rock. The frame shuddered. The groove turned into a fissure. While the other contestants continued, Ben stopped and turned to his equipment.

"That's an odd sight." Eva headed onto the field. "Come on, you two. Something peculiar is happening here."

"What?" Lily noticed nothing too out of the ordinary.

"Something in the crack." Eva tossed the cryptic remark over her shoulder.

"What?" Lily followed Eva and Becky along Ben's lane. Matt and Tom gestured to them to go back. The ladies ignored the men and continued.

"Ben," Becky called, "what happened?"

He stood beside the plow, pulling on something protruding from the crack. Concentration etched his face, and when he glanced at them, excitement sparkled in his eyes.

"This plow was never intended to be used for this purpose again." He yanked on what appeared to be a scrap of fabric. "It's been cobbled together—"

"What are you all doing?" Matt demanded, Tom right behind him.

"You're supposed to be judging the contest," Eva said.

"It's done." Tom frowned at her. "The Hastings lad won. They're all headed this way."

They were. Lily glanced around to see what appeared to be the entire town swarming toward them.

"I need a chisel," Ben said.

Someone ran for tent stakes and a hammer. Ben and Tom used the stakes to form wedges to pry the pieces of the plow apart far enough for Ben to extract a canvas bag.

A canvas bag that sagged in his hand.

"Let me have that." Sheriff Dodd stepped up beside Ben. "Hidden like that, it's probably contraband of some kind."

"I believe it is," Ben said. "This plow used to belong to Jim Mitchell."

Gasps rose from the crowd like a wave.

Lily opened her mouth, but no sound emerged. She met Ben's gaze, and both of them grinned.

"Ladies and gentlemen," Dodd announced, staring into the bag, "Mr. Purcell is right in his surmise. He has indeed found the gold."

Chapter 15

REGARDING YOUR LETTER *STOP* PURCELL WILL RECEIVE REWARD
STOP WILL DELIVER IN PERSON *STOP*

S carcely able to breathe, Lily read the telegram addressed to Sheriff Dodd and
signed by a general in Washington City. She wanted to dash from the telegraph office and race into town, shouting the news all the way—and more.

"We can build our house now."

But she could say nothing to anyone other than the sheriff. He would have
the privilege of telling Ben.

The sooner he received the news, the better.

She slid off her stool and yanked open the door. "Theo?" She waved the
telegram at him. "Please deliver this at once, and don't you dare read it."

"No, Miss Lily, you know I can't deliver telegrams right now. Afternoon
train's due any minute."

"But this is important."

"Is it, now?" Theo grinned. "Maybe you should take it yourself."

"You know I can't leave the office until Toby gets here."

"And he's slower'n the train in an ice storm." Theo peered down the road.
"No sign of him."

"He isn't late yet."

He wasn't due for another quarter hour. By the time he arrived and she got
into town, Dodd would have left his office. She would have to hunt him down.

She chafed at the delay then laughed at herself. They had waited two months
to hear if Ben would indeed receive the reward for the gold. They should be able
to wait another hour or more. Of course, who knew when the general would
arrive with the money. The sum the sheriff had mentioned staggered her. They
could build a fine house with it.

They could also buy a farm, and the notion of it still gave Lily pause. She
knew Ben still wanted land, lots of it, and that piece along the river was still
for sale. Lily kept telling herself it wasn't too far from town, not too far from
others. Doing so didn't help much. She felt comfortable being alone now, yet
preferred not to be, and still doubted her ability to remain content as the wife
of a farmer.

Often during the last two months, she'd thought perhaps she should tell Ben to find a lady who wanted to be a farm wife, feeding chickens and milking cows, slopping pigs and preserving vegetables.

Well, she liked the preserving part.

Now that everything looked as though it would work out for them, Lily stared at her telegraph machine, waiting for Toby to arrive, and wondered if maybe she didn't love Ben enough to marry him no matter where they lived. She had told him she would love him all her life, but if she couldn't be happy regardless of their circumstances, she might be mistaken.

Her insides knotted, she greeted Toby, grabbed the telegram, and headed for Dodd's office as fast as she could manage and remain ladylike. Through the window, she saw him seated at his desk, inspecting wanted posters.

"In case any of these men come through my town," he told her, stacking the posters. "How may I help you, Miss Lily?"

"Telegram." She handed it to him.

He read it and let out a low whistle. "The general himself. Well, what do you know? Guess I should run along and tell Ben."

"Please do." Lily hugged her arms across her middle. "He'll be at the store."

"Yes, ma'am." Dodd grinned. "And let me be the first one to congratulate you."

"For what, sir?"

Dodd guffawed. "For what indeed. You go home and make yourself pretty. I expect you'll have a caller later."

Laughing, Lily did as he suggested. She combed and pinned up her hair. She tucked a fresh collar around her neckline. She sat on the front porch to catch the warm air of the late afternoon and waited.

Thirty minutes passed. They felt like thirty hours. She reviewed Dodd's words and realized how embarrassed Ben and she would be if they didn't marry. Everyone expected them to tie the knot. She expected them to marry soon—had even made her wedding dress without telling anyone other than Becky and Eva, who were sworn to secrecy. She didn't think she was being presumptive, but now that the moment had arrived, Ben might have other plans.

"I want my farm to prosper first," she imagined him saying. "You said you'd wait for me."

She had said something of the kind. Silly female for making such a promise. No telling what notion he would come up with to postpone their union.

Because he was as scared as she was?

Lily shot to her feet, preparing to hide in her room.

She saw Ben striding toward her and sat down again.

He bounded up the steps to Mrs. Willoughby's porch and dropped onto the seat beside her. He sounded winded, as though he had run all the way, and carried the aromas of the store with him—cinnamon, cloves, and fresh coffee. She inhaled the rich fragrances and waited for him to speak.

"I just got some good news." He laughed. "You already know, though, don't you?"

"I do." She beamed at him. "Congratulations. And a general's coming to deliver it himself."

"Not *is* coming." Ben shook his head. "He's here. Came in on the train. Seems he's bought a farm here to live on with his family when he leaves the military, so he offered to deliver the reward in person."

"He bought a farm here for his old age?" Lily couldn't keep the astonishment from her tone. "Where is it?"

Ben gazed at the maple tree in Mrs. Willoughby's front yard. "The piece of land we visited in April."

"The one you wanted?"

"Yes." His voice remained neutral.

"Why, Ben, that's. . .um. . ."

She stumbled over saying it was terrible news. For her, it wasn't terrible at all.

"It's not too bad." Ben stretched his long legs ahead of him as though settling in for a lengthy chat. "I found another property about fifteen miles out."

"Fifteen?" Lily's voice squeaked.

She gripped the edge of her chair, reminding herself all would be well when she was married to the man she loved, the mate the Lord had found for her.

"Of course, it's got to be cleared and tilled. Lots of rocks." Ben shrugged. "I figure in a year or two we should be able to build something there."

"A year or two?" Lily frowned at him. "That's a long time, isn't it?"

"Not when compared with forev—" His voice broke, and he started to laugh. "Lily, don't look so horrified. I'm teasing you."

"You're not buying land that far from town?" She turned toward him.

Love and laughter filled his eyes. "No, my dear. I'm buying the store and the livery from Mr. Gilchrist."

"But your farm. You wanted it more than anything."

"So much that I knew I had to give it up. And when the opportunity came along to buy the business and have a wife who prefers town, I knew what I was supposed to be doing." He leaned toward her and grasped her hand. "That is, if you'll be my wife."

"You know I will."

He leaned forward and kissed her in front of anyone who might be watching.

"How soon can you put a wedding together?"

"I can have a wedding ready in a week. How soon can you build us a house?"

Epilogue

They waited to marry for another three months until after harvest so everyone could attend the wedding, including the general turning farmer and his family. Lily wore the dress she had finished making in June. Rather than trimming the gown with yards of lace, she had plied her needles to fashioning a lace veil. It floated around her as she walked down the aisle of the church, making her feel as though she drifted through a dream.

But everything was wonderfully real, from the rows of friends and neighbors on either side of her to the man waiting for her at the altar. Sunlight shone on his face, and she wondered how she could have once thought she wouldn't follow him anywhere the Lord led them.

When she reached his side, she slipped her hand into his and said, "I will."

"So will I." Ben grinned down at her.

The pastor chuckled. "You're getting ahead of me," he whispered. "But it's good to see a bride and groom so sure of what they're doing." Aloud, he added, "Now for all of the ceremony."

Lily knew she and Ben gave the right responses but didn't remember much else about it. Ben and she had already spoken their vows before God in their first, simple words to each other.

She didn't recall much of the festivities following the wedding, either. For once, no one had let her plan or prepare a thing. Eva, Becky, and Mary had taken over so Lily could see to more important things, like decorating their new home.

She expected to return there after the wedding, but Ben led her out of the church hall to a chorus of good wishes and lifted her into the livery's new buggy.

"We can walk," she protested.

"No we can't." Ben jumped up beside her. "We aren't even driving ourselves."

"But—"

Matt climbed in and took up the reins. "Keep her close to you, Ben."

"Where are we going?" Lily asked.

Ben tucked her close to his side. "The train depot."

"Train?" Lily nearly jumped up and down with excitement. "We're going on a train? Where?"

"Chicago." Ben rested his cheek against the top of her head. "I thought you might like an adventure before you become a staid matron in a small town."

Just as she knew she would enjoy their honeymoon in a real city, Lily knew life with Ben would be the best adventure she would ever live.

Laurie Alice Eakes

Award-winning author LAURIE ALICE EAKES has always loved books. When she ran out of available stories to entertain and encourage her, she began creating her own tales of love and adventure. In 2006, she celebrated the publication of her first hardcover novel. Much to her astonishment and delight, it won the National Readers Choice Award. Besides writing, she teaches classes to other writers, mainly on research, something she enjoys nearly as much as creating characters and their exploits. A graduate of Asbury College and Seton Hill University, she lives in Northern Virginia with her husband and sundry animals.

A Letter to Our Readers

Dear Readers:

In order that we might better contribute to your reading enjoyment, we would appreciate your taking a few minutes to respond to the following questions. When completed, please return to the following: Fiction Editor, Barbour Publishing, Inc., P.O. Box 719, Uhrichsville, OH 44683.

1. Did you enjoy reading *Wild Prairie Roses*?
   ❏ Very much—I would like to see more books like this.
   ❏ Moderately—I would have enjoyed it more if _____

_____

_____

2. What influenced your decision to purchase this book?
   (Check those that apply.)
   ❏ Cover   ❏ Back cover copy   ❏ Title   ❏ Price
   ❏ Friends   ❏ Publicity   ❏ Other

3. Which story was your favorite?
   ❏ *A Daughter's Quest*   ❏ *Better Than Gold*
   ❏ *Tara's Gold*

4. Please check your age range:
   ❏ Under 18   ❏ 18–24   ❏ 25–34
   ❏ 35–45   ❏ 46–55   ❏ Over 55

5. How many hours per week do you read? _____

Name _____

Occupation _____

Address _____

City_____ State _____ Zip _____

E-mail _____